FRIMLEY CHURCH
Harte's body lies in Frimley Churchyard

"ARGONAUT EDITION" OF
THE WORKS OF BRET HARTE

TALES
OF THE ARGONAUTS

ON THE FRONTIER

BY

BRET HARTE

ILLUSTRATED

VIGILANS ET AUDAX

P. F. COLLIER & SON
NEW YORK

CONTENTS.

———◆———

CONTENTS.

THE ROSE OF TUOLUMNE.

CHAPTER I.

IT was nearly two o'clock in the morning.
The lights were out in Robinson's Hall,
where there had been dancing and revelry; and
the moon, riding high, painted the black windows with silver. The cavalcade, that an hour
ago had shocked the sedate pines with song and
laughter, were all dispersed. One enamoured
swain had ridden east, another west, another
north, another south; and the object of their
adoration, left within her bower at Chemisal
Ridge, was calmly going to bed.

I regret that I am not able to indicate the
exact stage of that process. Two chairs were
already filled with delicate inwrappings and
white confusion; and the young lady herself,
half-hidden in the silky threads of her yellow
hair, had at one time borne a faint resemblance
to a partly-husked ear of Indian corn. But she
was now clothed in that one long, formless garment that makes all women equal; and the
round shoulders and neat waist, that an hour

1

ago had been so fatal to the peace of mind of
Four Forks, had utterly disappeared. The face
above it was very pretty: the foot below, albeit
shapely, was not small. "The flowers, as a
general thing, don't raise their heads *much* to
look after me," she had said with superb frankness to one of her lovers.

The expression of the "Rose" to-night was
contentedly placid. She walked slowly to the
window, and, making the smallest possible peep-
hole through the curtain, looked out. The
motionless figure of a horseman still lingered on
the road, with an excess of devotion that only a
coquette, or a woman very much in love, could
tolerate. The "Rose," at that moment, was
neither, and, after a reasonable pause, turned
away, saying quite audibly that it was "too
ridiculous for any thing." As she came back to
her dressing-table, it was noticeable that she
walked steadily and erect, without that slight
affectation of lameness common to people with
whom bare feet are only an episode. Indeed, it
was only four years ago, that without shoes or
stockings, a long-limbed, colty girl, in a waist-
less calico gown, she had leaped from the tail-
board of her father's emigrant-wagon when it
first drew up at Chemisal Ridge. Certain wild
habits of the "Rose" had outlived transplant-
ing and cultivation.

A knock at the door surprised her. In another moment she had leaped into bed, and with darkly-frowning eyes, from its secure recesses demanded " Who's there ? "

An apologetic murmur on the other side of the door was the response.

" Why, father ! — is that you ? "

There were further murmurs, affirmative, deprecatory, and persistent.

" Wait," said the " Rose." She got up, unlocked the door, leaped nimbly into bed again, and said, " Come."

The door opened timidly. The broad, stooping shoulders, and grizzled head, of a man past the middle age, appeared: after a moment's hesitation, a pair of large, diffident feet, shod with canvas slippers, concluded to follow. When the apparition was complete, it closed the door softly, and stood there, — a very shy ghost indeed, — with apparently more than the usual spiritual indisposition to begin a conversation. The " Rose " resented this impatiently, though, I fear, not altogether intelligibly.

" Do, father, I declare ! "

" You was abed, Jinny," said Mr. McClosky slowly, glancing, with a singular mixture of masculine awe and paternal pride, upon the two chairs and their contents, — " you was abed and ondressed."

"I was."

"Surely," said Mr. McClosky, seating himself on the extreme edge of the bed, and painfully tucking his feet away under it, — "surely." After a pause, he rubbed a short, thick, stumpy beard, that bore a general resemblance to a badly-worn blacking-brush, with the palm of his hand, and went on, "You had a good time, Jinny?"

"Yes, father."

"They was all there?"

"Yes, Rance and York and Ryder and Jack."

"And Jack!" Mr. McClosky endeavored to throw an expression of arch inquiry into his small, tremulous eyes; but meeting the unabashed, widely-opened lid of his daughter, he winked rapidly, and blushed to the roots of his hair.

"Yes, Jack was there," said Jenny, without change of color, or the least self-consciousness in her great gray eyes; "and he came home with me." She paused a moment, locking her two hands under her head, and assuming a more comfortable position on the pillow. "He asked me that same question again, father, and I said, 'Yes.' It's to be — soon. We're going to live at Four Forks, in his own house; and next winter we're going to Sacramento. I suppose it's all right, father, eh?" She emphasized the question with a slight kick through the bed-clothes, as the parental McClosky had fallen into an abstract revery.

"Yes, surely," said Mr. McClosky, recovering himself with some confusion. After a pause, he looked down at the bed-clothes, and, patting them tenderly, continued, "You couldn't have done better, Jinny. They isn't a girl in Tuolumne ez could strike it ez rich as you hev-- even if they got the chance." He paused again, and then said, "Jinny?"

"Yes, father."

"You'se in bed, and ondressed?"

"Yes."

"You couldn't," said Mr. McClosky, glancing hopelessly at the two chairs, and slowly rubbing his chin, — "you couldn't dress yourself again could yer?"

"Why, father!"

"Kinder get yourself into them things again?" he added hastily. "Not all of 'em, you know, but some of 'em. Not if I helped you'— sorter stood by, and lent a hand now and then with a strap, or a buckle, or a necktie, or a shoestring?" he continued, still looking at the chairs, and evidently trying to boldly familiarize himself with their contents.

"Are you crazy, father?" demanded Jenny

suddenly sitting up with a portentous switch of her yellow mane. Mr. McClosky rubbed one side of his beard, which already had the appearance of having been quite worn away by that process, and faintly dodged the question.

"Jinny," he said, tenderly stroking the bed-clothes as he spoke, "this yer's what's the matter. Thar is a stranger down stairs, — a stranger to you, lovey, but a man ez I've knowed a long time. He's been here about an hour; and he'll be here ontil fower o'clock, when the up-stage passes. Now I wants ye, Jinny dear, to get up and come down stairs, and kinder help me pass the time with him. It's no use, Jinny," he went on, gently raising his hand to deprecate any interruption, "it's no use! He won't go to bed; he won't play keerds; whiskey don't take no effect on him. Ever since I knowed him, he was the most on-satisfactory critter to hev round " —

"What do you have him round for, then?" interrupted Miss Jinny sharply.

Mr. McClosky's eyes fell. "Ef he hedn't kem out of his way to-night to do me a good turn, I wouldn't ask ye, Jinny. I wouldn't, so help me! But I thought, ez I couldn't do any thing with him, you might come down, and sorter fetch him, Jinny, as you did the others."

Miss Jenny shrugged her pretty shoulders.

"Is he old, or young?"

"He's young enough, Jinny; but he knows a power of things."

"What does he do?"

"Not much, I reckon. He's got money in the mill at Four Forks. He travels round a good deal. I've heard, Jinny that he's a poet — writes them rhymes, you know." Mr. McClosky here appealed submissively but directly to his daughter. He remembered that she had frequently been in receipt of printed elegaic couplets known as "mottoes," containing enclosures equally saccharine.

Miss Jenny slightly curled her pretty lip She had that fine contempt for the illusions of fancy which belongs to the perfectly healthy young animal.

"Not," continued Mr. McClosky, rubbing his head reflectively, "not ez I'd advise ye, Jinny, to say any thing to him about poetry. It ain't twenty minutes ago ez *I* did. I set the whiskey afore him in the parlor. I wound up the music-box, and set it goin'. Then I sez to him, sociable-like and free, ' Jest consider yourself in your own house, and repeat what you allow to be your finest production,' and he raged. That man, Jinny, jest raged! Thar's no end of the names he called me. You see, Jinny," continued Mr. McClosky apologetically, " he's known me a long time."

But his daughter had already dismissed the
question with her usual directness. "I'll be
down in a few moments, father," she said after
a pause, "but don't say any thing to him about
it — don't say I was abed."

Mr. McClosky's face beamed. "You was
allers a good girl, Jinny," he said, dropping on
one knee the better to imprint a respectful kiss
on her forehead. But Jenny caught him by
the wrists, and for a moment held him captive.
"Father," said she, trying to fix his shy eyes
with the clear, steady glance of her own, "all
the girls that were there to-night had some one
with them. Mame Robinson had her aunt;
Lucy Rance had her mother; Kate Pierson had
her sister — all, except me, had some other
woman. Father dear," her lip trembled just a
little, "I wish mother hadn't died when I was
so small. I wish there was some other woman
in the family besides me. I ain't lonely with
you, father dear; but if there was only some
one, you know, when the time comes for John
and me " —

Her voice here suddenly gave out, but not
her brave eyes, that were still fixed earnestly
upon his face. Mr. McClosky, apparently
tracing out a pattern on the bedquilt, essayed
words of comfort.

"Thar ain't one of them gals ez you've

named, Jinny, ez could do what you've done
with a whole Noah's ark of relations at their
backs! Thar ain't one ez wouldn't sacrifice
her nearest relation to make the strike that
you hev. Ez to mothers, maybe, my dear
you're doin' better without one." He rose
suddenly, and walked toward the door. When
he reached it, he turned, and, in his old deprecating manner, said, "Don't be long, Jinny,"
smiled, and vanished from the head downward,
his canvas slippers asserting themselves resolutely to the last.

When Mr. McClosky reached his parlor
again, his troublesome guest was not there.
The decanter stood on the table untouched;
three or four books lay upon the floor; a
number of photographic views of the Sierras
were scattered over the sofa ; two sofa-pillows,
a newspaper, and a Mexican blanket, lay on the
carpet, as if the late occupant of the room had
tried to read in a recumbent position. A
French window opening upon a veranda, which
never before in the history of the house had
been unfastened, now betrayed by its waving
lace curtain the way that the fugitive had
escaped. Mr. McClosky heaved a sigh of
despair. He looked at the gorgeous carpet
purchased in Sacramento at a fabulous price, at
the crimson satin and rosewood furniture un-

paralleled in the history of Tuolumne. at the massively-framed pictures on the walls, and looked beyond it, through the open window, to the reckless man, who, fleeing these sybaritic allurements, was smoking a cigar upon the moonlit road. This room, which had so often awed the youth of Tuolumne into filial respect, was evidently a failure. It remained to be seen if the "Rose" herself had lost her fragrance. "I reckon Jinny will fetch him yet," said Mr. McClosky with parental faith.

He stepped from the window upon the veranda ; but he had scarcely done this, before his figure was detected by the stranger, who at once crossed the road. When within a few feet of McClosky, he stopped. "You persistent old plantigrade !" he said in a low voice, audible only to the person addressed, and a face full of affected anxiety, "why don't you go to bed? Didn't I tell you to go and leave me here alone ? In the name of all that's idiotic and imbecile, why do you contiuue to shuffle about here ? Or are you trying to drive me crazy with your presence, as you have with that wretched music-box that I've just dropped under yonder tree ? It's an hour and a half yet before the stage passes : do you think, do you imagine for a single moment, that I can tolerate you until then, eh ? Why don't you speak?

Are you asleep? You don't mean to say that
you have the audacity to add somnambulism to
your other weaknesses? you're not low enough
to repeat yourself under any such weak pretext
as that, eh?"

A fit of nervous coughing ended this extraordinary exordium; and half sitting, half leaning
against the veranda, Mr. McClosky's guest
turned his face, and part of a slight elegant
figure, toward his host. The lower portion of
this upturned face wore an habitual expression
of fastidious discontent, with an occasional line
of physical suffering. But the brow above was
frank and critical; and a pair of dark, mirthful
eyes, sat in playful judgment over the super-
sensitive mouth and its suggestion.

" I allowed to go to bed, Ridgeway," said Mr.
McClosky meekly; "but my girl Jinny's jist
got back from a little tear up at Robinson's, and
ain't inclined to turn in yet. You know what
girls is. So I thought we three would jist have
a social chat together to pass away the time."

"You mendacious old hypocrite! She got
back an hour ago," said Ridgeway, "as that sav-
age-looking escort of hers, who has been haunt
ing the house ever since, can testify. My belief
is, that, like an enterprising idiot as you are,
you've dragged that girl out of her bed, that we
might mutually bore each other."

Mr. McClosky was too much stunned by this evidence of Ridgeway's apparently superhuman penetration to reply. After enjoying his host's confusion for a moment with his eyes, Ridgeway's mouth asked grimly, —

"And who is this girl, anyway?"

"Nancy's."

"Your wife's?"

"Yes. But look yar, Ridgeway," said McClosky, laying one hand imploringly on Ridgeway's sleeve, "not a word about her to Jinny. She thinks her mother's dead — died in Missouri. Eh!"

Ridgeway nearly rolled from the veranda in an excess of rage. "Good God! Do you mean to say that you have been concealing from her a fact that any day, any moment, may come to her ears? That you've been letting her grow up in ignorance of something that by this time she might have outgrown and forgotten? That you have been, like a besotted old ass, all these years slowly forging a thunderbolt that any one may crush her with? That" — but here Ridgeway's cough took possession of his voice, and even put a moisture into his dark eyes, as he looked at McClosky's aimless hand feebly employed upon his beard.

"But," said McClosky, "look how she's done! She's held her head as high as any of 'em. She's to be married in a month to the richest man in the county; and," he added cunningly, " Jack Ashe ain't the kind o' man to sit by and hear any thing said of his wife or her relations, you bet! But hush — that's her foot on the stairs. She's cummin'."

She came. I don't think the French window ever held a finer view than when she put aside the curtains, and stepped out. She had dressed herself simply and hurriedly, but with a woman's knowledge of her best points; so that you got the long curves of her shapely limbs, the shorter curves of her round waist and shoulders, the long sweep of her yellow braids, the light of her gray eyes, and even the delicate rose of her complexion, without knowing how it was delivered to you.

The introduction by Mr. McClosky was brief. When Ridgeway had got over the fact that it was two o'clock in the morning, and that the cheek of this Tuolumne goddess nearest him was as dewy and fresh as an infant's, that she looked like Marguerite, without, probably, ever having heard of Gœthe's heroine, he talked, I dare say, very sensibly. When Miss Jenny — who from her childhood had been brought up among the sons of Anak, and who was accustomed to have the supremacy of our noble sex presented to her as a physical fact — found her-

self in the presence of a new and strange
power in the slight and elegant figure beside
her, she was at first frightened and cold. But
finding that this power, against which the
weapons of her own physical charms were of
no avail, was a kindly one, albeit general, she
fell to worshipping it, after the fashion of
woman, and casting before it the fetishes and
other idols of her youth. She even confessed
to it. So that, in half an hour, Ridgeway was
in possession of all the facts connected with
her life, and a great many, I fear, of her fancies
—except one. When Mr. McClosky found the
young people thus amicably disposed, he calmly
went to sleep.

It was a pleasant time to each. To Miss
Jenny it had the charm of novelty; and she
abandoned herself to it, for that reason, much
more freely and innocently than her companion,
who knew something more of the inevitable logic
of the position. I do not think, however, he had
any intention of love-making. I do not think
he was at all conscious of being in the attitude.
I am quite positive he would have shrunk from
the suggestion of disloyalty to the one woman
whom he admitted to himself he loved. But,
like most poets, he was much more true to an
idea than a fact, and having a very lofty conception of womanhood, with a very sanguine nature,

he saw in each new face the possibilities of a
realization of his ideal. It was, perhaps, an
unfortunate thing for the women, particularly as
he brought to each trial a surprising freshness,
which was very deceptive, and quite distinct
from the *blasé* familiarity of the man of gallantry.
It was this perennial virginity of the affections
that most endeared him to the best women,
who were prone to exercise toward him a chivalrous protection, — as of one likely to go astray,
unless looked after, — and indulged in the dangerous combination of sentiment with the
highest maternal instincts. It was this quality
which caused Jenny to recognize in him a
certain boyishness that required her womanly
care, and even induced her to offer to accompany him to the cross-roads when the time for
his departure arrived. With her superior
knowledge of woodcraft and the locality, she
would have kept him from being lost. I wot
not but that she would have protected him from
bears or wolves, but chiefly, I think, from the
feline fascinations of Mame Robinson and Lucy
Rance, who might be lying in wait for this
tender young poet. Nor did she cease to be
thankful that Providence had, so to speak,
delivered him as a trust into her hands.

It was a lovely night. The moon swung low,
and languished softly on the snowy ridge

beyond. There were quaint odors in the still
air; and a strange incense from the woods per-
fumed their young blood, and seemed to swoon
in their pulses. Small wonder that they lingered on the white road, that their feet climbed,
unwillingly the little hill where they were to
part, and that, when they at last reached it,
even the saving grace of speech seemed to have
forsaken them.

For there they stood alone. There was no
sound nor motion in earth, or woods, or heaven.
They might have been the one man and woman
for whom this goodly earth that lay at their
feet, rimmed with the deepest azure, was
created. And, seeing this, they turned toward
each other with a sudden instinct, and their
hands met, and then their lips in one long kiss.

And then out of the mysterious distance
came the sound of voices, and the sharp clatter
of hoofs and wheels, and Jenny slid away — a
white moonbeam — from the hill. For a moment she glimmered through the trees, and
then, reaching the house, passed her sleeping
father on the veranda, and, darting into her
bedroom, locked the door, threw open the
window, and, falling on her knees beside it,
leaned her hot cheeks upon her hands, and
listened. In a few moments she was rewarded
by the sharp clatter of hoofs on the stony road:

but it was only a horseman, whose dark figure
was swiftly lost in the shadows of the lower
road. At another time she might have recognized the man; but her eyes and ears were now
all intent on something else. It came presently
with dancing lights, a musical rattle of harness,
a cadence of hoof-beats, that set her heart to
beating in unison—and was gone. A sudden
sense of loneliness came over her; and tears
gathered in her sweet eyes.

She arose, and looked around her. There was
the little bed, the dressing-table, the roses that
she had worn last night, still fresh and bloom-
ing in the little vase. Every thing was there;
but every thing looked strange. The roses should
have been withered, for the party seemed so
long ago. She could hardly remember when she
had worn this dress that lay upon the chair.
So she came back to the window, and sank down
beside it, with her cheek a trifle paler, leaning
on her hand, and her long braids reaching to
the floor. The stars paled slowly, like her
cheek; yet with eyes that saw not, she still
looked from her window for the coming dawn.

It came, with violet deepening into purple,
with purple flushing into rose, with rose shining
into silver, and glowing into gold. The straggling line of black picket-fence below, that had
faded away with the stars, came back with the

sun. What was that object moving by the fence? Jenny raised her head, and looked intently. It was a man endeavoring to climb the pickets, and falling backward with each attempt. Suddenly she started to her feet, as if the rosy flushes of the dawn had crimsoned her from forehead to shoulders; then she stood, white as the wall, with her hands clasped upon her bosom; then, with a single bound, she reached the door, and, with flying braids and fluttering skirt, sprang down the stairs, and out to the garden walk. When within a few feet of the fence, she uttered a cry, the first she had given, — the cry of a mother over her stricken babe, of a tigress over her mangled cub; and in another moment she had leaped the fence, and knelt beside Ridgeway, with his fainting head upon her breast.

"My boy, my poor, poor boy! who has done this?"

Who, indeed? His clothes were covered with dust; his waistcoat was torn open; and his handkerchief, wet with the blood it could not stanch, fell from a cruel stab beneath his shoulder.

"Ridgeway, my poor boy! tell me what has happened."

Ridgeway slowly opened his heavy blue-veined lids, and gazed upon her. Presently a gleam of mischief came into his dark eyes, a smile stole over his lips as he whispered slowly, —

" It — was — your kiss — did it, Jenny dear I had forgotten — how high-priced the article was here. Never mind, Jenny !" — he feebly raised her hand to his white lips, — " it was — worth it," and fainted away.

Jenny started to her feet, and looked wildly around her. Then, with a sudden resolution, she stooped over the insensible man, and with one strong effort lifted him in her arms as if he had been a child. When her father, a moment later, rubbed his eyes, and awoke from his sleep upon the veranda, it was to see a goddess, erect and triumphant, striding toward the house with the helpless body of a man lying across that breast where man had never lain before, — a goddess, at whose imperious mandate he arose, and cast open the doors be fore her. And then, when she had laid her unconscious burden on the sofa, the goddess fled ; and a woman, helpless and trembling, stood before him, — a woman that cried out that she had " killed him," that she was "wicked, wicked !" and that, even saying so, staggered, and fell beside her late burden. And all that Mr. McClosky could do was to feebly rub his beard, and say to himself vaguely and incoherently, that " Jinny had fetched him."

CHAPTER II.

BEFORE noon the next day, it was generally believed throughout Four Forks that Ridgeway Dent had been attacked and wounded at Chemisal Ridge by a highwayman, who fled on the approach of the Wingdam coach. It is to be presumed that this statement met with Ridgeway's approval, as he did not contradict it, nor supplement it with any details. His wound was severe, but not dangerous. After the first excitement had subsided, there was, I think, a prevailing impression common to the provincial mind, that his misfortune was the result of the defective moral quality of his being a stranger, and was, in a vague sort of a way, a warning to others, and a lesson to him. "Did you hear how that San-Francisco feller was took down the other night?" was the average tone of introductory remark. Indeed, there was a general suggestion that Ridgeway's presence was one that no self-respecting, high-minded highwayman, honorably conservative of the best interests of Tuolumne County, could for a moment tolerate.

Except for the few words spoken on that eventful morning, Ridgeway was reticent of the past. When Jenny strove to gather some details of the affray that might offer a clew to his unknown assailant, a subtle twinkle in his brown eyes was the only response. When Mr. McClosky attempted the same process, the young gentleman threw abusive epithets, and, eventually slippers, teaspoons, and other lighter articles within the reach of an invalid, at the head of his questioner. "I think he's coming round, Jinny," said Mr. McClosky: "he laid for me this morning with a candlestick."

It was about this time that Miss Jenny, having sworn her father to secrecy regarding the manner in which Ridgeway had been carried into the house, conceived the idea of addressing the young man as "Mr. Dent," and of apologizing for intruding whenever she entered the room in the discharge of her household duties. It was about this time that she became more rigidly conscientious to those duties, and less general in her attentions. It was at this time that the quality of the invalid's diet improved, and that she consulted him less frequently about it. It was about this time that she began to see more company, that the house was greatly frequented by her former admirers, with whom she rode, walked, and danced. It was at about this time also, and when Ridgeway was able to be brought out on the veranda in a chair, that, with great archness

of manner, she introduced to him Miss Lucy
Ashe, the sister of her betrothed, a flashing
brunette, and terrible heart-breaker of Four
Forks. And, in the midst of this gayety, she
concluded that she would spend a week with
the Robinsons, to whom she owed a visit. She
enjoyed herself greatly there, so much, indeed,
that she became quite hollow-eyed, the result,
as she explained to her father, of a too frequent
indulgence in festivity. "You see, father, I
won't have many chances after John and I are
married : you know how queer he is, and I must
make the most of my time ; " and she laughed
an odd little laugh, which had lately become
habitual to her. "And how is Mr. Dent
getting on?" Her father replied that he was
getting on very well indeed, — so well, in fact,
that he was able to leave for San Francisco two
days ago. "He wanted to be remembered to
you, Jinny, — 'remembered kindly,' — yes, they
is the very words he used," said Mr. McClosky,
looking down, and consulting one of his large
shoes for corroboration. Miss Jenny was glad
to hear that he was so much better. Miss
Jenny could not imagine any thing that pleased
her more than to know that he was so strong as
to be able to rejoin his friends again, who must
love him so much, and be so anxious about him.
Her father thought she would be pleased, and,

now that he was gone, there was really no necessity for her to hurry back. Miss Jenny, in a high metallic voice, did not know that she had expressed any desire to stay, still if her presence had become distasteful at home, if her own father was desirous of getting rid of her, if, when she was so soon to leave his roof forever, he still begrudged her those few days remaining, if— "My God, Jinny, so help me!" said Mr. McClosky, clutching despairingly at his beard, "I didn't go for to say any thing of the kind. I thought that you"— "Never mind, father," interrupted Jenny magnanimously, "you misunderstood me: of course you did, you couldn't help it—you're a MAN!" Mr. McClosky, sorely crushed, would have vaguely protested; but his daughter, having relieved herself, after the manner of her sex, with a mental personal application of an abstract statement, forgave him with a kiss.

Nevertheless, for two or three days after her return, Mr. McClosky followed his daughter about the house with yearning eyes, and occasionally with timid, diffident feet. Sometimes he came upon her suddenly at her household tasks, with an excuse so palpably false, and a careless manner so outrageously studied, that she was fain to be embarrassed for him. Later, he took to rambling about the house at night, and was often seen noiselessly passing and repassing through the hall after she had retired. On one occasion, he was surprised, first by sleep, and then by the early-rising Jenny, as he lay on the rug outside her chamber-door. "You treat me like a child, father," said Jenny. "I thought, Jinny," said the father apologetically, —"I thought I heard sounds as if you was takin' on inside, and, listenin' I fell asleep."—"You dear, old simple-minded baby!" said Jenny, looking past her father's eyes, and lifting his grizzled locks one by one with meditative fingers: "what should I be takin' on for? Look how much taller I am than you!" she said, suddenly lifting herself up to the extreme of her superb figure. Then rubbing his head rapidly with both hands, as if she were anointing his hair with some rare unguent, she patted him on the back, and returned to her room. The result of this and one or two other equally sympathetic interviews was to produce a change in Mr. McClosky's manner, which was, if possible, still more discomposing. He grew unjustifiably hilarious, cracked jokes with the servants, and repeated to Jenny humorous stories, with the attitude of facetiousness carefully preserved throughout the entire narration, and the point utterly ignored and forgotten. Certain incidents reminded him of funny things, which invariably turned out to have not the slightest relevancy or application. He occasionally brought home with him practical humorists, with a sanguine hope of setting them going, like the music-box, for his daughter's edification. He essayed the singing of melodies with great freedom of style, and singular limitation of note. He sang "Come haste to the Wedding, Ye Lasses and Maidens," of which he knew a single line, and that incorrectly, as being peculiarly apt and appropriate. Yet away from the house and his daughter's presence, he was silent and distraught. His absence of mind was particularly noted by his workmen at the Empire Quartz Mill. "Ef the old man don't look out and wake up," said his foreman, "he'll hev them feet of his yet under the stamps. When he ain't givin' his mind to 'em, they is altogether too promiskuss."

A few nights later, Miss Jenny recognized her father's hand in a timid tap at the door. She opened it, and he stood before her, with a valise in his hand, equipped as for a journey. "I takes the stage to-night, Jinny dear, from Four Forks to 'Frisco. Maybe I may drop in on Jack afore I go. I'll be back in a week. Good-by."

"Good-by." He still held her hand. Presently he drew her back into the room, closing

the door carefully, and glancing around. There
was a look of profound cunning in his eye as
he said slowly, —

" Bear up, and keep dark, Jinny dear, and
trust to the old man. Various men has various
ways. Thar is ways as is common, and ways as
is uncommon; ways as is easy, and ways as is
oneasy. Bear up, and keep dark." With this
Delphic utterance he put his finger to his lips,
and vanished.

It was ten o'clock when he reached Four
Forks. A few minutes later, he stood on the
threshold of that dwelling described by the
Four Forks " Sentinel " as " the palatial resi-
dence of John Ashe," and known to the local
satirist as the " ash-box." " Hevin' to lay by
two hours, John," he said to his prospective
son-in-law, as he took his hand at the door,
" a few words of social converse, not on business, but strictly private, seems to be about as
nat'ral a thing as a man can do." This introduction, evidently the result of some study, and
plainly committed to memory, seemed so satisfactory to Mr. McClosky, that he repeated it
again, after John Ashe had led him into his
private office, where, depositing his valise in
the middle of the floor, and sitting down before
it, he began carefully to avoid the eye of his
host. John Ashe, a tall, dark, handsome Ken·

tuckian, with whom even the trifles of life were evidently full of serious import, waited with a kind of chivalrous respect the further speech of his guest. Being utterly devoid of any sense of the ridiculous, he always accepted Mr. McClosky as a grave fact, singular only from his own want of experience of the class.

" Ores is running light now," said Mr. Mc-Closky with easy indifference.

John Ashe returned that he had noticed the same fact in the receipts of the mill at Four Forks.

Mr. McClosky rubbed his beard, and looked at his valise, as if for sympathy and suggestion.

" You don't reckon on having any trouble with any of them chaps as you cut out with Jinny?"

John Ashe, rather haughtily, had never thought of that. " I saw Rance hanging round your house the other night, when I took your daughter home; but he gave me a wide berth," he added carelessly.

" Surely," said Mr. McClosky, with a peculiar winking of the eye. After a pause, he took a fresh departure from his valise.

" A few words, John, ez between man and man, ez between my daughter's father and her husband who expects to be, is about the thing,

I take it, as is fair and square. I kem here to say them. They're about Jinny, my gal."

Ashe's grave face brightened, to Mr. Mc-Closky's evident discomposure.

"Maybe I should have said about her mother; but, the same bein' a stranger to you, I says naterally, 'Jinny.'"

Ashe nodded courteously. Mr. McClosky, with his eyes on his valise, went on, —

"It is sixteen year ago as I married Mrs. McClosky in the State of Missouri. She let on, at the time, to be a widder, — a widder with one child. When I say let on, I mean to imply that I subsekently found out that she was not a widder, nor a wife; and the father of the child was, so to speak, onbeknowst. Thet child was Jinny — my gal."

With his eyes on his valise, and quietly ignoring the wholly-crimsoned face and swiftly-darkening brow of his host, he continued, —

"Many little things sorter tended to make our home in Missouri onpleasant. A disposition to smash furniture, and heave knives around; an inclination to howl when drunk, and that frequent; a habitooal use of vulgar language, and a tendency to cuss the casooal visitor, — seemed to pint," added Mr. Mc-Closky with submissive hesitation "that — she — was — so to speak — quite onsuited to the marriage relation in its holiest aspeck."

"Damnation! Why didn't" — burst out John Ashe, erect and furious.

"At the end of two year," continued Mr. McClosky, still intent on the valise, "I allowed I'd get a diworce. Et about thet time, however, Providence sends a circus into thet town, and a feller ez rode three horses to onct. Hevin' allez a taste for athletic sports, she left town with this feller, leavin' me and Jinny behind. I sent word to her, thet, if she would give Jinny to me, we'd call it quits. And she did."

"Tell me," gasped Ashe, "did you ask your daughter to keep this from me? or did she do it of her own accord?"

"She doesn't know it," said Mr. McClosky. "She thinks I'm her father, and that her mother's dead."

"Then, sir, this is your" —

"I don't know," said Mr. McClosky slowly, "ez I've asked any one to marry my Jinny. I don't know ez I've persood that ez a biziness, or even taken it up as a healthful recreation."

John Ashe paced the room furiously. Mr. McClosky's eyes left the valise, and followed him curiously. "Where is this woman?" demanded Ashe suddenly. McClosky's eyes sought the valise again.

"She went to Kansas; from Kansas she went into Texas; from Texas she eventooally came

to Californy. Being here, I've purvided her
with money, when her business was slack,
through a friend."

John Ashe groaned. "She's gettin' rather
old and shaky for hosses, and now does the
tight-rope business and flying trapeze. Never
hevin' seen her perform," continued Mr. Mc-
Closky with conscientious caution, "I can't say
how she gets on. On the bills she looks well.
Thar is a poster, " said Mr. McClosky glancing at Ashe, and opening his valise, — "thar is
a poster givin' her performance at Marysville
next month." Mr. McClosky slowly unfolded
a large yellow-and-blue printed poster, pro-
fusely illustrated. "She calls herself 'Mam-
s'elle J. Miglawski, the great Russian Tra-
peziste.'"

John Ashe tore it from his hand. "Of
course," he said, suddenly facing Mr. McClosky,
"you don't expect me to go on with this?"

Mr. McClosky took up the poster, carefully
refolded it, and returned it to his valise.
"When you break off with Jinny," he said
quietly, "I don't want any thing said 'bout
this. She doesn't know it. She's a woman,
and I reckon you're a white man."

"But what am I to say? How am I to go
back of my word?"

"Write her a note. Say something hez come

to your knowledge (don't say what) that makes you break it off. You needn't be afeard Jinny'll ever ask you what."

John Ashe hesitated. He felt he had been cruelly wronged. No gentleman, no Ashe, could go on further in this affair. It was preposterous to think of it. But somehow he felt at the moment very unlike a gentleman, or an Ashe, and was quite sure he should break down under Jenny's steady eyes. But then — he could write to her.

"So ores is about as light here as on the Ridge. Well, I reckon they'll come up before the rains. Good-night." Mr. McClosky took the hand that his host mechanically extended, shook it gravely, and was gone.

When Mr. McClosky, a week later, stepped again upon his own veranda, he saw through the French window the figure of a man in his parlor. Under his hospitable roof, the sight was not unusual; but, for an instant, a subtle sense of disappointment thrilled him. When he saw it was not the face of Ashe turned toward him, he was relieved; but when he saw the tawny beard, and quick, passionate eyes of Henry Rance, he felt a new sense of apprehension, so that he fell to rubbing his beard almost upon his very threshold.

Jenny ran into the hall, and seized her father with a little cry of joy. "Father," said Jenny in a hurried whisper, "don't mind *him*," indicating Rance with a toss of her yellow braids: "he's going soon. And I think, father. I've done him wrong. But it's all over with John and me now. Read that note, and see how he's insulted me." Her lip quivered; but she went on, "It's Ridgeway that he means, father; and I believe it was *his* hand struck Ridgeway down, or that he knows who did. But hush now! not a word."

She gave him a feverish kiss, and glided back into the parlor, leaving Mr. McClosky, perplexed and irresolute, with the note in his hand. He glanced at it hurriedly, and saw that it was couched in almost the very words he had suggested. But a sudden, apprehensive recollection came over him. He listened; and, with an exclamation of dismay, he seized his hat, and ran out of the house, but too late. At the same moment a quick, nervous footstep was heard upon the veranda; the French window flew open, and, with a light laugh of greeting, Ridgeway stepped into the room.

Jenny's finer ear first caught the step. Jenny's swifter feelings had sounded the depths of hope, of joy, of despair, before he entered the room. Jenny's pale face was the only one that met his, self-possessed and self-reliant, when he stood before them. An angry flush suffused even the pink roots of Rance's beard as he rose to his feet. An ominous fire sprang into Ridgeway's eyes, and a spasm of hate and scorn passed over the lower part of his face, and left the mouth and jaw immobile and rigid.

Yet he was the first to speak. "I owe you an apology," he said to Jenny, with a suave scorn that brought the indignant blood back to her cheek, "for this intrusion; but I ask no pardon for withdrawing from the only spot where that man dare confront me with safety."

With an exclamation of rage, Rance sprang toward him. But as quickly Jenny stood between them, erect and menacing. "There must be no quarrel here," she said to Rance. "While I protect your right as my guest, don't oblige me to remind you of mine as your hostess." She turned with a half-deprecatory air to Ridgeway; but he was gone. So was her father. Only Rance remained with a look of ill-concealed triumph on his face.

Without looking at him, she passed toward the door. When she reached it, she turned. "You asked me a question an hour ago. Come to me in the garden, at nine o'clock to-night, and I will answer you. But promise me, first, to keep away from Mr. Dent. Give me your

word not to seek him — to avoid him, if he
seeks you. Do you promise? It is well."

He would have taken her hand; but she
waved him away. In another moment he heard
the swift rustle of her dress in the hall, the
sound of her feet upon the stair, the sharp
closing of her bedroom door, and all was quiet.

And even thus quietly the day wore away;
and the night rose slowly from the valley, and
overshadowed the mountains with purple wings
that fanned the still air into a breeze, until the
moon followed it, and lulled every thing to rest
as with the laying-on of white and benedictory
hands. It was a lovely night; but Henry Rance,
waiting impatiently beneath a sycamore at the
foot of the garden, saw no beauty in earth or
air or sky. A thousand suspicions common to a
jealous nature, a vague superstition of the spot,
filled his mind with distrust and doubt. "If
this should be a trick to keep my hands off that
insolent pup!" he muttered. But, even as the
thought passed his tongue, a white figure slid
from the shrubbery near the house, glided along
the line of picket-fence, and then stopped, mid-
way, motionless in the moonlight.

It was she. But he scarcely recognized her
in the white drapery that covered her head and
shoulders and breast. He approached her with
a hurried whisper. "Let us withdraw from the
moonlight. Everybody can see us here."

"We have nothing to say that cannot be said in the moonlight, Henry Rance," she replied, coldly receding from his proffered hand. She trembled for a moment, as if with a chill, and then suddenly turned upon him. "Hold up your head, and let me look at you! I've known only what men are: let me see what a traitor looks like!"

He recoiled more from her wild face than her words. He saw from the first that her hollow cheeks and hollow eyes were blazing with fever. He was no coward; but he would have fled.

"You are ill, Jenny," he said: "you had best return to the house. Another time"—

"Stop!" she cried hoarsely. "Move from this spot, and I'll call for help! Attempt to leave me now, and I'll proclaim you the assassin that you are!"

"It was a fair fight," he said doggedly.

"Was it a fair fight to creep behind an unarmed and unsuspecting man? Was it a fair fight to try to throw suspicion on some one else? Was it a fair fight to deceive me? Liar and coward that you are!"

He made a stealthy step toward her with evil eyes, and a wickeder hand that crept within his breast. She saw the motion; but it only stung her to newer fury.

"Strike!" she said with blazing eyes, throw-

ing her hands open before him. "Strike! **Are**
you afraid of the woman who dares you? **Or**
do you keep your knife for the backs of unsuspecting men? Strike, I tell you! No? Look,
then!" With a sudden movement, she tore
from her head and shoulders the thick lace
shawl that had concealed her figure, and stood
before him. "Look!" she cried passionately,
pointing to the bosom and shoulders of her
white dress, darkly streaked with faded stains
and ominous discoloration, — "look! This is
the dress I wore that morning when I found
him lying here, — *here*, — bleeding from your
cowardly knife. Look! Do you see? This is his
blood, — my darling boy's blood! — one drop of
which, dead and faded as it is, is more precious
to me than the whole living pulse of any other
man. Look! I come to you to-night, christened with his blood, and dare you to strike, —
dare you to strike him again through me, and
mingle my blood with his. Strike, I implore
you! Strike! if you have any pity on me, for
God's sake! Strike! if you are a man! Look!
Here lay his head on my shoulder; here I held
him to my breast, where never — so help me my
God! — another man — Ah!" —

She reeled against the fence, and something
that had flashed in Rance's hand dropped at her
feet; for another flash and report rolled him

over in the dust: and across his writhing body two men strode, and caught her ere she fell.

"She has only fainted," said Mr. McClosky "Jinny dear, my girl, speak to me!"

"What is this on her dress?" said Ridgeway, kneeling beside her, and lifting his set and colorless face. At the sound of his voice, the color came faintly back to her cheek: she opened her eyes, and smiled.

"It's only your blood, dear boy," she said; "but look a little deeper, and you'll find my own."

She put up her two yearning hands, and drew his face and lips down to her own. When Ridgeway raised his head again, her eyes were closed; but her mouth still smiled as with the memory of a kiss.

They bore her to the house, still breathing, but unconscious. That night the road was filled with clattering horsemen; and the summoned skill of the countryside for leagues away gathered at her couch. The wound, they said, was not essentially dangerous; but they had grave fears of the shock to a system that already seemed suffering from some strange and unaccountable nervous exhaustion. The best medical skill of Tuolumne happened to be young and observing, and waited patiently an opportunity to account for it. He was presently rewarded.

For toward morning she rallied, and looked feebly around. Then she beckoned her father toward her, and whispered, " Where is he?"

" They took him away, Jinny dear, in a cart. He won't trouble you agin." He stopped; for Miss Jenny had raised herself on her elbow, and was levelling her black brows at him. But two kicks from the young surgeon, and a significant motion towards the door, sent Mr. McClosky away muttering. " How should I know that ' he' meant Ridgeway?" he said apologetically, as he went and returned with the young gentleman. The surgeon, who was still holding her pulse, smiled, and thought that — with a little care — and attention — the stimulants — might be — diminished — and — he — might leave — the patient for some hours with perfect safety. He would give further directions to Mr. McClosky — down stairs.

It was with great archness of manner, that, half an hour later, Mr. McClosky entered the room with a preparatory cough; and it was with some disappointment that he found Ridgeway standing quietly by the window, and his daughter apparently fallen into a light doze. He was still more concerned, when, after Ridgeway had retired, noticing a pleasant smile playing about her lips, he said softly —

" You was thinking of some one, Jinny?"

'Yes, father," the gray eyes met his steadily, — "of poor John Ashe!"

Her recovery was swift. Nature, that had seemed to stand jealously aloof from her in her mental anguish, was kind to the physical hurt of her favorite child. The suberb physique, which had been her charm and her trial, now stood her in good stead. The healing balsam of the pine, the balm of resinous gums, and the rare medicaments of Sierran altitudes, touched her as it might have touched the wounded doe; so that in two weeks she was able to walk about. And when, at the end of the month, Ridgeway returned from a flying visit to San Francisco, and jumped from the Wingdam coach at four o'clock in the morning, the Rose of Tuolumne, with the dewy petals of either cheek fresh as when first unfolded to his kiss, confronted him on the road.

With a common instinct, their young feet both climbed the little hill now sacred to their thought. When they reached its summit, they were both, I think, a little disappointed. There is a fragrance in the unfolding of a passion, that escapes the perfect flower. Jenny thought the night was not as beautiful; Ridgeway, that the long ride had blunted his perceptions. But they had the frankness to confess it to each other, with the rare delight of such a

confession, and the comparison of details which
they thought each had forgotten. And with
this, and an occasional pitying reference to the
blank period when they had not known each
other, hand in hand they reached the house.

Mr. McClosky was awaiting them impatiently
upon the veranda. When Miss Jenny had
slipped up stairs to replace a collar that stood
somewhat suspiciously awry, Mr. McClosky
drew Ridgeway solemnly aside. He held a
large theatre poster in one hand, and an open
newspaper in the other.

"I allus said," he remarked slowly, with the
air of merely renewing a suspended conversation,
—"I allus said that riding three horses to onct
wasn't exactly in her line. It would seem that
it ain't. From remarks in this yer paper, it
would appear that she tried it on at Marysville
last week, and broke her neck."

A PASSAGE IN THE LIFE OF MR. JOHN OAKHURST.

HE always thought it must have been fate. Certainly nothing could have been more inconsistent with his habits than to have been in the Plaza at seven o'clock of that midsummer morning. The sight of his colorless face in Sacramento was rare at that season, and, indeed, at any season, anywhere publicly, before two o'clock in the afternoon. Looking back upon it in after-years in the light of a chanceful life, he determined, with the characteristic philosophy of his profession, that it must have been fate.

Yet it is my duty, as a strict chronicler of facts, to state that Mr. Oakhurst's presence there that morning was due to a very simple cause. At exactly half-past six, the bank being then a winner to the amount of twenty thousand dollars, he had risen from the faro-table, relinquished his seat to an accomplished assistant, and withdrawn quietly, without attracting a glance from the silent, anxious faces bowed over the table. But when he entered his luxurious sleeping-room, across the passage-way, he was a little shocked at finding the sun streaming through an inadvertently opened window. Something in the rare beauty of the morning. perhaps something in the novelty of the idea, struck him as he was about to close the blinds; and he hesitated. Then, taking his hat from the table, he stepped down a private staircase into the street.

The people who were abroad at that early hour were of a class quite unknown to Mr. Oakhurst. There were milkmen and hucksters delivering their wares, small tradespeople opening their shops, housemaids sweeping doorsteps, and occasionally a child. These Mr. Oakhurst regarded with a certain cold curiosity, perhaps quite free from the cynical disfavor with which he generally looked upon the more pretentious of his race whom he was in the habit of meeting. Indeed, I think he was not altogether displeased with the admiring glances which these humble women threw after his handsome face and figure, conspicuous even in a country of fine-looking men. While it is very probable that this wicked vagabond, in the pride of his social isolation, would have been coldly indifferent to the advances of a fine lady, a little girl who ran admiringly by his side in a ragged dress had the power to call a faint flush into his colorless cheek. He dismissed her at last, but not until she had found out — what, sooner or later, her large-hearted and discriminating sex inevitably did — that he was exceedingly free and open-handed with his money, and also — what, perhaps, none other of her sex ever did — that the bold black eyes of this fine gentleman were in reality of a brownish and even tender gray.

There was a small garden before a white cottage in a side-street, that attracted Mr. Oakhurst's attention. It was filled with roses, heliotrope, and verbena, — flowers familiar enough to him in the expensive and more portable form of bouquets, but, as it seemed to him then, never before so notably lovely. Perhaps it was because the dew was yet fresh upon them; perhaps it was because they were unplucked: but Mr. Oakhurst admired them — not as a possible future tribute to the fascinating and accomplished Miss Ethelinda, then performing at the Varieties, for Mr. Oakhurst's especial benefit, as she had often assured him; nor yet as a *douceur* to the inthralling Miss Montmorrissy, with whom Mr. Oakhurst expected to sup that evening; but simply for himself, and, mayhap, for the flowers' sake. Howbeit he passed on, and so out into the open Plaza, where, finding a bench under a cottonwood-tree, he first dusted the seat with his handkerchief, and then sat down.

It was a fine morning. The air was so still and calm, that a sigh from the sycamores seemed like the deep-drawn breath of the just awakening tree, and the faint rustle of its boughs as the outstretching of cramped and reviving limbs. Far away the Sierras stood out against a sky so remote as to be of no positive color, — so remote, that even the sun despaired of ever reaching it, and so expended its strength recklessly on the whole landscape, until it fairly glittered in a white and vivid contrast. With a very rare impulse, Mr. Oakhurst took off his hat, and half reclined on the bench, with his face to the sky. Certain birds who had taken a critical attitude on a spray above him, apparently began an animated discussion regarding his possible malevolent intentions. One or two, emboldened by the silence, hopped on the ground at his feet, until the sound of wheels on the gravel-walk frightened them away.

Looking up, he saw a man coming slowly toward him, wheeling a nondescript vehicle, in which a woman was partly sitting, partly reclining. Without knowing why, Mr. Oakhurst instantly conceived that the carriage was the invention and workmanship of the man, partly from its oddity, partly from the strong, mechanical hand that grasped it, and partly from a certain pride and visible consciousness in the

manner in which the man handled it. Then
Mr. Oakhurst saw something more: the man's
face was familiar. With that regal faculty of
not forgetting a face that had ever given him
professional audience, he instantly classified it
under the following mental formula: "At
'Frisco, Polka Saloon. Lost his week's wages.
I reckon — seventy dollars — on red. Never
came again." There was, however, no trace of
this in the calm eyes and unmoved face that
he turned upon the stranger, who, on the contrary, blushed, looked embarrassed, hesitated
and then stopped with an involuntary motion
that brought the carriage and its fair occupant
face to face with Mr. Oakhurst.

I should hardly do justice to the position she
will occupy in this veracious chronicle by describing the lady now, if, indeed, I am able to
do it at all. Certainly the popular estimate
was conflicting. The late Col. Starbottle — to
whose large experience of a charming sex I have
before been indebted for many valuable suggestions — had, I regret to say, depreciated her fascinations. "A yellow-faced cripple, by dash!
a sick woman, with mahogany eyes; one of your
blanked spiritual creatures — with no flesh on
her bones." On the other hand, however, she
enjoyed later much complimentary disparage-
ment from her own sex. Miss Celestina Howard,

second leader in the *ballet* at the Varieties, **had,** with great alliterative directness, in after-years, denominated her as an "aquiline asp." Mlle. Brimborion remembered that she had always warned "Mr. Jack" that this woman would "empoison" him. But Mr. Oakhurst, whose impressions are perhaps the most important, only saw a pale, thin, deep-eyed woman, raised above the level of her companion by the refinement of long suffering and isolation, and a certain shy virginity of manner. There was a suggestion of physical purity in the folds of her fresh-looking robe, and a certain picturesque tastefulness in the details, that, without knowing why, made him think that the robe was her invention and handiwork, even as the carriage she occupied was evidently the work of her companion. Her own hand, a trifle too thin, but well-shaped, subtle-fingered, and gentlewomanly, rested on the side of the carriage, the counterpart of the strong mechanical grasp of her companion's.

There was some obstruction to the progress of the vehicle; and Mr. Oakhurst stepped forward to assist. While the wheel was being lifted over the curbstone, it was necessary that she should hold his arm; and for a moment her thin hand rested there, light and cold as a snowflake, and then, as it seemed to him, like a snow-flake melted away. Then there was a pause, and then conversation, the lady joining occasionally and shyly.

It appeared that they were man and wife; that for the past two years she had been a great invalid, and had lost the use of her lower limbs from rheumatism; that until lately she had been confined to her bed, until her husband — who was a master-carpenter — had bethought himself to make her this carriage. He took her out regularly for an airing before going to work, because it was his only time, and — they attracted less attention. They had tried many doctors, but without avail. They had been advised to go to the Sulphur Springs; but it was expensive. Mr. Decker, the husband, had once saved eighty dollars for that purpose, but while in San Francisco had his pocket picked — Mr Decker was so senseless! (The intelligent reader need not be told that it is the lady who is speaking.) They had never been able to make up the sum again, and they had given up the idea. It was a dreadful thing to have one's pocket picked. Did he not think so?

Her husband's face was crimson; but Mr. Oakhurst's countenance was quite calm and unmoved, as he gravely agreed with her, and walked by her side until they passed the little garden that he had admired. Here Mr. Oakhurst commanded a halt, and, going to the door, astounded the proprietor by a preposterously extravagant offer for a choice of the flowers. Presently he returned to the carriage with his arms full of roses, heliotrope, and verbena, and cast them in the lap of the invalid. While she was bending over them with childish delight, Mr. Oakhurst took the opportunity of drawing her husband aside.

"Perhaps," he said in a low voice, and a manner quite free from any personal annoyance, — "perhaps it's just as well that you lied to her as you did. You can say now that the pickpocket was arrested the other day, and you got your money back." Mr. Oakhurst quietly slipped four twenty-dollar gold-pieces into the broad hand of the bewildered Mr. Decker. "Say that — or any thing you like — but the truth. Promise me you won't say that."

The man promised. Mr. Oakhurst quietly returned to the front of the little carriage. The sick woman was still eagerly occupied with the flowers, and, as she raised her eyes to his, her faded cheek seemed to have caught some color from the roses, and her eyes some of their dewy freshness. But at that instant Mr. Oakhurst lifted his hat, and before she could thank him was gone.

I grieve to say that Mr. Decker shamelessly

broke his promise. That night, in the very goodness of his heart and uxorious self-abnegation, he, like all devoted husbands, not only offered himself, but his friend and benefactor, as a sacrifice on the family-altar. It is only fair, however, to add that he spoke with great fervor of the generosity of Mr. Oakhurst, and dwelt with an enthusiasm quite common with his class on the mysterious fame and prodigal vices of the gambler.

"And now, Elsie dear, say that you'll forgive me," said Mr. Decker, dropping on one knee beside his wife's couch. "I did it for the best. It was for you, dearey, that I put that money on them cards that night in 'Frisco. I thought to win a heap — enough to take you away, and enough left to get you a new dress."

Mrs. Decker smiled, and pressed her husband's hand. "I do forgive you, Joe dear," she said, still smiling, with eyes abstractedly fixed on the ceiling; "and you ought to be whipped for deceiving me so, you bad boy! and making me make such a speech. There, say no more about it. If you'll be very good hereafter, and will just now hand me that cluster of roses, I'll forgive you." She took the branch in her fingers, lifted the roses to her face, and presently said, behind their leaves, —

"Joe!"

" What is it, lovey ? "

" Do you think that this Mr. — what do you
call him? — Jack Oakhurst would have given
that money back to you, if I hadn't made that
speech ? "

" Yes."

" If he hadn't seen me at all ? "

Mr. Decker looked up. His wife had managed in some way to cover up her whole face
with the roses, except her eyes, which were
dangerously bright.

" No ! It was you, Elsie — it was all along of
seeing you that made him do it."

" A poor sick woman like me ? "

" A sweet, little, lovely, pooty Elsie — Joe's
own little wifey ! How could he help it ? "

Mrs. Decker fondly cast one arm around her
husband's neck, still keeping the roses to her
face with the other. From behind them she
began to murmur gently and idiotically, " Dear,
ole square Joey. Elsie's oney booful big bear."
But, really, I do not see that my duty as a
chronicler of facts compels me to continue this
little lady's speech any further; and, out of
respect to the unmarried reader, I stop.

Nevertheless, the next morning Mrs. Decker
betrayed some slight and apparently uncalled
for irritability on reaching the Plaza, and presently desired her husband to wheel her back

home. Moreover, she was very much astonished at meeting Mr. Oakhurst just as they were returning, and even doubted if it were he, and questioned her husband as to his identity with the stranger of yesterday as he approached. Her manner to Mr. Oakhurst, also, was quite in contrast with her husband's frank welcome. Mr. Oakhurst instantly detected it. "Her husband has told her all, and she dislikes me," he said to himself, with that fatal appreciation of the half-truths of a woman's motives that causes the wisest masculine critic to stumble, He lingered only long enough to take the business address of the husband, and then lifting his hat gravely, without looking at the lady, went his way. It struck the honest master-carpenter as one of the charming anomalies of his wife's character, that, although the meeting was evidently very much constrained and unpleasant, instantly afterward his wife's spirits began to rise. "You was hard on him, a leetle hard; wasn't you, Elsie?" said Mr. Decker deprecatingly. "I'm afraid he may think I've broke my promise." — "Ah, indeed!" said the lady indifferently. Mr. Decker instantly stepped round to the front of the vehicle. "You look like an A 1 first-class lady riding down Broadway in her own carriage, Elsie," said he. "I never seed you lookin' so peart and sassy before."

A few days later, the proprietor of the San
Isabel Sulphur Springs received the following
note in Mr. Oakhurst's well-known, dainty
hand : —

"DEAR STEVE, — I've been thinking over your prop-
osition to buy Nichols's quarter-interest, and have concluded to go in.   But I don't see how the thing will pay
until you have more accommodation down there, and for
the best class, — I mean *my* customers.   What we want
is an extension to the main building, and two or three
cottages put up.   I send down a builder to take hold of
the job at once.   He takes his sick wife with him; and
you are to look after them as you would for one of us.

"I may run down there myself after the races, just
to look after things; but I sha'n't set up any game this
season.

"Yours always,

"'JOHN OAKHURST.'"

It was only the last sentence of this letter
that provoked criticism.   "I can understand,"
said Mr. Hamlin, a professional brother, to whom
Mr. Oakhurst's letter was shown, — "I can
understand why Jack goes in heavy and builds;
for it's a sure spec, and is bound to be a mighty
soft thing in time, if he comes here regularly.
But why in blank he don't set up a bank this
season, and take the chance of getting some of
the money back that he puts into circulation in
building, is what gets me.   I wonder now," he
mused deeply, "what *is* his little game."

The season had been a prosperous one to Mr. Oakhurst, and proportionally disastrous to several members of the legislature, judges, colonels, and others who had enjoyed but briefly the pleasure of Mr. Oakhurst's midnight society. And yet Sacramento had become very dull to him. He had lately formed a habit of early morning walks, so unusual and startling to his friends, both male and female, as to occasion the intensest curiosity. Two or three of the latter set spies upon his track; but the inquisition resulted only in the discovery that Mr. Oakhurst walked to the Plaza, sat down upon one particular bench for a few moments, and then returned without seeing anybody; and the theory that there was a woman in the case was abandoned. A few superstitious gentlemen of his own profession believed that he did it for "luck." Some others, more practical, declared that he went out to "study points."

After the races at Marysville, Mr. Oakhurst went to San Francisco; from that place he returned to Marysville, but a few days after was seen at San José, Santa Cruz, and Oakland. Those who met him declared that his manner was restless and feverish, and quite unlike his ordinary calmness and phlegm. Col. Starbottle pointed out the fact, that at San Francisco, at the club, Jack had declined to deal. "Hand

shaky, sir; depend upon it. Don't stimulate
enough — blank him!"

From San José he started to go to Oregon by
land with a rather expensive outfit of horses
and camp equipage; but, on reaching Stockton,
he suddenly diverged, and four hours later
found him with a single horse entering the
cañon of the San Isabel Warm Sulphur Springs.

It was a pretty triangular valley lying at the
foot of three sloping mountains, dark with pines,
and fantastic with madrono and manzanita.
Nestling against the mountain-side, the straggling buildings and long piazza of the hotel
glittered through the leaves, and here and there
shone a white toy-like cottage. Mr. Oakhurst
was not an admirer of Nature; but he felt something of the same novel satisfaction in the view,
that he experienced in his first morning walk in
Sacramento. And now carriages began to pass
him on the road filled with gayly-dressed women;
and the cold California outlines of the landscape began to take upon themselves somewhat
of a human warmth and color. And then the
long hotel piazza came in view, efflorescent
with the full-toiletted fair. Mr. Oakhurst, a
good rider after the California fashion, did not
check his speed as he approached his destination, but charged the hotel at a gallop, threw
his horse on his haunches within a foot of the

piazza, and then quietly emerged from the cloud of dust that veiled his dismounting.

Whatever feverish excitement might have raged within, all his habitual calm returned as he stepped upon the piazza. With the instinct of long habit, he turned and faced the battery of eyes with the same cold indifference with which he had for years encountered the half-hidden sneers of men and the half-frightened admiration of women. Only one person stepped forward to welcome him. Oddly enough, it was Dick Hamilton, perhaps the only one present, who by birth, education, and position, might have satisfied the most fastidious social critic. Happily for Mr. Oakhurst's reputation, he was also a very rich banker and social leader. " Do you know who that is you spoke to ? " asked young Parker with an alarmed expression. " Yes," replied Hamilton with characteristic effrontery. " The man you lost a thousand dollars to last week. *I* only know him *socially*." " But isn't he a gambler ? " queried the youngest Miss Smith. " He is," replied Hamilton; " but I wish, my dear young lady, that we all played as open and honest a game as our friend yonder, and were as willing as he is to abide by its fortunes."

But Mr. Oakhurst was happily out of hearing of this colloquy, and was even then loun-

ging listlessly yet watchfully along the upper
hall. Suddenly he heard a light footstep
behind him, and then his name called in a familiar voice that drew the blood quickly to his
heart. He turned, and she stood before him.

But how transformed! If I have hesitated
to describe the hollow-eyed cripple, the
quaintly-dressed artisan's wife, a few pages ago,
what shall I do with this graceful, shapely,
elegantly-attired gentlewoman into whom she
has been merged within these two months? In
good faith she was very pretty. You and I, my
dear madam, would have been quick to see
that those charming dimples were misplaced for
true beauty, and too fixed in their quality for
honest mirthfulness ; that the delicate lines
around these aquiline nostrils were cruel and
selfish ; that the sweet virginal surprise of these
lovely eyes were as apt to be opened on her
plate as upon the gallant speeches of her dinner
partner; that her sympathetic color came and
went more with her own spirits than yours.
But you and I are not in love with her, dear
madam, and Mr. Oakhurst is. And, even in the
folds of her Parisian gown, I am afraid this
poor fellow saw the same subtle strokes of
purity that he had seen in her homespun robe.
And then there was the delightful revelation
that she could walk, and that she had dear

little feet of her own in the tiniest slippers of her French shoemaker, with such preposterous blue bows, and Chappell's own stamp — Rue de something or other, Paris — on the narrow sole.

He ran toward her with a heightened color and outstretched hands. But she whipped her own behind her, glanced rapidly up and down the long hall, and stood looking at him with a half-audacious, half-mischievous admiration, in utter contrast to her old reserve.

"I've a great mind not to shake hands with you at all. You passed me just now on the piazza without speaking; and I ran after you, as I suppose many another poor woman has done."

Mr. Oakhurst stammered that she was so changed.

"The more reason why you should know me. Who changed me? You. You have re-created me. You found a helpless, crippled, sick, poverty-stricken woman, with one dress to her back, and that her own make, and you gave her life, health, strength, and fortune. You did; and you know it, sir. How do you like your work?" She caught the side-seams of her gown in either hand, and dropped him a playful courtesy. Then, with a sudden, relenting gesture, she gave him both her hands.

Outrageous as this speech was, and unfemi- nine as I trust every fair reader will deem it,

I fear it pleased Mr. Oakhurst. Not but that
he was accustomed to a certain frank female
admiration; but then it was of the *coulisse*,
and not of the cloister, with which he always
persisted in associating Mrs. Decker. To be
addressed in this way by an invalid Puritan, a
sick saint with the austerity of suffering still
clothing her, a woman who had a Bible on the
dressing-table, who went to church three times
a day, and was devoted to her husband, com
pletely bowled him over. He still held her
hands as she went on, —

"Why didn't you come before? What were
you doing in Marysville, in San José, in Oakland? You see I have followed you. I saw
you as you came down the cañon, and knew
you at once. I saw your letter to Joseph, and
knew you were coming. Why didn't you write
to me? You will some time! — Good-evening,
Mr. Hamilton."

She had withdrawn her hands, but not until
Hamilton, ascending the staircase, was nearly
abreast of them. He raised his hat to her
with well-bred composure, nodded familiarly to
Oakhurst, and passed on. When he had gone,
Mrs. Decker lifted her eyes to Mr. Oakhurst
"Some day I shall ask a great favor of you."

Mr. Oakhurst begged that it should be now
"No, not until you know me better. Then,
some day, I shall want you to — kill that man!"

She laughed such a pleasant little ringing laugh, such a display of dimples,—albeit a little fixed in the corners of her mouth,—such an innocent light in her brown eyes, and such a lovely color in her cheeks, that Mr. Oakhurst (who seldom laughed) was fain to laugh too. It was as if a lamb had proposed to a fox a foray into a neighboring sheepfold.

A few evenings after this, Mrs. Decker arose from a charmed circle of her admirers on the hotel piazza, excused herself for a few moments. laughingly declined an escort, and ran over to her little cottage — one of her husband's creation — across the road.   Perhaps from the sudden and unwonted exercise in her still convalescent state, she breathed hurriedly and feverishly as she entered her boudoir, and once or twice placed her hand upon her breast.   She was startled on turning up the light to find her husband lying on the sofa.

" You look hot and excited, Elsie love," said Mr. Decker.   " You ain't took worse, are you?"

Mrs Decker's face had paled, but now flushed again.   " No," she said; " only a little pain here," as she again placed her hand upon her corsage.

" Can I do any thing for you?" said Mr. Desker, rising with affectionate concern.

" Run over to the hotel and get me some brandy, quick!"

Mr. Decker ran. Mrs Decker closed and bolted the door, and then, putting her hand to her bosom, drew out the pain. It was folded foursquare, and was, I grieve to say, in Mr. Oakhurst's handwriting.

She devoured it with burning eyes and cheeks until there came a step upon the porch; then she hurriedly replaced it in her bosom, and unbolted the door. Her husband entered. She raised the spirits to her lips, and declared herself better.

" Are you going over there again to-night?" asked Mr. Decker submissively.

" No," said Mrs. Decker, with her eyes fixed dreamily on the floor.

" I wouldn't if I was you," said Mr. Decker with a sigh of relief. After a pause, he took a seat on the sofa, and, drawing his wife to his side, said, " Do you know what I was thinking of when you came in, Elsie?" Mrs. Decker ran her fingers through his stiff black hair, and couldn't imagine.

" I was thinking of old times, Elsie: I was thinking of the days when I built that kerridge for you, Elsie,—when I used to take you out to ride, and was both hoss and driver. We was poor then, and you was sick, Elsie; but we was happy. We've got money now, and a house; and you're quite another woman. I may say, dear, that you're a *new* woman. And that's where the trouble comes in. I could build you a kerridge, Elsie; I could build you a house, Elsie — but there I stopped. I couldn't build up *you*. You're strong and pretty, Elsie, and fresh and new. But somehow, Elsie, you ain't no work of mine!"

He paused. With one hand laid gently on his forehead, and the other pressed upon her bosom, as if to feel certain of the presence of her pain, she said sweetly and soothingly, —

" But it was your work, dear."

Mr. Decker shook his head sorrowfully. " No, Elsie, not mine. I had the chance to do it once, and I let it go. It's done now — but not by me."

Mrs. Decker raised her surprised, innocent eyes to his. He kissed her tenderly, and then went on in a more cheerful voice, —

" That ain't all I was thinking of, Elsie. I was thinking that maybe you give too much of your company to that Mr. Hamilton. Not that there's any wrong in it, to you or him; but it might make people talk. You're the only one here, Elsie," said the master-carpenter, looking fondly at his wife, " who isn't talked about, whose work ain't inspected or condemned."

Mrs. Decker was glad he had spoken about it. She had thought so too. But she could not well be uncivil to Mr. Hamilton, who was a fine gen tleman, without making a powerful enemy. "And he's always treated me as if I was a born lady in his own circle," added the little woman, with a certain pride that made her husband fondly smile. "But I have thought of a plan. He will not stay here if I should go away. If, for instance, I went to San Francisco to visit ma for a few days, he would be gone before I should return."

Mr. Decker was delighted. "By all means," he said, "go to-morrow. Jack Oakhurst is going down; and I'll put you in his charge."

Mrs. Decker did not think it was prudent. "Mr. Oakhurst is our friend, Joseph; but you know his reputation." In fact, she did not know that she ought to go now, knowing that he was going the same day; but, with a kiss, Mr. Decker overcame her scruples. She yielded gracefully. Few women, in fact, knew how to give up a point as charmingly as she.

She staid a week in San Francisco. When she returned, she was a trifle thinner and paler than she had been. This she explained as the result of perhaps too active exercise and excitement. "I was out of doors nearly all the time, as ma will tell you," she said to her husband, "and always alone. I am getting quite inde pendent now," she added gayly. "I don't want any escort. I believe, Joey dear, I could get along even without you, I'm so brave!"

But her visit, apparently, had not been pro-ductive of her impelling design. Mr. Hamilton had not gone, but had remained, and called upon them that very evening. "I've thought of a plan, Joey dear," said Mrs. Decker, when he had departed. "Poor Mr. Oakhurst has a miserable room at the hotel. Suppose you ask him, when he returns from San Francisco, to stop with us. He can have our spare-room. I don't think," she added archly, "that Mr. Hamilton will call often." Her husband laughed, intimated that she was a little coquette, pinched her cheek, and complied. "The queer thing about a woman," he said afterward confidentially to Mr. Oak-hurst, "is, that, without having any plan of her own, she'll take anybody's, and build a house on it entirely different to suit herself. And dern my skin if you'll be able to say whether or not you didn't give the scale and measurements yourself! That's what gets me!"

The next week Mr. Oakhurst was installed in the Deckers' cottage. The business relations of her husband and himself were known to all, and her own reputation was above suspicion. In-deed, few women were more popular. She was domestic, she was prudent, she was pious. In a country of great feminine freedom and latitude,

she never rode or walked with anybody but her
husband. In an epoch of slang and ambiguous
expression, she was always precise and formal
in her speech. In the midst of a fashion of ostentatious decoration, she never wore a diamond,
nor a single valuable jewel. She never permitted an indecorum in public. She never coun-
tenanced the familiarities of California society.
She declaimed against the prevailing tone of
infidelity and scepticism in religion. Few people who were present will ever forget the dignified yet stately manner with which she
rebuked Mr. Hamilton in the public parlor for
entering upon the discussion of a work on ma·
terialism, lately published; and some among
them, also, will not forget the expression of
amused surprise on Mr. Hamilton's face, that
gradually changed to sardonic gravity, as he
courteously waived his point; certainly not Mr.
Oakhurst, who, from that moment, began to be
uneasily impatient of his friend, and even — if
such a term could be applied to any moral quali·
ty in Mr. Oakhurst — to fear him.

For during this time Mr. Oakhurst had begun
to show symptoms of a change in his usual
habits. He was seldom, if ever, seen in his old
haunts, in a bar-room, or with his old associates.
Pink and white notes, in distracted handwriting,
accumulated on the dressing-table in his rooms

at Sacramento. It was given out in San Francisco that he had some organic disease of the heart, for which his physician had prescribed perfect rest. He read more; he took long walks; he sold his fast horses; he went to church.

I have a very vivid recollection of his first appearance there. He did not accompany the Deckers, nor did he go into their pew, but came in as the service commenced, and took a seat quietly in one of the back-pews. By some mysterious instinct, his presence became presently known to the congregation, some of whom so far forgot themselves, in their curiosity, as to face around, and apparently address their responses to him. Before the service was over, it was pretty well understood that "miserable sinners" meant Mr. Oakhurst. Nor did this mysterious influence fail to affect the officiating clergyman, who introduced an allusion to Mr. Oakhurst's calling and habits in a sermon on the architecture of Solomon's temple, and in a manner so pointed, and yet labored, as to cause the youngest of us to flame with indignation. Happily, however, it was lost upon Jack: I do not think he even heard it. His handsome, colorless face, albeit a trifle worn and thoughtful, was inscrutable. Only once, during the singing of a hymn, at a certain note in the contralto's voice, there crept into his dark eyes a look of wistful

tenderness, so yearning and yet so hopeless, that
those who were watching him felt their own
glisten.   Yet I retain a very vivid remembrance
of his standing up to receive the benediction,
with the suggestion, in his manner and tightly-
buttoned coat, of taking the fire of his adversary at ten paces.   After church, he disappeared
as quietly as he had entered, and fortunately
escaped hearing the comments on his rash act.
His appearance was generally considered as an
impertinence, attributable only to some wanton
fancy, or possibly a bet.   One or two thought
that the sexton was exceedingly remiss in not
turning him out after discovering who he was ;
and a prominent pew-holder remarked, that if he
couldn't take his wife and daughters to that
church, without exposing them to such an influence, he would try to find some church where
he could.   Another traced Mr. Oakhurst's presence to certain Broad Church radical tendencies,
which he regretted to say he had lately noted
in their pastor.   Deacon Sawyer, whose deli-
cately-organized, sickly wife had already borne
him eleven children, and died in an ambitious
attempt to complete the dozen, avowed that the
presence of a person of Mr. Oakhurst's various
and indiscriminate gallantries was an insult to
the memory of the deceased, that, as a man, he
could not brook.

It was about this time that Mr. Oakhurst, contrasting himself with a conventional world in which he had hitherto rarely mingled, became aware that there was something in his face, figure, and carriage quite unlike other men,— something, that, if it did not betray his former career, at least showed an individuality and originality that was suspicious. In this belief, he shaved off his long, silken mustache, and religiously brushed out his clustering curls every morning. He even went so far as to affect a negligence of dress, and hid his small, slim, arched feet in the largest and heaviest walking-shoes. There is a story told that he went to his tailor in Sacramento, and asked him to make him a suit of clothes like everybody else. The tailor, familiar with Mr. Oakhurst's fastidiousness, did not know what he meant. "I mean," said Mr. Oakhurst savagely, "something *respectable*,—something that doesn't exactly fit me, you know." But, however Mr. Oakhurst might hide his shapely limbs in homespun and home-made garments, there was something in his carriage, something in the pose of his beautiful head, something in the strong and fine manliness of his presence, something in the perfect and utter discipline and control of his muscles, something in the high repose of his nature,—a repose not so much a matter of intellectual rul-

ing as of his very nature, — that, go where he
would, and with whom, he was always a notable
man in ten thousand. Perhaps this was never
so clearly intimated to Mr. Oakhurst, as when,
emboldened by Mr. Hamilton's advice and assistance, and his own predilections, he became a
San-Francisco broker. Even before objection
was made to his presence in the Board, — the objection, I remember, was urged very eloquently
by Watt Sanders, who was supposed to be the
inventor of the "freezing-out" system of disposing of poor stockholders, and who also
enjoyed the reputation of having been the impelling cause of Briggs of Tuolumne's ruin and
suicide, — even before this formal protest of
respectability against lawlessness, the aquiline
suggestions of Mr. Oakhurst's mien and countenance, not only prematurely fluttered the
pigeons, but absolutely occasioned much uneasiness among the fish-hawks who circled below
him with their booty. "Dash me ! but he's as
likely to go after us as anybody," said Joe
Fielding.

It wanted but a few days before the close of
the brief summer season at San Isabel Warm
Springs. Already there had been some migra-
tion of the more fashionable ; and there was an
uncomfortable suggestion of dregs and lees in

the social life that remained.   Mr. Oakhurst
was moody. It was hinted that even the secure
reputation of Mrs. Decker could no longer protect her from the gossip which his presence
excited. It is but fair to her to say, that, during
the last few weeks of this trying ordeal, she
looked like a sweet, pale martyr, and conducted
herself toward her traducers with the gentle,
forgiving manner of one who relied not upon
the idle homage of the crowd, but upon the
security of a principle that was dearer than
popular favor. "They talk about myself and
Mr. Oakhurst, my dear," she said to a friend ;
"but heaven and my husband can best answer
their calumny. It never shall be said that my
husband ever turned his back upon a friend in
the moment of his adversity, because the position was changed, — because his friend was poor,
and he was rich." This was the first intimation
to the public that Jack had lost money, although
it was known generally that the Deckers had
lately bought some valuable property in San
Francisco.

A few evenings after this, an incident occurred
which seemed to unpleasantly discord with the
general social harmony that had always existed
at San Isabel. It was at dinner ; and Mr. Oakhurst and Mr. Hamilton, who sat together at a
separate table, were observed to rise in some

agitation. When they reached the hall, by a common instinct they stepped into a little breakfast-room which was vacant, and closed the door. Then Mr. Hamilton turned with a half-amused, half-serious smile toward his friend, and said, —

"If we are to quarrel, Jack Oakhurst, — you and I, — in the name of all that is ridiculous, don't let it be about a" —

I do not know what was the epithet intended. It was either unspoken or lost; for at that very instant Mr. Oakhurst raised a wineglass, and dashed its contents into Hamilton's face.

As they faced each other, the men seemed to have changed natures. Mr. Oakhurst was trembling with excitement, and the wineglass that he returned to the table shivered between his fingers. Mr. Hamilton stood there, grayish white, erect, and dripping. After a pause, he said coldly, —

"So be it. But remember, our quarrel commences here. If I fall by your hand, you shall not use it to clear her character: if you fall by mine, you shall not be called a martyr. I am sorry it has come to this; but amen, the sooner now, the better."

He turned proudly, dropped his lids over his cold steel-blue eyes, as if sheathing a rapier bowed, and passed coldly out.

They met, twelve hours later, in a little hollow two miles from the hotel, on the Stockton road. As Mr. Oakhurst received his pistol from Col. Starbottle's hands, he said to him in a low voice, " Whatever turns up or down, I shall not return to the hotel. You will find some directions in my room. Go there " — But his voice suddenly faltered, and he turned his glistening eyes away, to his second's intense astonishment. " I've been out a dozen times with Jack Oakhurst," said Col. Starbottle afterward, " and I never saw him anyways cut before. Blank me if I didn't think he was losing his sand, till he walked to position."

The two reports were almost simultaneous. Mr. Oakhurst's right arm dropped suddenly to his side, and his pistol would have fallen from his paralyzed fingers; but the discipline of trained nerve and muscle prevailed, and he kept his grasp until he had shifted it to the other hand, without changing his position. Then there was a silence that seemed interminable, a gathering of two or three dark figures where a smoke-curl still lazily floated, and then the hurried, husky, panting voice of Col. Starbottle in his ear, " He's hit hard — through the lungs — you must run for it ! "

Jack turned his dark, questioning eyes upon his second, but did not seem to listen, — rather seemed to hear some other voice, remoter in the distance. He hesitated, and then made a step forward in the direction of the distant group. Then he paused again as the figures separated, and the surgeon came hastily toward him.

" He would like to speak with you a moment," said the man. " You have little time to lose, I know ; but," he added in a lower voice, " it is my duty to tell you he has still less."

A look of despair, so hopeless in its intensity, swept over Mr. Oakhurst's usually impassive face, that the surgeon started. " You are hit," he said, glancing at Jack's helpless arm.

" Nothing — a mere scratch," said Jack hastily. Then he added with a bitter laugh, " I'm not in luck to-day. But come : we'll see what he wants."

His long, feverish stride outstripped the surgeon's ; and in another moment he stood where the dying man lay, — like most dying men, — the one calm, composed, central figure of an anxious group. Mr. Oakhurst's face was less calm as he dropped on one knee beside him, and took his hand. " I want to speak with this gentleman alone," said Hamilton, with something of his old imperious manner, as he turned to those about him. When they drew back, he looked up in Oakhurst's face.

" I've something to tell you, Jack."

His own face was white, but not so white as that which Mr. Oakhurst bent over him, — a face so ghastly, with haunting doubts, and a hopeless presentiment of coming evil, — a face so piteous in its infinite weariness and envy of death, that the dying man was touched, even in the languor of dissolution, with a pang of compassion; and the cynical smile faded from his lips.

" Forgive me, Jack," he whispered more feebly, " for what I have to say. I don't say it in anger, but only because it must be said. I could not do my duty to you, I could not die contented, until you knew it all. It's a miserable business at best, all around. But it can't be helped now. Only I ought to have fallen by Decker's pistol, and not yours."

A flush like fire came into Jack's cheek, and he would have risen; but Hamilton held him fast.

" Listen! In my pocket you will find two letters. Take them — there! You will know the handwriting. But promise you will not read them until you are in a place of safety. Promise me."

Jack did not speak, but held the letters between his fingers as if they had been burning coals.

" Promise me," said Hamilton faintly.

"Why?" asked Oakhurst, dropping his friend's hand coldly.

"Because," said the dying man with a bitter smile, — " because — when you have read them — you — will — go back — to capture — and death !"

They were his last words. He pressed Jack's hand faintly. Then his grasp relaxed, and he fell back a corpse.

It was nearly ten o'clock at night, and Mrs. Decker reclined languidly upon the sofa with a novel in her hand, while her husband discussed the politics of the country in the bar-room of the hotel. It was a warm night; and the French window looking out upon a little balcony was partly open. Suddenly she heard a foot upon the balcony, and she raised her eyes from the book with a slight start. The next moment the window was hurriedly thrust wide, and a man entered.

Mrs. Decker rose to her feet with a little cry of alarm.

"For Heaven's sake, Jack, are you mad? He has only gone for a little while — he may return at any moment. Come an hour later, to-morrow, any time when I can get rid of him — but go, now, dear, at once."

Mr. Oakhurst walked toward the door, bolted it, and then faced her without a word. His face was haggard; his coat-sleeve hung loosely over an arm that was bandaged and bloody.

Nevertheless her voice did not falter as she turned again toward him. "What has happened, Jack. Why are you here?"

He opened his coat, and threw two letters in her lap.

"To return your lover's letters; to kill you — and then myself," he said in a voice so low as to be almost inaudible.

Among the many virtues of this admirable woman was invincible courage. She did not faint; she did not cry out; she sat quietly down again, folded her hands in her lap, and said calmly, —

"And why should you not?"

Had she recoiled, had she shown any fear or contrition, had she essayed an explanation or apology, Mr. Oakhurst would have looked upon it as an evidence of guilt. But there is no quality that courage recognizes so quickly as courage. There is no condition that desperation bows before but desperation. And Mr. Oakhurst's power of analysis was not so keen as to prevent him from confounding her courage with a moral quality. Even in his fury, he could not help admiring this dauntless invalid.

"Why should you not?" she repeated with a smile. "You gave me life, health, and happi-

ness, Jack. You gave me your love. Why
should you not take what you have given? Go
on. I am ready."

She held out her hands with that same infinite grace of yielding with which she had taken
his own on the first day of their meeting at the
hotel. Jack raised his head, looked at her for
one wild moment, dropped upon his knees beside her, and raised the folds of her dress to his
feverish lips. But she was too clever not to
instantly see her victory: she was too much
of a woman, with all her cleverness, to refrain
from pressing that victory home. At the same
moment, as with the impulse of an outraged
and wounded woman, she rose, and, with an imperious gesture, pointed to the window. Mr.
Oakhurst rose in his turn, cast one glance upon
her, and without another word passed out of
her presence forever.

When he had gone, she closed the window
and bolted it, and, going to the chimney-piece,
placed the letters, one by one, in the flame of
the candle until they were consumed. I would
not have the reader think, that, during this
painful operation, she was unmoved. Her hand
trembled, and — not being a brute — for some
minutes (perhaps longer) she felt very badly,
and the corners of her sensitive mouth were
depressed. When her husband arrived, it was

with a genuine joy that she ran to him, and nestled against his broad breast with a feeling of security that thrilled the honest fellow to the core.

"But I've heard dreadful news to-night, Elsie," said Mr. Decker, after a few endearments were exchanged.

"Don't tell me any thing dreadful, dear: I'm not well to-night," she pleaded sweetly.

"But it's about Mr. Oakhurst and Hamilton."

"Please!" Mr. Decker could not resist the petitionary grace of those white hands and that sensitive mouth, and took her to his arms. Suddenly he said, "What's that?"

He was pointing to the bosom of her white dress. Where Mr. Oakhurst had touched her, there was a spot of blood.

It was nothing: she had slightly cut her hand in closing the window; it shut so hard! If Mr. Decker had remembered to close and bolt the shutter before he went out, he might have saved her this. There was such a genuine irritability and force in this remark, that Mr. Decker was quite overcome by remorse. But Mrs. Decker forgave him with that graciousness which I have before pointed out in these pages. And with the halo of that forgiveness and marital confidence still lingering above the pair, with the reader's permission we will leave them, and return to Mr. Oakhurst.

But not for two weeks. At the end of that time, he walked into his rooms in Sacramento, and in his old manner took his seat at the faro-table.

"How's your arm, Jack?" asked an incautious player.

There was a smile followed the question, which, however, ceased as Jack looked up quietly at the speaker.

"It bothers my dealing a little; but I can shoot as well with my left."

The game was continued in that decorous silence which usually distinguished the table at which Mr. John Oakhurst presided.

WAN LEE, THE PAGAN.

A S I opened Hop Sing's letter, there flut tered to the ground a square strip of yellow paper covered with hieroglyphics, which, at first glance, I innocently took to be the label from a pack of Chinese fire-crackers. But the same envelope also contained a smaller strip of rice-paper, with two Chinese characters traced in India ink, that I at once knew to be Hop Sing's visiting-card. The whole, as afterwards literally translated, ran as follows : —

"To the stranger the gates of my house are not closed : the rice-jar is on the left, and the sweetmeats on the right, as you enter.
Two sayings of the Master : —
Hospitality is the virtue of the son and the wisdom of the ancestor.
The Superior man is light hearted after the crop-gathering : he makes a festival.
When the stranger is in your melon-patch, observe him not too closely : inattention is often the highest form of civility.
Happiness, Peace, and Prosperity.
HOP SING."

Admirable, certainly, as was this morality and proverbial wisdom, and although this last axiom was very characteristic of my friend Hop Sing, who was that most sombre of all humorists, a Chinese philosopher, I must confess, that, even after a very free translation, I was at a loss to make any immediate application of the message. Luckily I discovered a third enclosure in the shape of a little note in English, and Hop Sing's own commercial hand. It ran thus: —

" The pleasure of your company is requested at No. — Sacramento Street, on Friday evening at eight o'clock. A cup of tea at nine, — sharp.

"HOP SING."

This explained all. It meant a visit to Hop Sing's warehouse, the opening and exhibition of some rare Chinese novelties and *curios*, a chat in the back office, a cup of tea of a perfection unknown beyond these sacred precincts, cigars, and a visit to the Chinese theatre or temple. This was, in fact, the favorite programme of Hop Sing when he exercised his functions of hospi-tality as the chief factor or superintendent of the Ning Foo Company.

At eight o'clock on Friday evening, I entered the warehouse of Hop Sing. There was that deliciously commingled mysterious foreign odor that I had so often noticed; there was the old array of uncouth-looking objects, the long procession of jars and crockery, the same singular blending of the grotesque and the mathematically neat and exact, the same endless suggestions of frivolity and fragility, the same want of harmony in colors, that were each, in themselves, beautiful and rare. Kites in the shape of enormous dragons and gigantic butterflies; kites so ingeniously arranged as to utter at intervals, when facing the wind, the cry of a hawk; kites so large as to be beyond any boy's power of restraint, — so large that you understood why kite-flying in China was an amusement for adults; gods of china and bronze so gratuitously ugly as to be beyond any human interest or sympathy from their very impossibility; jars of sweetmeats covered all over with moral sentiments from Confucius; hats that looked like baskets, and baskets that looked like hats; silks so light that I hesitate to record the incredible number of square yards that you might pass through the ring on your little finger, — these, and a great many other indescribable objects, were all familiar to me. I pushed my way through the dimly-lighted warehouse, until I reached the back office, or parlor, where I found Hop Sing waiting to receive me.

Before I describe him, I want the average reader to discharge from his mind any idea of a

Chinaman that he may have gathered from the pantomime. He did not wear beautifully scalloped drawers fringed with little bells (I never met a Chinaman who did); he did not habitually carry his forefinger extended before him at right angles with his body; nor did I ever hear him utter the mysterious sentence, "Ching a ring a ring chaw;" nor dance under any provocation. He was, on the whole, a rather grave, decorous, handsome gentleman. His complexion, which extended all over his head, except where his long pig-tail grew, was like a very nice piece of glazed brown paper-muslin. His eyes were black and bright, and his eyelids set at an angle of fifteen degrees; his nose straight, and delicately formed; his mouth small; and his teeth white and clean. He wore a dark blue silk blouse; and in the streets, on cold days, a short jacket of astrachan fur. He wore, also, a pair of drawers of blue brocade gathered tightly over his calves and ankles, offering a general sort of suggestion, that he had forgotten his trousers that morning, but that, so gentlemanly were his manners, his friends had forborne to mention the fact to him. His manner was urbane, although quite serious. He spoke French and English fluently. In brief, I doubt if you could have found the equal of this Pagan shopkeeper among the Christian traders of San Francisco.

There were a few others present, — a judge of the Federal Court, an editor, a high government official, and a prominent merchant. After we had drunk our tea, and tasted a few sweetmeats from a mysterious jar, that looked as if it might contain a preserved mouse among its other nondescript treasures, Hop Sing arose, and, gravely beckoning us to follow him, began to descend to the basement. When we got there, we were amazed at finding it brilliantly lighted, and that a number of chairs were arranged in a half-circle on the asphalt pavement. When he had courteously seated us, he said, —

" I have invited you to witness a performance which I can at least promise you no other foreigners but yourselves have ever seen. Wang, the court-juggler, arrived here yesterday morning. He has never given a performance outside of the palace before. I have asked him to entertain my friends this evening. He requires no theatre, stage accessories, or any confederate, — nothing more than you see here. Will you be pleased to examine the ground yourselves, gentlemen."

Of course we examined the premises. It was the ordinary basement or cellar of the San-Francisco storehouse, cemented to keep out the damp. We poked our sticks into the pavement, and rapped on the walls, to satisfy our polite

host — but for no other purpose. We were quite
content to be the victims of any clever deception. For myself, I knew I was ready to be
deluded to any extent, and, if I had been offered
an explanation of what followed, I should have
probably declined it.

Although I am satisfied that Wang's general
performance was the first of that kind ever
given on American soil, it has, probably, since
become so familiar to many of my readers, that
I shall not bore them with it here. He began
by setting to flight, with the aid of his fan, the
usual number of butterflies, made before our
eyes of little bits of tissue-paper, and kept them
in the air during the remainder of the performance. I have a vivid recollection of the judge
trying to catch one that had lit on his knee, and
of its evading him with the pertinacity of a living insect. And, even at this time, Wang, still
plying his fan, was taking chickens out of hats,
making oranges disappear, pulling endless yards
of silk from his sleeve, apparently filling the
whole area of the basement with goods that
appeared mysteriously from the ground, from
his own sleeves, from nowhere! He swallowed
knives to the ruin of his digestion for years to
come; he dislocated every limb of his body; he
reclined in the air, apparently upon nothing.
But his crowning performance, which I have

never yet seen repeated, was the most weird, mysterious, and astounding. It is my apology for this long introduction, my sole excuse for writing this article, and the genesis of this veracious history.

He cleared the ground of its encumbering articles for a space of about fifteen feet square, and then invited us all to walk forward, and again examine it. We did so gravely. There was nothing but the cemented pavement below to be seen or felt. He then asked for the loan of a handkerchief; and, as I chanced to be nearest him, I offered mine. He took it, and spread it open upon the floor. Over this he spread a large square of silk, and over this, again, a large shawl nearly covering the space he had cleared. He then took a position at one of the points of this rectangle, and began a monotonous chant, rocking his body to and fro in time with the somewhat lugubrious air.

We sat still and waited. Above the chant we could hear the striking of the city clocks, and the occasional rattle of a cart in the street overhead. The absolute watchfulness and expectation, the dim, mysterious half-light of the cellar falling in a grewsome way upon the misshapen bulk of a Chinese deity in the back ground, a faint smell of opium-smoke mingling with spice, and the dreadful uncertainty of what we were really waiting for, sent an uncomfortable thrill down our backs, and made us look at each other with a forced and unnatural smile. This feeling was heightened when Hop Sing slowly rose, and, without a word, pointed with his finger to the centre of the shawl.

There was something beneath the shawl Surely — and something that was not there before; at first a mere suggestion in relief, a faint outline, but growing more and more distinct and visible every moment. The chant still continued; the perspiration began to roll from the singer's face; gradually the hidden object took upon itself a shape and bulk that raised the shawl in its centre some five or six inches. It was now unmistakably the outline of a small but perfect human figure, with extended arms and legs. One or two of us turned pale. There was a feeling of general uneasiness, until the editor broke the silence by a gibe, that, poor as it was, was received with spontaneous enthusiasm. Then the chant suddenly ceased. Wang arose, and with a quick, dexterous movement, stripped both shawl and silk away, and discovered, sleeping peacefully upon my handkerchief, a tiny Chinese baby.

The applause and uproar which followed this revelation ought to have satisfied Wang, even if his audience was a small one: it was loud enough to awaken the baby, — a pretty little boy about a year old, looking like a Cupid cut out of sandal-wood. He was whisked away almost as mysteriously as he appeared. When Hop Sing returned my handkerchief to me with a bow, I asked if the juggler was the father of the baby. "No sabe!" said the imperturbable Hop Sing, taking refuge in that Spanish form of non-committalism so common in California.

"But does he have a new baby for every performance?" I asked. "Perhaps: who knows?" — "But what will become of this one?" — "Whatever you choose, gentlemen," replied Hop Sing with a courteous inclination. "It was born here: you are its godfathers."

There were two characteristic peculiarities of any Californian assemblage in 1856, — it was quick to take a hint, and generous to the point of prodigality in its response to any charitable appeal. No matter how sordid or avaricious the individual, he could not resist the infection of sympathy. I doubled the points of my handkerchief into a bag, dropped a coin into it, and, without a word, passed it to the judge. He quietly added a twenty-dollar gold-piece, and passed it to the next. When it was returned to me, it contained over a hundred dollars. I knotted the money in the handkerchief, and gave it to Hop Sing.

" For the baby, from its godfathers."

" But what name?" said the judge. There was a running fire of " Erebus," " Nox," " Plutus," " Terra Cotta," " Antæus," &c. Finally the question was referred to our host.

" Why not keep his own name?" he said quietly, — " Wan Lee." And he did.

And thus was Wan Lee, on the night of Friday, the 5th of March, 1856, born into this veracious chronicle.

The last form of " The Northern Star " for the 19th of July, 1865, — the only daily paper published in Klamath County, — had just gone to press; and at three, A.M., I was putting aside my proofs and manuscripts, preparatory to going home, when I discovered a letter lying under some sheets of paper, which I must have overlooked. The envelope was considerably soiled: it had no post-mark; but I had no difficulty in recognizing the hand of my friend Hop Sing. I opened it hurriedly, and read as follows: —

" MY DEAR SIR, — I do not know whether the bearer will suit you; but, unless the office of ' devil ' in your newspaper is a purely technical one, I think he has all the qualities required. He is very quick, active, and intelligent; understands English better than he speaks it; and makes up for any defect by his habits of observation and imitation. You have only to show him how to do a thing once, and he will repeat it, whether it is an offence or a virtue. But you certainly know him already. You are one of his godfathers; for is he not Wan Lee, the reputed son of Wang the conjurer, to whose performances I had the honor to introduce you? But perhaps you have forgotten it.

"I shall send him with a gang of coolies to Stockton, thence by express to your town. If you can use him there, you will do me a favor, and probably save his life, which is at present in great peril from the hands of the younger members of your Christian and highly-civilized race who attend the enlightened schools in San Francisco.

"He has acquired some singular habits and customs from his experience of Wang's profession, which he followed for some years, — until he became too large to go in a hat, or be produced from his father's sleeve. The money you left with me has been expended on his education. He has gone through the Tri-literal Classics, but, I think, without much benefit. He knows but little of Confucius, and absolutely nothing of Mencius. Owing to the negligence of his father, he associated, perhaps, too much with American children.

"I should have answered your letter before, by post; but I thought that Wan Lee himself would be a better messenger for this.

"Yours respectfully,
"HOP SING."

And this was the long-delayed answer to my letter to Hop Sing. But where was "the bearer"? How was the letter delivered? I summoned hastily the foreman, printers, and office-boy, but without eliciting any thing. No one

had seen the letter delivered, nor knew any
thing of the bearer. A few days later, I had
a visit from my laundry-man, Ah Ri.

" You wantee debbil? All lightee: me
catchee him."

He returned in a few moments with a bright-
looking Chinese boy, about ten years old, with
whose appearance and general intelligence I was
so greatly impressed, that I engaged him on the
spot. When the business was concluded, I
asked his name.

" Wan Lee," said the boy.

" What! Are you the boy sent out by Hop
Sing? What the devil do you mean by not
coming here before? and how did you deliver
that letter?"

Wan Lee looked at me, and laughed. " Me
pitchee in top side window."

I did not understand. He looked for a moment perplexed, and then, snatching the letter
out of my hand, ran down the stairs. After a
moment's pause, to my great astonishment, the
letter came flying in the window, circled twice
around the room, and then dropped gently, like
a bird upon my table. Before I had got over
my surprise, Wan Lee re-appeared, smiled, looked
at the letter and then at me, said, " So, John,"
and then remained gravely silent. I said noth
ing further; but it was understood that this was
his first official act.

His next performance, I grieve to say, was not attended with equal success. One of our regular paper-carriers fell sick, and, at a pinch, Wan Lee was ordered to fill his place. To prevent mistakes, he was shown over the route the previous evening, and supplied at about daylight with the usual number of subscribers' copies. He returned, after an hour, in good spirits, and without the papers. He had delivered them all, he said.

Unfortunately for Wan Lee, at about eight o'clock, indignant subscribers began to arrive at the office. They had received their copies; but how ? In the form of hard-pressed cannon-balls, delivered by a single shot, and a mere *tour de force*, through the glass of bedroom-windows. They had received them full in the face, like a base ball, if they happened to be up and stirring; they had received them in quarter-sheets, tucked in at separate windows; they had found them in the chimney, pinned against the door, shot through attic-windows, delivered in long slips through convenient keyholes, stuffed into ventilators, and occupying the same can with the morning's milk. One subscriber, who waited for some time at the office-door to have a personal interview with Wan Lee (then comfortably locked in my bedroom), told me, with tears of rage in his eyes, that he had been awakened at five o'clock by a most hideous yelling below his windows; that, on rising in great agitation, he was startled by the sudden appearance of " The Northern Star," rolled hard, and bent into the form of a boomerang, or East-Indian club, that sailed into the window, described a number of fiendish circles in the room, knocked over the light, slapped the baby's face, " took " him (the subscriber) " in the jaw," and then returned out of the window, and dropped helplessly in the area. During the rest of the day, wads and strips of soiled paper, purporting to be copies of " The Northern Star " of that morning's issue, were brought indignantly to the office. An admirable editorial on " The Resources of Humboldt County," which I had constructed the evening before, and which, I had reason to believe, might have changed the whole balance of trade during the ensuing year, and left San Francisco bankrupt at her wharves, was in this way lost to the public.

It was deemed advisable for the next three weeks to keep Wan Lee closely confined to the printing-office, and the purely mechanical part of the business. Here he developed a surprising quickness and adaptability, winning even the favor and good will of the printers and foreman, who at first looked upon his introduction into the secrets of their trade as fraught with the gravest political significance. He learned to set type readily and neatly, his wonderful skill in manipulation aiding him in the mere mechanical act, and his ignorance of the language confining him simply to the mechanical effort, confirming the printer's axiom, that the printer who considers or follows the ideas of his copy makes a poor compositor. He would set up deliberately long diatribes against himself, composed by his fellow-printers, and hung on his hook as copy, and even such short sentences as " Wan Lee is the devil's own imp," " Wan Lee is a Mongolian rascal," and bring the proof to me with happiness beaming from every tooth, and satisfaction shining in his huckleberry eyes.

It was not long, however, before he learned to retaliate on his mischievous persecutors. I remember one instance in which his reprisal came very near involving me in a serious misunderstanding. Our foreman's name was Webster; and Wan Lee presently learned to know and recognize the individual and combined letters of his name. It was during a political campaign; and the eloquent and fiery Col. Starbottle of Siskyou had delivered an effective speech, which was reported especially for " The Northern Star." In a very sublime peroration, Col. Starbottle had said, " In the language of the godlike Webster, I repeat "— and here followed the quotation, which I have forgotten. Now, it chanced that Wan Lee, looking over the galley after it had been revised, saw the name of his chief persecutor, and, of course, imagined the quotation his. After the form was locked up, Wan Lee took advantage of Webster's absence to remove the quotation, and substitute a thin piece of lead, of the same size as the type, engraved with Chinese characters, making a sentence, which, I had reason to believe, was an utter and abject confession of the incapacity and offensiveness of the Webster family generally, and exceedingly eulogistic of Wan Lee himself personally.

The next morning's paper contained Col. Starbottle's speech in full, in which it appeared that the "godlike" Webster had, on one occasion, uttered his thoughts in excellent but perfectly enigmatical Chinese. The rage of Col. Starbottle knew no bounds. I have a vivid recollection of that admirable man walking into my office, and demanding a retraction of the statement.

"But my dear sir," I asked, "are you willing to deny, over your own signature, that Webster ever uttered such a sentence? Dare you deny, that, with Mr. Webster's well-known attainments, a knowledge of Chinese might not have been among the number? Are you willing to

submit a translation suitable to the capacity of
our readers, and deny, upon your honor as a
gentleman, that the late Mr. Webster ever
uttered such a sentiment? If you are, sir, I am
willing to publish your denial."

The colonel was not, and left, highly indignant.

Webster, the foreman, took it more coolly.
Happily, he was unaware, that, for two days
after, Chinamen from the laundries, from the
gulches, from the kitchens, looked in the front
office-door, with faces beaming with sardonic
delight; that three hundred extra copies of the
" Star " were ordered for the wash-houses on the
river. He only knew, that, during the day, Wan
Lee occasionally went off into convulsive spasms,
and that he was obliged to kick him into consciousness again. A week after the occurrence,
I called Wan Lee into my office.

" Wan," I said gravely, " I should like you
to give me, for my own personal satisfaction, a
translation of that Chinese sentence which my
gifted countryman, the late godlike Webster,
uttered upon a public occasion." Wan Lee
looked at me intently, and then the slightest
possible twinkle crept into his black eyes. Then
he replied with equal gravity, —

" Mishtel Webstel, he say, ' China boy makee
me belly much foolee. China boy makee me

heap sick.'" Which I have reason to think was true.

But I fear I am giving but one side, and not the best, of Wan Lee's character. As he imparted it to me, his had been a hard life. He had known scarcely any childhood: he had no recollection of a father or mother. The conjurer Wang had brought him up. He had spent the first seven years of his life in appearing from baskets, in dropping out of hats, in climbing ladders, in putting his little limbs out of joint in posturing. He had lived in an atmosphere of trickery and deception. He had learned to look upon mankind as dupes of their senses: in fine, if he had thought at all, he would have been a sceptic; if he had been a little older, he would have been a cynic; if he had been older still, he would have been a philosopher. As it was, he was a little imp. A good-natured imp it was, too, — an imp whose moral nature had never been awakened, — an imp up for a holiday, and willing to try virtue as a diversion. I don't know that he had any spiritual nature. He was very superstitious. He carried about with him a hideous little porcelain god, which he was in the habit of alternately reviling and propitiating. He was too intelligent for the commoner Chinese vices of stealing or gratuitous lying. Whatever discipline he practised was taught by his intellect.

I am inclined to think that his feelings were not altogether unimpressible, although it was almost impossible to extract an expression from him; and I conscientiously believe he became attached to those that were good to him. What he might have become under more favorable conditions than the bondsman of an overworked, under-paid literary man, I don't know: I only know that the scant, irregular, impulsive kindnesses that I showed him were gratefully received. He was very loyal and patient, two qualities rare in the average American servant. He was like Malvolio, "sad and civil" with me. Only once, and then under great provocation, do I remember of his exhibiting any impatience. It was my habit, after leaving the office at night, to take him with me to my rooms, as the bearer of any supplemental or happy after-thought, in the editorial way, that might occur to me before the paper went to press. One night I had been scribbling away past the usual hour of dismissing Wan Lee, and had become quite oblivious of his presence in a chair near my door, when suddenly I became aware of a voice saying in plaintive accents, something that sounded like "Chy Lee."

I faced around sternly.

" What did you say ?"

"Me say, ' Chy Lee.' "

"Well?" I said impatiently.

"You sabe, ' How do, John?' "

" Yes."

"You sabe, ' So long, John'?"

" Yes."

"Well, ' Chy Lee ' allee same!"

I understood him quite plainly. It appeared that "Chy Lee" was a form of "good-night," and that Wan Lee was anxious to go home. But an instinct of mischief, which, I fear, I possessed in common with him, impelled me to act as if oblivious of the hint. I muttered something about not understanding him, and again bent over my work. In a few minutes I heard his wooden shoes pattering pathetically over the floor. I looked up. He was standing near the door.

"You no sabe, ' Chy Lee '?"

"No," I said sternly.

"You sabe muchee big foolee! allee same!"

And, with this audacity upon his lips, he fled The next morning, however, he was as meek and patient as before, and I did not recall his offence. As a probable peace-offering, he blacked all my boots, — a duty never required of him, — including a pair of buff deer-skin slippers and an immense pair of horseman's jack-boots, on which he indulged his remorse for two hours.

I have spoken of his honesty as being a quality of his intellect rather than his principle but I recall about this time two exceptions to the rule. I was anxious to get some fresh eggs as a change to the heavy diet of a mining-town; and, knowing that Wan Lee's country-men were great poultry-raisers, I applied to him. He furnished me with them regularly every morning, but refused to take any pay, saying that the man did not sell them, — a remarkable instance of self-abnegation, as eggs were then worth half a dollar apiece. One morning my neighbor Forster dropped in upon me at breakfast, and took occasion to bewail his own ill fortune, as his hens had lately stopped laying, or wandered off in the bush. Wan Lee, who was present during our colloquy, preserved his characteristic sad taciturnity. When my neighbor had gone, he turned to me with a slight chuckle : " Flostel's hens — Wan Lee's hens allee same ! " His other offence was more serious and ambitious. It was a season of great irregularities in the mails, and Wan Lee had heard me deplore the delay in the delivery of my letters and newspapers. On arriving at my office one day, I was amazed to find my table covered with letters, evidently just from the post-office, but, unfortunately, not one addressed to me. I turned to Wan Lee, who was surveying them with a calm satisfaction, and demanded an explanation. To my horror he pointed to an empty mail-bag in the corner, and said, " Postman he say, ' No lettee, John; no lettee, John.' Postman plentee lie! Postman no good. Me catchee lettee last night allee same!" Luckily it was still early: the mails had not been distributed. I had a hurried interview with the postmaster; and Wan Lee's bold attempt at robbing the United States mail was finally condoned by the purchase of a new mail-bag, and the whole affair thus kept a secret.

If my liking for my little Pagan page had not been sufficient, my duty to Hop Sing was enough, to cause me to take Wan Lee with me when I returned to San Francisco after my two years' experience with " The Northern Star." I do not think he contemplated the change with pleasure. I attributed his feelings to a nervous dread of crowded public streets (when he had to go across town for me on an errand, he always made a circuit of the outskirts), to his dislike for the discipline of the Chinese and English school to which I proposed to send him, to his fondness for the free, vagrant life of the mines, to sheer wilfulness. That it might have been a superstitious premonition did not occur to me until long after.

Nevertheless it really seemed as if the opportunity I had long looked for and confidently expected had come, — the opportunity of placing Wan Lee under gently restraining influences, of subjecting him to a life and experience that would draw out of him what good my superficial care and ill-regulated kindness could not reach. Wan Lee was placed at the school of a Chinese missionary, — an intelligent and kind-hearted clergyman, who had shown great interest in the boy, and who, better than all, had a wonderful faith in him. A home was found for him in the family of a widow, who had a bright and interesting daughter about two years younger than Wan Lee. It was this bright, cheery, innocent, and artless child that touched and reached a depth in the boy's nature that hitherto had been unsuspected; that awakened a moral susceptibility which had lain for years insensible alike to the teachings of society, or the ethics of the theologian.

These few brief months — bright with a promise that we never saw fulfilled — must have been happy ones to Wan Lee. He worshipped his little friend with something of the same superstition, but without any of the caprice, that he bestowed upon his porcelain Pagan god. It was his delight to walk behind her to school, carrying her books — a service always fraught with danger to him from the little hands of his Caucasian Christian brothers. He made her the most marvellous toys; he would cut out of carrots and turnips the most astonishing roses and tulips; he made life-like chickens out of melon-seeds; he constructed fans and kites, and was singularly proficient in the making of dolls' paper dresses. On the other hand, she played and sang to him, taught him a thousand little prettinesses and refinements only known to girls, gave him a yellow ribbon for his pig-tail, as best suiting his complexion, read to him, showed him wherein he was original and valuable, took him to Sunday school with her, against the precedents of the school, and, small-woman-like, triumphed. I wish I could add here, that she effected his conversion, and made him give up his porcelain idol. But I am telling a true story; and this little girl was quite content to fill him with her own Christian goodness, without letting him know that he was changed. So they got along very well together, — this little Christian girl with her shining cross hanging around her plump, white little neck; and this dark little Pagan, with his hideous porcelain god hidden away in his blouse.

There were two days of that eventful year which will long be remembered in San Fran cisco, — two days when a mob of her citizens set upon and killed unarmed, defenceless foreigners because they were foreigners, and of another race, religion, and color, and worked for what wages they could get. There were some public men so timid, that, seeing this, they thought that the end of the world had come. There were some eminent statesmen, whose names I am ashamed to write here, who began to think that the passage in the Constitution which guarantees civil and religious liberty to every citizen or foreigner was a mistake. But there were, also, some men who were not so easily frightened; and in twenty-four hours we had things so arranged, that the timid men could wring their hands in safety, and the eminent statesmen utter their doubts without hurting any body or any thing. And in the midst of this I got a note from Hop Sing, asking me to come to him immediately.

I found his warehouse closed, and strongly guarded by the police against any possible attack of the rioters. Hop Sing admitted me through a barred grating with his usual imperturbable calm, but, as it seemed to me, with more than his usual seriousness. Without a word, he took my hand, and led me to the rear of the room, and thence down stairs into the basement. It was dimly lighted; but there was something lying on the floor covered by a shawl

As I approached he drew the shawl away with a sudden gesture, and revealed Wan Lee, the Pagan, lying there dead.

Dead, my reverend friends, dead, — stoned to death in the streets of San Francisco, in the year of grace 1869, by a mob of half-grown boys and Christian school-children !

As I put my hand reverently upon his breast, I felt something crumbling beneath his blouse. I looked inquiringly at Hop Sing. He put his hand between the folds of silk, and drew out something with the first bitter smile I had ever seen on the face of that Pagan gentleman.

It was Wan Lee's porcelain god, crushed by a stone from the hands of those Christian iconoclasts !

HOW OLD MAN PLUNKETT WENT HOME.

I THINK we all loved him. Even after he mismanaged the affairs of the Amity Ditch Company, we commiserated him, although most of us were stockholders, and lost heavily. I remember that the blacksmith went so far as to say that "them chaps as put that responsibility on the old man oughter be lynched." But the blacksmith was not a stockholder; and the expression was looked upon as the excusable extravagance of a large, sympathizing nature, that, when combined with a powerful frame, was unworthy of notice. At least, that was the way they put it. Yet I think there was a general feeling of regret that this misfortune would interfere with the old man's long-cherished plan of "going home."

Indeed, for the last ten years he had been "going home." He was going home after a six-months' sojourn at Monte Flat; he was going home after the first rains; he was going home

when the rains were over; he was going home
when he had cut the timber on Buckeye Hill,
when there was pasture on Dow's Flat, when he
struck pay-dirt on Eureka Hill, when the Amity
Company paid its first dividend, when the elec-
tion was over, when he had received an answer
from his wife. And so the years rolled by,
the spring rains came and went, the woods of
Buckeye Hill were level with the ground, the
pasture on Dow's Flat grew sear and dry, Eureka
Hill yielded its pay-dirt and swamped its owner,
the first dividends of the Amity Company were
made from the assessments of stockholders,
there were new county officers at Monte Flat,
his wife's answer had changed into a persistent
question, and still old man Plunkett remained.

It is only fair to say that he had made several
distinct essays toward going. Five years before,
he had bidden good-by to Monte Hill with
much effusion and hand-shaking. But he never
got any farther than the next town. Here
he was induced to trade the sorrel colt he was
riding for a bay mare, — a transaction that at
once opened to his lively fancy a vista of vast
and successful future speculation. A few days
after, Abner Dean of Angel's received a letter
from him, stating that he was going to Visalia to
buy horses. "I am satisfied," wrote Plunkett,
with that elevated rhetoric for which his corre·

spondence was remarkable, — " I am satisfied
that we are at last developing the real resources
of California. The world will yet look to Dow's
Flat as the great stock-raising centre. In view
of the interests involved, I have deferred my
departure for a month." It was two before he
again returned to us — penniless. Six months
later, he was again enabled to start for the East
ern States ; and this time he got as far as San
Francisco. I have before me a letter which I
received a few days after his arrival, from which
I venture to give an extract : " You know, my
dear boy, that I have always believed that gam
bling, as it is absurdly called, is still in its in
fancy in California. I have always maintained
that a perfect system might be invented, by
which the game of poker may be made to yield
a certain percentage to the intelligent player.
I am not at liberty at present to disclose the
system ; but before leaving this city I intend to
perfect it." He seems to have done so, and
returned to Monte Flat with two dollars and
thirty-seven cents, the absolute remainder of
his capital after such perfection.

It was not until 1868 that he appeared to
have finally succeeded in going home. He left
us by the overland route, — a route which he
declared would give great opportunity for the
discovery of undeveloped resources. His last

letter was dated Virginia City. He was absent three years. At the close of a very hot day in midsummer, he alighted from the Wingdam stage, with hair and beard powdered with dust and age. There was a certain shyness about his greeting, quite different from his usual frank volubility, that did not, however, impress us as any accession of character. For some days he was reserved regarding his recent visit, content-ing himself with asserting, with more or less aggressiveness, that he had " always said he was going home, and now he had been there." Later he grew more communicative, and spoke freely and critically of the manners and customs of New York and Boston, commented on the social changes in the years of his absence, and, I remember, was very hard upon what he deemed the follies incidental to a high state of civiliza-tion. Still later he darkly alluded to the moral laxity of the higher planes of Eastern society ; but it was not long before he completely tore away the veil, and revealed the naked wicked-ness of New York social life in a way I even now shudder to recall. Vinous intoxication, it appeared, was a common habit of the first ladies of the city. Immoralities which he scarcely dared name were daily practised by the refined of both sexes. Niggardliness and greed were the common vices of the rich. " I have always asserted," he continued, " that corruption must exist where luxury and riches are rampant, and capital is not used to develop the natural resources of the country. Thank you — I will take mine without sugar." It is possible that some of these painful details crept into the local journals. I remember an editorial in " The Monte Flat Monitor," entitled " The Effete East," in which the fatal decadence of New York and New England was elaborately stated, and California offered as a means of natural salvation. " Perhaps," said " The Monitor," " we might add that Calaveras County offers superior inducements to the Eastern visitor with capital."

Later he spoke of his family. The daughter he had left a child had grown into beautiful womanhood. The son was already taller and larger than his father; and, in a playful trial of strength, " the young rascal," added Plunkett, with a voice broken with paternal pride and humorous objurgation, had twice thrown his doting parent to the ground. But it was of his daughter he chiefly spoke. Perhaps emboldened by the evident interest which masculine Monte Flat held in feminine beauty, he expatiated at some length on her various charms and accomplishments, and finally produced her photograph, — that of a very pretty girl, — to their infinite peril. But his account of his first meeting with her was so peculiar, that I must fain give it after his own methods, which were, perhaps, some shades less precise and elegant than his written style.

"You see, boys, it's always been my opinion that a man oughter be able to tell his own flesh and blood by instinct. It's ten years since I'd seen my Melindy; and she was then only seven, and about so high. So, when I went to New York, what did I do? Did I go straight to my house, and ask for my wife and daughter, like other folks? No, sir! I rigged myself up as a peddler, as a peddler, sir; and I rung the bell. When the servant came to the door, I wanted — don't you see? — to show the ladies some trinkets. Then there was a voice over the banister says, 'Don't want any thing: send him away.' — 'Some nice laces, ma'am, smuggled,' I says, looking up. 'Get out, you wretch!' says she. I knew the voice, boys: it was my wife, sure as a gun. Thar wasn't any instinct thar. 'Maybe the young ladies want somethin',' I said. 'Did you hear me?' says she; and with that she jumps forward, and I left. It's ten years, boys, since I've seen the old woman; but somehow, when she fetched that leap, I naterally left."

He had been standing beside the bar — his usual attitude — when he made this speech; but at this point he half faced his auditors with a look that was very effective. Indeed, a few who had exhibited some signs of scepticism and lack of interest, at once assumed an appearance of intense gratification and curiosity as he went on, —

"Well, by hangin round there for a day or two, I found out at last it was to be Melindy's birthday next week, and that she was goin' to have a big party. I tell ye what, boys, it weren't no slouch of a reception. The whole house was bloomin' with flowers, and blazin' with lights; and there was no end of servants and plate and refreshments and fixin's " —

"Uncle Joe."

"Well?"

"Where did they get the money?"

Plunkett faced his interlocutor with a severe glance. "I always said," he replied slowly, "that, when I went home, I'd send on ahead of me a draft for ten thousand dollars. I always said that, didn't I? Eh? And I said I was goin' home — and I've been home, haven't I? Well?"

Either there was something irresistibly conclusive in this logic, or else the desire to hear the remainder of Plunkett's story was stronger; but there was no more interruption. His ready good-humor quickly returned, and, with a slight chuckle, he went on, —

"I went to the biggest jewelry shop in town, and I bought a pair of diamond ear-rings, and put them in my pocket, and went to the house. 'What name?' says the chap who opened the door; and he looked like a cross 'twixt a restaurant waiter and a parson. 'Skeesicks,' said I. He takes me in; and pretty soon my wife comes sailin' into the parlor, and says, 'Excuse me; but I don't think I recognize the name.' She was mighty polite; for I had on a red wig and side-whiskers. 'A friend of your husband's from California, ma'am, with a present for your daughter, Miss ——,' and I made as I had forgot the name. But all of a sudden a voice said, 'That's too thin;' and in walked Melindy. 'It's playin' it rather low down, father, to pretend you don't know your daughter's name; ain't it, now? How are you, old man?' And with that she tears off my wig and whiskers, and throws her arms around my neck — instinct, sir, pure instinct!"

Emboldened by the laughter which followed his description of the filial utterances of Melinda, he again repeated her speech, with more or less elaboration, joining in with, and indeed often leading, the hilarity that accompanied it, and returning to it, with more or less incoherency, several times during the evening.

And so, at various times and at various

places, but chiefly in bar-rooms, did this
Ulysses of Monte Flat recount the story of
his wanderings. There were several discrep-
ancies in his statement; there was sometimes
considerable prolixity of detail; there was occasional change of character and scenery; there
was once or twice an absolute change in the
denoûment: but always the fact of his having
visited his wife and children remained. Of
course, in a sceptical community like that of
Monte Flat, — a community accustomed to great
expectation and small realization, — a community wherein, to use the local dialect, "they got
the color, and struck hardpan," more frequently
than any other mining-camp, — in such a community, the fullest credence was not given to
old man Plunkett's facts. There was only one
exception to the general unbelief, — Henry York
of Sandy Bar. It was he who was always an
attentive listener; it was his scant purse that
had often furnished Plunkett with means to
pursue his unprofitable speculations; it was to
him that the charms of Melinda were more frequently rehearsed; it was he that had borrowed
her photograph; and it was he that, sitting
alone in his little cabin one night, kissed that
photograph, until his honest, handsome face
glowed again in the firelight.

It was dusty in Monte Flat. The ruins of

the long dry season were crumbling every where: everywhere the dying summer had strewn its red ashes a foot deep, or exhaled its last breath in a red cloud above the troubled highways. The alders and cottonwoods, that marked the line of the water-courses, were grimy with dust, and looked as if they might have taken root in the open air. The gleaming stones of the parched water-courses themselves were as dry bones in the valley of death. The dusty sunset at times painted the flanks of the distant hills a dull, coppery hue: on other days, there was an odd, indefinable earthquake halo on the volcanic cones of the farther coast-spurs. Again an acrid, resinous smoke from the burning wood on Heavytree Hill smarted the eyes, and choked the free breath of Monte Flat; or a fierce wind, driving every thing, including the shrivelled summer, like a curled leaf before it, swept down the flanks of the Sierras, and chased the inhabitants to the doors of their cabins, and shook its red fist in at their windows. And on such a night as this, the dust having in some way choked the wheels of material progress in Monte Flat, most of the inhabitants were gathered listlessly in the gilded bar-room of the Moquelumne Hotel, spitting silently at the red-hot stove that tempered the mountain winds to the shorn lambs of Monte Flat, and waiting for the rain.

Every method known to the Flat of beguiling
the time until the advent of this long-looked-
for phenomenon had been tried. It is true, the
methods were not many, being limited chiefly
to that form of popular facetiæ known as practical joking; and even this had assumed the
seriousness of a business-pursuit. Tommy Roy,
who had spent two hours in digging a ditch in
front of his own door, into which a few friends
casually dropped during the evening, looked
ennuyé and dissatisfied. The four prominent
citizens, who, disguised as foot-pads, had
stopped the county treasurer on the Wingdam
road, were jaded from their playful efforts
next morning. The principal physician and
lawyer of Monte Flat, who had entered into an
unhallowed conspiracy to compel the sheriff
of Calaveras and his *posse* to serve a writ of
ejectment on a grizzly bear, feebly disguised
under the name of one "Major Ursus," who
haunted the groves of Heavytree Hill, wore
an expression of resigned weariness. Even the
editor of "The Monte Flat Monitor," who had
that morning written a glowing account of a
battle with the Wipneck Indians, for the benefit of Eastern readers, — even *he* looked grave
and worn. When, at last, Abner Dean of Angel's, who had been on a visit to San Francisco,
walked into the room, he was, of course, vic-

timized in the usual way by one or two apparently honest questions, which ended in his
answering them, and then falling into the trap
of asking another, to his utter and complete
shame and mortification; but that was all. Nobody laughed; and Abner, although a victim,
did not lose his good-humor. He turned quietly
on his tormentors, and said, —

"I've got something better than that — you
know old man Plunkett?"

Everybody simultaneously spat at the stove,
and nodded his head.

"You know he went home three years ago?"
Two or three changed the position of their legs
from the backs of different chairs; and one man
said, "Yes."

"Had a good time, home?"

Everybody looked cautiously at the man who
had said, "Yes;" and he, accepting the responsibility with a faint-hearted smile, said, "Yes,"
again, and breathed hard. "Saw his wife and
child — purty gal?" said Abner cautiously.
"Yes," answered the man doggedly. "Saw
her photograph, perhaps?" continued Abner
Dean quietly.

The man looked hopelessly around for support. Two or three, who had been sitting near
him, and evidently encouraging him with a look
of interest, now shamelessly abandoned him

and looked another way. Henry York flushed
a little, and veiled his gray eyes. The man
hesitated, and then with a sickly smile, that
was intended to convey the fact that he was
perfectly aware of the object of this questioning, and was only humoring it from abstract
good feeling, returned, "Yes," again.

"Sent home — let's see — ten thousand dollars, wasn't it?" Abner Dean went on "Yes,"
reiterated the man with the same smile.

"Well, I thought so," said Abner quietly.
"But the fact is, you see, that he never went
home at all — nary time."

Everybody stared at Abner in genuine surprise and interest, as, with provoking calmness
and a half-lazy manner, he went on, —

"You see, thar was a man down in 'Frisco as
knowed him, and saw him in Sonora during the
whole of that three years. He was herding
sheep, or tending cattle, or spekilating all that
time, and hadn't a red cent. Well it 'mounts
to this, — that 'ar Plunkett ain't been east of
the Rocky Mountains since '49."

The laugh which Abner Dean had the right
to confidently expect came; but it was bitter
and sardonic. I think indignation was apparent in the minds of his hearers. It was felt,
for the first time, that there was a limit to practical joking. A deception carried on for a year,

compromising the sagacity of Monte Flat, was deserving the severest reprobation. Of course, nobody had believed Plunkett; but then the supposition that it might be believed in adjacent camps that they *had* believed him was gall and bitterness. The lawyer thought that an indictment for obtaining money under false pretences might be found. The physician had long suspected him of insanity, and was not certain but that he ought to be confined. The four prominent merchants thought that the business-interests of Monte Flat demanded that something should be done. In the midst of an excited and angry discussion, the door slowly opened, and old man Plunkett staggered into the room.

He had changed pitifully in the last six months. His hair was a dusty, yellowish gray, like the chemisal on the flanks of Heavytree Hill; his face was waxen white, and blue and puffy under the eyes; his clothes were soiled and shabby, streaked in front with the stains of hurriedly eaten luncheons, and fluffy behind with the wool and hair of hurriedly-extemporized couches. In obedience to that odd law, that, the more seedy and soiled a man's garments become, the less does he seem inclined to part with them, even during that portion of the twenty-four hours when they are deemed less essential, Plunkett's clothes had gradually taken on the appearance of a kind of a bark, or an outgrowth from within, for which their possessor was not entirely responsible. Howbeit, as he entered the room, he attempted to button his coat over a dirty shirt, and passed his fingers, after the manner of some animal, over his cracker-strewn beard, in recognition of a cleanly public sentiment. But, even as he did so, the weak smile faded from his lips; and his hand, after fumbling aimlessly around a button, dropped helplessly at his side. For as he leaned his back against the bar, and faced the group, he, for the first time, became aware that every eye but one was fixed upon him. His quick, nervous apprehension at once leaped to the truth. His miserable secret was out, and abroad in the very air about him. As a last resort, he glanced despairingly at Henry York; but his flushed face was turned toward the windows.

No word was spoken. As the bar-keeper silently swung a decanter and glass before him, he took a cracker from a dish, and mumbled it with affected unconcern. He lingered over his liquor until its potency stiffened his relaxed sinews, and dulled the nervous edge of his apprehension, and then he suddenly faced around. "It don't look as if we were goin' to hev any rain much afore Christmas," he said with defiant ease.

No one made any reply.

"Just like this in '52, and again in '60. It's always been my opinion that these dry seasons come reg'lar. I've said it afore. I say it again. It's jist as I said about going home, you know," he added with desperate recklessness.

"Thar's a man," said Abner Dean lazily, "ez sez you never went home. Thar's a man ez sez you've been three years in Sonora. Thar's a man ez sez you hain't seen your wife and daughter since '49. Thar's a man ez sez you've been playin' this camp for six months."

There was a dead silence. Then a voice said quite as quietly, —

"That man lies."

It was not the old man's voice. Everybody turned as Henry York slowly rose, stretching out his six feet of length, and, brushing away the ashes that had fallen from his pipe upon his breast, deliberately placed himself beside Plunkett, and faced the others.

"That man ain't here," continued Abner Dean, with listless indifference of voice, and a gentle pre-occupation of manner, as he carelessly allowed his right hand to rest on his hip near his revolver. "That man ain't here; but, if I'm called upon to make good what he says, why, I'm on hand."

All rose as the two men — perhaps the least externally agitated of them all — approached each other. The lawyer stepped in between them.

"Perhaps there's some mistake here. York, do you *know* that the old man has been home?"

"Yes."

"How do you know it?"

York turned his clear, honest, frank eyes on his questioner, and without a tremor told the only direct and unmitigated lie of his life. "Because I've seen him there."

The answer was conclusive. It was known that York had been visiting the East during the old man's absence. The colloquy had diverted attention from Plunkett, who, pale and breathless, was staring at his unexpected deliverer. As he turned again toward his tormentors, there was something in the expression of his eye that caused those that were nearest to him to fall back, and sent a strange, indefinable thrill through the boldest and most reckless. As he made a step forward, the physician, almost unconsciously, raised his hand with a warning gesture; and old man Plunkett, with his eyes fixed upon the red-hot stove, and an odd smile playing about his mouth, began, —

"Yes — of course you did. Who says you didn't? It ain't no lie. I said I was goin' home — and I've been home. Haven't I? My God! I have. Who says I've been lyin'? Who says I m dreamin'? Is it true — why don't you speak? It is true, after all. You say you saw me there: why don't you speak again? Say, say! — is it true? It's going now. O my God! it's going again. It's going now. Save me!" And with a fierce cry he fell forward in a fit upon the floor.

When the old man regained his senses, he found himself in York's cabin. A flickering fire of pine-boughs lit up the rude rafters, and fell upon a photograph tastefully framed with fir-cones, and hung above the brush whereon he lay. It was the portrait of a young girl. It was the first object to meet the old man's gaze; and it brought with it a flush of such painful consciousness, that he started, and glanced quickly around. But his eyes only encountered those of York, — clear, gray, critical, and patient, — and they fell again.

"Tell me, old man," said York not unkindly, but with the same cold, clear tone in his voice that his eye betrayed a moment ago, — "tell me, is *that* a lie too?" and he pointed to the picture.

The old man closed his eyes, and did not reply. Two hours before, the question would have stung him into some evasion or bravado.

But the revelation contained in the question, as well as the tone of York's voice, was to him now, in his pitiable condition, a relief. It was plain, even to his confused brain, that York had lied when he had indorsed his story in the bar-room; it was clear to him now that he had not been home, that he was not, as he had begun to fear, going mad. It was such a relief, that, with characteristic weakness, his former recklessness and extravagance returned. He began to chuckle, finally to laugh uproariously.

York, with his eyes still fixed on the old man, withdrew the hand with which he had taken his.

"Didn't we fool 'em nicely; eh, Yorky! He, he! The biggest thing yet ever played in this camp! I always said I'd play 'em all some day, and I have — played 'em for six months. Ain't it rich? — ain't it the richest thing you ever seed? Did you see Abner's face when he spoke 'bout that man as seed me in Sonora? Warn't it good as the minstrels? Oh, it's too much!" and, striking his leg with the palm of his hand, he almost threw himself from the bed in a paroxysm of laughter, — a paroxysm that, nevertheless, appeared to be half real and half affected.

"Is that photograph hers?" said York in a low voice, after a slight pause.

"Hers? No! It's one of the San Francisco actresses. He, he! Don't you see? I bought it for two bits in one of the bookstores. I never thought they'd swaller *that* too; but they did! Oh, but the old man played 'em this time didn't he — eh?" and he peered curiously in York's face.

"Yes, and he played *me* too," said York, looking steadily in the old man's eye.

"Yes, of course," interposed Plunkett hastily; "but you know, Yorky, you got out of it well! You've sold 'em too. We've both got 'em on a string now — you and me — got to stick together now. You did it well, Yorky: you did it well. Why, when you said you'd seen me in York City, I'm d——d if I didn't "——

"Didn't what?" said York gently; for the old man had stopped with a pale face and wandering eye.

"Eh?"

"You say when I said I had seen you in New York you thought"——

"You lie!" said the old man fiercely. "I didn't say I thought any thing. What are you trying to go back on me for, eh?" His hands were trembling as he rose muttering from the bed, and made his way toward the hearth.

"Gimme some whiskey," he said presently "and dry up. You oughter treat **anyway**

Them fellows oughter treated last night. By hookey, I'd made 'em — only I fell sick."

York placed the liquor and a tin cup on the table beside him, and, going to the door, turned his back upon his guest, and looked out on the night. Although it was clear moonlight, the familiar prospect never to him seemed so dreary. The dead waste of the broad Wingdam highway never seemed so monotonous, so like the days that he had passed, and were to come to him, so like the old man in its suggestion of going sometime, and never getting there. He turned, and going up to Plunkett put his hand upon his shoulder, and said, —

"I want you to answer one question fairly and squarely."

The liquor seemed to have warmed the torpid blood in the old man's veins, and softened his acerbity; for the face he turned up to York was mellowed in its rugged outline, and more thoughtful in expression, as he said, —

"Go on, my boy."

"Have you a wife and — daughter?"

"Before God I have!"

The two men were silent for a moment, both gazing at the fire. Then Plunkett began rubbing his knees slowly.

"The wife, if it comes to that, ain't much," he began cautiously, "being a little on the shoulder, you know, and wantin', so to speak, a liberal California education, which makes, you know, a bad combination. It's always been my opinion, that there ain't any worse. Why, she's as ready with her tongue as Abner Dean is with his revolver, only with the difference that she shoots from principle, as she calls it; and the consequence is, she's always layin' for you. It's the effete East, my boy, that's ruinin' her. It's them ideas she gets in New York and Boston that's made her and me what we are. I don't mind her havin' 'em, if she didn't shoot. But, havin' that propensity, them principles oughtn't to be lying round loose no more'n fire-arms."

"But your daughter?" said York.

The old man's hands went up to his eyes here, and then both hands and head dropped forward on the table. "Don't say any thing 'bout her, my boy, don't ask me now." With one hand concealing his eyes, he fumbled about with the other in his pockets for his handkerchief — but vainly. Perhaps it was owing to this fact, that he repressed his tears; for, when he removed his hand from his eyes, they were quite dry. Then he found his voice.

"She's a beautiful girl, beautiful, though I say it; and you shall see her, my boy, — you shall see her sure. I've got things about fixed now

I shall have my plan for reducin' ores perfected in a day or two; and I've got proposals from all the smeltin' works here " (here he hastily produced a bundle of papers that fell upon the floor), 'and I'm goin' to send for 'em. I've got the papers here as will give me ten thousand dollars clear in the next month," he added, as he strove to collect the valuable documents again. "I'll have 'em here by Christmas, if I live; and you shall eat your Christmas dinner with me, York, my boy, — you shall sure."

With his tongue now fairly loosened by liquor and the suggestive vastness of his prospects, he rambled on more or less incoherently, elaborating and amplifying his plans, occasionally even speaking of them as already accomplished, until the moon rode high in the heavens, and York led him again to his couch. Here he lay for some time muttering to himself, until at last he sank into a heavy sleep. When York had satisfied himself of the fact, he gently took down the picture and frame, and, going to the hearth, tossed them on the dying embers, and sat down to see them burn.

The fir-cones leaped instantly into flame; then the features that had entranced San Francisco audiences nightly, flashed up and passed away (as such things are apt to pass); and even the cynical smile on York's lips faded too.

And then there came a supplemental and un-expected flash as the embers fell together, and by its light York saw a paper upon the floor. It was one that had fallen from the old man's pocket. As he picked it up listlessly, a photo-graph slipped from its folds. It was the portrait of a young girl; and on its reverse was written in a scrawling hand, "Melinda to father."

It was at best a cheap picture, but, ah me! I fear even the deft graciousness of the highest art could not have softened the rigid angulari-ties of that youthful figure, its self-complacent vulgarity, its cheap finery, its expressionless ill-favor. York did not look at it a second time. He turned to the letter for relief.

It was misspelled; it was unpunctuated; it was almost illegible; it was fretful in tone, and selfish in sentiment. It was not, I fear, even original in the story of its woes. It was the harsh recital of poverty, of suspicion, of mean makeshifts and compromises, of low pains and lower longings, of sorrows that were degrading, of a grief that was pitiable. Yet it was sincere in a certain kind of vague yearning for the presence of the degraded man to whom it was written, — an affection that was more like a con-fused instinct than a sentiment.

York folded it again carefully, and placed it beneath the old man's pillow. Then he returned to his seat by the fire. A smile that had been playing upon his face, deepening the curves behind his mustache, and gradually overrunning his clear gray eyes, presently faded away. It was last to go from his eyes; and it left there, oddly enough to those who did not know him, a tear.

He sat there for a long time, leaning forward, his head upon his hands. The wind that had been striving with the canvas roof all at once lifted its edges, and a moonbeam slipped suddenly in, and lay for a moment like a shining blade upon his shoulder; and, knighted by its touch, straightway plain Henry York arose, sustained, high-purposed and self-reliant.

The rains had come at last. There was already a visible greenness on the slopes of Heavy-tree Hill; and the long, white track of the Wingdam road was lost in outlying pools and ponds a hundred rods from Monte Flat. The spent water-courses, whose white bones had been sinuously trailed over the flat, like the vertebræ of some forgotten saurian, were full again; the dry bones moved once more in the valley; and there was joy in the ditches, and a pardonable extravagance in the columns of " The Monte Flat Monitor." " Never before in the history of the county has the yield been so satisfactory. Our contemporary of 'The Hillside Beacon,' who yesterday facetiously alluded to the fact (?) that our best citizens were leaving town in 'dugouts,' on account of the flood, will be glad to hear that our distinguished fellow-townsman, Mr. Henry York, now on a visit to his relatives in the East, lately took with him in his 'dugout' the modest sum of fifty thousand dollars, the result of one week's clean-up. We can imagine," continued that sprightly journal, "that no such misfortune is likely to overtake Hillside this season. And yet we believe 'The Beacon' man wants a railroad." A few journals broke out into poetry. The operator at Simpson's Crossing telegraphed to "The Sacramento Universe" "All day the low clouds have shook their garnered fulness down." A San-Francisco journal lapsed into noble verse, thinly disguised as editorial prose: "Rejoice: the gentle rain has come, the bright and pearly rain, which scatters blessings on the hills, and sifts them o'er the plain. Rejoice," &c. Indeed, there was only one to whom the rain had not brought blessing, and that was Plunkett. In some mysterious and darksome way, it had interfered with the perfection of his new method of reducing ores, and thrown the advent of that invention back another season. It had brought him down to an habitual seat in the bar-room, where, to heedless and inattentive ears, he sat and discoursed of the East and his family.

No one disturbed him. Indeed, it was rumored that some funds had been lodged with the landlord, by a person or persons unknown, whereby his few wants were provided for. His mania — for that was the charitable construction which Monte Flat put upon his conduct — was indulged, even to the extent of Monte Flat's accepting his invitation to dine with his family on Christmas Day, — an invitation extended frankly to every one with whom the old man drank or talked. But one day, to everybody's astonishment, he burst into the bar-room, holding an open letter in his hand. It read as follows: —

"Be ready to meet your family at the new cottage on Heavytree Hill on Christmas Day. Invite what friends you choose.

"HENRY YORK."

The letter was handed round in silence. The old man, with a look alternating between hope and fear, gazed in the faces of the group. The doctor looked up significantly, after a pause. "It's a forgery evidently," he said in a low voice. "He's cunning enough to conceive it (they always are); but you'll find he'll fail in executing it. Watch his face ! — Old man," he said suddenly, in a loud peremptory tone, "this is a trick, a forgery, and you know it. Answer me squarely, and look me in the eye. Isn't it so?"

The eyes of Plunkett stared a moment, and then dropped weakly. Then, with a feebler smile, he said, "You're too many for me, boys. The Doc's right. The little game's up. You can take the old man's hat;" and so, tottering, trembling, and chuckling, he dropped into silence and his accustomed seat. But the next day he seemed to have forgotten this episode, and talked as glibly as ever of the approaching festivity.

And so the days and weeks passed until Christmas — a bright, clear day, warmed with south winds, and joyous with the resurrection of springing grasses — broke upon Monte Flat. And then there was a sudden commotion in the hotel bar-room ; and Abner Dean stood beside the old man's chair, and shook him out of a slumber to his feet. "Rouse up, old man. York is here, with your wife and daughter, at the cottage on Heavytree. Come, old man. Here, boys, give him a lift;" and in another moment a dozen strong and willing hands had raised the old man, and bore him in triumph to the street up the steep grade of Heavytree Hill, and deposited him, struggling and confused, in the porch of a little cottage. At the same instant two women rushed forward, but were restrained by a gesture from Henry York. The old man was struggling to his feet. With an effort at last, he stood erect, trembling, his eye fixed, a gray pallor on his cheek, and a deep resonance in his voice.

"It's all a trick, and a lie! They ain't no flesh and blood or kin o' mine. It ain't my wife, nor child. My daughter's a beautiful girl — a beautiful girl, d'ye hear? She's in New York with her mother, and I'm going to fetch her here I said I'd go home, and I've been home: d'ye hear me?' I've been home! It's a mean trick you're playin' on the old man. Let me go: d'ye hear? Keep them women off me! Let me go! I'm going — I'm going — home!"

His hands were thrown up convulsively in the air, and, half turning round, he fell sideways on the porch, and so to the ground. They picked him up hurriedly, but too late. He had gone home.

THE FOOL OF FIVE FORKS.

HE lived alone. I do not think this
peculiarity arose from any wish to withdraw his foolishness from the rest of the camp;
nor was it probable that the combined wisdom
of Five Forks ever drove him into exile. My
impression is, that he lived alone from choice, —
a choice he made long before the camp indulged
in any criticism of his mental capacity. He
was much given to moody reticence, and,
although to outward appearances a strong man,
was always complaining of ill-health. Indeed,
one theory of his isolation was, that it afforded
him better opportunities for taking medicine, of
which he habitually consumed large quantities.

His folly first dawned upon Five Forks
through the post-office windows. He was, for
a long time, the only man who wrote home by
every mail; his letters being always directed to
the same person, — a woman. Now, it so happened that the bulk of the Five Forks corre-
spondence was usually the other way. There
were many letters received (the majority being

in the female hand), but very few answered.
The men received them indifferently, or as a
matter of course. A few opened and read them
on the spot, with a barely repressed smile of
self-conceit, or quite as frequently glanced over
them with undisguised impatience. Some of
the letters began with " My dear husband ; " and
some were never called for. But the fact that
the only regular correspondent of Five Forks
never received any reply became at last quite
notorious. Consequently, when an envelope was
received, bearing the stamp of the " dead letter
office," addressed to " The Fool," under the
more conventional title of " Cyrus Hawkins,"
there was quite a fever of excitement. I do
not know how the secret leaked out ; but it was
eventually known to the camp, that the envelope contained Hawkins's own letters returned.
This was the first evidence of his weakness.
Any man who repeatedly wrote to a woman who
did not reply must be a fool. I think Hawkins suspected that his folly was known to the
camp ; but he took refuge in symptoms of chills
and fever, which he at once developed, and
effected a diversion with three bottles of Indian
cholagogue and two boxes of pills. At all
events, at the end of a week, he resumed a pen
stiffened by tonics, with all his old epistolatory
pertinacity. This time the letters had a new
address.

In those days a popular belief obtained in the mines, that luck particularly favored the foolish and unscientific. Consequently, when Hawkins struck a " pocket " in the hillside near his solitary cabin, there was but little surprise. " He will sink it all in the next hole " was the prevailing belief, predicated upon the usual manner in which the possessor of "nigger luck" disposed of his fortune. To everybody's astonishment, Hawkins, after taking out about eight thousand dollars, and exhausting the pocket, did not prospect for another. The camp then waited patiently to see what he would do with his money. I think, however, that it was with the greatest difficulty their indignation was kept from taking the form of a personal assault when it became known that he had purchased a draft for eight thousand dollars, in favor of " that woman." More than this, it was finally whispered that the draft was returned to him as his letters had been, and that he was ashamed to reclaim the money at the express-office. " It wouldn't be a bad speculation to go East, get some smart gal, for a hundred dollars, to dress herself up and represent that ' Hag,' and jest freeze onto that eight thousand," suggested a far-seeing financier. I may state here, that we always alluded to Hawkins's fair unknown as the " Hag " without having, I am confident, the least justification for that epithet.

That the "Fool" should gamble seemed eminently fit and proper. That he should occasionally win a large stake, according to that popular theory which I have recorded in the preceding paragraph, appeared, also, a not improbable or inconsistent fact. That he should, however, break the faro bank which Mr. John Hamlin had set up in Five Forks, and carry off a sum variously estimated at from ten to twenty thousand dollars, and not return the next day, and lose the money at the same table, really appeared incredible. Yet such was the fact. A day or two passed without any known investment of Mr. Hawkins's recently-acquired capital. " Ef he allows to send it to that ' Hag,' " said one prominent citizen, " suthin' ought to be done. It's jest ruinin' the reputation of this yer camp, — this sloshin' around o' capital on non-residents ez don't claim it!" "It's settin' an example o' extravagance," said another, " ez is little better nor a swindle. Thais mor'n five men in this camp, thet, hearin' thet Hawkins hed sent home eight thousand dollars, must jest rise up and send home their hard earnings too! And then to think thet thet eight thousand was only a bluff, after all, and thet it's lyin' there on call in Adams &

Co.'s bank! Well, I say it's one o' them things a vigilance committee oughter look into."

When there seemed no possibility of this repetition of Hawkins's folly, the anxiety to know what he had really done with his money became intense. At last a self-appointed committee of four citizens dropped artfully, but to outward appearances carelessly, upon him in his seclusion. When some polite formalities had been exchanged, and some easy vituperation of a backward season offered by each of the parties, Tom Wingate approached the subject.

" Sorter dropped heavy on Jack Hamlin the other night, didn't ye? He allows you didn't give him no show for revenge. I said you wasn't no such d—d fool; didn't I, Dick?" continued the artful Wingate, appealing to a confederate.

" Yes," said Dick promptly. " You said twenty thousand dollars wasn't goin' to be thrown around recklessly. You said Cyrus had suthin' better to do with his capital," superadded Dick with gratuitous mendacity. " I disremember now what partickler investment you said he was goin' to make with it," he continued, appealing with easy indifference to his friend.

Of course Wingate did not reply, but looked at the " Fool," who, with a troubled face, was rubbing his legs softly. After a pause, he turned deprecatingly toward his visitors.

"Ye didn't enny of ye ever hev a sort of tremblin' in your legs, a kind o' shakiness from the knee down? Suthin'," he continued, slightly brightening with his topic, — "suthin' that begins like chills, and yet ain't chills? A kind o' sensation of goneness here, and a kind o' feelin' as if you might die suddint? — when Wright's Pills don't somehow reach the spot, and quinine don't fetch you?"

"No!" said Wingate with a curt directness, and the air of authoritatively responding for his friends, — "no, never had. You was speakin' of this yer investment."

"And your bowels all the time irregular?" continued Hawkins, blushing under Wingate's eye, and yet clinging despairingly to his theme, like a shipwrecked mariner to his plank.

Wingate did not reply, but glanced significantly at the rest. Hawkins evidently saw this recognition of his mental deficiency, and said apologetically, "You was saying suthin' about my investment?"

"Yes," said Wingate, so rapidly as to almost take Hawkins's breath away, — "the investment you made in" —

"Rafferty's Ditch," said the "Fool" timidly. For a moment, the visitors could only stare

blankly at each other. " Rafferty's Ditch," the
one notorious failure of Five Forks!—Rafferty's
Ditch, the impracticable scheme of an utterly
unpractical man!—Rafferty's Ditch, a ridiculous plan for taking water that could not be
got to a place where it wasn't wanted!—Rafferty's Ditch, that had buried the fortunes of
Rafferty and twenty wretched stockholders in
its muddy depths!

" And thet's it, is it?" said Wingate, after a
gloomy pause. " Thet's it! I see it all now,
boys. That's how ragged Pat Rafferty went
down to San Francisco yesterday in store-
clothes, and his wife and four children went off
in a kerridge to Sacramento. Thet's why them
ten workmen of his, ez hadn't a cent to bless
themselves with, was playin' billiards last night,
and eatin' isters. Thet's whar that money kum
frum,—one hundred dollars to pay for the
long advertisement of the new issue of ditch
stock in the " Times " yesterday. Thet's why
them six strangers were booked at the Magnolia
Hotel yesterday. Don't you see? It's thet
money—and that 'Fool'!"

The " Fool " sat silent. The visitors rose
without a word.

" You never took any of them Indian Vegetable Pills?" asked Hawkins timidly of Wingate.

"No!" roared Wingate as he opened the door.

"They tell me, that, took with the Panacea,— they was out o' the Panacea when I went to the drug-store last week,—they say, that, took with the Panacea, they always effect a certin cure." But by this time, Wingate and his disgusted friends had retreated, slamming the door on the "Fool" and his ailments.

Nevertheless, in six months the whole affair was forgotten : the money had been spent; the "Ditch" had been purchased by a company of Boston capitalists, fired by the glowing descrip- tion of an Eastern tourist, who had spent one drunken night at Five Forks; and I think even the mental condition of Hawkins might have remained undisturbed by criticism, but for a singular incident.

It was during an exciting political campaign, when party-feeling ran high, that the irascible Capt. McFadden of Sacramento visited Five Forks. During a heated discussion in the Prairie Rose Saloon, words passed between the captain and the Hon. Calhoun Bungstarter, ending in a challenge. The captain bore the in- felicitous reputation of being a notorious duellist and a dead-shot. The captain was unpopular. The captain was believed to have been sent by the opposition for a deadly purpose; and the

captain was, moreover, a stranger. I am sorry
to say that with Five Forks this latter condition did not carry the quality of sanctity or
reverence that usually obtains among other
nomads. There was, consequently, some little
hesitation when the captain turned upon the
crowd, and asked for some one to act as his
friend. To everybody's astonishment, and to
the indignation of many, the " Fool " stepped
forward, and offered himself in that capacity.
I do not know whether Capt. McFadden would
have chosen him voluntarily; but he was constrained, in the absence of a better man, to
accept his services.

The duel never took place. The prelimina-
ries were all arranged, the spot indicated; the
men were present with their seconds; there
was no interruption from without; there was no
explanation or apology passed — but the duel
did not take place. It may be readily imagined
that these facts, which were all known to Five
Forks, threw the whole community into a fever
of curiosity. The principals, the surgeon, and
one second left town the next day. Only the
" Fool " remained. *He* resisted all questioning,
declaring himself held in honor not to divulge:
in short, conducted himself with consistent
but exasperating folly. It was not until six
months had passed, that Col. Starbottle, the

second of Calhoun Bungstarter, in a moment of
weakness, superinduced by the social glass,
condescended to explain. I should not do
justice to the parties, if I did not give that
explanation in the colonel's own words. I may
remark, in passing, that the characteristic
dignity of Col. Starbottle always became intensified by stimulants, and that, by the same
process, all sense of humor was utterly elimi-
nated.

"With the understanding that I am addressing myself confidentially to men of honor,"
said the colonel, elevating his chest above the
bar-room counter of the Prairie Rose Saloon,
"I trust that it will not be necessary for me to
protect myself from levity, as I was forced to
do in Sacramento on the only other occasion
when I entered into an explanation of this
delicate affair by — er — er — calling the individual to a personal account — er. I do not
believe," added the colonel, slightly waving his
glass of liquor in the air with a graceful gesture
of courteous deprecation, "knowing what I
do of the present company, that such a course
of action is required here. Certainly not,
sir, in the home of Mr. Hawkins — er — the
gentleman who represented Mr. Bungstarter,
whose conduct, ged, sir, is worthy of praise,
blank me!"

Apparently satisfied with the gravity and respectful attention of his listeners, Col. Starbottle smiled relentingly and sweetly, closed his eyes half-dreamily, as if to recall his wandering thoughts, and began, —

"As the spot selected was nearest the tenement of Mr. Hawkins, it was agreed that the parties should meet there. They did so promptly at half-past six. The morning being chilly, Mr. Hawkins extended the hospitalities of his house with a bottle of Bourbon whiskey, of which all partook but myself. The reason for that exception is, I believe, well known. It is my invariable custom to take brandy — a wineglassful in a cup of strong coffee — immediately on rising. It stimulates the functions, sir, without producing any blank derangement of the nerves."

The barkeeper, to whom, as an expert, the colonel had graciously imparted this information, nodded approvingly; and the colonel, amid a breathless silence, went on.

"We were about twenty minutes in reaching the spot. The ground was measured, the weapons were loaded, when Mr. Bungstarter confided to me the information that he was unwell, and in great pain. On consultation with Mr. Hawkins, it appeared that his prin cipal, in a distant part of the field, was also suffering, and in great pain. The symptoms were such as a medical man would pronounce 'choleraic.' I say *would* have pronounced; for, on examination, the surgeon was also found to be — er — in pain, and, I regret to say, expressing himself in language unbecoming the occasion. His impression was, that some powerful drug had been administered. On referring the question to Mr. Hawkins, he remembered that the bottle of whiskey partaken by them contained a medicine which he had been in the habit of taking, but which, having failed to act upon him, he had concluded to be generally ineffective, and had forgotten. His perfect willingness to hold himself personally responsible to each of the parties, his genuine concern at the disastrous effect of the mistake, mingled with his own alarm at the state of his system, which — er — failed to — er — respond to the peculiar qualities of the medicine, was most becoming to him as a man of honor and a gentleman. After an hour's delay, both principals being completely exhausted, and abandoned by the surgeon, who was unreasonably alarmed at his own condition, Mr. Hawkins and I agreed to remove our men to Markleville. There, after a further consultation with Mr. Hawkins, an amicable adjustment of all difficulties, honorable to both parties, and governed by profound secrecy, was arranged. I believe," added the colonel, looking around, and setting down his glass, "no gentleman has yet expressed himself other than satisfied with the result."

Perhaps it was the colonel's manner; but, whatever was the opinion of Five Forks regarding the intellectual display of Mr. Hawkins in this affair, there was very little outspoken criticism at the moment. In a few weeks the whole thing was forgotten, except as part of the necessary record of Hawkins's blunders, which was already a pretty full one. Again, some later follies conspired to obliterate the past, until, a year later, a valuable lead was discovered in the "Blazing Star" tunnel, in the hill where he lived; and a large sum was offered him for a portion of his land on the hilltop. Accustomed as Five Forks had become to the exhibition of his folly, it was with astonishment that they learned that he resolutely and decidedly refused the offer. The reason that he gave was still more astounding, — he was about to build.

To build a house upon property available for mining-purposes was preposterous; to build at all, with a roof already covering him, was an act of extravagance; to build a house of the style he proposed was simply madness.

Yet here were facts. The plans were made, and the lumber for the new building was already on the ground, while the shaft of the "Blazing Star" was being sunk below. The site was, in reality, a very picturesque one, the building itself of a style and quality hitherto unknown in Five Forks. The citizens, at first sceptical, during their moments of recreation and idleness gathered doubtingly about the locality. Day by day, in that climate of rapid growths, the building, pleasantly known in the slang of Five Forks as the "Idiot Asylum," rose beside the green oaks and clustering firs of Hawkins Hill, as if it were part of the natural phenomena. At last it was completed. Then Mr. Hawkins proceeded to furnish it with an expensiveness and extravagance of outlay quite in keeping with his former idiocy. Carpets, sofas, mirrors, and finally a piano, — the only one known in the county, and brought at great expense from Sacramento, — kept curiosity at a fever-heat. More than that, there were articles and ornaments which a few married experts declared only fit for women. When the furnishing of the house was complete, — it had occupied two months of the speculative and curious attention of the camp, — Mr. Hawkins locked the front-door, put the key in his pocket, and quietly retired to his more humble roof, lower on the hillside.

I have not deemed it necessary to indicate to the intelligent reader all of the theories which obtained in Five Forks during the erection of the building. Some of them may be readily imagined. That the "Hag" had, by artful coyness and systematic reticence, at last completely subjugated the "Fool," and that the new house was intended for the nuptial bower of the (predestined) unhappy pair, was, of course, the prevailing opinion. But when, after a reasonable time had elapsed, and the house still remained untenanted, the more exasperating conviction forced itself upon the general mind, that the "Fool" had been for the third time imposed upon; when two months had elapsed, and there seemed no prospect of a mistress for the new house, — I think public indignation became so strong, that, had the "Hag" arrived, the marriage would have been publicly prevented. But no one appeared that seemed to answer to this idea of an available tenant; and all inquiry of Mr. Hawkins as to his intention in building a house, and not renting it, or occupying it, failed to elicit any further information. The reasons that he gave were felt to be vague, evasive, and unsatisfactory. He was in no hurry to move, he said. When he *was* ready, it surely

was not strange that he should like to have his
house all ready to receive him. He was often
seen upon the veranda, of a summer evening,
smoking a cigar. It is reported that one night
the house was observed to be brilliantly lighted
from garret to basement; that a neighbor, observing this, crept toward the open parlor-window,
and, looking in, espied the "Fool" accurately
dressed in evening costume, lounging upon a sofa
in the drawing-room, with the easy air of socially
entertaining a large party. Notwithstanding
this, the house was unmistakably vacant that
evening, save for the presence of the owner, as
the witness afterward testified. When this
story was first related, a few practical men sug
gested the theory that Mr. Hawkins was simply
drilling himself in the elaborate duties of hospitality against a probable event in his history.
A few ventured the belief that the house was
haunted. The imaginative editor of the Five
Forks "Record" evolved from the depths of
his professional consciousness a story that Haw
kins's sweetheart had died, and that he regularly entertained her spirit in this beautifully
furnished mausoleum. The occasional spectacle
of Hawkins's tall figure pacing the veranda on
moonlight nights lent some credence to this
theory, until an unlooked-for incident diverted
all speculation into another channel.

It was about this time that a certain wild, rude valley, in the neighborhood of Five Forks, had become famous as a picturesque resort. Travellers had visited it, and declared that there were more cubic yards of rough stone cliff, and a waterfall of greater height, than any they had visited. Correspondents had written it up with extravagant rhetoric and inordinate poetical quotation. Men and women who had never enjoyed a sunset, a tree, or a flower, who had never appreciated the graciousness or meaning of the yellow sunlight that flecked their homely doorways, or the tenderness of a midsummer's night, to whose moonlight they bared their shirt-sleeves or their *tulle* dresses, came from thousands of miles away to calculate the height of this rock, to observe the depth of this chasm, to remark upon the enormous size of this unsightly tree, and to believe with ineffable self-complacency that they really admired Nature. And so it came to pass, that, in accordance with the tastes or weaknesses of the individual, the more prominent and salient points of the valley were christened; and there was a "Lace Handkerchief Fall," and the "Tears of Sympathy Cataract," and one distinguished orator's "Peak," and several "Mounts" of various noted people, living or dead, and an "Exclamation-Point," and a "Valley of Silent

Adoration." And, in course of time, empty soda-water bottles were found at the base of the cataract, and greasy newspapers, and fragments of ham-sandwiches, lay at the dusty roots of giant trees. With this, there were frequent irruptions of closely-shaven and tightly-cravated men, and delicate, flower-faced women, in the one long street of Five Forks, and a scampering of mules, and an occasional procession of dusty brown-linen cavalry.

A year after " Hawkins's Idiot Asylum " was completed, one day there drifted into the valley a riotous cavalcade of " school-marms," teachers of the San-Francisco public schools, out for a holiday. Not severely-spectacled Minervas, and chastely armed and mailed Pallases, but, I fear, for the security of Five Forks, very human, charming, and mischievous young women. At least, so the men thought, working in the ditches, and tunnelling on the hillside; and when, in the interests of science, and the mental advancement of juvenile posterity, it was finally settled that they should stay in Five Forks two or three days for the sake of visiting the various mines, and particularly the " Blazing Star " tunnel, there was some flutter of masculine anxiety. There was a considerable inquiry for " store-clothes," a hopeless overhauling of old and disused raiment, and a general demand for " boiled shirts " and the barber.

Meanwhile, with that supreme audacity and impudent hardihood of the sex when gregarious, the school-marms rode through the town, admiring openly the handsome faces and manly figures that looked up from the ditches, or rose behind the cars of ore at the mouths of tunnels. Indeed, it is alleged that Jenny Forester, backed and supported by seven other equally shameless young women, had openly and publicly waved her handkerchief to the florid Hercules of Five Forks, one Tom Flynn, formerly of Virginia, leaving that good-natured but not over-bright giant pulling his blonde mustaches in bashful amazement.

It was a pleasant June afternoon that Miss Milly Arnot, principal of the primary department of one of the public schools of San Francisco, having evaded her companions, resolved to put into operation a plan which had lately sprung up in her courageous and mischief-loving fancy. With that wonderful and mysterious instinct of her sex, from whom no secrets of the affections are hid, and to whom all hearts are laid open, she had heard the story of Hawkins's folly, and the existence of the "Idiot Asylum." Alone, on Hawkins Hill, she had determined to penetrate its seclusion. Skirting the underbrush at the foot of the hill, she managed to keep the heaviest timber between

herself and the " Blazing Star " tunnel at its
base, as well as the cabin of Hawkins, half-way
up the ascent, until, by a circuitous route,
at last she reached, unobserved, the summit.
Before her rose, silent, darkened, and motionless, the object of her search. Here her
courage failed her, with all the characteristic
inconsequence of her sex. A sudden fear of
all the dangers she had safely passed — bears,
tarantulas, drunken men, and lizards — came
upon her. For a moment, as she afterward
expressed it, " she thought she should die."
With this belief, probably, she gathered three
large stones, which she could hardly lift, for the
purpose of throwing a great distance; put two
hair-pins in her mouth; and carefully re-adjusted
with both hands two stray braids of her lovely
blue-black mane, which had fallen in gathering
the stones. Then she felt in the pockets of her
linen duster for her card-case, handkerchief,
pocket-book, and smelling-bottle, and, finding
them intact, suddenly assumed an air of easy,
ladylike unconcern, went up the steps of the
veranda, and demurely pulled the front door-
bell, which she knew would not be answered.
After a decent pause, she walked around the
encompassing veranda, examining the closed
shutters of the French windows until she found
one that yielded to her touch. Here she paused

again to adjust her coquettish hat by the mirror-like surface of the long sash-window, that reflected the full length of her pretty figure. And then she opened the window, and entered the room.

Although long closed, the house had a smell of newness and of fresh paint, that was quite unlike the mouldiness of the conventional haunted house. The bright carpets, the cheerful walls, the glistening oil-cloths, were quite inconsistent with the idea of a ghost. With childish curiosity, she began to explore the silent house, at first timidly, — opening the doors with a violent push, and then stepping back from the threshold to make good a possible retreat, — and then more boldly, as she became convinced of her security and absolute loneliness. In one of the chambers — the largest — there were fresh flowers in a vase, evidently gathered that morning; and, what seemed still more remarkable, the pitchers and ewers were freshly filled with water. This obliged Miss Milly to notice another singular fact, namely, that the house was free from dust, the one most obtrusive and penetrating visitor of Five Forks. The floors and carpets had been recently swept, the chairs and furniture carefully wiped and dusted. If the house *was* haunted, it was possessed by a spirit who had none of the usual indifference to decay and mould. And yet

the beds had evidently never been slept in, the
very springs of the chair in which she sat
creaked stiffly at the novelty; the closet-doors
opened with the reluctance of fresh paint and
varnish; and in spite of the warmth, cleanli-
ness, and cheerfulness of furniture and decoration, there was none of the ease of tenancy and
occupation. As Miss Milly afterward confessed,
she longed to "tumble things around;" and, when
she reached the parlor or drawing-room again,
she could hardly resist the desire. Particularly
was she tempted by a closed piano, that stood
mutely against the wall. She thought she would
open it just to see who was the maker. That
done, it would be no harm to try its tone. She
did so, with one little foot on the soft pedal.
But Miss Milly was too good a player, and too
enthusiastic a musician, to stop at half-measures.
She tried it again, this time so sincerely, that
the whole house seemed to spring into voice.
Then she stopped and listened. There was no
response: the empty rooms seemed to have re-
lapsed into their old stillness. She stepped out
on the veranda. A woodpecker recommenced his
tapping on an adjacent tree: the rattle of a cart
in the rocky gulch below the hill came faintly
up. No one was to be seen far or near. Miss
Milly, re-assured, returned. She again ran her
fingers over the keys, stopped, caught at a mel-

ody running in her mind, half played it, and
then threw away all caution. Before five minutes had elapsed, she had entirely forgotten herself, and with her linen duster thrown aside,
her straw hat flung on the piano, her white
hands bared, and a black loop of her braided
hair hanging upon her shoulder, was fairly
embarked upon a flowing sea of musical recollection.

She had played, perhaps, half an hour, when
having just finished an elaborate symphony, and
resting her hands on the keys, she heard very
distinctly and unmistakably the sound of applause from without. In an instant the fires of
shame and indignation leaped into her cheeks;
and she rose from the instrument, and ran to the
window, only in time to catch sight of a dozen
figures in blue and red flannel shirts vanishing
hurriedly through the trees below.

Miss Milly's mind was instantly made up. I
think I have already intimated, that, under the
stimulus of excitement, she was not wanting in
courage; and as she quietly resumed her gloves,
hat, and duster, she was not, perhaps, exactly
the young person that it would be entirely safe
for the timid, embarrassed, or inexperienced of
my sex to meet alone. She shut down the
piano; and having carefully reclosed all the
windows and doors, and restored the house to

its former desolate condition, she stepped from
the veranda, and proceeded directly to the cabin
of the unintellectual Hawkins, that reared its
adobe chimney above the umbrage a quarter of
a mile below.

The door opened instantly to her impulsive
knock, and the "Fool of Five Forks" stood before
her. Miss Milly had never before seen the man
designated by this infelicitous title; and as he
stepped backward, in half courtesy and half
astonishment, she was, for the moment, discon-
certed. He was tall, finely formed, and dark-
bearded. Above cheeks a little hollowed by
care and ill-health shone a pair of hazel eyes,
very large, very gentle, but inexpressibly sad
and mournful. This was certainly not the kind
of man Miss Milly had expected to see; yet,
after her first embarrassment had passed, the
very circumstance, oddly enough, added to her
indignation, and stung her wounded pride still
more deeply. Nevertheless, the arch hypocrite
instantly changed her tactics with the swift
intuition of her sex.

"I have come," she said with a dazzling smile,
infinitely more dangerous than her former dignified severity, — "I have come to ask your pardon
for a great liberty I have just taken. I believe
the new house above us on the hill is yours. I
was so much pleased with its exterior, that I left

my friends for a moment below here," she con
tinued artfully, with a slight wave of the hand,
as if indicating a band of fearless Amazons without, and waiting to avenge any possible insult
offered to one of their number, "and ventured
to enter it. Finding it unoccupied, as I had
been told, I am afraid I had the audacity to sit
down and amuse myself for a few moments at
the piano, while waiting for my friends."

Hawkins raised his beautiful eyes to hers. He
saw a very pretty girl, with frank gray eyes
glistening with excitement, with two red, slightly freckled cheeks glowing a little under his
eyes, with a short scarlet upper-lip turned back,
like a rose-leaf, over a little line of white teeth,
as she breathed somewhat hurriedly in her nervous excitement. He saw all this calmly, quietly, and, save for the natural uneasiness of a shy,
reticent man, I fear without a quickening of his
pulse.

"I knowed it," he said simply. "I heerd ye
as I kem up."

Miss Milly was furious at his grammar, his
dialect, his coolness, and, still more, at the suspicion that he was an active member of her in
visible *claque*.

"Ah!" she said, still smiling. "Then I think I
heard *you*" —

"I reckon not," he interrupted gravely. "I

didn't stay long. I found the boys hanging round the house, and I allowed at first I'd go in and kinder warn you; but they promised to keep still: and you looked so comfortable, and wrapped up in your music, that I hadn't the heart to disturb you, and kem away. I hope," he added earnestly, "they didn't let on ez they heerd you. They ain't a bad lot, — them Blazin' Star boys — though they're a little hard at times. But they'd no more hurt ye then they would a — a — a cat!" continued Mr. Hawkins, blushing with a faint apprehension of the inelegance of his simile.

"No, no!" said Miss Milly, feeling suddenly very angry with herself, the "Fool," and the entire male population of Five Forks. "No! I have behaved foolishly, I suppose — and, if they *had*, it would have served me right. But I only wanted to apologize to you. You'll find every thing as you left it. Good-day!"

She turned to go. Mr. Hawkins began to feel embarrassed. "I'd have asked ye to sit down," he said finally, "if it hed been a place fit for a lady. I oughter done so, enny way. I don't know what kept me from it. But I ain't well, miss. Times I get a sort o' dumb ager, — it's the ditches, I think, miss, — and I don't seem to hev my wits about me."

Instantly Miss Arnot was all sympathy: her quick woman's heart was touched.

" Can I — can any thing be done?" she asked more timidly than she had before spoken.

" No — not onless ye remember suthin' about these pills." He exhibited a box containing about half a dozen. "I forget the direction — I don't seem to remember much, any way, these times. They're ' Jones's Vegetable Compound.' If ye've ever took 'em, ye'll remember whether the reg'lar dose is eight. They ain't but six here. But perhaps ye never tuk any," he added deprecatingly.

" No," said Miss Milly curtly. She had usually a keen sense of the ludicrous ; but somehow Mr. Hawkins's eccentricity only pained her.

" Will you let me see you to the foot of the hill?" he said again, after another embarrassing pause.

Miss Arnot felt instantly that such an act would condone her trespass in the eyes of the world. She might meet some of her invisible admirers, or even her companions ; and, with all her erratic impulses, she was, nevertheless, a woman, and did not entirely despise the verdict of conventionality. She smiled sweetly, and assented ; and in another moment the two were lost in the shadows of the wood.

Like many other apparently trivial acts in an uneventful life, it was decisive. As she expected, she met two or three of her late

applauders, whom, she fancied, looked sheepish
and embarrassed; she met, also, her companions
looking for her in some alarm, who really
appeared astonished at her escort, and, she
fancied, a trifle envious of her evident success.
I fear that Miss Arnot, in response to their
anxious inquiries, did not state entirely the
truth, but, without actual assertion, led them
to believe that she had, at a very early stage
of the proceeding, completely subjugated this
weak-minded giant, and had brought him triumphantly to her feet. From telling this story
two or three times, she got finally to believing
that she had some foundation for it, then to a
vague sort of desire that it would eventually
prove to be true, and then to an equally vague
yearning to hasten that consummation. That
it would redound to any satisfaction of the
" Fool " she did not stop to doubt. That it would
cure him of his folly she was quite confident.
Indeed, there are very few of us, men or
women, who do not believe that even a hopeless love for ourselves is more conducive to
the salvation of the lover than a requited affection for another.

The criticism of Five Forks was, as the
reader may imagine, swift and conclusive.
When it was found out that Miss Arnot was
not the " Hag " masquerading as a young and

pretty girl, to the ultimate deception of Five Forks in general, and the "Fool" in particular, it was at once decided that nothing but the speedy union of the "Fool" and the "pretty school-marm" was consistent with ordinary common sense. The singular good-fortune of Hawkins was quite in accordance with the theory of his luck as propounded by the camp. That, after the "Hag" failed to make her appearance, he should "strike a lead" in his own house, without the trouble of "prospect-in'," seemed to these casuists as a wonderful but inevitable law. To add to these fateful probabilities, Miss Arnot fell, and sprained her ankle, in the ascent of Mount Lincoln, and was confined for some weeks to the hotel after her companions had departed. During this period, Hawkins was civilly but grotesquely attentive. When, after a reasonable time had elapsed, there still appeared to be no immediate prospect of the occupancy of the new house, public opinion experienced a singular change in regard to its theories of Mr. Hawkins's conduct. The "Hag" was looked upon as a saint-like and long-suffering martyr to the weaknesses and incon-sistency of the "Fool." That, after erecting this new house at her request, he had suddenly "gone back" on her; that his celibacy was the result of a long habit of weak proposal and subsequent shameless rejection; and that he was now trying his hand on the helpless school-marm, was perfectly plain to Five Forks. That he should be frustrated in his attempts at any cost was equally plain. Miss Milly suddenly found herself invested with a rude chivalry that would have been amusing, had it not been at times embarrassing; that would have been impertinent, but for the almost superstitious respect with which it was proffered. Every day somebody from Five Forks rode out to inquire the health of the fair patient. "Hez Hawkins bin over yer to-day?" queried Tom Flynn, with artful ease and indifference, as he leaned over Miss Milly's easy-chair on the veranda. Miss Milly, with a faint pink flush on her cheek, was constrained to answer, "No." "Well, he sorter sprained his foot agin a rock yesterday," continued Flynn with shameless untruthfulness. "You mus'n't think any thing o' that, Miss Arnot. He'll be over yer to-mor-rer; and meantime he told me to hand this yer bookay with his re-gards, and this yer speci-men." And Mr. Flynn laid down the flowers he had picked *en route* against such an emer-gency, and presented respectfully a piece of quartz and gold, which he had taken that morn-ing from his own sluice-box. "You mus'n't mind Hawkins's ways, Miss Milly," said another sympathizing miner. " There ain't a better man in camp than that theer Cy Hawkins — but he don't understand the ways o' the world with wimen. He hasn't mixed as much with society as the rest of us," he added, with an elaborate Chesterfieldian ease of manner; " but he means well." Meanwhile a few other sympathetic tunnel-men were impressing upon Mr. Hawkins the necessity of the greatest attention to the invalid. " It won't do, Hawkins," they explained, " to let that there gal go back to San Francisco and say, that, when she was sick and alone, the only man in Five Forks under whose roof she had rested, and at whose table she had sat" (this was considered a natural but pardonable exaggeration of rhetoric) " ever threw off on her; and it sha'n't be done. It ain't the square thing to Five Forks." And then the " Fool" would rush away to the valley, and be received by Miss Milly with a certain reserve of manner that finally disappeared in a flush of color, some increased vivacity, and a pardonable coquetry. And so the days passed. Miss Milly grew better in health, and more troubled in mind; and Mr. Hawkins became more and more embarrassed; and Five Forks smiled, and rubbed its hands, and waited for the approaching *denoûment*. And then it came — but not, perhaps, in the manner that Five Forks had imagined.

It was a lovely afternoon in July that a party of Eastern tourists rode into Five Forks. They had just "done" the Valley of Big Things; and, there being one or two Eastern capitalists among the party, it was deemed advisable that a proper knowledge of the practical mining-resources of California should be added to their experience of the merely picturesque in Nature. Thus far every thing had been satisfactory; the amount of water which passed over the Fall was large, owing to a backward season; some snow still remained in the cañons near the highest peaks; they had ridden round one of the biggest trees, and through the prostrate trunk of another. To say that they were delighted is to express feebly the enthusiasm of these ladies and gentlemen, drunk with the champagny hospitality of their entertainers, the utter novelty of scene, and the dry, exhilarating air of the valley. One or two had already expressed themselves ready to live and die there; another had written a glowing account to the Eastern press, depreciating all other scenery in Europe and America; and, under these circumstances, it was reasonably expected that Five Forks would do its duty, and equally impress the stranger after its own fashion.

Letters to this effect were sent from San Francisco by prominent capitalists there; and,

under the able superintendence of one of their
agents, the visitors were taken in hand, shown
"what was to be seen," carefully restrained
from observing what ought not to be visible,
and so kept in a blissful and enthusiastic condition. And so the graveyard of Five Forks, in
which but two of the occupants had died natural deaths; the dreary, ragged cabins on the
hillsides, with their sad-eyed, cynical, broken-
spirited occupants, toiling on day by day for
a miserable pittance, and a fare that a self-
respecting Eastern mechanic would have scornfully rejected, — were not a part of the Eastern
visitors' recollection. But the hoisting works
and machinery of the "Blazing Star Tunnel
Company" was, — the Blazing Star Tunnel Company, whose "gentlemanly superintendent" had
received private information from San Francisco to do the "proper thing" for the party.
Wherefore the valuable heaps of ore in the
company's works were shown; the oblong bars
of gold, ready for shipment, were playfully
offered to the ladies who could lift and carry
them away unaided; and even the tunnel itself,
gloomy, fateful, and peculiar, was shown as
part of the experience; and, in the noble language of one correspondent, "The wealth of
Five Forks, and the peculiar inducements that
it offered to Eastern capitalists," were estab-

lished beyond a doubt. And then occurred a little incident, which, as an unbiassed spectator, I am free to say offered no inducements to anybody whatever, but which, for its bearing upon the central figure of this veracious chronicle, I cannot pass over.

It had become apparent to one or two more practical and sober-minded in the party, that certain portions of the " Blazing Star " tunnel (owing, perhaps, to the exigencies of a flattering annual dividend) were economically and imperfectly " shored " and supported, and were, consequently, unsafe, insecure, and to be avoided. Nevertheless, at a time when champagne corks were popping in dark corners, and enthusiastic voices and happy laughter rang through the half-lighted levels and galleries, there came a sudden and mysterious silence. A few lights dashed swiftly by in the direction of a distant part of the gallery, and then there was a sudden sharp issuing of orders, and a dull, ominous rumble. Some of the visitors turned pale : one woman fainted.

Something had happened. What ? " Nothing " (the speaker is fluent, but uneasy) — " one of the gentlemen, in trying to dislodge a ' specimen ' from the wall, had knocked away a support. There had been a ' cave ' — the gentleman was caught, and buried below his shoulders. It

was all right, they'd get him out in a moment
—only it required great care to keep from extending the 'cave.' Didn't know his name.
It was that little man, the husband of that
lively lady with the black eyes. Eh! Hullo,
there! Stop her! For God's sake! Not that
way! She'll fall from that shaft. She'll be
killed!"

But the lively lady was already gone. With
staring black eyes, imploringly trying to pierce
the gloom, with hands and feet that sought to
batter and break down the thick darkness, with
incoherent cries and supplications following the
moving of *ignis fatuus* lights ahead, she ran, and
ran swiftly!—ran over treacherous foundations,
ran by yawning gulfs, ran past branching galleries and arches, ran wildly, ran despairingly,
ran blindly, and at last ran into the arms of
the "Fool of Five Forks."

In an instant she caught at his hand. "Oh,
save him!" she cried. "You belong here; you
know this dreadful place: bring me to him.
Tell me where to go, and what to do, I implore
you! Quick, he is dying! Come!"

He raised his eyes to hers, and then, with a
sudden cry, dropped the rope and crowbar he
was carrying, and reeled against the wall.

"Annie!" he gasped slowly. "Is it you?"
She caught at both his hands, brought her

face to his with staring eyes, murmured, " Good God, Cyrus ! " and sank upon her knees before him.

He tried to disengage the hand that she wrung with passionate entreaty.

" No, no ! Cyrus, you will forgive me — you will forget the past ! God has sent you here to-day. You will come with me. You will — you must — save him ! "

" Save who ? " cried Cyrus hoarsely.

" My husband ! "

The blow was so direct, so strong and overwhelming, that, even through her own stronger and more selfish absorption, she saw it in the face of the man, and pitied him.

" I thought — you — knew — it, " she faltered.

He did not speak, but looked at her with fixed, dumb eyes. And then the sound of distant voices and hurrying feet started her again into passionate life. She once more caught his hand.

" O Cyrus, hear me ! If you have loved me through all these years, you will not fail me now. You must save him ! You can ! You are brave and strong — you always were, Cyrus. You will save him, Cyrus, for my sake, for the sake of your love for me ! You will — I know it. God bless you ! "

She rose as if to follow him; but, at a gesture of command, she stood still. He picked up the rope and crowbar slowly, and in a dazed, blinded way, that, in her agony of impatience and alarm, seemed protracted to cruel infinity. Then he turned, and, raising her hand to his lips, kissed it slowly, looked at her again, and the next moment was gone.

He did not return; for at the end of the next half-hour, when they laid before her the half-conscious, breathing body of her husband, safe and unharmed, but for exhaustion and some slight bruises, she learned that the worst fears of the workmen had been realized. In releasing him, a second cave had taken place. They had barely time to snatch away the helpless body of her husband, before the strong frame of his rescuer, Cyrus Hawkins, was struck and smitten down in his place.

For two hours he lay there, crushed and broken-limbed, with a heavy beam lying across his breast, in sight of all, conscious and patient. For two hours they had labored around him, wildly, despairingly, hopefully, with the wills of gods and the strength of giants; and at the end of that time they came to an upright timber, which rested its base upon the beam. There was a cry for axes, and one was already swinging in the air, when the dying man called to them feebly, —

"Don't cut that upright!"

"Why?"

"It will bring down the whole gallery with it."

"How?"

"It's one of the foundations of my house."

The axe fell from the workman's hand, and with a blanched face he turned to his fellows. It was too true. They were in the uppermost gallery; and the "cave" had taken place directly below the new house. After a pause, the "Fool" spoke again more feebly.

"The lady — quick!"

They brought her, — a wretched, fainting creature, with pallid face and streaming eyes, — and fell back as she bent her face above him.

"It was built for you, Annie darling," he said in a hurried whisper, "and has been waiting up there for you and me all these long days. It's deeded to you, Annie; and you must — live there — with *him!* He will not mind that I shall be always near you; for it stands above — my grave."

And he was right. In a few minutes later, when he had passed away, they did not move him, but sat by his body all night with a torch at his feet and head. And the next day they walled up the gallery as a vault; but they put no mark or any sign thereon, trusting, rather, to

the monument, that, bright and cheerful, rose
above him in the sunlight of the hill. And
those who heard the story said, " This is not an
evidence of death and gloom and sorrow, as are
other monuments, but is a sign of life and
light and hope, wherefore shall all know that
he who lies under it is what men call — " **a fool.**"

BABY SYLVESTER.

IT was at a little mining-camp in the California Sierras that he first dawned upon me in all his grotesque sweetness.

I had arrived early in the morning, but not in time to intercept the friend who was the object of my visit. He had gone "prospecting," — so they told me on the river, — and would not probably return until late in the afternoon. They could not say what direction he had taken; they could not suggest that I would be likely to find him if I followed. But it was the general opinion that I had better wait.

I looked around me. I was standing upon the bank of the river; and apparently the only other human beings in the world were my interlocutors, who were even then just disappearing from my horizon, down the steep bank, toward the river's dry bed. I approached the edge of the bank.

Where could I wait?

Oh! anywhere, — down with them on the river-bar, where they were working, if I liked. Or I could make myself at home in any of those cabins that I found lying round loose. Or perhaps it would be cooler and pleasanter for me in my friend's cabin on the hill. Did I see those three large sugar-pines, and, a little to the right, a canvas roof and chimney, over the bushes? Well, that was my friend's, — that was Dick Sylvester's cabin. I could stake my horse in that little hollow, and just hang round there till he came. I would find some books in the shanty. I could amuse myself with them, or I could play with the baby.

Do what?

But they had already gone. I leaned over the bank, and called after their vanishing figures, —

" What did you say I could do? "

The answer floated slowly up on the hot, sluggish air, —

" Pla-a-y with the ba-by."

The lazy echoes took it up, and tossed it languidly from hill to hill, until Bald Mountain opposite made some incoherent remark about the baby; and then all was still.

I must have been mistaken. My friend was not a man of family; there was not a woman within forty miles of the river camp; he never was so passionately devoted to children as to import a luxury so expensive. I must have been mistaken.

I turned my horse's head toward the hill.
As we slowly climbed the narrow trail, the little
settlement might have been some exhumed
Pompeiian suburb, so deserted and silent were
its habitations. The open doors plainly disclosed each rudely-furnished interior, — the
rough pine table, with the scant equipage of
the morning meal still standing; the wooden
bunk, with its tumbled and dishevelled blankets.
A golden lizard, the very genius of desolate
stillness, had stopped breathless upon the
threshold of one cabin; a squirrel peeped im-
pudently into the window of another; a woodpecker, with the general flavor of undertaking
which distinguishes that bird, withheld his
sepulchral hammer from the coffin-lid of the
roof on which he was professionally engaged,
as we passed. For a moment I half regretted
that I had not accepted the invitation to the
river-bed; but, the next moment, a breeze
swept up the long, dark cañon, and the waiting
files of the pines beyond bent toward me in salutation. I think my horse understood, as well
as myself, that it was the cabins that made the
solitude human, and therefore unbearable; for
he quickened his pace, and with a gentle trot
brought me to the edge of the wood, and the
three pines that stood like vedettes before the
Sylvester outpost.

Unsaddling my horse in the little hollow, I
unslung the long *riata* from the saddle-bow,
and, tethering him to a young sapling, turned
toward the cabin. But I had gone only a few
steps, when I heard a quick trot behind me; and
poor Pomposo, with every fibre tingling with
fear, was at my heels. I looked hurriedly
around. The breeze had died away; and only
an occasional breath from the deep-chested
woods, more like a long sigh than any articulate
sound, or the dry singing of a cicala in the
heated cañon, were to be heard. I examined
the ground carefully for rattlesnakes, but in
vain. Yet here was Pomposo shivering from
his arched neck to his sensitive haunches, his
very flanks pulsating with terror. I soothed
him as well as I could, and then walked to the
edge of the wood, and peered into its dark
recesses. The bright flash of a bird's wing, or
the quick dart of a squirrel, was all I saw. I
confess it was with something of superstitious
expectation that I again turned towards the
cabin. A fairy-child, attended by Titania and
her train, lying in an expensive cradle, would
not have surprised me: a Sleeping Beauty,
whose awakening would have repeopled these
solitudes with life and energy, I am afraid I
began to confidently look for, and would have
kissed without hesitation.

But I found none of these. Here was the evidence of my friend's taste and refinement, in the hearth swept scrupulously clean, in the picturesque arrangement of the fur-skins that covered the floor and furniture, and the striped *serápe*[1] lying on the wooden couch. Here were the walls fancifully papered with illustrations from " The London News;" here was the woodcut portrait of Mr. Emerson over the chimney, quaintly framed with blue-jays' wings; here were his few favorite books on the swinging-shelf; and here, lying upon the couch, the latest copy of " Punch." Dear Dick! The flour-sack was sometimes empty; but the gentle satirist seldom missed his weekly visit.

I threw myself on the couch, and tried to read. But I soon exhausted my interest in my friend's library, and lay there staring through the open door on the green hillside beyond. The breeze again sprang up; and a delicious coolness, mixed with the rare incense of the woods, stole through the cabin. The slumbrous droning of bumblebees outside the canvas roof, the faint cawing of rooks on the opposite mountain, and the fatigue of my morning ride, began to droop my eyelids. I pulled the *serápe* over me, as a

---

[1] A fine Mexican blanket, used as an outer garment for dding

precaution against the freshening mountain
breeze, and in a few moments was asleep.

I do not remember how long I slept. I must
have been conscious, however, during my slumber, of my inability to keep myself covered by
the *serápe;* for I awoke once or twice, clutching
it with a despairing hand as it was disappearing
over the foot of the couch. Then I became
suddenly aroused to the fact that my efforts to
retain it were resisted by some equally persistent
force; and, letting it go, I was horrified at seeing it swiftly drawn under the couch. At this
point I sat up, completely awake; for immediately after, what seemed to be an exaggerated
muff began to emerge from under the couch.
Presently it appeared fully, dragging the *serápe*
after it. There was no mistaking it now: it
was a baby-bear, — a mere suckling, it was true,
a helpless roll of fat and fur, but unmistakably
a grizzly cub!

I cannot recall any thing more irresistibly
ludicrous than its aspect as it slowly raised its
small, wondering eyes to mine. It was so much
taller on its haunches than its shoulders, its
forelegs were so disproportionately small, that,
in walking, its hind-feet invariably took prece-
dence. It was perpetually pitching forward over
its pointed, inoffensive nose, and recovering itself always, after these involuntary somersaults

with the gravest astonishment. To add to its
preposterous appearance, one of its hind-feet
was adorned by a shoe of Sylvester's, into which
it had accidentally and inextricably stepped.
As this somewhat impeded its first impulse to
fly, it turned to me ; and then, possibly recognizing in the stranger the same species as its
master, it paused. Presently it slowly raised
itself on its hind-legs, and vaguely and deprecatingly waved a baby-paw, fringed with little
hooks of steel. I took the paw, and shook it
gravely. From that moment we were friends.
The little affair of the *serápe* was forgotten.

Nevertheless, I was wise enough to cement
our friendship by an act of delicate courtesy.
Following the direction of his eyes, I had no
difficulty in finding on a shelf near the ridge-
pole the sugar-box and the square lumps of
white sugar that even the poorest miner is
never without. While he was eating them, I had
time to examine him more closely. His body
was a silky, dark, but exquisitely-modulated
gray, deepening to black in his paws and muzzle.
His fur was excessively long, thick, and soft as
eider-down ; the cushions of flesh beneath perfectly infantine in their texture and contour.
He was so very young, that the palms of his
half-human feet were still tender as a baby's.
Except for the bright blue, steely hooks, half

sheathed in his little toes, there was not a single
harsh outline or detail in his plump figure. He
was as free from angles as one of Leda's off-
spring. Your caressing hand sank away in his
fur with dreamy languor. To look at him long
was an intoxication of the senses; to pat him
was a wild delirium; to embrace him, an utter
demoralization of the intellectual faculties.

When he had finished the sugar, he rolled
out of the door with a half-diffident, half-
inviting look in his eyes as if he expected me
to follow. I did so; but the sniffing and snort-
ing of the keen-scented Pomposo in the hollow
not only revealed the cause of his former terror,
but decided me to take another direction.
After a moment's hesitation, he concluded to go
with me, although I am satisfied, from a certain
impish look in his eye, that **he** fully understood
and rather enjoyed the fright of Pomposo. As
he rolled along at my side, with a gait not unlike a drunken sailor, I discovered that his long
hair concealed a leather collar around his neck,
which bore for its legend the single word
" Baby ! " I recalled the mysterious suggestion
of the two miners. This, then, was the " baby "
with whom I was to " play."

How we " played; " how Baby allowed me
to roll him down hill, crawling and puffing up
again each time with perfect good-humor; how

he climbed a young sapling after my Panama
hat, which I had "shied" into one of the top-
most branches; how, after getting it, he refused
to descend until it suited his pleasure; how,
when he did come down, he persisted in
walking about on three legs, carrying my hat, a
crushed and shapeless mass, clasped to his breast
with the remaining one; how I missed him at
last, and finally discovered him seated on a
table in one of the tenantless cabins, with a
bottle of sirup between his paws, vainly
endeavoring to extract its contents, — these and
other details of that eventful day I shall not
weary the reader with now. Enough that, when
Dick Sylvester returned, I was pretty well
fagged out, and the baby was rolled up, an immense bolster, at the foot of the couch, asleep.
Sylvester's first words after our greeting
were, —

"Isn't he delicious?"

"Perfectly. Where did you get him?"

"Lying under his dead mother, five miles
from here," said Dick, lighting his pipe.
"Knocked her over at fifty yards: perfectly
clean shot; never moved afterwards. Baby
crawled out, scared, but unhurt. She must
have been carrying him in her mouth, and
dropped him when she faced me; for he wasn't
more than three days old, and not steady on his

pins. He takes the only milk that comes to the settlement, brought up by Adams Express at seven o'clock every morning. They say he looks like me. Do you think so?" asked Dick with perfect gravity, stroking his hay-colored mustachios, and evidently assuming his best expression.

I took leave of the baby early the next morning in Sylvester's cabin, and, out of respect to Pomposo's feelings, rode by without any postscript of expression. But the night before I had made Sylvester solemnly swear, that, in the event of any separation between himself and Baby, it should revert to me. "At the same time," he had added, "it's only fair to say that I don't think of dying just yet, old fellow; and I don't know of anything else that would part the cub and me."

Two months after this conversation, as I was turning over the morning's mail at my office in San Francisco, I noticed a letter bearing Sylvester's familiar hand. But it was post-marked "Stockton," and I opened it with some anxiety at once. Its contents were as follows:—

"O FRANK!— Don't you remember what we agreed upon anent the baby? Well, consider me as dead for the next six months, or gone where cubs can't follow me,— East. I know you love the baby; but do you think, dear boy,— now, really, do you think you *could* be a father to it? Consider this well. You are young, thoughtless, well-meaning enough; but dare you take upon yourself the functions of guide, genius, or guardian to one so young and guileless? Could you be the Mentor to this Telemachus? Think of the temptations of a metropolis. Look at the question well, and let me know speedily; for I've got him as far as this place, and he's kicking up an awful row in the hotel-yard, and rattling his chain like a maniac. Let me know by telegraph at once.

" Sylvester.

" P.S. — Of course he's grown a little, and doesn't take things always as quietly as he did. He dropped rather heavily on two of Watson's 'purps' last week, and snatched old Watson himself bald headed, for interfering. You remember Watson? For an intelligent man. he knows very little of California fauna. How are you fixed for bears on Montgomery Street, I mean in regard to corrals and things? S.

" P.P.S. — He's got some new tricks. The boys have been teaching him to put up his hands with them. He slings an ugly left. S."

I am afraid that my desire to possess myself of Baby overcame all other considerations; and I telegraphed an affirmative at once to Sylvester. When I reached my lodgings late that afternoon, my landlady was awaiting me with a telegram. It was two lines from Sylvester, —

" All right. Baby goes down on night-boat. Be a father to him. S."

It was due, then, at one o'clock that night.

For a moment I was staggered at my own pre-
cipitation. I had as yet made no preparations,
had said nothing to my landlady about her new
guest. I expected to arrange every thing in
time; and now, through Sylvester's indecent
haste, that time had been shortened twelve
hours.

Something, however, must be done at once.
I turned to Mrs. Brown. I had great reliance
in her maternal instincts: I had that still
greater reliance common to our sex in the
general tender-heartedness of pretty women.
But I confess I was alarmed. Yet, with a
feeble smile, I tried to introduce the subject
with classical ease and lightness. I even said,
"If Shakspeare's Athenian clown, Mrs. Brown,
believed that a lion among ladies was a dreadful thing, what must"— But here I broke
down; for Mrs. Brown, with the awful intuition
of her sex, I saw at once was more occupied
with my manner than my speech. So I tried a
business *brusquerie,* and, placing the telegram
in her hand, said hurriedly, "We must do something about this at once. It's perfectly absurd;
but he will be here at one to-night. Beg
thousand pardons; but business prevented my
speaking before" — and paused out of breath
and courage.

Mrs. Brown read the telegram gravely, lifted

her pretty eyebrows, turned the paper over, and looked on the other side, and then, in a remote and chilling voice, asked me if she understood me to say that the mother was coming also.

" Oh, dear no!" I exclaimed with considerable relief. " The mother is dead, you know. Sylvester, that is my friend who sent this, shot her when the baby was only three days old." But the expression of Mrs. Brown's face at this moment was so alarming, that I saw that nothing but the fullest explanation would save me. Hastily, and I fear not very coherently, I told her all.

She relaxed sweetly. She said I had frightened her with my talk about lions. Indeed, I think my picture of poor Baby, albeit a trifle highly colored, touched her motherly heart. She was even a little vexed at what she called Sylvester's " hardheartedness." Still I was not without some apprehension. It was two months since I had seen him; and Sylvester's vague allusion to his " slinging an ugly left " pained me. I looked at sympathetic little Mrs. Brown; and the thought of Watson's pups covered me with guilty confusion.

Mrs. Brown had agreed to sit up with me until he arrived. One o'clock came, but no Baby. Two o'clock, three o'clock, passed. It was almost four when there was a wild clatter of horses' hoofs outside, and with a jerk a wagon stopped at the door. In an instant I had opened it, and confronted a stranger. Almost at the same moment, the horses attempted to run away with the wagon.

The stranger's appearance was, to say the least, disconcerting. His clothes were badly torn and frayed; his linen sack hung from his shoulders like a herald's apron; one of his hands was bandaged; his face scratched; and there was no hat on his dishevelled head. To add to the general effect, he had evidently sought relief from his woes in drink; and he swayed from side to side as he clung to the door-handle, and, in a very thick voice, stated that he had "suthin" for me outside. When he had finished, the horses made another plunge.

Mrs. Brown thought they must be frightened at something.

"Frightened!" laughed the stranger with bitter irony. "Oh, no! Hossish ain't frightened! On'y ran away four timesh comin' here. Oh, no! Nobody's frightened. Every thin's all ri'. Ain't it, Bill?" he said, addressing the driver. "On'y been overboard twish; knocked down a hatchway once. Thash nothin'! On'y two men unner doctor's han's at Stockton. Thash nothin'! Six hunner dollarsh cover all dam mish."

I was too much disheartened to reply, but moved toward the wagon. The stranger eyed me with an astonishment that almost sobered him.

"Do you reckon to tackle that animile yourself?" he asked, as he surveyed me from head to foot.

I did not speak, but, with an appearance of boldness I was far from feeling, walked to the wagon, and called "Baby!"

"All ri'. Cash loose them straps, Bill, and stan' clear."

The straps were cut loose; and Baby, the re morseless, the terrible, quietly tumbled to the ground, and, rolling to my side, rubbed his foolish head against me.

I think the astonishment of the two men was beyond any vocal expression. Without a word, the drunken stranger got into the wagon, and drove away.

And Baby? He had grown, it is true, a trifle larger; but he was thin, and bore the marks of evident ill usage. His beautiful coat was matted and unkempt; and his claws, those bright steel hooks, had been ruthlessly pared to the quick. His eyes were furtive and restless; and the old expression of stupid good humor had changed to one of intelligent distrust. His intercourse with mankind had evidently quick ened his intellect, without broadening his moral nature.

I had great difficulty in keeping Mrs. Brown from smothering him in blankets, and ruining his digestion with the delicacies of her larder; but I at last got him completely rolled up in the corner of my room, and asleep. I lay awake some time later with plans for his future. I finally determined to take him to Oakland — where I had built a little cottage, and always spent my Sundays — the very next day. And in the midst of a rosy picture of domestic felicity, I fell asleep.

When I awoke, it was broad day. My eyes at once sought the corner where Baby had been lying; but he was gone. I sprang from the bed, looked under it, searched the closet, but in vain. The door was still locked; but there were the marks of his blunted claws upon the sill of the window that I had forgotten to close. He had evidently escaped that way. But where? The window opened upon a balcony, to which the only other entrance was through the hall. He must be still in the house.

My hand was already upon the bell-rope; but I stayed it in time. If he had not made himself known, why should I disturb the house? I dressed myself hurriedly, and slipped into the hall. The first object that met my eyes was a boot lying upon the stairs. It bore the marks of Baby's teeth; and, as I looked along the hall, I saw too plainly that the usual array of freshly-blackened boots and shoes before the lodgers' doors was not there. As I ascended the stairs, I found another, but with the blacking carefully licked off. On the third floor were two or three more boots, slightly mouthed; but at this point Baby's taste for blacking had evidently palled. A little farther on was a ladder, leading to an open scuttle. I mounted the ladder, and reached the flat roof, that formed a continuous level over the row of houses to the corner of the street. Behind the chimney on the very last roof, something was lurking. It was the fugitive Baby. He was covered with dust and dirt and fragments of glass. But he was sitting on his hind-legs, and was eating an enormous slab of peanut candy, with a look of mingled guilt and infinite satisfaction. He even, I fancied, slightly stroked his stomach with his disengaged fore-paw as I approached. He knew that I was looking for him; and the expression of his eye said plainly, "The past, at least, is secure."

I hurried him, with the evidences of his guilt, back to the scuttle, and descended on tiptoe to the floor beneath. Providence favored

us: I met no one on the stairs; and his own
cushioned tread was inaudible. I think he was
conscious of the dangers of detection; for he
even forebore to breathe, or much less chew the
last mouthful he had taken; and he skulked
at my side with the sirup dropping from his
motionless jaws. I think he would have silently
choked to death just then, for my sake; and
it was not until I had reached my room again,
and threw myself panting on the sofa, that I
saw how near strangulation he had been. He
gulped once or twice apologetically, and then
walked to the corner of his own accord, and
rolled himself up like an immense sugarplum,
sweating remorse and treacle at every pore.

I locked him in when I went to breakfast,
when I found Mrs. Brown's lodgers in a state
of intense excitement over certain mysterious
events of the night before, and the dreadful
revelations of the morning. It appeared that
burglars had entered the block from the scut-
tles; that, being suddenly alarmed, they had
quitted our house without committing any
depredation, dropping even the boots they had
collected in the halls; but that a desperate
attempt had been made to force the till in the
confectioner's shop on the corner, and that the
glass show-cases had been ruthlessly smashed.
A courageous servant in No. 4 had seen a

masked burglar, on his hands and knees, attempting to enter their scuttle; but, on her shouting, "Away wid yees!" he instantly fled.

I sat through this recital with cheeks that burned uncomfortably; nor was I the less embarrassed, on raising my eyes, to meet Mrs. Brown's fixed curiously and mischievously on mine. As soon as I could make my escape from the table, I did so, and, running rapidly up stairs, sought refuge from any possible inquiry in my own room. Baby was still asleep in the corner. It would not be safe to remove him until the lodgers had gone down town; and I was revolving in my mind the expediency of keeping him until night veiled his obtrusive eccentricity from the public eye, when there came a cautious tap at my door. I opened it. Mrs. Brown slipped in quietly, closed the door softly, stood with her back against it, and her hand on the knob, and beckoned me mysteriously towards her. Then she asked in a low voice, —

" Is hair-dye poisonous?"

I was too confounded to speak.

"Oh, do! you know what I mean," she said impatiently. "This stuff." She produced suddenly from behind her a bottle with a Greek label so long as to run two or three times spirally around it from top to bottom. "He says it isn't a dye: it's a vegetable preparation, for invigorating " —

"Who says?" I asked despairingly.

"Why, Mr. Parker, of course!" said Mrs. Brown severely, with the air of having repeated the name a great many times, — "the old gentleman in the room above. The simple question I want to ask," she continued with the calm manner of one who has just convicted another of gross ambiguity of language, "is only this: If some of this stuff were put in a saucer, and left carelessly on the table, and a child, or a baby, or a cat, or any young animal, should come in at the window, and drink it up, — a whole saucer full, — because it had a sweet taste, would it be likely to hurt them?"

I cast an anxious glance at Baby, sleeping peacefully in the corner, and a very grateful one at Mrs. Brown, and said I didn't think it would.

"Because," said Mrs. Brown loftily as she opened the door, "I thought, if it was poisonous, remedies might be used in time. Because," she added suddenly, abandoning her lofty manner, and wildly rushing to the corner with a frantic embrace of the unconscious Baby, "because, if any nasty stuff should turn its booful hair a horrid green, or a naughty pink, it would break its own muzzer's heart, it would!'

But, before I could assure Mrs. Brown of the inefficiency of hair-dye as an internal application, she had darted from the room.

That night, with the secrecy of defaulters, Baby and I decamped from Mrs. Brown's. Distrusting the too emotional nature of that noble animal, the horse, I had recourse to a hand-cart, drawn by a stout Irishman, to convey my charge to the ferry. Even then, Baby refused to go, unless I walked by the cart, and at times rode in it.

"I wish," said Mrs. Brown, as she stood by the door, wrapped in an immense shawl, and saw us depart, "I wish it looked less solemn,— less like a pauper's funeral."

I must admit, that, as I walked by the cart that night, I felt very much as if I were accompanying the remains of some humble friend to his last resting-place; and that, when I was obliged to ride in it, I never could entirely convince myself that I was not helplessly overcome by liquor, or the victim of an accident, *en route* to the hospital. But at last we reached the ferry. On the boat, I think no one discovered Baby, except a drunken man, who approached me to ask for a light for his cigar, but who suddenly dropped it, and fled in dismay to the gentlemen's cabin, where his incoherent ravings were luckily taken for the earlier indications of *delirium tremens.*

It was nearly midnight when I reached my
little cottage on the outskirts of Oakland; and
it was with a feeling of relief and security that
I entered, locked the door, and turned him
loose in the hall, satisfied that henceforward
his depredations would be limited to my own
property. He was very quiet that night; and
after he had tried to mount the hat-rack, under
the mistaken impression that it was intended
for his own gymnastic exercise, and knocked
all the hats off, he went peaceably to sleep on
the rug.

In a week, with the exercise afforded him by
the run of a large, carefully-boarded enclosure,
he recovered his health, strength, spirits, and
much of his former beauty. His presence was
unknown to my neighbors, although it was
noticeable that horses invariably "shied" in
passing to the windward of my house, and that
the baker and milkman had great difficulty in
the delivery of their wares in the morning, and
indulged in unseemly and unnecessary profanity
in so doing.

At the end of the week, I determined to invite
a few friends to see the Baby, and to that purpose wrote a number of formal invitations.
After descanting, at some length, on the great
expense and danger attending his capture and
training, I offered a programme of the perform

ance, of the "Infant Phenomenon of Sierran Solitudes," drawn up into the highest professional profusion of alliteration and capital letters. A few extracts will give the reader some idea of his educational progress: —

1. He will, rolled up in a Round Ball, roll down the Wood-Shed Rapidly, illustrating His manner of Escaping from His Enemy in His Native Wilds.
2. He will Ascend the Well-Pole, and remove from the Very Top a Hat, and as much of the Crown and Brim thereof, as May be Permitted.
3. He will perform in a pantomime, descriptive of the Conduct of the Big Bear, The Middle-Sized Bear, and The Little Bear of the Popular Nursery Legend.
4. He will shake his chain Rapidly, showing his Manner of striking Dismay and Terror in the Breasts of Wanderers in Ursine Wildernesses.

The morning of the exhibition came; but an hour before the performance the wretched Baby was missing. The Chinese cook could not indicate his whereabouts. I searched the premises thoroughly; and then, in despair, took my hat, and hurried out into the narrow lane that led toward the open fields and the woods beyond. But I found no trace nor track of Baby Sylvester. I returned, after an hour's fruitless search, to find my guests already assembled on the rear veranda. I briefly re counted my disappointment, my probable loss, and begged their assistance.

"Why," said a Spanish friend, who prided himself on his accurate knowledge of English, to Barker, who seemed to be trying vainly to rise from his reclining position on the veranda, "why do you not disengage yourself from the veranda of our friend? And why, in the name of Heaven, do you attach to yourself so much of this thing, and make to yourself such unnecessary contortion? Ah," he continued, suddenly withdrawing one of his own feet from the veranda with an evident effort, "I am myself attached! Surely it is something here!"

It evidently was. My guests were all rising with difficulty. The floor of the veranda was covered with some glutinous substance. It was — sirup!

I saw it all in a flash. I ran to the barn. The keg of "golden sirup," purchased only the day before, lay empty upon the floor. There were sticky tracks all over the enclosure, but still no Baby.

"There's something moving the ground over there by that pile of dirt," said Barker.

He was right. The earth was shaking in one corner of the enclosure like an earthquake. I approached cautiously. I saw, what I had not before noticed, that the ground was thrown up; and there, in the middle of an immense grave-like cavity, crouched Baby Sylvester, stil digging, and slowly but surely sinking from sight in a mass of dust and clay.

What were his intentions? Whether he was stung by remorse, and wished to hide himself from my reproachful eyes, or whether he was simply trying to dry his sirup-besmeared coat, I never shall know; for that day, alas! was his last with me.

He was pumped upon for two hours, at the end of which time he still yielded a thin treacle. He was then taken, and carefully inwrapped in blankets, and locked up in the store-room. The next morning he was gone! The lower portion of the window sash and pane were gone too. His successful experiments on the fragile texture of glass at the confectioner's, on the first day of his entrance to civilization, had not been lost upon him. His first essay at combining cause and effect ended in his escape.

Where he went, where he hid, who captured him, if he did not succeed in reaching the foothills beyond Oakland, even the offer of a large reward, backed by the efforts of an intelligent police, could not discover. I never saw him again from that day until —

Did I see him? I was in a horse-car on Sixth Avenue, a few days ago, when the horses suddenly became unmanageable, and left the track for the sidewalk, amid the oaths and exe-

erations of the driver. Immediately in front
of the car a crowd had gathered around two
performing bears and a showman. One of the
animals, thin, emaciated, and the mere wreck
of his native strength, attracted my attention.
I endeavored to attract his. He turned a pair
of bleared, sightless eyes in my direction; but
there was no sign of recognition. I leaned
from the car-window, and called softly, " Baby! "
But he did not heed. I closed the window.
The car was just moving on, when he suddenly
turned, and, either by accident or design, thrust
a callous paw through the glass.

"It's worth a dollar and half to put in a new
pane," said the conductor, "if folks will play
with bears!" —

AN EPISODE OF FIDDLETOWN.

IN 1858 Fiddletown considered her a very pretty woman. She had a quantity of light chestnut hair, a good figure, a dazzling complexion, and a certain languid grace which passed easily for gentlewomanliness. She always dressed becomingly, and in what Fiddletown accepted as the latest fashion. She had only two blemishes: one of her velvety eyes, when examined closely, had a slight cast; and her left cheek bore a small scar left by a single drop of vitriol — happily the only drop of an entire phial — thrown upon her by one of her own jealous sex, that reached the pretty face it was intended to mar. But, when the observer had studied the eyes sufficiently to notice this defect, he was generally incapacitated for criticism; and even the scar on her cheek was thought by some to add piquancy to her smile. The youthful editor of "The Fiddletown Avalanche" had said privately that it was "an exaggerated dimple." Col. Starbottle was instantly "reminded of the beautifying patches of the days of Queen Anne,

but more particularly, sir, of the blankest beautiful women, that, blank you, you ever laid your
two blank eyes upon, — a Creole woman, sir, in
New Orleans. And this woman had a scar, — a
line extending, blank me, from her eye to her
blank chin. And this woman, sir, thrilled you,
sir; maddened you, sir; absolutely sent your
blank soul to perdition with her blank fascina-
tion! And one day I said to her, ' Celeste, how
in blank did you come by that beautiful scar,
blank you?' And she said to me, 'Star, there
isn't another white man that I'd confide in but
you; but I made that scar myself, purposely, I
did, blank me.' These were her very words,
sir, and perhaps you think it a blank lie, sir;
but I'll put up any blank sum you can name
and prove it, blank me."

Indeed, most of the male population of Fiddletown were or had been in love with her. Of
this number, about one-half believed that their
love was returned, with the exception, possibly,
of her own husband. He alone had been known
to express scepticism.

The name of the gentleman who enjoyed this
infelicitous distinction was Tretherick. He had
been divorced from an excellent wife to marry
this Fiddletown enchantress. She, also, had been
divorced; but it was hinted that some previous
experiences of hers in that legal formality had

made it perhaps less novel, and probably less
sacrificial. I would not have it inferred from
this that she was deficient in sentiment, or
devoid of its highest moral expression. Her
intimate friend had written (on the occasion of
her second divorce), " The cold world does not
understand Clara yet;" and Col. Starbottle had
remarked blankly, that with the exception of
a single woman in Opelousas Parish, La., she
had more soul than the whole caboodle of
them put together. Few indeed could read
those lines entitled " Infelissimus," commencing,
" Why waves no cypress o'er this brow?" origi
nally published in " The Avalanche," over the
signature of " The Lady Clare," without feeling
the tear of sensibility tremble on his eyelids, or
the glow of virtuous indignation mantle his
cheek, at the low brutality and pitiable jocularity
of " The Dutch Flat Intelligencer," which the
next week had suggested the exotic character
of the cypress, and its entire absence from Fiddletown, as a reasonable answer to the query.

Indeed, it was this tendency to elaborate her
feelings in a metrical manner, and deliver them
to the cold world through the medium of the
newspapers, that first attracted the attention of
Tretherick. Several poems descriptive of the
effects of California scenery upon a too sensitive
soul, and of the vague yearnings for the infinite,

which an enforced study of the heartlessness of
California society produced in the poetic breast,
impressed Mr. Tretherick, who was then driving
a six-mule freight-wagon between Knight's
Ferry and Stockton, to seek out the unknown
poetess. Mr. Tretherick was himself dimly
conscious of a certain hidden sentiment in his
own nature; and it is possible that some reflections on the vanity of his pursuit, — he supplied
several mining-camps with whiskey and tobacco,
— in conjunction with the dreariness of the
dusty plain on which he habitually drove, may
have touched some chord in sympathy with this
sensitive woman. Howbeit, after a brief courtship, — as brief as was consistent with some
previous legal formalities, — they were married;
and Mr. Tretherick brought his blushing bride
to Fiddletown, or "Fidéletown," as Mrs. Tretherick preferred to call it in her poems.

The union was not a felicitous one. It was
not long before Mr. Tretherick discovered that
the sentiment he had fostered while freighting
between Stockton and Knight's Ferry was different from that which his wife had evolved from
the contemplation of California scenery and
her own soul. Being a man of imperfect logic,
this caused him to beat her; and she, being
equally faulty in deduction, was impelled to a
certain degree of unfaithfulness on the same

premise.   Then Mr. Tretherick began to drink, and Mrs. Tretherick to contribute regularly to the columns of " The Avalanche." It was at this time that Col. Starbottle discovered a similarity in Mrs. Tretherick's verse to the genius of Sappho, and pointed it out to the citizens of Fiddletown in a two-columned criticism, signed " A. S.," also published in " The Avalanche," and supported by extensive quotation.   As " The Avalanche " did not possess a font of Greek type, the editor was obliged to reproduce the Leucadian numbers in the ordinary Roman letter, to the intense disgust of Col. Starbottle, and the vast delight of Fiddletown, who saw fit to accept the text as an excellent imitation of Choctaw, — a language with which the colonel, as a whilom resident of the Indian Territories, was supposed to be familiar.   Indeed, the next week's " Intelligencer " contained some vile doggerel, supposed to be an answer to Mrs. Tretherick's poem, ostensibly written by the wife of a Digger Indian chief, accompanied by a glowing eulogium, signed " A. S. S."

The result of this jocularity was briefly given in a later copy of " The Avalanche."   " An unfortunate rencounter took place on Monday last, between the Hon. Jackson Flash of " The Dutch Flat Intelligencer " and the well-known Col. Starbottle of this place, in front of the Eureka

Saloon. Two shots were fired by the parties without injury to either, although it is said that a passing Chinaman received fifteen buckshot in the calves of his legs from the colonel's double-barrelled shot-gun, which were not intended for him. John will learn to keep out of the way of Melican man's fire-arms hereafter. The cause of the affray is not known, although it is hinted that there is a lady in the case. The rumor that points to a well-known and beautiful poetess whose lucubrations have often graced our columns seems to gain credence from those that are posted."

Meanwhile the passiveness displayed by Tretherick under these trying circumstances was fully appreciated in the gulches. "The old man's head is level," said one long-booted philosopher. "Ef the colonel kills Flash, Mrs. Tretherick is avenged: if Flash drops the colonel, Tretherick is all right. Either way, he's got a sure thing." During this delicate condition of affairs, Mrs. Tretherick one day left her husband's home, and took refuge at the Fiddletown Hotel, with only the clothes she had on her back. Here she staid for several weeks, during which period it is only justice to say that she bore herself with the strictest propriety.

It was a clear morning in early spring that

Mrs. Tretherick, unattended, left the hotel, and walked down the narrow street toward the fringe of dark pines which indicated the extreme limits of Fiddletown. The few loungers at that early hour were pre-occupied with the departure of the Wingdown coach at the other extremity of the street; and Mrs. Tretherick reached the suburbs of the settlement without discomposing observation. Here she took a cross street or road, running at right angles with the main thoroughfare of Fiddletown, and passing through a belt of woodland. It was evidently the exclusive and aristocratic avenue of the town. The dwellings were few, ambitious, and uninterrupted by shops. And here she was joined by Col. Starbottle.

The gallant colonel, notwithstanding that he bore the swelling port which usually distinguished him, that his coat was tightly buttoned, and his boots tightly fitting, and that his cane, hooked over his arm, swung jauntily, was not entirely at his ease. Mrs. Tretherick, however, vouchsafed him a gracious smile and a glance of her dangerous eyes ; and the colonel, with an embarrassed cough and a slight strut, took his place at her side.

" The coast is clear," said the colonel, " and Tretherick is over at Dutch Flat on a spree. There is no one in the house but a Chinaman :

and you need fear no trouble from him. *I*," he
continued, with a slight inflation of the chest
that imperilled the security of his button, " I
will see that you are protected in the removal
of your property."

" I'm sure it's very kind of you, and so dis-
interested ! " simpered the lady as they walked
along. " It's so pleasant to meet some one who
has soul, — some one to sympathize with in a
community so hardened and heartless as this."
And Mrs. Tretherick cast down her eyes, but
not until they wrought their perfect and accepted work upon her companion.

" Yes, certainly, of course," said the colonel,
glancing nervously up and down the street, —
" yes, certainly."   Perceiving, however, that
there was no one in sight or hearing, he proceeded at once to inform Mrs. Tretherick that
the great trouble of his life, in fact, had been
the possession of too much soul. That many
women — as a gentleman she would excuse
him, of course, from mentioning names — but
many beautiful women had often sought his
society, but being deficient, madam, absolutely
deficient, in this quality, he could not recipro-
cate.   But when two natures thoroughly in
sympathy, despising alike the sordid trammels
of a low and vulgar community, and the con
ventional restraints of a hypocritical society, —

when two souls in perfect accord met and mingled in poetical union, then — but here the colonel's speech, which had been remarkable for a certain whiskey-and-watery fluency, grew husky, almost inaudible, and decidedly incoherent. Possibly Mrs. Tretherick may have heard something like it before, and was enabled to fill the hiatus. Nevertheless, the cheek that was on the side of the colonel was quite virginal and bashfully conscious until they reached their destination.

It was a pretty little cottage, quite fresh and warm with paint, very pleasantly relieved against a platoon of pines, some of whose fore· most files had been displaced to give freedom to the fenced enclosure in which it sat. In the vivid sunlight and perfect silence, it had a new, uninhabited look, as if the carpenters and painters had just left it. At the farther end of the lot, a Chinaman was stolidly digging; but there was no other sign of occupancy. " The coast," as the colonel had said, was indeed " clear." Mrs. Tretherick paused at the gate. The colonel would have entered with her, but was stopped by a gesture. " Come for me in a couple of hours, and I shall have every thing packed," she said, as she smiled, and extended her hand. The colonel seized and pressed it with great fervor. Perhaps the pressure was

slightly returned; for the gallant colonel was
impelled to inflate his chest, and trip away as
smartly as his stubby-toed, high-heeled boots
would permit. When he had gone, Mrs. Tretherick opened the door, listened a moment in
the deserted hall, and then ran quickly up stairs
to what had been her bedroom.

Every thing there was unchanged as on the
night she left it. On the dressing-table stood
her bandbox, as she remembered to have left it
when she took out her bonnet. On the mantle
lay the other glove she had forgotten in her
flight. The two lower drawers of the bureau
were half open (she had forgotten to shut them);
and on its marble top lay her shawl-pin and a
soiled cuff. What other recollections came upon
her I know not; but she suddenly grew quite
white, shivered, and listened with a beating
heart, and her hand upon the door. Then she
stepped to the mirror, and half fearfully, half
curiously, parted with her fingers the braids of
her blonde hair above her little pink ear, until
she came upon an ugly, half-healed scar. She
gazed at this, moving her pretty head up and
down to get a better light upon it, until the
sligh⁺ cast in her velvety eyes became very
strongly marked indeed. Then she turned
away with a light, reckless, foolish laugh, and
ran to the closet where hung her precious

dresses. These she inspected nervously, and missing suddenly a favorite black silk from its accustomed peg, for a moment, thought she should have fainted. But discovering it the next instant lying upon a trunk where she had thrown it, a feeling of thankfulness to a superior Being who protects the friendless, for the first time sincerely thrilled her. Then, albeit she was hurried for time, she could not resist trying the effect of a certain lavender neck-ribbon upon the dress she was then wearing, before the mirror. And then suddenly she became aware of a child's voice close beside her, and she stopped. And then the child's voice repeated, " Is it mamma ? "

Mrs. Tretherick faced quickly about. Standing in the doorway was a little girl of six or seven. Her dress had been originally fine, but was torn and dirty ; and her hair, which was a very violent red, was tumbled serio-comically about her forehead. For all this, she was a picturesque little thing, even through whose childish timidity there was a certain self-sustained air which is apt to come upon children who are left much to themselves. She was holding under her arm a rag doll, apparently of her own workmanship, and nearly as large as herself, — a doll with a cylindrical head, and features roughly indicated with charcoal. A long shawl, evidently belonging to a grown person, dropped from her shoulders, and swept the floor.

The spectacle did not excite Mrs. Trether ick's delight. Perhaps she had but a small sense of humor. Certainly, when the child, still standing in the doorway, again asked, " Is it mamma?" she answered sharply, " No, it isn't," and turned a severe look upon the intruder.

The child retreated a step, and then, gaining courage with the distance, said in deliciously imperfect speech, —

" Dow 'way then! why don't you dow away?"

But Mrs. Tretherick was eying the shawl. Suddenly she whipped it off the child's shoulders, and said angrily, —

" How dared you take my things, you bad child?"

" Is it yours? Then you are my mamma; ain't you? You are mamma!" she continued gleefully; and, before Mrs. Tretherick could avoid her, she had dropped her doll, and, catch- ing the woman's skirts with both hands, was dancing up and down before her.

" What's your name, child?" said Mrs. Treth- erick coldly, removing the small and not very white hands from her garments.

" Tarry."

" Tarry ? "

" Yeth. Tarry. Tarowline."

" Caroline ? "

" Yeth. Tarowline Tretherick."

" Whose child *are* you ? " demanded **Mrs.**
Tretherick still more coldly, to keep down a
rising fear.

" Why, yours," said the little creature with a
laugh. " I'm your little durl. You're my
mamma, my new mamma. Don't you know my
ole mamma's dorn away, never to tum back
any more? I don't live wid my ol' mamma
now. I live wid you and papa."

" How long have you been here ? " asked Mrs.
Tretherick snappishly.

" I fink it's free days," said Carry reflectively.

" You think ! Don't you know ? " sneered
Mrs. Tretherick. " Then, where did you come
from ? "

Carry's lip began to work under this sharp
cross-examination. With a great effort and a
small gulp, she got the better of it, and answered, —

" Papa, papa fetched me, — from Miss Sim
mons — from Sacramento, last week."

" Last week ! You said three days just now,"
returned Mrs Tretherick with severe deliberation.

" I mean a monf," said Carry, now utterly
adrift in sheer helplessness and confusion.

" Do you know what you are talking about?" demanded Mrs. Tretherick shrilly, restraining an impulse to shake the little figure before her, and precipitate the truth by specific gravity.

But the flaming red head here suddenly disappeared in the folds of Mrs. Tretherick's dress, as if it were trying to extinguish itself forever.

" There now — stop that sniffling," said Mrs. Tretherick, extricating her dress from the moist embraces of the child, and feeling exceedingly uncomfortable. " Wipe your face now, and run away, and don't bother. Stop," she continued, as Carry moved away. " Where's your papa?"

" He's dorn away too. He's sick. He's been dorn " — she hesitated — " two, free, days."

" Who takes care of you, child?" said Mrs. Tretherick, eying her curiously.

" John, the Chinaman. I tresses myselth. John tooks and makes the beds."

" Well, now, run away and behave yourself, and don't bother me any more," said Mrs. Tretherick, remembering the object of her visit. " Stop — where are you going?" she added, as the child began to ascend the stairs, dragging the long doll after her by one helpless leg.

" Doin up stairs to play and be dood, and no bother mamma."

" I ain't your mamma," shouted Mrs. Trether-

ick, and then she swiftly re-entered her bedroom, and slammed the door.

Once inside, she drew forth a large trunk
from the closet, and set to work with querulous
and fretful haste to pack her wardrobe. She
tore her best dress in taking it from the hook
on which it hung : she scratched her soft hands
twice with an ambushed pin. All the while,
she kept up an indignant commentary on the
events of the past few moments. She said to
herself she saw it all. Tretherick had sent for
this child of his first wife — this child of whose
existence he had never seemed to care — just to
insult her, to fill her place. Doubtless the first
wife herself would follow soon, or perhaps
there would be a third. Red hair, not auburn,
but *red*, — of course the child, this Caroline,
looked like its mother, and, if so, she was any
thing but pretty. Or the whole thing had
been prepared : this red-haired child, the image
of its mother, had been kept at a convenient
distance at Sacramento, ready to be sent for
when needed. She remembered his occasional
visits there on — business, as he said. Perhaps
the mother already was there ; but no, she had
gone East. Nevertheless, Mrs. Tretherick, in
her then state of mind, preferred to dwell upon
the fact that she might be there. She was
dimly conscious, also, of a certain satisfaction

in exaggerating her feelings. Surely no woman had ever been so shamefully abused. In fancy, she sketched a picture of herself sitting alone and deserted, at sunset, among the fallen columns of a ruined temple, in a melancholy yet graceful attitude, while her husband drove rapidly away in a luxurious coach-and-four, with a red-haired woman at his side. Sitting upon the trunk she had just packed, she partly composed a lugubrious poem, describing her sufferings, as, wandering alone, and poorly clad, she came upon her husband and " another " flaunting in silks and diamonds. She pictured herself dying of consumption, brought on by sorrow, — a beautiful wreck, yet still fascinating, gazed upon adoringly by the editor of " The Avalanche," and Col. Starbottle. And where was Col. Starbottle all this while? Why didn't he come? He, at least, understood her. He — she laughed the reckless, light laugh of a few moments before; and then her face suddenly grew grave, as it had not a few moments before.

What was that little red-haired imp doing all this time? Why was she so quiet? She opened the door noiselessly, and listened. She fancied that she heard, above the multitudinous small noises and creakings and warpings of the vacant house, a smaller voice singing on the floor above This, as she remembered, was only an open attic that had been used as a store-room. With a half-guilty consciousness, she crept softly up stairs, and, pushing the door partly open, looked within.

Athwart the long, low-studded attic, a slant sunbeam from a single small window lay, filled with dancing motes, and only half illuminating the barren, dreary apartment. In the ray of this sunbeam she saw the child's glowing hair, as if crowned by a red aureola, as she sat upon the floor with her exaggerated doll between her knees. She appeared to be talking to it; and it was not long before Mrs. Tretherick observed that she was rehearsing the interview of a half-hour before. She catechised the doll severely, cross-examining it in regard to the duration of its stay there, and generally on the measure of time. The imitation of Mrs. Tretherick's manner was exceedingly successful, and the conversation almost a literal reproduction, with a single exception. After she had informed the doll that she was not her mother, at the close of the interview she added pathetically, "that if she was dood, very dood, she might be her mamma, and love her very much."

I have already hinted that Mrs. Tretherick was deficient in a sense of humor. Perhaps it was for this reason that this whole scene affected her most unpleasantly; and the conclusion sent the blood tingling to her cheek. There was something, too, inconceivably lonely in the situation. The unfurnished vacant room, the half-lights, the monstrous doll, whose very size seemed to give a pathetic significance to its speechlessness, the smallness of the one animate, self-centred figure, — all these touched more or less deeply the half-poetic sensibilities of the woman. She could not help utilizing the impression as she stood there, and thought what a fine poem might be constructed from this material, if the room were a little darker, the child lonelier, — say, sitting beside a dead mother's bier, and the wind wailing in the turrets. And then she suddenly heard footsteps at the door below, and recognized the tread of the colonel's cane.

She flew swiftly down the stairs, and encountered the colonel in the hall. Here she poured into his astonished ear a voluble and exaggerated statement of her discovery, and indignant recital of her wrongs. "Don't tell me the whole thing wasn't arranged beforehand; for I know it was!" she almost screamed. "And think," she added, "of the heartlessness of the wretch, leaving his own child alone here in that way."

"It's a blank shame!" stammered the colonel without the least idea of what he was talking

about. In fact, utterly unable as he was to
comprehend a reason for the woman's excitement with his estimate of her character, I fear
he showed it more plainly than he intended.
He stammered, expanded his chest, looked
stern, gallant, tender, but all unintelligently.
Mr. Tretherick, for an instant, experienced a
sickening doubt of the existence of natures in
perfect affinity.

"It's of no use," said Mrs. Tretherick with
sudden vehemence, in answer to some inaudible
remark of the colonel's, and withdrawing her
hand from the fervent grasp of that ardent and
sympathetic man. "It's of no use: my mind
is made up. You can send for my trunk as soon
as you like; but I shall stay here, and confront
that man with the proof of his vileness. I will
put him face to face with his infamy."

I do not know whether Col. Starbottle
thoroughly appreciated the convincing proof
of Tretherick's unfaithfulness and malignity
afforded by the damning evidence of the exist
ence of Tretherick's own child in his own
house. He was dimly aware, however, of some
unforeseen obstacle to the perfect expression
of the infinite longing of his own sentimental
nature. But, before he could say any thing,
Carry appeared on the landing above them,
looking timidly, and yet half-critically at the
pair.

" That's her," said Mrs. Tretherick excitedly.
In her deepest emotions, either in verse or prose,
she rose above a consideration of grammatical
construction.

" Ah!" said the colonel, with a sudden
assumption of parental affection and jocularity
that was glaringly unreal and affected. " Ah!
pretty little girl, pretty little girl! How do you
do? How are you? You find yourself pretty
well, do you, pretty little girl?" The colonel's
impulse also was to expand his chest, and swing
his cane, until it occurred to him that this action
might be ineffective with a child of six or seven.
Carry, however, took no immediate notice of this
advance, but further discomposed the chivalrous
colonel by running quickly to Mrs. Tretherick,
and hiding herself, as if for protection, in the
folds of her gown. Nevertheless, the colonel
was not vanquished. Falling back into an attitude of respectful admiration, he pointed out a
marvellous resemblance to the " Madonna and
Child." Mrs. Tretherick simpered, but did not
dislodge Carry as before. There was an awkward pause for a moment; and then Mrs. Tretherick, motioning significantly to the child, said
in a whisper, " Go now. Don't come here
again, but meet me to-night at the hotel." She
extended her hand: the colonel bent over it
gallantly, and, raising his hat, the next moment
was gone.

"Do you think," said Mrs. Tretherick with an embarrassed voice and a prodigious blush, looking down, and addressing the fiery curls just visible in the folds of her dress, — "do you think you will be 'dood,' if I let you stay in here and sit with me?"

"And let me tall you mamma?" queried Carry, looking up.

"And let you call me mamma!" assented Mrs. Tretherick with an embarrassed laugh.

"Yeth," said Carry promptly.

They entered the bedroom together. Carry's eye instantly caught sight of the trunk.

"Are you dowin away adain, mamma?" she said with a quick nervous look, and a clutch at the woman's dress.

"No-o," said Mrs. Tretherick, looking out of the window.

"Only playing your dowin away," suggested Carry with a laugh. "Let me play too."

Mrs. Tretherick assented. Carry flew into the next room, and presently re-appeared, dragging a small trunk, into which she gravely proceeded to pack her clothes. Mrs. Tretherick noticed that they were not many. A question or two regarding them brought out some further replies from the child; and, before many minutes had elapsed, Mrs. Tretherick was in possession of all her earlier history. But, to do this, Mrs

Tretherick had been obliged to take Carry
upon her lap, pending the most confidential
disclosures. They sat thus a long time after
Mrs. Tretherick had apparently ceased to be
interested in Carry's disclosures; and, when lost
in thought, she allowed the child to rattle on
unheeded, and ran her fingers through the
scarlet curls.

" You don't hold me right, mamma," said
Carry at last, after one or two uneasy shiftings
of position.

" How should I hold you? " asked Mrs. Tretherick with a half-amused, half-embarrassed
laugh.

" Dis way," said Carry, curling up into position, with one arm around Mrs. Tretherick's
neck, and her cheek resting on her bosom, —
" dis way, — dere." After a little preparatory
nestling, not unlike some small animal, she
closed her eyes, and went to sleep.

For a few moments the woman sat silent,
scarcely daring to breathe in that artificial attitude. And then, whether from some occult
sympathy in the touch, or God best knows
what, a sudden fancy began to thrill her. She
began by remembering an old pain that she
had forgotten, an old horror that she had resolutely put away all these years. She recalled
days of sickness and distrust, — days of an

overshadowing fear, — days of preparation for something that was to be prevented, that *was* prevented, with mortal agony and fear. She thought of a life that might have been, — she dared not say *had* been, — and wondered. It was six years ago: if it had lived, it would have been as old as Carry. The arms which were folded loosely around the sleeping child began to tremble, and tighten their clasp. And then the deep potential impulse came, and with a half-sob, half-sigh, she threw her arms out, and drew the body of the sleeping child down, down, into her breast, down again and again as if she would hide it in the grave dug there years before. And the gust that shook her passed, and then, ah me! the rain.

A drop or two fell upon the curls of Carry, and she moved uneasily in her sleep. But the woman soothed her again, — it was *so* easy to do it now, — and they sat there quiet and undisturbed, so quiet that they might have seemed incorporate of the lonely silent house, the slowly-declining sunbeams, and the general air of desertion and abandonment, yet a desertion that had in it nothing of age, decay, or despair.

Col. Starbottle waited at the Fiddletown Hotel all that night in vain. And the next morning, when Mr. Tretherick returned to his husks,

he found the house vacant and untenanted,
except by motes and sunbeams.

When it was fairly known that Mrs. Tretherick had run away, taking Mr. Tretherick's own
child with her, there was some excitement, and
much diversity of opinion, in Fiddletown. "The
Dutch Flat Intelligencer" openly alluded to
the "forcible abduction" of the child with the
same freedom, and it is to be feared the same
prejudice, with which it had criticised the
abductor's poetry. All of Mrs. Tretherick's
own sex, and perhaps a few of the opposite sex,
whose distinctive quality was not, however,
very strongly indicated, fully coincided in the
views of "The Intelligencer." The majority,
however, evaded the moral issue: that Mrs.
Tretherick had shaken the red dust of Fiddletown from her dainty slippers was enough for
them to know. They mourned the loss of the
fair abductor more than her offence. They
promptly rejected Tretherick as an injured husband and disconsolate father, and even went
so far as to openly cast discredit on the sincerity
of his grief. They reserved an ironical con-
dolence for Col. Starbottle, overbearing that
excellent man with untimely and demonstra-
tive sympathy in bar-rooms, saloons, and other
localities not generally deemed favorable to
the display of sentiment. "She was alliz a

skittish thing, kernel," said one sympathizer, with a fine affectation of gloomy concern, and great readiness of illustration; "and it's kinder nat'ril thet she'd get away some day, and stampede that theer colt: but thet she should shake *you*, kernel, thet she should just shake you — is what gits me. And they do say thet you jist hung around thet hotel all night, and payrolled them corriders, and histed yourself up and down them stairs, and meandered in and out o' thet piazzy, and all for nothing?" It was another generous and tenderly commiserating spirit that poured additional oil and wine on the colonel's wounds. "The boys yer let on thet Mrs. Tretherick prevailed on ye to pack her trunk and a baby over from the house to the stage-offis, and that the chap ez did go off with her thanked you, and offered you two short bits, and sed ez how he liked your looks, and ud employ you agin — and now you say it ain't so? Well, I'll tell the boys it aint so, and I'm glad I met you, for stories *do* get round."

Happily for Mrs. Tretherick's reputation, however, the Chinaman in Tretherick's employment, who was the only eye-witness of her flight, stated that she was unaccompanied, except by the child. He further deposed, that, obeying her orders, he had stopped the Sacramento coach, and secured a passage for herself and child to San Francisco. It was true that Ah Fe's testimony was of no legal value. But nobody doubted it. Even those who were sceptical of the Pagan's ability to recognize the sacredness of the truth admitted his passionless, unprejudiced unconcern. But it would appear, from a hitherto unrecorded passage of this veracious chronicle, that herein they were mistaken.

It was about six months after the disappearance of Mrs. Tretherick, that Ah Fe, while working in Tretherick's lot, was hailed by two passing Chinamen. They were the ordinary mining coolies, equipped with long poles and baskets for their usual pilgrimages. An animated conversation at once ensued between Ah Fe and his brother Mongolians, — a conversation characterized by that usual shrill volubility and apparent animosity which was at once the delight and scorn of the intelligent Caucasian who did not understand a word of it. Such, at least, was the feeling with which Mr. Tretherick on his veranda, and Col. Starbottle who was passing, regarded their heathenish jargon. The gallant colonel simply kicked them out of his way: the irate Tretherick, with an oath, threw a stone at the group, and dispersed them. but not before one or two slips of yellow rice paper, marked with hieroglyphics, were ex changed, and a small parcel put into Ah Fe's hands. When Ah Fe opened this in the dim solitude of his kitchen, he found a little girl's apron, freshly washed, ironed, and folded. On the corner of the hem were the initials "C. T." Ah Fe tucked it away in a corner of his blouse, and proceeded to wash his dishes in the sink with a smile of guileless satisfaction.

Two days after this, Ah Fe confronted his master. "Me no likee Fiddletown. Me belly sick. Me go now." Mr. Tretherick violently suggested a profane locality. Ah Fe gazed at him placidly, and withdrew.

Before leaving Fiddletown, however, he accidentally met Col. Starbottle, and dropped a few incoherent phrases which apparently interested that gentleman. When he concluded, the colonel handed him a letter and a twenty-dollar gold-piece. "If you bring me an answer, I'll double that — Sabe, John?" Ah Fe nodded. An interview equally accidental, with precisely the same result, took place between Ah Fe and another gentleman, whom I suspect to have been the youthful editor of "The Avalanche." Yet I regret to state, that, after proceeding some distance on his journey, Ah Fe calmly broke the seals of both letters, and, after trying to read them upside down and sideways, finally divided them into accurate squares, and in this

condition disposed of them to a brother **Celes-**
tial whom he met on the road, for a trifling
gratuity.   The agony of Col. Starbottle on
finding his wash-bill made out on the unwritten
side of one of these squares, and delivered to
him with his weekly clean clothes, and the subsequent discovery that the remaining portions
of his letter were circulated by the same method
from the Chinese laundry of one Fung Ti of
Fiddletown, has been described to me as peculiarly affecting.   Yet I am satisfied that a higher
nature, rising above the levity induced by the
mere contemplation of the insignificant details
of this breach of trust, would find ample retrib-
utive justice in the difficulties that subsequently
attended Ah Fe's pilgrimage.

On the road to Sacramento he was twice playfully thrown from the top of the stage-coach by
an intelligent but deeply-intoxicated Caucasian,
whose moral nature was shocked at riding with
one addicted to opium-smoking.   At Hangtown
he was beaten by a passing stranger, — purely
an act of Christian supererogation.   At Dutch
Flat he was robbed by well-known hands from
unknown motives.   At Sacramento he was arrested on suspicion of being something or other,
and discharged with a severe reprimand — possibly for not being it, and so delaying the course
of justice.   At San Francisco he was freely

stoned by children of the public schools; but, by carefully avoiding these monuments of enlightened progress, he at last reached, in comparative safety, the Chinese quarters, where his abuse was confined to the police, and limited by the strong arm of the law.

The next day he entered the wash-house of Chy Fook as an assistant, and on the following Friday was sent with a basket of clean clothes to Chy Fook's several clients.

It was the usual foggy afternoon as he climbed the long wind-swept hill of California Street, — one of those bleak, gray intervals that made the summer a misnomer to any but the liveliest San-Franciscan fancy. There was no warmth or color in earth or sky, no light nor shade within or without, only one monotonous, universal neutral tint over every thing. There was a fierce unrest in the wind-whipped streets: there was a dreary vacant quiet in the gray houses. When Ah Fe reached the top of the hill, the Mission Ridge was already hidden; and the chill sea-breeze made him shiver. As he put down his basket to rest himself, it is possible, that, to his defective intelligence and heathen experience, this " God's own climate," as it was called, seemed to possess but scant tenderness, softness, or mercy. But it is possible that Ah Fe illogically confounded this season with his old persecutors, the school-children, who, being released from studious confinement, at this hour were generally most aggressive. So he hastened on, and, turning a corner, at last stopped before a small house.

It was the usual San-Franciscan urban cottage. There was the little strip of cold green shrubbery before it; the chilly, bare veranda, and above this, again, the grim balcony, on which no one sat. Ah Fe rang the bell. A servant appeared, glanced at his basket, and reluctantly admitted him, as if he were some necessary domestic animal. Ah Fe silently mounted the stairs, and, entering the open door of the front-chamber, put down the basket, and stood passively on the threshold.

A woman, who was sitting in the cold gray light of the window, with a child in her lap, rose listlessly, and came toward him. Ah Fe instantly recognized Mrs. Tretherick; but not a muscle of his immobile face changed, nor did his slant eyes lighten as he met her own placidly. She evidently did not recognize him as she began to count the clothes. But the child, curiously examining him, suddenly uttered a short, glad cry.

"Why, it's John, mamma! It's our old John what we had in Fiddletown."

For an instant Ah Fe's eyes and teeth electrirally lightened. The child clapped her hands, and caught at his blouse. Then he said shortly, "Me John — Ah Fe — allee same. Me know you. How do?"

Mrs. Tretherick dropped the clothes nervously, and looked hard at Ah Fe. Wanting the quick-witted instinct of affection that sharpened Carry's perception, she even then could not distinguish him above his fellows. With a recollection of past pain, and an obscure suspicion of impending danger, she asked him when he had left Fiddletown.

"Longee time. No likee Fiddletown, no likee Tlevelick. Likee San Flisco. Likee washee. Likee Tally."

Ah Fe's laconics pleased Mrs. Tretherick. She did not stop to consider how much an imperfect knowledge of English added to his curt directness and sincerity. But she said, "Don't tell anybody you have seen me," and took out her pocket-book.

Ah Fe, without looking at it, saw that it was nearly empty. Ah Fe, without examining the apartment, saw that it was scantily furnished. Ah Fe, without removing his eyes from blank vacancy, saw that both Mrs. Tretherick and Carry were poorly dressed. Yet it is my duty to state that Ah Fe's long fingers closed promptly and firmly over the half-dollar which Mrs. Tretherick extended to him.

Then he began to fumble in his blouse with a series of extraordinary contortions. After a few moments, he extracted from apparently no particular place a child's apron, which he laid upon the basket with the remark, —

"One piecee washman flagittee."

Then he began anew his fumblings and contortions. At last his efforts were rewarded by his producing, apparently from his right ear, a many-folded piece of tissue-paper. Unwrapping this carefully, he at last disclosed two twenty-dollar gold-pieces, which he handed to Mrs. Tretherick.

"You leavee money top-side of blulow, Fiddletown. Me findee money. Me fetchee money to you. All lightee."

"But I left no money on the top of the bureau, John," said Mrs. Tretherick earnestly. "There must be some mistake. It belongs to some other person. Take it back, John."

Ah Fe's brow darkened. He drew away from Mrs. Tretherick's extended hand, and began hastily to gather up his basket.

"Me no takee it back. No, no! Bimeby pleesman he catchee me. He say, 'God damn thief! — catchee flowty dollar: come to jailee.' Me no takee back. You leavee money top-side blulow, Fiddletown. Me fetchee money you. Me no takee back."

Mrs. Tretherick hesitated. In the confusion of her flight, she *might* have left the money in the manner he had said. In any event, she had no right to jeopardize this honest Chinaman's safety by refusing it. So she said, " Very well. John, I will keep it. But you must come again and see me " — here Mrs. Tretherick hesitated with a new and sudden revelation of the fact that any man could wish to see any other than herself — " and, and — Carry."

Ah Fe's face lightened. He even uttered a short ventriloquistic laugh without moving his mouth. Then shouldering his basket, he shut the door carefully, and slid quietly down stairs. In the lower hall he, however, found an unexpected difficulty in opening the front-door, and, after fumbling vainly at the lock for a moment, looked around for some help or instruction. But the Irish handmaid who had let him in was contemptuously oblivious of his needs, and did not appear.

There occurred a mysterious and painful incident, which I shall simply record without attempting to explain. On the hall-table a scarf, evidently the property of the servant before alluded to, was lying. As Ah Fe tried the lock with one hand, the other rested lightly on the table. Suddenly, and apparently of its own volition, the scarf began to creep slowly

towards Ah Fe's hand; from Ah Fe's hand it
began to creep up his sleeve slowly, and with
an insinuating, snake-like motion; and then
disappeared somewhere in the recesses of his
blouse. Without betraying the least interest
or concern in this phenomenon, Ah Fe still
repeated his experiments upon the lock. A
moment later the tablecloth of red damask,
moved by apparently the same mysterious impulse, slowly gathered itself under Ah Fe's
fingers, and sinuously disappeared by the same
hidden channel. What further mystery might
have followed, I cannot say; for at this moment
Ah Fe discovered the secret of the lock, and
was enabled to open the door coincident with the
sound of footsteps upon the kitchen-stairs. Ah
Fe did not hasten his movements, but, patiently
shouldering his basket, closed the door carefully behind him again, and stepped forth into the
thick encompassing fog that now shrouded
earth and sky.

From her high casement-window, Mrs.
Tretherick watched Ah Fe's figure until it disappeared in the gray cloud. In her present
loneliness, she felt a keen sense of gratitude
toward him, and may have ascribed to the
higher emotions and the consciousness of a
good deed, that certain expansiveness of the
chest, and swelling of the bosom, that was really

due to the hidden presence of the scarf and tablecloth under his blouse. For Mrs. Tretherick was still poetically sensitive. As the gray fog deepened into night, she drew Carry closer towards her, and, above the prattle of the child, pursued a vein of sentimental and egotistic recollection at once bitter and dangerous. The sudden apparition of Ah Fe linked her again with her past life at Fiddletown. Over the dreary interval between, she was now wandering, — a journey so piteous, wilful, thorny, and useless, that it was no wonder that at last Carry stopped suddenly in the midst of her voluble confidences to throw her small arms around the woman's neck, and bid her not to cry.

Heaven forefend that I should use a pen that should be ever dedicated to an exposition of unalterable moral principle to transcribe Mrs. Tretherick's own theory of this interval and episode, with its feeble palliations, its illogical deductions, its fond excuses, and weak apologies. It would seem, however, that her experience had been hard. Her slender stock of money was soon exhausted. At Sacramento she found that the composition of verse, although appealing to the highest emotions of the human heart, and compelling the editorial breast to the noblest commendation in the editorial pages, was singu

larly inadequate to defray the expenses of herself and Carry. Then she tried the stage, but
failed signally. Possibly her conception of the
passions was different from that which obtained
with a Sacramento audience ; but it was certain
that her charming presence, so effective at short
range, was not sufficiently pronounced for the
footlights. She had admirers enough in the
green-room, but awakened no abiding affection
among the audience. In this strait, it occurred
to her that she had a voice,— a contralto of no
very great compass or cultivation, but singularly sweet and touching ; and she finally obtained
position in a church-choir. She held it for
three months, greatly to her pecuniary advantage, and, it is said, much to the satisfaction of
the gentlemen in the back-pews, who faced
toward her during the singing of the last
hymn.

I remember her quite distinctly at this time.
The light that slanted through the oriel of St.
Dives choir was wont to fall very tenderly on
her beautiful head with its stacked masses of
deerskin-colored hair, on the low black arches
of her brows, and to deepen the pretty fringes
that shaded her eyes of Genoa velvet. Very
pleasant it was to watch the opening and shut-
ting of that small straight mouth, with its quick
revelation of little white teeth, and to see the

foolish blood faintly deepen her satin cheek as you watched. For Mrs. Tretherick was very sweetly conscious of admiration, and, like most pretty women, gathered herself under your eye like a racer under the spur.

And then, of course, there came trouble. I have it from the soprano, — a little lady who possessed even more than the usual unprejudiced judgment of her sex, — that Mrs. Tretherick's conduct was simply shameful; that her conceit was unbearable; that, if she considered the rest of the choir as slaves, she (the soprano) would like to know it; that her conduct on Easter Sunday with the basso had attracted the attention of the whole congregation; and that she herself had noticed Dr. Cope twice look up during the service; that her (the soprano's) friends had objected to her singing in the choir with a person who had been on the stage, but she had waived this. Yet she had it from the best authority that Mrs. Tretherick had run away from her husband, and that this red-haired child who sometimes came in the choir was not her own. The tenor confided to me behind the organ, that Mrs. Tretherick had a way of sustaining a note at the end of a line in order that her voice might linger longer with the con· gregation, -— an act that could be attributed only to a defective moral nature; that as a man

(he was a very popular dry-goods clerk on
week-days, and sang a good deal from apparently behind his eyebrows on the sabbath) — that
as a man, sir, he would put up with it no longer.
The basso alone — a short German with a heavy
voice, for which he seemed reluctantly responsible, and rather grieved at its possession — stood
up for Mrs. Tretherick, and averred that they
were jealous of her because she was "bretty."
The climax was at last reached in an open quarrel, wherein Mrs. Tretherick used her tongue
with such precision of statement and epithet,
that the soprano burst into hysterical tears, and
had to be supported from the choir by her husband and the tenor.   This act was marked
intentionally to the congregation by the omis-
sion of the usual soprano solo.   Mrs. Tretherick went home flushed with triumph, but on
reaching her room frantically told Carry that
they were beggars henceforward; that she — her
mother — had just taken the very bread out of
her darling's mouth, and ended by bursting into
a flood of penitent tears. They did not come
so quickly as in her old poetical days; but when
they came they stung deeply. She was roused
by a formal visit from a vestryman, — one of the
music committee.   Mrs. Tretherick dried her
long lashes, put on a new neck-ribbon, and
went down to the parlor. She staid there two

hours, — a fact that might have occasioned some remark, but that the vestryman was married, and had a family of grown-up daughters. When Mrs. Tretherick returned to her room, she sang to herself in the glass and scolded Carry — but she retained her place in the choir.

It was not long, however. In due course of time, her enemies received a powerful addition to their forces in the committee-man's wife. That lady called upon several of the church-members and on Dr. Cope's family. The result was, that, at a later meeting of the music committee, Mrs. Tretherick's voice was declared inadequate to the size of the building and she was invited to resign. She did so. She had been out of a situation for two months, and her scant means were almost exhausted, when Ah Fe's unexpected treasure was tossed into her lap.

The gray fog deepened into night, and the street-lamps started into shivering life, as, absorbed in these unprofitable memories, Mrs. Tretherick still sat drearily at her window. Even Carry had slipped away unnoticed; and her abrupt entrance with the damp evening paper in her hand roused Mrs. Tretherick, and brought her back to an active realization of the present. For Mrs. Tretherick was wont to scan the advertisements in the faint hope of finding some avenue of employment — she knew not what — open to her needs; and Carry had noted this habit.

Mrs. Tretherick mechanically closed the shutters, lit the lights, and opened the paper. Her eye fell instinctively on the following paragraph in the telegraphic column : —

"FIDDLETOWN, 7th. — Mr. James Tretherick, an old resident of this place, died last night of delirium tremens. Mr. Tretherick was addicted to intemperate habits, said to have been induced by domestic trouble."

Mrs. Tretherick did not start. She quietly turned over another page of the paper, and glanced at Carry. The child was absorbed in a book. Mrs. Tretherick uttered no word, but, during the remainder of the evening, was unusually silent and cold. When Carry was undressed and in bed, Mrs. Tretherick suddenly dropped on her knees beside the bed, and, taking Carry's flaming head between her hands, said, —

"Should you like to have another papa, Carry darling?"

"No," said Carry, after a moment's thought.

"But a papa to help mamma take care of you, to love you, to give you nice clothes, to make a lady of you when you grow up?"

Carry turned her sleepy eyes toward the questioner. "Should *you*, mamma?"

Mrs. Tretherick suddenly flushed to the roots of her hair. "Go to sleep," she said sharply, and turned away.

But at midnight the child felt two white arms close tightly around her, and was drawn down into a bosom that heaved, fluttered, and at last was broken up by sobs.

"Don't ky, mamma," whispered Carry, with a vague retrospect of their recent conversation. "Don't ky. I fink I *should* like a new papa, if he loved you very much — very, very much!"

A month afterward, to everybody's astonishment, Mrs. Tretherick was married. The happy bridegroom was one Col. Starbottle, recently elected to represent Calaveras County in the legislative councils of the State. As I cannot record the event in finer language than that used by the correspondent of "The Sacramento Globe," I venture to quote some of his graceful periods. "The relentless shafts of the sly god have been lately busy among our gallant Solons. We quote 'one more unfortunate.' The latest victim is the Hon. C. Starbottle of Calaveras. The fair enchantress in the case is a beautiful widow, a former votary of Thespis, and lately a fascinating St. Cecilia of one of the most fashionable churches of San Francisco, where she commanded a high salary."

"The Dutch Flat Intelligencer" saw fit,

however, to comment upon the fact with tha. humorous freedom characteristic of an unfettered press. "The new Democratic war-horse from Calaveras has lately advented in the legislature with a little bill to change the name of Tretherick to Starbottle. They call it a marriage-certificate down there. Mr. Tretherick has been dead just one month; but we presume the gallant colonel is not afraid of ghosts." It is but just to Mrs. Tretherick to state that the colonel's victory was by no means an easy one. To a natural degree of coyness on the part of the lady was added the impediment of a rival, — a prosperous undertaker from Sacramento, who had first seen and loved Mrs. Tretherick at the theatre and church; his professional habits debarring him from ordinary social intercourse, and indeed any other than the most formal public contact with the sex. As this gentleman had made a snug fortune during the felicitous prevalence of a severe epidemic, the colonel regarded him as a dangerous rival. Fortunately, however, the undertaker was called in professionally to lay out a brother-senator, who had unhappily fallen by the colonel's pistol in an affair of honor; and either deterred by physical consideration from rivalry, or wisely concluding that the colonel was professionally valuable, he withdrew from the field.

The honeymoon was brief, and brought to a close by an untoward incident. During their bridal-trip, Carry had been placed in the charge of Col. Starbottle's sister. On their return to the city, immediately on reaching their lodgings, Mrs. Starbottle announced her intention of at once proceeding to Mrs. Culpepper's to bring the child home. Col. Starbottle, who had been exhibiting for some time a certain uneasiness which he had endeavored to overcome by repeated stimulation, finally buttoned his coat tightly across his breast, and, after walking unsteadily once or twice up and down the room, suddenly faced his wife with his most imposing manner.

"I have deferred," said the colonel with an exaggeration of port that increased with his inward fear, and a growing thickness of speech. — "I have deferr — I may say poshponed statement o' fack thash my duty ter dishclose ter ye. I did no wish to mar sushine mushal happ'ness, to bligh bud o' promise, to darken conjuglar sky by unpleasht revelashun. Musht be done — by G—d, m'm, musht do it now. The chile is gone!"

"Gone!" echoed Mrs. Starbottle.

There was something in the tone of her voice, in the sudden drawing-together of the pupils of her eyes, that for a moment nearly sobered the colonel, and partly collapsed his chest

"I'll splain all in a minit," he said with a deprecating wave of the hand. "Every thing shall be splained. The-the-the-melencholly event wish preshipitate our happ'ness — the myster'us prov'nice wish releash you — releash chile ! hunerstan? — releash chile. The mom't Tretherick die — all claim you have in chile through him — die too. Thash law. Whose chile b'long to? Tretherick? Tretherick dead. Chile can't b'long dead man. Damn nonshense b'long dead man. I'sh your chile ? no ! who's chile then? Chile b'long to 'ts mother. Unnerstan?"

"Where is she ?" said Mrs. Starbottle with a very white face and a very low voice.

"I'll splain all. Chile b'long to 'ts mother. Thash law. I'm lawyer, leshlator, and American sis'n. Ish my duty as lawyer, as leshlator, and 'merikan sis'n to reshtore chile to suff'rin mother at any coss — any coss."

"Where is she ?" repeated Mrs. Starbottle with her eyes still fixed on the colonel's face.

"Gone to 'ts m'o'r. Gone East on shteamer, yesserday. Waffed by fav'rin gales to suff'rin p'rent. Thash so !"

Mrs. Starbottle did not move. The colonel felt his chest slowly collapsing, but steadied himself against a chair, and endeavored to beam with chivalrous gallantry not unmixed with magisterial firmness upon her as she sat.

"Your feelin's, m'm, do honor to yer sex, but conshider situashun. Conshider m'or's feelings — conshider *my* feelin's." The colonel paused, and, flourishing a white handkerchief, placed it negligently in his breast, and then smiled tenderly above it, as over laces and ruffles, on the woman before him. "Why should dark shedder cass bligh on two sholes with single beat? Chile's fine chile, good chile, but summonelse chile! Chile's gone, Clar'; but all ish'n't gone, Clar'. Conshider dearesht, you all's have me!"

Mrs. Starbottle started to her feet. "*You!*" she cried, bringing out a chest note that made the chandeliers ring, — "YOU that I married to give my darling food and clothes, — *you!* a dog that I whistled to my side to keep the men off me, — *you!*"

She choked up, and then dashed past him into the inner room, which had been Carry's; then she swept by him again into her own bedroom, and then suddenly re-appeared before him, erect, menacing, with a burning fire over her cheek-bones, a quick straightening of her arched brows and mouth, a squaring of jaw, and ophidian flattening of the head.

"Listen!" she said in a hoarse, half-grown boy's voice. "Hear me! If you ever expect to set eyes on me again, you must find the child. If you ever expect to speak to me again, to

touch me, you must bring her back. For
where she goes, I go : you hear me! Where
she has gone, look for me. ''

She struck out past him again with a quick
feminine throwing-out of her arms from the
elbows down, as if freeing herself from some
imaginary bonds, and, dashing into her chamber,
slammed and locked the door. Col. Starbottle, although no coward, stood in superstitious
fear of an angry woman, and, recoiling as she
swept by, lost his unsteady foothold, and rolled
helplessly on the sofa. Here, after one or two
unsuccessful attempts to regain his foothold, he
remained, uttering from time to time profane
but not entirely coherent or intelligible protests,
until at last he succumbed to the exhausting
quality of his emotions, and the narcotic quantity of his potations.

Meantime, within, Mrs. Starbottle was excitedly gathering her valuables, and packing her
trunk, even as she had done once before in the
course of this remarkable history. Perhaps
some recollection of this was in her mind; for
she stopped to lean her burning cheeks upon
her hand, as if she saw again the figure of the
child standing in the doorway, and heard once
more a childish voice asking, " Is it mamma ? "
But the epithet now stung her to the quick
and with a quick, passionate gesture she dashed

it away with a tear that had gathered in her eye. And then it chanced, that, in turning over some clothes, she came upon the child's slipper with a broken sandal-string. She uttered a great cry here, — the first she had uttered, — and caught it to her breast, kissing it passionately again and again, and rocking from side to side with a motion peculiar to her sex. And then she took it to the window, the better to see it through her now streaming eyes. Here she was taken with a sudden fit of coughing that she could not stifle with the handkerchief she put to her feverish lips. And then she suddenly grew very faint. The window seemed to recede before her, the floor to sink beneath her feet; and, staggering to the bed, she fell prone upon it with the sandal and handkerchief pressed to her breast. Her face was quite pale, the orbit of her eyes dark; and there was a spot upon her lip, another on her handkerchief, and still another on the white counterpane of the bed.

The wind had risen, rattling the window-sashes, and swaying the white curtains in a ghostly way. Later, a gray fog stole softly over the roofs, soothing the wind-roughened surfaces, and inwrapping all things in an uncertain light and a measureless peace. She lay there very quiet — for all her troubles, still a very pretty bride. And on the other side of the bolted door the gallant bridegroom, from his temporary couch, snored peacefully.

A week before Christmas Day, 1870, the little town of Genoa, in the State of New York, exhibited, perhaps more strongly than at any other time, the bitter irony of its founders and sponsors. A driving snow-storm, that had whitened every windward hedge, bush, wall, and telegraph-pole, played around this soft Italian Capitol, whirled in and out of the great staring wooden Doric columns of its post-office and hotel, beat upon the cold green shutters of its best houses, and powdered the angular, stiff, dark figures in its streets. From the level of the street, the four principal churches of the town stood out starkly, even while their mis-shapen spires were kindly hidden in the low, driving storm. Near the railroad-station, the new Methodist chapel, whose resemblance to an enormous locomotive was further heightened by the addition of a pyramidal row of front-steps, like a cowcatcher, stood as if waiting for a few more houses to be hitched on to proceed to a pleasanter location. But the pride of Genoa — the great Crammer Institute for Young Ladies — stretched its bare brick length, and reared its cupola plainly from the bleak Parnassian hill

above the principal avenue.   There was no evasion in the Crammer Institute of the fact that
it was a public institution.   A visitor upon its
doorsteps, a pretty face at its window, were
clearly visible all over the township.

The shriek of the engine of the four-o'clock
Northern express brought but few of the usual
loungers to the depot.   Only a single passenger
alighted, and was driven away in the solitary
waiting sleigh toward the Genoa Hotel.   And
then the train sped away again, with that passionless indifference to human sympathies or
curiosity peculiar to express-trains; the one
baggage-truck was wheeled into the station
again; the station-door was locked; and the sta-
tion-master went home.

The locomotive-whistle, however, awakened
the guilty consciousness of three young ladies
of the Crammer Institute, who were even
then surreptitiously regaling themselves in the
bake-shop and confectionery-saloon of Mistress
Phillips in a by-lane.   For even the admirable
regulations of the Institute failed to entirely
develop the physical and moral natures of its
pupils.   They conformed to the excellent dietary
rules in public, and in private drew upon the
luxurious rations of their village caterer.   They
attended church with exemplary formality, and
flirted informally during service with the village

beaux. They received the best and most judicious instruction during school-hours, and devoured the trashiest novels during recess. The result of which was an aggregation of quite healthy, quite human, and very charming young creatures, that reflected infinite credit on the Institute. Even Mistress Phillips, to whom they owed vast sums, exhilarated by the exuberant spirits and youthful freshness of her guests, declared that the sight of " them young things " did her good ; and had even been known to shield them by shameless equivocation.

" Four o'clock, girls ! and, if we're not back to prayers by five, we'll be missed," said the tallest of these foolish virgins, with an aquiline nose, and certain quiet *élan* that bespoke the leader, as she rose from her seat. " Have you got the books, Addy ? " Addy displayed three dissipated-looking novels under her waterproof. ' And the provisions, Carry ? " Carry showed a suspicious parcel filling the pocket of her sack. " All right, then. Come girls, trudge. — Charge it," she added, nodding to her host as they passed toward the door. " I'll pay you when my quarter's allowance comes."

" No, Kate," interposed Carry, producing **her** purse, " let me pay : it's my turn."

" Never ! " said Kate, arching her black brows loftily, " even if you do have rich relatives, and

regular remittances from California. **Never!**—
Come, girls, forward, march!"

As they opened the door, a gust of wind
nearly took them off their feet. Kind-hearted
Mrs. Phillips was alarmed. "Sakes alive, galls!
ye mussn't go out in sich weather. Better let
me send word to the Institoot, and make ye up
a nice bed to-night in my parlor." But the last
sentence was lost in a chorus of half-suppressed
shrieks, as the girls, hand in hand, ran down the
steps into the storm, and were at once whirled
away.

The short December day, unlit by any sunset
glow, was failing fast. It was quite dark
already; and the air was thick with driving
snow. For some distance their high spirits,
youth, and even inexperience, kept them bravely
up; but, in ambitiously attempting a short-cut
from the high-road across an open field, their
strength gave out, the laugh grew less frequent,
and tears began to stand in Carry's brown eyes.
When they reached the road again, they were
utterly exhausted. "Let us go back," said
Carry.

"We'd never get across that field again," said
Addy.

"Let's stop at the first house, then," said
Carry.

"The first house," said Addy, peering through

the gathering darkness, "is Squire Robinson's."
She darted a mischievous glance at Carry, that,
even in her discomfort and fear, brought the
quick blood to her cheek.

"Oh, yes!" said Kate with gloomy irony, "certainly; stop at the squire's by all means, and be
invited to tea, and be driven home after tea by
your dear friend Mr. Harry, with a formal apology from Mrs. Robinson, and hopes that the
young ladies may be excused this time. No!"
continued Kate with sudden energy. "That
may suit *you;* but I'm going back as I came, —
by the window, or not at all." Then she
pounced suddenly, like a hawk, on Carry, who
was betraying a tendency to sit down on a
snowbank, and whimper, and shook her briskly.
"You'll be going to sleep next. Stay, hold your
tongues, all of you, — what's that?"

It was the sound of sleigh-bells. Coming
down toward them out of the darkness was a
sleigh with a single occupant. "Hold down
your heads, girls: if it's anybody that knows
us, we're lost." But it was not; for a voice
strange to their ears, but withal very kindly
and pleasant, asked if its owner could be of any
help to them. As they turned toward him,
they saw it was a man wrapped in a handsome
sealskin cloak, wearing a sealskin cap; his face,
half concealed by a muffler of the same material,

disclosing only a pair of long mustaches, and two keen dark eyes. " It's a son of old Santa Claus ! " whispered Addy. The girls tittered audibly as they tumbled into the sleigh : they had regained their former spirits. " Where shall I take you ? " said the stranger quietly. There was a hurried whispering ; and then Kate said boldly, " To the Institute." They drove silently up the hill, until the long, ascetic building loomed up before them. The stranger reined up suddenly. " You know the way better than I," he said. " Where do you go in ? " — " Through the back-window," said Kate with sudden and appalling frankness. " I see ! " responded their strange driver quietly, and, alighting quickly, removed the bells from the horses. " We can drive as near as you please now," he added by way of explanation. " He certainly is a son of Santa Claus," whispered Addy. " Hadn't we better ask after his father ? " " Hush ! " said Kate decidedly. " He is an angel, I dare say." She added with a delicious irrelevance, which was, however, perfectly understood by her feminine auditors, " We are looking like three frights."

Cautiously skirting the fences, they at last pulled up a few feet from a dark wall. The stranger proceeded to assist them to alight. There was still some light from the reflected snow; and, as he handed his fair companions to the ground, each was conscious of undergoing an intense though respectful scrutiny. He assisted them gravely to open the window, and then discreetly retired to the sleigh until the difficult and somewhat discomposing ingress was made. He then walked to the window. "Thank you and good-night!" whispered three voices. A single figure still lingered. The stranger leaned over the window-sill. "Will you permit me to light my cigar here? it might attract attention if I struck a match outside." By the upspringing light he saw the figure of Kate very charmingly framed in by the window. The match burnt slowly out in his fingers. Kate smiled mischievously. The astute young woman had detected the pitiable subterfuge. For what else did she stand at the head of her class, and had doting parents paid three years' tuition?

The storm had passed, and the sun was shining quite cheerily in the eastern recitation-room the next morning, when Miss Kate, whose seat was nearest the window, placing her hand pathetically upon her heart, affected to fall in bashful and extreme agitation upon the shoulder of Carry her neighbor. "*He* has come," she gasped in a thrilling whisper. "Who?" asked Carry sympathetically, who never clearly understood when Kate was in earnest. "Who?—

why, the man who rescued us last night! I saw
him drive to the door this moment.   Don't
speak: I shall be better in a moment — there!"
she said; and the shameless hypocrite passed
her hand pathetically across her forehead with
a tragic air.

"What can he want?" asked Carry, whose
curiosity was excited.

"I don't know," said Kate, suddenly relaps-
ing into gloomy cynicism.   "Possibly to put his
five daughters to school; perhaps to finish his
young wife, and warn her against us."

"He didn't look old, and he didn't seem like
a married man," rejoined Addy thoughtfully.

"That was his art, you poor creature!" returned Kate scornfully.   "You can never tell
any thing of these men, they are so deceitful
Besides, it's just my fate!"

"Why, Kate," began Carry, in serious concern.

"Hush! Miss Walker is saying something,"
said Kate, laughing.

" The young ladies will please give attention,"
said a slow, perfunctory voice.   "Miss Carry
Tretherick is wanted in the parlor."

Meantime Mr. Jack Prince, the name given
on the card, and various letters and credentials
submitted to the Rev. Mr. Crammer, paced the
somewhat severe apartment known publicly as

the "reception parlor," and privately to the
pupils as "purgatory." His keen eyes had
taken in the various rigid details, from the flat
steam "radiacor," like an enormous japanned
soda-cracker, that heated one end of the room,
to the monumental bust of Dr. Crammer, that
hopelessly chilled the other; from the Lord's
Prayer, executed by a former writing-master in
such gratuitous variety of elegant calligraphic
trifling as to considerably abate the serious value
of the composition, to three views of Genoa
from the Institute, which nobody ever recognized,
taken on the spot by the drawing-teacher; from
two illuminated texts of Scripture in an English
letter, so gratuitously and hideously remote as
to chill all human interest, to a large photograph of the senior class, in which the prettiest
girls were Ethiopian in complexion, and sat,
apparently, on each other's heads and shoulders.
His fingers had turned listlessly the leaves of
school-catalogues, the "Sermons" of Dr. Crammer, the "Poems" of Henry Kirke White, the
"Lays of the Sanctuary" and "Lives of Celebrated Women." His fancy, and it was a nervously active one, had gone over the partings and
greetings that must have taken place here, and
wondered why the apartment had yet caught so
little of the flavor of humanity; indeed, I am
afraid he had almost forgotten the object of his

visit, when the door opened, and Carry Tretherick stood before him.

It was one of those faces he had seen the night
before, prettier even than it had seemed then;
and yet I think he was conscious of some disappointment, without knowing exactly why. Her
abundant waving hair was of a guinea-golden
tint, her complexion of a peculiar flower-like
delicacy, her brown eyes of the color of seaweed
in deep water. It certainly was not her beauty
that disappointed him.

Without possessing his sensitiveness to impression, Carry was, on her part, quite as vaguely
ill at ease. She saw before her one of those
men whom the sex would vaguely generalize as
" nice," that is to say, correct in all the superficial appointments of style, dress, manners and
feature. Yet there was a decidedly unconven-
tional quality about him : he was totally unlike
any thing or anybody that she could remember ;
and, as the attributes of originality are often as
apt to alarm as to attract people, she was not
entirely prepossessed in his favor.

" I can hardly hope," he began pleasantly,
" that you remember me. It is eleven years
ago, and you were a very little girl. I am
afraid I cannot even claim to have enjoyed that
familiarity that might exist beween a child of
six and a young man of twenty-one. I don't

think I was fond of children. But I knew your
mother very well.   I was editor of 'The Avalanche' in Fiddletown, when she took you to
San Francisco."

"You mean my stepmother: she wasn't my
mother, you know," interposed Carry hastily.

Mr. Prince looked at her curiously. "I mean
your stepmother," he said gravely. "I never
had the pleasure of meeting your mother."

"No: *mother* hasn't been in California these
twelve years."

There was an intentional emphasizing of the
title and of its distinction, that began to coldly
interest Prince after his first astonishment was
past.

"As I come from your stepmother now," he
went on with a slight laugh, "I must ask you
to go back for a few moments to that point.
After your father's death, your mother — I
mean your stepmother — recognized the fact
that your mother, the first Mrs. Tretherick,
was legally and morally your guardian, and,
although much against her inclination and
affections, placed you again in her charge."

"My stepmother married again within a month
after father died, and sent me home," said Carry
with great directness, and the faintest toss of
her head.

Mr. Prince smiled so sweetly, and apparently

so sympathetically, that Carry began to like him. With no other notice of the interruption he went on, "After your stepmother had performed this act of simple justice, she entered into an agreement with your mother to defray the expenses of your education until your eighteenth year, when you were to elect and choose which of the two should thereafter be your guardian, and with whom you would make your home. This agreement, I think, you are already aware of, and, I believe, knew at the time."

"I was a mere child then," said Carry.

"Certainly," said Mr. Prince, with the same smile. "Still the conditions, I think, have never been oppressive to you nor your mother; and the only time they are likely to give you the least uneasiness will be when you come to make up your mind in the choice of your guardian. That will be on your eighteenth birthday, — the 20th, I think, of the present month."

Carry was silent.

"Pray do not think that I am here to receive your decision, even if it be already made. I only came to inform you that your stepmother, Mrs. Starbottle, will be in town to-morrow, and will pass a few days at the hotel. If it is your wish to see her before you make up your mind,

she will be glad to meet you. She does not,
however, wish to do any thing to influence your
judgment."

"Does mother know she is coming?" said
Carry hastily.

"I do not know," said Prince gravely. "I
only know, that, if you conclude to see Mrs.
Starbottle, it will be with your mother's permission. Mrs. Starbottle will keep sacredly this
part of the agreement, made ten years ago.
But her health is very poor; and the change
and country quiet of a few days may benefit
her." Mr. Prince bent his keen, bright eyes
upon the young girl, and almost held his breath
until she spoke again.

"Mother's coming up to-day or to-morrow,"
she said, looking up.

"Ah!" said Mr. Prince with a sweet and
languid smile.

"Is Col. Starbottle here too?" asked Carry,
after a pause.

"Col. Starbottle is dead. Your stepmother
is again a widow."

"Dead!" repeated Carry.

"Yes," replied Mr. Prince. "Your stepmother has been singularly unfortunate in sur-
viving her affections."

Carry did not know what he meant, and
looked so. Mr. Prince smiled re-assuringly.

Presently Carry began to whimper.

Mr. Prince softly stepped beside her chair.

"I am afraid," he said with a very peculiar light in his eye, and a singular dropping of the corners of his mustache,—"I am afraid you are taking this too deeply. It will be some days before you are called upon to make a decision. Let us talk of something else. I hope you caught no cold last evening."

Carry's face shone out again in dimples.

"You must have thought us so queer! It was too bad to give you so much trouble."

"None, whatever, I assure you. My sense of propriety," he added demurely, "which might have been outraged, had I been called upon to help three young ladies out of a schoolroom window at night, was deeply gratified at being able to assist them in again." The door-bell rang loudly, and Mr. Prince rose. "Take your own time, and think well before you make your decision." But Carry's ear and attention were given to the sound of voices in the hall. At the same moment, the door was thrown open, and a servant announced, "Mrs. Tretherick and Mr. Robinson."

The afternoon train had just shrieked out its usual indignant protest at stopping at Genoa at all, as Mr. Jack Prince entered the outskirts of the town, and drove towards his hotel. He was wearied and cynical. A drive of a dozen miles through unpicturesque outlying villages, past small economic farmhouses, and hideous villas that violated his fastidious taste, had, I fear, left that gentleman in a captious state of mind. He would have even avoided his taciturn land-lord as he drove up to the door; but that functionary waylaid him on the steps. "There's a lady in the sittin'-room, waitin' for ye." Mr. Prince hurried up stairs, and entered the room as Mrs. Starbottle flew towards him.

She had changed sadly in the last ten years. Her figure was wasted to half its size. The beautiful curves of her bust and shoulders were broken or inverted. The once full, rounded arm was shrunken in its sleeve; and the golden hoops that encircled her wan wrists almost slipped from her hands as her long, scant fingers closed convulsively around Jack's. Her cheek-bones were painted that afternoon with the hectic of fever: somewhere in the hollows of those cheeks were buried the dimples of long ago; but their graves were forgotten. Her lustrous eyes were still beautiful, though the orbits were deeper than before. Her mouth was still sweet, although the lips parted more easily over the little teeth, and even in breathing, and showed more of them than she was wont to do before. The glory of her blonde hair

was still left: it was finer, more silken **and** **ethereal**, yet it failed even in its plenitude to **cover** the hollows of the blue-veined temples.

"Clara!" said Jack reproachfully.

"Oh, forgive me, Jack!" she said, falling into a chair, but still clinging to his hand,— "forgive me, dear; but I could not wait longer. I should have died, Jack,—died before another night. Bear with me a little longer (it will not be long), but let me stay. I may not see her, I know; I shall not speak to her: but it's so sweet to feel that I am at last near her, that I breathe the same air with my darling. I am better already, Jack, I am indeed. And you have seen her to-day? How did she look? What did she say? Tell me all, every thing, Jack. Was she beautiful? They say she is. Has she grown? Would you have known her again? Will she come, Jack? Perhaps she has been here already; perhaps," she had risen with tremulous excitement, and was glancing at the door,—"perhaps she is here now. Why don't you speak, Jack? Tell me all."

The keen eyes that looked down into hers were glistening with an infinite tenderness that none, perhaps, but she would have deemed them capable of. "Clara," he said gently and cheerily, "try and compose yourself. You are trembling now with the fatigue and excitement of your journey. I have seen Carry: she is well and beautiful. Let that suffice you now."

His gentle firmness composed and calmed her now, as it had often done before. Stroking her thin hand, he said, after a pause, " Did Carry ever write to you?"

" Twice, thanking me for some presents. They were only school-girl letters," she added, nervously answering the interrogation of his eyes.

" Did she ever know of your own troubles? of your poverty, of the sacrifices you made to pay her bills, of your pawning your clothes and jewels, of your " —

" No, no !" interrupted the woman quickly: "no! How could she? I have no enemy cruel enough to tell her that."

" But if she — or if Mrs. Tretherick — had heard of it? If Carry thought you were poor, and unable to support her properly, it might influence her decision. Young girls are fond of the position that wealth can give. She may have rich friends, maybe a lover."

Mrs. Starbottle winced at the last sentence. " But," she said eagerly, grasping Jack's hand, "when you found me sick and helpless at Sacramento, when you — God bless you for it, Jack ! — offered to help me to the East, you said you knew of something, you had some plan, that would make me and Carry independent."

"Yes," said Jack hastily; "but I want you to get strong and well first. And, now that you are calmer, you shall listen to my visit to the school."

It was then that Mr. Jack Prince proceeded to describe the interview already recorded, with a singular felicity and discretion that shames my own account of that proceeding. Without suppressing a single fact, without omitting a word or detail, he yet managed to throw a poetic veil over that prosaic episode, to invest the heroine with a romantic roseate atmosphere, which, though not perhaps entirely imaginary, still, I fear, exhibited that genius which ten years ago had made the columns of "The Fiddletown Avalanche" at once fascinating and instructive. It was not until he saw the heightening color, and heard the quick breathing, of his eager listener, that he felt a pang of self-reproach. "God help her and forgive me!" he muttered between his clinched teeth, "but how can I tell her *all* now!"

That night, when Mrs. Starbottle laid her weary head upon her pillow, she tried to picture to herself Carry at the same moment sleeping peacefully in the great schoolhouse on the hill; and it was a rare comfort to this yearning, foolish woman to know that she was so near. But at this moment Carry was sitting on the

edge of her bed, half undressed, pouting her
pretty lips, and twisting her long, leonine locks
between her fingers, as Miss Kate Van Corlear
— dramatically wrapped in a long white counterpane, her black eyes sparkling, and her thor-
ough-bred nose thrown high in air, — stood over
her like a wrathful and indignant ghost; for
Carry had that evening imparted her woes and
her history to Miss Kate, and that young lady
had "proved herself no friend" by falling into
a state of fiery indignation over Carry's "ingrati-
tude," and openly and shamelessly espousing
the claims of Mrs. Starbottle. "Why, if the
half you tell me is true, your mother and those
Robinsons are making of you not only a little
coward, but a little snob, miss. Respectability,
forsooth! Look you, my family are centuries
before the Trethericks; but if my family had
ever treated me in this way, and then asked me
to turn my back on my best friend, I'd whistle
them down the wind;" and here Kate snapped
her fingers, bent her black brows, and glared
around the room as if in search of a recreant
Van Corlear.

"You just talk this way, because you have
taken a fancy to that Mr. Prince," said Carry.

In the debasing slang of the period, that had
even found its way into the virgin cloisters of
the Crammer Institute, Miss Kate, as she afterwards expressed it, instantly "went for her."

First, with a shake of her head, she threw her long black hair over one shoulder, then, dropping one end of the counterpane from the other like a vestal tunic, she stepped before Carry with a purposely-exaggerated classic stride. "And what if I have, miss! What if I happen to know a gentleman when I see him! What if I happen to know, that among a thousand such traditional, conventional, feeble editions of their grandfathers as Mr. Harry Robinson, you cannot find one original, independent, individualized gentleman like your Prince! Go to bed, miss, and pray to Heaven that he may be *your* Prince indeed. Ask to have a contrite and grateful heart, and thank the Lord in particular for having sent you such a friend as Kate Van Corlear." Yet, after an imposing dramatic exit, she re-appeared the next moment as a straight white flash, kissed Carry between the brows, and was gone.

The next day was a weary one to Jack Prince. He was convinced in his mind that Carry would not come; yet to keep this consciousness from Mrs. Starbottle, to meet her simple hopefulness with an equal degree of apparent faith, was a hard and difficult task. He would have tried to divert her mind by taking her on a long drive; but she was fearful that Carry might come during her absence; and her strength, he was obliged to admit, had failed greatly. As he looked into her large and awe-inspiring clear eyes, a something he tried to keep from his mind — to put off day by day from contemplation — kept asserting itself directly to his inner consciousness. He began to doubt the expediency and wisdom of his management. He recalled every incident of his interview with Carry, and half believed that its failure was due to himself. Yet Mrs. Starbottle was very patient and confident: her very confidence shook his faith in his own judgment. When her strength was equal to the exertion, she was propped up in her chair by the window, where she could see the school and the entrance to the hotel. In the intervals she would elaborate pleasant plans for the future, and would sketch a country home. She had taken a strange fancy, as it seemed to Prince, to the present location; but it was notable that the future, always thus outlined, was one of quiet and repose. She believed she would get well soon: in fact, she thought she was now much better than she had been; but it might be long before she should be quite strong again. She would whisper on in this way until Jack would dash madly down into the bar-room, order liquors that he did not drink, light cigars that he did not smoke, talk with men that he did not

listen to, and behave generally as our stronger
sex is apt to do in periods of delicate trials and
perplexity.

The day closed with a clouded sky and a
bitter, searching wind. With the night fell a
few wandering flakes of snow. She was still
content and hopeful; and, as Jack wheeled her
from the window to the fire, she explained to
him, how, that, as the school-term was drawing
near its close, Carry was probably kept closely
at her lessons during the day, and could only
leave the school at night. So she sat up the
greater part of the evening, and combed her
silken hair, and, as far as her strength would
allow, made an undress toilet to receive her
guest. " We must not frighten the child, Jack,"
she said apologetically, and with something of
her old coquetry.

It was with a feeling of relief, that, at ten
o'clock, Jack received a message from the land-
lord, saying that the doctor would like to see
him for a moment down stairs. As Jack entered the grim, dimly-lighted parlor, he observed
the hooded figure of a woman near the fire. He
was about to withdraw again, when a voice that
he remembered very pleasantly said, —

" Oh, it's all right! I'm the doctor."

The hood was thrown back; and Prince saw
the shining black hair, and black, audacious
eyes, of Kate Van Corlear.

"Don't ask any questions. I'm the doctor and there's my prescription," and she pointed to the half-frightened, half-sobbing Carry in the corner — "to be taken at once."

"Then Mrs. Tretherick has given her permission?"

"Not much, if I know the sentiments of that lady," replied Kate saucily.

"Then how did you get away?" asked Prince gravely.

"BY THE WINDOW."

When Mr. Prince had left Carry in the arms of her stepmother, he returned to the parlor.

"Well?" demanded Kate.

"She will stay — *you* will, I hope, also — tonight."

"As I shall not be eighteen, and my own mistress on the 20th, and as I haven't a sick stepmother, I won't."

"Then you will give me the pleasure of seeing you safely through the window again?"

When Mr. Prince returned an hour later, he found Carry sitting on a low stool at Mrs. Starbottle's feet. Her head was in her stepmother's lap; and she had sobbed herself to sleep. Mrs. Starbottle put her finger to her lip. "I told you she would come. God bless you, Jack! and good-night."

The next morning Mrs. Tretherick, indig

nant, the Rev. Asa Crammer, principal, injured, and Mr. Joel Robinson, sen., complacently respectable, called upon Mr. Prince. There was a stormy meeting, ending in a demand for Carry. "We certainly cannot admit of this interference," said Mrs. Tretherick, a fashionably dressed, indistinctive looking woman. "It is several days before the expiration of our agreement; and we do not feel, under the circumstances, justified in releasing Mrs. Starbottle from its conditions." "Until the expiration of the school-term, we must consider Miss Tretherick as complying entirely with its rules and discipline," imposed Dr. Crammer. "The whole proceeding is calculated to injure the prospects, and compromise the position, of Miss Tretherick in society," suggested Mr. Robinson.

In vain Mr. Prince urged the failing condition of Mrs. Starbottle, her absolute freedom from complicity with Carry's flight, the pardonable and natural instincts of the girl, and his own assurance that they were willing to abide by her decision. And then with a rising color in his cheek, a dangerous look in his eye, but a singular calmness in his speech, he added, —

"One word more. It becomes my duty to inform you of a circumstance which would certainly justify me, as an executor of the late

Mr. Tretherick, in fully resisting your demands. A few months after Mr. Tretherick's death, through the agency of a Chinaman in his employment, it was discovered that he had made a will, which was subsequently found among his papers The insignificant value of his bequest — mostly land, then quite valueless — prevented his executors from carrying out his wishes, or from even proving the will, or making it otherwise publicly known, until within the last two or three years, when the property had enormously increased in value. The provisions of that bequest are simple, but unmistakable. The property is divided between Carry and her stepmother, with the explicit condition that Mrs. Starbottle shall become her legal guardian, provide for her education, and in all details stand to her *in loco parentis*."

"What is the value of this bequest?" asked Mr. Robinson. "I cannot tell exactly, but not far from half a million, I should say," returned Prince. "Certainly, with this knowledge, as a friend of Miss Tretherick, I must say that her conduct is as judicious as it is honorable to her," responded Mr. Robinson. "I shall not presume to question the wishes, or throw any obstacles in the way of carrying out the intentions, of my dead husband," added Mrs. Tretherick; and the interview was closed.

When its result was made known to Mrs. Starbottle, she raised Jack's hand to her feverish lips. "It cannot add to *my* happiness now, Jack; but tell me, why did you keep it from her?" Jack smiled, but did not reply.

Within the next week the necessary legal formalities were concluded; and Carry was restored to her stepmother. At Mrs. Starbottle's request, a small house in the outskirts of the town was procured; and thither they removed to wait the spring, and Mrs. Starbottle's convalescence. Both came tardily that year.

Yet she was happy and patient. She was fond of watching the budding of the trees beyond her window, — a novel sight to her Californian experience, — and of asking Carry their names and seasons. Even at this time she projected for that summer, which seemed to her so mysteriously withheld, long walks with Carry through the leafy woods, whose gray, misty ranks she could see along the hilltop. She even thought she could write poetry about them, and recalled the fact as evidence of her gaining strength; and there is, I believe, still treasured by one of the members of this little household a little carol so joyous, so simple, and so innocent, that it might have been an echo of the robin that called to her from the window, as perhaps it was.

And then, without warning, there dropped from Heaven a day so tender, so mystically soft, so dreamily beautiful, so throbbing, and alive with the fluttering of invisible wings, so replete and bounteously overflowing with an awakening and joyous resurrection not taught by man or limited by creed, that they thought it fit to bring her out, and lay her in that glorious sunshine that sprinkled like the droppings of a bridal torch the happy lintels and doors. And there she lay beatified and calm.

Wearied by watching, Carry had fallen asleep by her side; and Mrs. Starbottle's thin fingers lay like a benediction on her head. Presently she called Jack to her side.

"Who was that," she whispered, "who just came in?"

"Miss Van Corlear," said Jack, answering the look in her great hollow eyes.

"Jack," she said, after a moment's silence, "sit by me a moment, dear Jack: I've something I must say. If I ever seemed hard, or cold, or coquettish to you in the old days, it was because I loved you, Jack, too well to mar your future by linking it with my own. I always loved you, dear Jack, even when I seemed least worthy of you. That is gone now. But I had a dream lately, Jack, a foolish woman's dream, — that you might find what I lacked in *her*," and she glanced lovingly at the sleeping girl at her side; "that you might love her as you have loved me. But even that is not to be, Jack, is it?" and she glanced wistfully in his face. Jack pressed her hand, but did not speak. After a few moments' silence, she again said, "Perhaps you are right in your choice. She is a good-hearted girl, Jack — but a little bold."

And with this last flicker of foolish, weak humanity in her struggling spirit, she spoke no more. When they came to her a moment later, a tiny bird that had lit upon her breast flew away; and the hand that they lifted from Carry's head fell lifeless at her side.

A JERSEY CENTENARIAN.

I HAVE seen her at last. She is a hundred
and seven years old, and remembers George
Washington quite distinctly. It is somewhat
confusing, however, that she also remembers a
contemporaneous Josiah W. Perkins of Basking Ridge, N.J., and, I think, has the impression that Perkins was the better man. Perkins,
at the close of the last century, paid her some
little attention. There are a few things that a
really noble woman of a hundred and seven
never forgets.

It was Perkins, who said to her in 1795, in
the streets of Philadelphia, "Shall I show thee
Gen. Washington?" Then she said careless-
like (for you know, child, at that time it wasn't
what it is now to see Gen. Washington), she
said, "So do, Josiah, so do!" Then he pointed
to a tall man who got out of a carriage, and
went into a large house. He was larger than
you be. He wore his own hair — not powdered;
had a flowered chintz vest, with yellow breeches
and blue stockings, and a broad-brimmed hat

274

In summer he wore a white straw hat, and at his farm at Basking Ridge he always wore it. At this point, it became too evident that she was describing the clothes of the all-fascinating Perkins: so I gently but firmly led her back to Washington. Then it appeared that she did not remember exactly what he wore. To assist her, I sketched the general historic dress of that period. She said she thought he was dressed like that. Emboldened by my success, I added a hat of Charles II., and pointed shoes of the eleventh century. She indorsed these with such cheerful alacrity, that I dropped the subject.

The house upon which I had stumbled, or, rather, to which my horse — a Jersey hack, accustomed to historic research — had brought me, was low and quaint. Like most old houses, it had the appearance of being encroached upon by the surrounding glebe, as if it were already half in the grave, with a sod or two, in the shape of moss thrown on it, like ashes on ashes, and dust on dust. A wooden house, instead of acquiring dignity with age, is apt to lose its youth and respectability together. A porch, with scant, sloping seats, from which even the winter's snow must have slid uncomfortably, projected from a doorway that opened most unjustifiably into a small sitting-room. There was no vestibule, or *locus pœnitentiæ*, for the embarrassed or bashful visitor: he passed at once from the security of the public road into shameful privacy. And here, in the mellow autumnal sunlight, that, streaming through the maples and sumach on the opposite bank, flickered and danced upon the floor, she sat and discoursed of George Washington, and thought of Perkins. She was quite in keeping with the house and the season, albeit a little in advance of both; her skin being of a faded russet, and her hands so like dead November leaves, that I fancied they even rustled when she moved them.

For all that, she was quite bright and cheery; her faculties still quite vigorous, although performing irregularly and spasmodically. It was somewhat discomposing, I confess, to observe, that at times her lower jaw would drop, leaving her speechless, until one of the family would notice it, and raise it smartly into place with a slight snap, — an operation always performed in such an habitual, perfunctory manner, generally in passing to and fro in their household duties, that it was very trying to the spectator. It was still more embarrassing to observe that the dear old lady had evidently no knowledge of this, but believed she was still talking, and that, on resuming her actual vocal utterance, she was often abrupt and incoherent, beginning always in the middle of a sentence, and often in the middle of a word. "Sometimes," said her daughter, a giddy, thoughtless young thing of eighty-five, — "sometimes just moving her head sort of unhitches her jaw; and, if we don't happen to see it, she'll go on talking for hours without ever making a sound." Although I was convinced, after this, that during my interview I had lost several important revelations regarding George Washington through these peculiar lapses, I could not help reflecting how beneficent were these provisions of the Creator, — how, if properly studied and applied, they might be fraught with happiness to mankind, — how a slight jostle or jar at a dinner-party might make the post-prandial eloquence of garrulous senility satisfactory to itself, yet harmless to others, — how a more intimate knowledge of anatomy, introduced into the domestic circle, might make a home tolerable at least, if not happy, — how a long-suffering husband, under the pretence of a conjugal caress, might so unhook his wife's condyloid process as to allow the flow of expostulation, criticism, or denunciation, to go on with gratification to her, and perfect immunity to himself.

But this was not getting back to George Washington and the early struggles of the

Republic. So I returned to the commander
in-chief, but found, after one or two leading
questions, that she was rather inclined to re-
sent his re-appearance on the stage. Her rem·
iniscences here were chiefly social and local,
and more or less flavored with Perkins. We
got back as far as the Revolutionary epoch, or,
rather, her impressions of that epoch, when it
was still fresh in the public mind. And here
I came upon an incident, purely personal and
local, but, withal, so novel, weird, and uncanny,
that for a while I fear it quite displaced
George Washington in my mind, and tinged the
autumnal fields beyond with a red that was not
of the sumach. I do not remember to have
read of it in the books. I do not know that it
is entirely authentic. It was attested to me by
mother and daughter, as an uncontradicted tradition.

In the little field beyond, where the plough still
turns up musket-balls and cartridge-boxes, took
place one of those irregular skirmishes between
the militiamen and Knyphausen's stragglers,
that made the retreat historical. A Hessian
soldier, wounded in both legs and utterly helpless, dragged himself to the cover of a hazel-
copse, and lay there hidden for two days. On
the third day, maddened by thirst, he managed
to creep to the rail-fence of an adjoining farm

house, but found himself unable to mount it or pass through. There was no one in the house but a little girl of six or seven years. He called to her, and in a faint voice asked for water. She returned to the house, as if to comply with his request, but, mounting a chair, took from the chimney a heavily-loaded Queen Anne musket, and, going to the door, took deliberate aim at the helpless intruder, and fired. The man fell back dead, without a groan. She replaced the musket, and, returning to the fence, covered the body with boughs and leaves, until it was hidden. Two or three days after, she related the occurrence in a careless, casual way, and leading the way to the fence, with a piece of bread and butter in her guileless little fingers, pointed out the result of her simple, unsophisticated effort. The Hessian was decently buried, but I could not find out what became of the little girl. Nobody seemed to remember. I trust, that, in after-years, she was happily married; that no Jersey Lovelace attempted to trifle with a heart whose impulses were so prompt, and whose purposes were so sincere. They did not seem to know if she had married or not. Yet it does not seem probable that such simplicity of conception, frankness of expression, and deftness of execution, were lost to posterity, or that they failed, in their time and season, to give flavor to the domestic felicity of the period. Beyond this, the story perhaps has little value, except as an offset to the usual anecdotes of Hessian atrocity.

They had their financial panics even in Jersey, in the old days. She remembered when Dr. White married your cousin Mary — or was it Susan? — yes, it was Susan. She remembers that your Uncle Harry brought in an armful of bank-notes, — paper money, you know, — and threw them in the corner, saying they were no good to anybody. She remembered playing with them, and giving them to your Aunt Anna — no, child, it was your own mother, bless your heart! Some of them was marked as high as a hundred dollars. Everybody kept gold and silver in a stocking, or in a "chaney" vase, like that. You never used money to buy any thing. When Josiah went to Springfield to buy any thing, he took a cartload of things with him to exchange. That yaller picture-frame was paid for in greenings. But then people knew jest what they had. They didn't fritter their substance away in unchristian trifles, like your father, Eliza Jane, who doesn't know that there is a God who will smite him hip and thigh; for vengeance is mine, and those that believe in me. But here, singularly enough, the inferior maxillaries gave out, and her jaw dropped. (I noticed that her giddy daughter of eighty-five was sitting near her; but I do not pretend to connect this fact with the arrested flow of personal disclosure.) Howbeit, when she recovered her speech again, it appeared that she was complaining of the weather.

The seasons had changed very much since your father went to sea. The winters used to be terrible in those days. When she went over to Springfield, in June, she saw the snow still on Watson's Ridge. There were whole days when you couldn't git over to William Henry's, their next neighbor, a quarter of a mile away. It was that drefful winter that the Spanish sailor was found. You don't remember the Spanish sailor, Eliza Jane — it was before your time. There was a little personal skirmishing here, which I feared, at first, might end in a suspension of maxillary functions, and the loss of the story; but here it is. Ah, me! it is a pure white winter idyl: how shall I sing it this bright, gay autumnal day?

It was a terrible night, that winter's night, when she and the century were young together. The sun was lost at three o'clock: the snowy night came down like a white sheet, that flapped around the house, beat at the windows with its edges, and at last wrapped it in a close embrace. In the middle of the right, **they** thought they heard above the wind a voice crying, "Christus, Christus!" in a foreign tongue. They opened the door, — no easy task in the north wind that pressed its strong shoulders against it, — but nothing was to be seen but the drifting snow. The next morning dawned on fences hidden, and a landscape changed and obliterated with drift. During the day, they again heard the cry of "Christus!" this time faint and hidden, like a child's voice. They searched in vain: the drifted snow hid its secret. On the third day they broke a path to the fence, and then they heard the cry distinctly. Digging down, they found the body of a man, — a Spanish sailor, dark and bearded, with ear-rings in his ears. As they stood gazing down at his cold and pulseless figure, the cry of "Christus!" again rose upon the wintry air; and they turned and fled in superstitious terror to the house. And then one of the children, bolder than the rest, knelt down, and opened the dead man's rough pea-jacket, and found — what think you? — a little blue-and-green parrot, nestling against his breast. It was the bird that had echoed mechanically the last despairing cry of the life that was given to save it. It was the bird, that ever after, amid outlandish oaths and wilder sailor-songs, that I fear often shocked the pure ears of its gentle mistress, and brought scandal into the Jerseys, still retained that one weird and mournful cry.

The sun meanwhile was sinking behind the steadfast range beyond, and I could not help feeling that I must depart with my wants unsatisfied. I had brought away no historic fragment: I absolutely knew little or nothing new regarding George Washington. I had been addressed variously by the names of different members of the family who were dead and forgotten; I had stood for an hour in the past: yet I had not added to my historical knowledge, nor the practical benefit of your readers. I spoke once more of Washington, and she replied with a reminiscence of Perkins.

Stand forth, O Josiah W. Perkins of Basking Ridge, N.J. Thou wast of little account in thy life, I warrant; thou didst not even feel the greatness of thy day and time; thou didst criticise thy superiors; thou wast small and narrow in thy ways; thy very name and grave are unknown and uncared for: but thou wast once kind to a woman who survived thee, and, lo! thy name is again spoken of men, and for a moment lifted up above thy betters.

ON THE FRONTIER.

CONTENTS.

CONTENTS.

AT THE MISSION OF SAN CARMEL.

PROLOGUE.

IT was noon of the 10th of August, 1838. The monotonous coast line between Monterey and San Diego had set its hard outlines against the steady glare of the Californian sky and the metallic glitter of the Pacific Ocean. The weary succession of rounded, dome-like hills obliterated all sense of distance; the rare whaling vessel or still rarer trader, drifting past, saw no change in these rusty undulations, barren of distinguishing peak or headland, and bald of wooded crest or timbered ravine. The withered ranks of wild oats gave a dull procession of uniform color to the hills, unbroken by any relief of shadow in their smooth, round curves. As far as the eye could reach, sea and shore met in one bleak monotony, flecked by no passing cloud, stirred by no sign of life or motion. Even sound was absent; the Angelus, rung from the invisible Mission tower far inland, was driven back again by the steady northwest trades, that for half the year had swept the coast line and left it abraded of all umbrage and color.

But even this monotony soon gave way to a change and another monotony as uniform and depressing. The western horizon, slowly contracting before a wall of vapor, by four o'clock had become a mere cold, steely strip of sea, into which gradually the northern trend of the coast faded and was lost. As the fog stole with soft step southward, all distance, space, character, and locality again vanished; the hills upon which the sun still shone bore the same monotonous outlines as those just wiped into space. Last of all, before the red sun sank like the descending Host, it gleamed upon the sails of a trading vessel close in shore. It was the last object visible. A damp breath breathed upon it, a soft hand passed over the slate, the sharp pencilling of the picture faded and became a confused gray cloud.

The wind and waves, too, went down in the fog; the now invisible and hushed breakers occasionally sent the surf over the sand in a quick whisper, with grave intervals of silence, but with no continuous murmur as before. In a curving bight of the shore the creaking of oars in their rowlocks began to be distinctly heard, but the boat itself, although apparently only its length from the sands, was invisible.

"Steady, now; way enough." The voice came from the sea, and was low, as if unconsciously affected by the fog. "Silence!"

The sound of a keel grating the sand was followed by the order, "Stern all!" from the invisible speaker.

"Shall we beach her?" asked another vague voice.

"Not yet. Hail again, and all together."

"Ah hoy—oi—oi—oy!"

There were four voices, but the hail appeared weak and ineffectual, like a cry in a dream, and seemed hardly to reach beyond the surf before it was suffocated in the creeping cloud. A silence followed, but no response.

"It's no use to beach her and go ashore until we find the boat," said the first voice, gravely; "and we'll do that if the current has brought her here. Are you sure you've got the right bearings?"

"As near as a man could off a shore with not a blasted pint to take his bearings by."

There was a long silence again, broken only by the occasional dip of oars, keeping the invisible boat-head to the sea.

"Take my word for it, lads, it's the last we'll

see of that boat again, or of Jack Cranch, or the captain's baby."

"It *does* look mighty queer that the painter should slip. Jack Cranch ain't the man to tie a granny knot."

"Silence!" said the invisible leader. "Listen."

A hail, so faint and uncertain that it might have been the long-deferred, far-off echo of their own, came from the sea, abreast of them.

"It's the captain. He hasn't found anything, or he couldn't be so far north. Hark!"

The hail was repeated again faintly, dreamily. To the seamen's trained ears it seemed to have an intelligent significance, for the first voice gravely responded, "Aye, aye!" and then said softly, "Oars."

The word was followed by a splash. The oars clicked sharply and simultaneously in the rowlocks, then more faintly, then still fainter, and then passed out into the darkness.

The silence and shadow both fell together; for hours sea and shore were impenetrable. Yet at times the air was softly moved and troubled, the surrounding gloom faintly lightened as with a misty dawn, and then was dark again; or drowsy, far-off cries and confused noises seemed to grow out of the silence, and, when they had attracted the weary ear, sank away as in a mocking dream, and showed themselves unreal. Nebulous gatherings in the fog seemed to indicate stationary objects that, even as one gazed, moved away; the recurring lap and ripple on the shingle sometimes took upon itself the semblance of faint articulate laughter or spoken words. But towards morning a certain monotonous grating on the sand, that had for many minutes alternately cheated and piqued the ear, asserted itself more strongly, and a moving, vacillating shadow in the gloom became an opaque object on the shore.

With the first rays of the morning light the fog lifted. As the undraped hills one by one bared their cold bosoms to the sun, the long line of coast struggled back to life again. Everything was unchanged, except that a stranded boat lay upon the sands, and in its stern sheets a sleeping child.

CHAPTER I.

THE 10th of August, 1852, brought little change to the dull monotony of wind, fog, and treeless coast line. Only the sea was occasionally flecked with racing sails that outstripped the old, slow-creeping trader, or was at times streaked and blurred with the trailing smoke of a steamer. There were a few strange footprints on those virgin sands, and a fresh track, that led from the beach over the rounded hills, dropped into the bosky recesses of a hidden valley beyond the coast range.

It was here that the refectory windows of the Mission of San Carmel had for years looked upon the reverse of that monotonous picture presented to the sea. It was here that the trade winds, shorn of their fury and strength in the heated, oven-like air that rose from the valley, lost their weary way in the tangled recesses of the wooded slopes, and breathed their last at the foot of the stone cross before the Mission. It was on the crest of those slopes that the fog halted and walled in the sun-illumined plain below; it was in this plain that limitless fields of grain clothed the fat adobe soil; here the Mission garden smiled over its hedges of fruitful vines, and through the leaves of fig and gnarled pear trees; and it was here that Father Pedro had lived for fifty years, found the prospect good, and had smiled also.

Father Pedro's smile was rare. He was not a Las Casas, nor a Junipero Serra, but he had the deep seriousness of all disciples laden with the responsible wording of a gospel not their own. And his smile had an ecclesiastical as well as a human significance, the pleasantest object in his prospect being the fair and curly head of his boy acolyte and chorister, Francisco, which appeared among the vines, and his sweetest pastoral music, the high soprano humming of a chant with which the boy accompanied his gardening.

Suddenly the acolyte's chant changed to a cry of terror. Running rapidly to Father Pedro's side, he grasped his *sotana,* and even tried to hide his curls among its folds.

" 'St! 'st!" said the Padre, disengaging himself with some impatience. "What new alarm is this? Is it Luzbel hiding among our Catalan vines, or one of those heathen Americanos from Monterey? Speak!"

"Neither, holy father," said the boy, the color struggling back into his pale cheeks, and an apologetic, bashful smile lighting his clear eyes. "Neither; but oh! such a gross, lethargic toad! And it almost leaped upon me."

"A toad leaped upon thee!" repeated the good father with evident vexation. "What next? I tell thee, child, those foolish fears are most unmeet for thee, and must be overcome, if necessary, with prayer and penance. Frightened by a toad! Blood of the Martyrs! 'Tis like any foolish girl!"

Father Pedro stopped and coughed.

"I am saying that no Christian child should shrink from any of God's harmless creatures.

And only last week thou wast disdainful of poor Murieta's pig, forgetting that San Antonio himself did elect one his faithful companion, even in glory."

"Yes, but it was so fat, and so uncleanly, holy father," replied the young acolyte, "and it smelt so."

"Smelt so?" echoed the father doubtfully. "Have a care, child, that this is not luxuriousness of the senses. I have noticed of late you gather overmuch of roses and syringa, excellent in their way and in moderation, but still not to be compared with the flower of Holy Church, the lily."

"But lilies don't look well on the refectory table, and against the adobe wall," returned the acolyte, with a pout of a spoilt child; "and surely the flowers cannot help being sweet, any more than myrrh or incense. And I am not frightened of the heathen Americanos either *now*. There was a small one in the garden yesterday, a boy like me, and he spoke kindly and with a pleasant face."

"What said he to thee, child?" asked Father Pedro, anxiously.

"Nay, the matter of his speech I could not understand," laughed the boy, "but the manner was as gentle as thine, holy father."

"'St, child," said the Padre impatiently.

"Thy likings are as unreasonable as thy fears. Besides, have I not told thee it ill becomes a child of Christ to chatter with those sons of Belial? But canst thou not repeat the words— the *words* he said?" he continued suspiciously.

" 'Tis a harsh tongue the Americanos speak in their throat," replied the boy. "But he said 'Devilishnisse' and 'pretty-as-a-girl,' and looked at me."

The good father made the boy repeat the words gravely, and as gravely repeated them after him with infinite simplicity. "They are but heretical words," he replied in answer to the boy's inquiring look; "it is well you understand not English. Enough. Run away, child, and be ready for the Angelus. I will commune with myself awhile under the pear trees."

Glad to escape so easily, the young acolyte disappeared down the alley of fig trees, not without a furtive look at the patches of chickweed around their roots, the possible ambuscade of creeping or saltant vermin. The good priest heaved a sigh and glanced round the darkening prospect. The sun had already disappeared over the mountain wall that lay between him and the sea, rimmed with a faint white line of outlying fog. A cool zephyr fanned his cheek; it was the dying breath of the *vientos generales* beyond the wall. As Father Pedro's eyes were

raised to this barrier, which seemed to shut out
the boisterous world beyond, he fancied he noticed for the first time a slight breach in the
parapet, over which an advanced banner of the
fog was fluttering. Was it an omen? His
speculations were cut short by a voice at his
very side.

He turned quickly and beheld one of those
"heathens" against whom he had just warned
his young acolyte; one of that straggling band
of adventurers whom the recent gold discoveries
had scattered along the coast. Luckily the
fertile alluvium of these valleys, lying parallel
with the sea, offered no "indications" to attract
the gold seekers. Nevertheless to Father Pedro
even the infrequent contact with the Americanos was objectionable; they were at once in-
quisitive and careless; they asked questions with
the sharp perspicacity of controversy; they received his grave replies with the frank indifference of utter worldliness. Powerful enough to
have been tyrannical oppressors, they were singularly tolerant and gentle, contenting themselves with a playful, good-natured irreverence,
which tormented the good father more than
opposition. They were felt to be dangerous and
subversive.

The Americano, however, who stood before
him did not offensively suggest these national

qualities. A man of middle height, strongly built, bronzed and slightly gray from the vicissitudes of years and exposure, he had an air of practical seriousness that commended itself to Father Pedro. To his religious mind it suggested self-consciousness; expressed in the dialect of the stranger it only meant "business."

"I'm rather glad I found you out here alone," began the latter; "it saves time. I haven't got to take my turn with the rest, in there"—he indicated the church with his thumb—"and you haven't got to make an appointment. You have got a clear forty minutes before the Angelus rings," he added, consulting a large silver chronometer, "and I reckon I kin git through my part of the job inside of twenty, leaving you ten minutes for remarks. I want to confess."

Father Pedro drew back with a gesture of dignity. The stranger, however, laid his hand upon the Padre's sleeve with the air of a man anticipating objection, but never refusal, and went on.

"Of course, I know. You want me to come at some other time, and in *there*. You want it in the reg'lar style. That's your way and your time. My answer is: it ain't *my* way and *my* time. The main idea of confession, I take it, is gettin' at the facts. I'm ready to give 'em if you'll take 'em out here, now. If you're willing to drop the Church and confessional, and all that sort o' thing, I, on my side, am willing to give up the absolution, and all that sort o' thing. You might," he added, with an unconscious touch of pathos in the suggestion, "heave in a word or two of advice after I get through; for instance, what *you'd* do in the circumstances, you see! That's all. But that's as you please. It ain't part of the business."

Irreverent as this speech appeared, there was really no trace of such intention in his manner, and his evident profound conviction that his suggestion was practical, and not at all inconsistent with ecclesiastical dignity, would alone have been enough to touch the Padre, had not the stranger's dominant personality already overridden him. He hesitated. The stranger seized the opportunity to take his arm, and lead him with the half familiarity of powerful protection to a bench beneath the refectory window. Taking out his watch again, he put it in the passive hands of the astonished priest, saying, "Time me," cleared his throat, and began :—

"Fourteen years ago there was a ship cruisin' in the Pacific, jest off this range, that was ez nigh on to a Hell afloat as anything rigged kin be. If a chap managed to dodge the cap'en's belayin-pin for a time, he was bound to be fetched up in the ribs at last by the mate's boots.

There was a chap knocked down the fore hatch with a broken leg in the Gulf, and another jumped overboard off Cape Corrientes, crazy as a loon, along a clip of the head from the cap'en's trumpet. Them's facts. The ship was a brigantine, trading along the Mexican coast. The cap'en had his wife aboard, a little timid Mexican woman he'd picked up at Mazatlan. I reckon she didn't get on with him any better than the men, for she ups and dies one day, leavin' her baby, a year-old gal. One of the crew was fond o' that baby. He used to get the black nurse to put it in the dingy, and he'd tow it astern, rocking it with the painter like a cradle. He did it—hatin' the cap'en all the same. One day the black nurse got out of the dingy for a moment, when the baby was asleep, leavin' him alone with it. An idea took hold on him, jest from cussedness, you'd say, but it was partly from revenge on the cap'en and partly to get away from the ship. The ship was well inshore, and the current settin' towards it. He slipped the painter—that man—and set himself adrift with the baby. It was a crazy act, you'd reckon, for there wasn't any oars in the boat; but he had a crazy man's luck, and he contrived, by sculling the boat with one of the seats he tore out, to keep her out of the breakers, till he could find a bight in the shore to run her in.

The alarm was given from the ship, but the fog shut down upon him; he could hear the other boats in pursuit. They seemed to close in on him, and by the sound he judged the cap'en was just abreast of him in the gig, bearing down upon him in the fog. He slipped out of the dingy into the water without a splash, and struck out for the breakers. He got ashore after havin' been knocked down and dragged in four times by the undertow. He had only one idea then, thankfulness that he had not taken the baby with him in the surf. You kin put that down for him: it's a fact. He got off into the hills, and made his way up to Monterey."

"And the child?" asked the Padre, with a sudden and strange asperity that boded no good to the penitent; "the child thus ruthlessly abandoned—what became of it?"

"That's just it, the child," assented the stranger, gravely. "Well, if that man was on his death-bed instead of being here talking to you, he'd swear that he thought the cap'en was sure to come up to it the next minit. That's a fact. But it wasn't until one day that he—that's me—ran across one of that crew in Frisco. 'Hallo, Cranch,' sez he to me, 'so you got away, didn't you? And how's the cap'en's baby? Grown a young gal by this time, ain't she?' 'What are you talkin about,' sez I; 'how should

I know?' He draws away from me, and sez, 'D—— it,' sez he, 'you don't mean that you' . . . I grabs him by the throat and makes him tell me all. And then it appears that the boat and the baby were never found again, and every man of that crew, cap'en and all, believed I had stolen it."

He paused. Father Pedro was staring at the prospect with an uncompromising rigidity of head and shoulder.

"It's a bad lookout for me, ain't it?" the stranger continued, in serious reflection.

"How do I know," said the priest harshly, without turning his head, "that you did not make away with this child?"

"Beg pardon."

"That you did not complete your revenge by —by—killing it, as your comrade suspected you? Ah! Holy Trinity," continued Father Pedro, throwing out his hands with an impatient gesture, as if to take the place of unutterable thought.

"How do *you* know?" echoed the stranger coldly.

"Yes."

The stranger linked his fingers together and threw them over his knee, drew it up to his chest caressingly, and said quietly, "Because you *do* know."

The Padre rose to his feet.

"What mean you?" he said, sternly fixing his eyes upon the speaker. Their eyes met. The stranger's were gray and persistent, with hanging corner lids that might have concealed even more purpose than they showed. The Padre's were hollow, open, and the whites slightly brown, as if with tobacco stains. Yet they were the first to turn away.

"I mean," returned the stranger, with the same practical gravity, "that you know it wouldn't pay me to come here, if I'd killed the baby, unless I wanted you to fix things right with me up there," pointing skywards, "and get absolution; and I've told you *that* wasn't in my line."

"Why do you seek me, then?" demanded the Padre, suspiciously.

"Because I reckon I thought a man might be allowed to confess something short of a murder. If you're going to draw the line below that—"

"This is but sacrilegious levity," interrupted Father Pedro, turning as if to go. But the stranger did not make any movement to detain him.

"Have you implored forgiveness of the father—the man you wronged—before you came here?" asked the priest, lingering.

"Not much. It wouldn't pay if he was living, and he died four years ago."

"You are sure of that?"

"I am."

"There are other relations, perhaps?"

"None."

Father Pedro was silent. When he spoke again, it was with a changed voice. "What is your purpose, then?" he asked, with the first indication of priestly sympathy in his manner. "You cannot ask forgiveness of the earthly father you have injured, you refuse the intercession of Holy Church with the Heavenly Father you have disobeyed. Speak, wretched man! What is it you want?"

"I want to find the child."

"But if it were possible, if she were still living, are you fit to seek her, to even make yourself known to her, to appear before her?"

"Well, if I made it profitable to her, perhaps."

"Perhaps," echoed the priest, scornfully. "So be it. But why come here?"

"To ask your advice. To know how to begin my search. You know this country. You were here when that boat drifted ashore beyond that mountain."

"Ah, indeed. I have much to do with it. It is an affair of the alcalde—the authorities—of your—your police."

"Is it?"

The Padre again met the stranger's eyes. He stopped, with the snuff box he had somewhat ostentatiously drawn from his pocket still open in his hand.

"Why is it not, Señor?" he demanded.

"If she lives, she is a young lady by this time, and might not want the details of her life known to any one."

"And how will you recognize your baby in this young lady?" asked Father Pedro, with a rapid gesture, indicating the comparative heights of a baby and an adult.

"I reckon I'll know her, and her clothes too; and whoever found her wouldn't be fool enough to destroy them."

"After fourteen years! Good! you have faith, Señor—"

"Cranch," supplied the stranger, consulting his watch. "But time's up. Business is business. Good-by; don't let me keep you."

He extended his hand.

The Padre met it with a dry, unsympathetic palm, as sere and yellow as the hills. When their hands separated, the father still hesitated, looking at Cranch. If he expected further speech or entreaty from him he was mistaken, for the American, without turning his head, walked in the same serious, practical fashion down the avenue of fig trees, and disappeared beyond the hedge of vines. The outlines of the mountain beyond were already lost in the fog. Father Pedro turned into the refectory.

"Antonio."

A strong flavor of leather, onions, and stable preceded the entrance of a short, stout *vaquero* from the little *patio*.

"Saddle Pinto and thine own mule to accompany Francisco, who will take letters from me to the Father Superior at San José to-morrow at daybreak."

"At daybreak, reverend father?"

"At daybreak. Hark ye, go by the mountain trails and avoid the highway. Stop at no *posada* nor *fonda,* but if the child is weary, rest then awhile at Don Juan Briones' or at the rancho of the Blessed Fisherman. Have no converse with stragglers, least of all those gentile Americanos. So . . ."

The first strokes of the Angelus came from the nearer tower. With a gesture Father Pedro waved Antonio aside, and opened the door of the sacristy.

"Ad Majorem Dei Gloria."

CHAPTER II.

THE hacienda of Don Juan Briones, nestling in a wooded cleft of the foot-hills, was hidden, as Father Pedro had wisely reflected, from the straying feet of travelers along the dusty highway to San José. As Francisco, emerging from the *cañada,* put spurs to his mule at the sight of the whitewashed walls, Antonio grunted:—

"Oh aye, little priest! thou wast tired enough a moment ago, and though we are not three leagues from the Blessed Fisherman, thou couldst scarce sit thy saddle longer. Mother of God! and all to see that little mongrel, Juanita."

"But, good Antonio, Juanita was my play-fellow, and I may not soon again chance this way. And Juanita is not a mongrel, no more than I am."

"She is a *mestiza,* and thou art a child of the Church, though this following of gypsy wenches does not show it."

"But Father Pedro does not object," urged the boy.

"The reverend father has forgotten he was ever young," replied Antonio, sententiously, "or he wouldn't set fire and tow together."

"What sayest thou, good Antonio?" asked

Francisco quickly, opening his blue eyes in frank curiosity; "who is fire, and who is tow?"

The worthy muleteer, utterly abashed and confounded by this display of the acolyte's direct simplicity, contented himself by shrugging his shoulders, and a vague *"Quien sabe?"*

"Come," said the boy, gayly, "confess it is only the *aguardiente* of the Blessed Fisherman thou missest. Never fear, Juanita will find thee some. And see! here she comes."

There was a flash of white flounces along the dark brown corridor, the twinkle of satin slippers, the flying out of long black braids, and with a cry of joy a young girl threw herself upon Francisco as he entered the *patio,* and nearly dragged him from his mule.

"Have a care, little sister," laughed the acolyte, looking at Antonio, "or there will be a conflagration. Am I the fire?" he continued, submitting to the two sounding kisses the young girl placed upon either cheek, but still keeping his mischievous glance upon the muleteer.

"Quien sabe?" repeated Antonio, gruffly, as the young girl blushed under his significant eyes. "It is no affair of mine," he added to himself, as he led Pinto away. "Perhaps Father Pedro is right, and this young twig of the Church is as dry and sapless as himself. Let the *mestiza* burn if she likes."

"Quick, Pancho," said the young girl, eagerly leading him along the corridor. "This way. I must talk with thee before thou seest Don Juan; that is why I ran to intercept thee, and not as that fool Antonio would signify, to shame thee. Wast thou ashamed, my Pancho?"

The boy threw his arm familiarly round the supple, stayless little waist, accented only by the belt of the light flounced *saya*, and said, "But why this haste and feverishness, 'Nita? And now I look at thee, thou hast been crying."

They had emerged from a door in the corridor into the bright sunlight of a walled garden. The girl dropped her eyes, cast a quick glance around her, and said,—

"Not here, to the *arroyo*," and half leading, half dragging him, made her way through a copse of *manzanita* and alder until they heard the faint tinkling of water. "Dost thou remember," said the girl, "it was here," pointing to an embayed pool in the dark current, "that I baptized thee, when Father Pedro first brought thee here, when we both played at being monks? They were dear old days, for Father Pedro would trust no one with thee but me, and always kept us near him."

"Aye, and he said I would be profaned by the touch of any other, and so himself always washed and dressed me, and made my bed near his."

"And took thee away again, and I saw thee not till thou camest with Antonio, over a year ago, to the cattle branding. And now, my Pancho, I may never see thee again." She buried her face in her hands and sobbed aloud.

The little acolyte tried to comfort her, but with such abstraction of manner and inadequacy of warmth that she hastily removed his caressing hand.

"But why? What has happened?" he asked eagerly.

The girl's manner had changed. Her eyes flashed, and she put her brown fist on her waist and began to rock from side to side.

"But I'll not go," she said viciously.

"Go where?" asked the boy.

"Oh, where?" she echoed, impatiently. "Hear me, Francisco; thou knowest I am, like thee, an orphan; but I have not, like thee, a parent in the Holy Church. For, alas," she added, bitterly, "I am not a boy, and have not a lovely voice borrowed from the angels. I was, like thee, a foundling, kept by the charity of the reverend fathers, until Don Juan, a childless widower, adopted me. I was happy, not knowing and caring who were the parents who had abandoned me, happy only in the love of him

who became my adopted father. And now—"
She paused.

"And now?" echoed Francisco, eagerly.

"And now they say it is discovered who are
my parents."—"And they live?"

"Mother of God! no," said the girl, with
scarcely filial piety. "There is some one, a
thing, a mere Don Fulano, who knows it all, it
seems, who is to be my guardian."

"But how? tell me all, dear Juanita," said
the boy with a feverish interest, that contrasted
so strongly with his previous abstraction that
Juanita bit her lips with vexation.

"Ah! How? Santa Barbara! an extrava-
ganza for children. A necklace of lies. I am
lost from a ship of which my father—Heaven
rest him—is General, and I am picked up
among the weeds on the sea-shore, like Moses
in the bulrushes. A pretty story, indeed."

"Oh, how beautiful!" exclaimed Francisco,
enthusiastically. "Ah, Juanita, would it had
been me."

"*Thee!*" said the girl bitterly,—"thee! No!
—it was a girl wanted. Enough, it was me."

"And when does the guardian come?" persisted the boy, with sparkling eyes.

"He is here even now, with that pompous
fool the American alcalde from Monterey, a
wretch who knows nothing of the country or

the people, but who helped the other American to claim me. I tell thee, Francisco, like as not it is all a folly, some senseless blunder of those Americanos that imposes upon Don Juan's simplicity and love for them."

"How looks he, this Americano who seeks thee?" asked Francisco.

"What care I how he looks," said Juanita, "or what he is? He may have the four S's, for all I care. Yet," she added with a slight touch of coquetry, "he is not bad to look upon, now I recall him."

"Had he a long moustache and a sad, sweet smile, and a voice so gentle and yet so strong that you felt he ordered you to do things without saying it? And did his eye read your thoughts?—that very thought that you must obey him?"

"Saints preserve thee, Pancho! Of whom dost thou speak?"

"Listen, Juanita. It was a year ago, the eve of Natividad, he was in the church when I sang. Look where I would, I always met his eye. When the canticle was sung and I was slipping into the sacristy, he was beside me. He spoke kindly, but I understood him not. He put into my hand gold for an *aguinaldo*. I pretended I understood not that also, and put it into the box for the poor. He smiled and went away. Often have I seen him since, and last night, when I left the Mission, he was there again with Father Pedro."

"And Father Pedro, what said he of him?" asked Juanita.

"Nothing." The boy hesitated. "Perhaps —because I said nothing of the stranger."

Juanita laughed. "So thou canst keep a secret from the good father when thou carest. But why dost thou think this stranger is my new guardian?"

"Dost thou not see, little sister? he was even then seeking thee," said the boy with joyous excitement. "Doubtless he knew we were friends and playmates—may be the good father has told him thy secret. For it is no idle tale of the alcalde, believe me. I see it all! It is true!"

"Then thou wilt let him take me away," exclaimed the girl bitterly, withdrawing the little hand he had clasped in his excitement.

"Alas, Juanita, what avails it now? I am sent to San José, charged with a letter to the Father Superior, who will give me further orders. What they are, or how long I must stay, I know not. But I know this: the good Father Pedro's eyes were troubled when he gave me his blessing, and he held me long in his embrace. Pray Heaven I have committed no fault. Still it may be that the reputation of my gift hath

reached the Father Superior, and he would advance me." And Francisco's eyes lit up with
youthful pride at the thought.

Not so Juanita. Her black eyes snapped suddenly with suspicion, she drew in her breath,
and closed her little mouth firmly. Then she
began a *crescendo*.

Mother of God! was that all? Was he a
child, to be sent away for such time or for such
purpose as best pleased the fathers? Was he to
know no more than that? With such gifts as
God had given him, was he not at least to have
some word in disposing of them? Ah! *she*
would not stand it.

The boy gazed admiringly at the piquant
energy of the little figure before him, and envied
her courage. "It is the *mestizo* blood," he
murmured to himself. Then aloud, "Thou
shouldst have been a man, 'Nita."

"And thou a woman."

"Or a priest. Eh, what is that?"

They had both risen, Juanita defiantly, her
black braids flying as she wheeled and suddenly
faced the thicket, Francisco clinging to her with
trembling hands and whitened lips. A stone,
loosened from the hillside, had rolled to their
feet; there was a crackling in the alders on the
slope above them.

"Is it a bear, or a brigand?" whispered Francisco, hurriedly, sounding the uttermost depths of his terror in the two words.

"It is an eavesdropper," said Juanita, impetuously; "and who and why, I intend to know," and she started towards the thicket.

"Do not leave me, good Juanita," said the young acolyte, grasping the girl's skirt.

"Nay; run to the hacienda quickly, and leave me to search the thicket. Run!"

The boy did not wait for a second injunction, but scuttled away, his long coat catching in the brambles, while Juanita darted like a kitten into the bushes. Her search was fruitless, however, and she was returning impatiently when her quick eye fell upon a letter lying amidst the dried grass where she and Francisco had been seated the moment before. It had evidently fallen from his breast when he had risen suddenly, and been overlooked in his alarm. It was Father Pedro's letter to the Father Superior of San José.

In an instant she had pounced upon it as viciously as if it had been the interloper she was seeking. She knew that she held in her fingers the secret of Francisco's sudden banishment. She felt instinctively that this yellowish envelope, with its red string and its blotch of red seal, was his sentence and her own. The little *mestiza* had not been brought up to respect the integrity of either locks or seals, both being unknown in the patriarchal life of the hacienda. Yet with a certain feminine instinct she looked furtively around her, and even managed to dislodge the clumsy wax without marring the pretty effigy of the crossed keys impressed upon it. Then she opened the letter and read.

Suddenly she stopped and put back her hair from her brown temples. Then a succession of burning blushes followed each other in waves from her neck up, and died in drops of moisture in her eyes. This continued until she was fairly crying, dropping the letter from her hands and rocking to and fro. In the midst of this she quickly stopped again; the clouds broke, a sunshine of laughter started from her eyes, she laughed shyly, she laughed loudly, she laughed hysterically. Then she stopped again as suddenly, knitted her brows, swooped down once more upon the letter, and turned to fly. But at the same moment the letter was quietly but firmly taken from her hand, and Mr. Jack Cranch stood beside her.

Juanita was crimson, but unconquered. She mechanically held out her hand for the letter; the American took her little fingers, kissed them, and said:—

"How are you again?"

"The letter," replied Juanita, with a strong disposition to stamp her foot.

"But," said Cranch, with business directness, "you've read enough to know it isn't for you."

"Nor for you either," responded Juanita.

"True. It is for the Reverend Father Superior of San José Mission. I'll give it to him."

Juanita was becoming alarmed, first at this prospect, second at the power the stranger seemed to be gaining over her. She recalled Francisco's description of him with something like superstitious awe.

"But it concerns Francisco. It contains a secret he should know."

"Then you can tell him it. Perhaps it would come easier from you."

Juanita blushed again. "Why?" she asked, half dreading his reply.

"Because," said the American, quietly, "you are old playmates; you are attached to each other."

Juanita bit her lips. "Why don't you read it yourself?" she asked bluntly.

"Because I don't read other people's letters, and if it concerns me you'll tell me."

"What if I don't?"

"Then the Father Superior will."

"I believe you know Francisco's secret already," said the girl, boldly.

"Perhaps."

"Then, Mother of God! Señor Crancho, what do you want?"

"I do not want to separate two such good friends as you and Francisco."

"Perhaps you'd like to claim us both," said the girl, with a sneer that was not devoid of coquetry.

"I should be delighted."

"Then here is your occasion, Señor, for here comes my adopted father, Don Juan, and your friend, Señor Br—r—own, the American alcalde."

Two men appeared in the garden path below them. The stiff, glazed, broad-brimmed black hat, surmounting a dark face of Quixotic gravity and romantic rectitude, indicated Don Juan Briones. His companion, lazy, specious, and red-faced, was Señor Brown, the American alcalde.

"Well, I reckon we kin about call the thing fixed," said Señor Brown, with a large wave of the hand, suggesting a sweeping away of all trivial details. "Ez I was saying to the Don yer, when two high-toned gents like you and him come together in a delicate matter of this kind, it ain't no hoss trade nor sharp practice. The Don is that lofty in principle that he's willin' to sacrifice his affections for the good of the gal; and you, on your hand, kalkilate to see all he's done for her, and go your whole pile better. You'll make the legal formalities good. I reckon that old Injin woman who can swear to the finding of the baby on the shore will set things all right yet. For the matter o' that, if you want anything in the way of a certificate, I'm on hand always."

"Juanita and myself are at your disposition, *caballeros*," said Don Juan, with a grave exaltation. "Never let it be said that the Mexican nation was outdone by the great Americanos in deeds of courtesy and affection. Let it rather stand that Juanita was a sacred trust put into my hands years ago by the goddess of American liberty, and nurtured in the Mexican eagle's nest. Is it not so, my soul?" he added, more humanly, to the girl, when he had quite recovered from the intoxication of his own speech. "We love thee, little one, but we keep our honor."

"There's nothing mean about the old man," said Brown, admiringly, with a slight dropping of his left eyelid; "his head is level, and he goes with his party."

"Thou takest my daughter, Señor Cranch," continued the old man, carried away by his emotion; "but the American nation gives me a son."

"You know not what you say, father," said

the young girl, angrily, exasperated by a slight twinkle in the American's eye.

"Not so," said Cranch. "Perhaps one of the American nation may take him at his word."

"Then, *caballeros,* you will, for the moment at least, possess yourselves of the house and its poor hospitality," said Don Juan, with time-honored courtesy, producing the rustic key of the gate of the *patio.* "It is at your disposition, *caballeros,*" he repeated, leading the way as his guests passed into the corridor.

Two hours passed. The hills were darkening on their eastern slopes; the shadows of the few poplars that sparsedly dotted the dusty highway were falling in long black lines that looked like ditches on the dead level of the tawny fields; the shadows of slowly moving cattle were mingling with their own silhouettes, and becoming more and more grotesque. A keen wind rising in the hills was already creeping from the *cañada* as from the mouth of a funnel, and sweeping the plains. Antonio had forgathered with the servants, had pinched the ears of the maids, had partaken of *aguardiente,* had saddled the mules,—Antonio was becoming impatient.

And then a singular commotion disturbed the peaceful monotony of the patriarchal household of Don Juan Briones. The stagnant court-yard was suddenly alive with *peons* and servants, running hither and thither. The alleys and gardens were filled with retainers. A confusion of questions, orders, and outcrys rent the air, the plains shook with the galloping of a dozen horsemen. For the acolyte Francisco, of the Mission San Carmel, had disappeared and vanished, and from that day the hacienda of Don Juan Briones knew him no more.

CHAPTER III.

WHEN Father Pedro saw the yellow mules vanish under the low branches of the oaks beside the little graveyard, caught the last glitter of the morning sun on Pinto's shining headstall, and heard the last tinkle of Antonio's spurs, something very like a mundane sigh escaped him. To the simple wonder of the majority of early worshipers—the half-breed converts who rigorously attended the spiritual ministrations of the Mission, and ate the temporal provisions of the reverend fathers—he deputed the functions of the first mass to a coadjutor, and, breviary in hand, sought the orchard of venerable pear trees. Whether there was any occult sympathy in his reflections with the contemplation of their gnarled, twisted, gouty, and knotty limbs, still bearing gracious and goodly fruit, I know not, but it was his private retreat, and under one of the most rheumatic and misshapen trunks there was a rude seat. Here Father Pedro sank, his face towards the mountain wall between him and the invisible sea. The relentless, dry, practical Californian sunlight falling on his face grimly pointed out a night of vigil and suffering. The snuffy yellow of his eyes was injected yet burning, his temples were ridged and veined like a tobacco leaf; the odor of desiccation which his garments always exhaled was hot and feverish, as if the fire had suddenly awakened among the ashes.

Of what was Father Pedro thinking?

He was thinking of his youth, a youth spent under the shade of those pear trees, even then venerable as now. He was thinking of his youthful dreams of heathen conquest, emulating the sacrifices and labors of Junipero Serra; a dream cut short by the orders of the archbishop, that sent his companion, Brother Diego, north on a mission to strange lands, and condemned him to the isolation of San Carmel. He was thinking of that fierce struggle with envy of a fellow creature's better fortune that, conquered by prayer and penance, left him patient, submissive, and devoted to his humble work; how he raised up converts to the faith, even taking them from the breast of heretic mothers.

He recalled how once, with the zeal of
propagandism quickening in the instincts of a
childless man, he had dreamed of perpetuating
his work through some sinless creation of his
own; of dedicating some virgin soul, one over
whom he could have complete control, restricted
by no human paternal weakness, to the task he
had begun. But how? Of all the boys eagerly
offered to the Church by their parents there
seemed none sufficiently pure and free from
parental taint. He remembered how one night,
through the intercession of the Blessed Virgin
herself, as he firmly then believed, this dream
was fulfilled. An Indian woman brought him a
Waugee child—a baby-girl that she had picked
up on the sea-shore. There were no parents to
divide the responsibility, the child had no past
to confront, except the memory of the ignorant
Indian woman, who deemed her duty done, and
whose interest ceased in giving it to the Padre.
The austere conditions of his monkish life compelled him to the first step in his adoption of
it—the concealment of its sex. This was easy
enough, as he constituted himself from that moment its sole nurse and attendant, and boldly
baptized it among the other children by the
name of Francisco. No others knew its origin,
nor cared to know. Father Pedro had taken a
muchacho foundling for adoption; his jealous

seclusion of it and his personal care was doubtless some sacerdotal formula at once high and
necessary.

He remembered with darkening eyes and impeded breath how his close companionship and
daily care of this helpless child had revealed to
him the fascinations of that paternity denied to
him; how he had deemed it his duty to struggle
against the thrill of baby fingers laid upon his
yellow cheeks, the pleading of inarticulate
words, the eloquence of wonder-seeing and
mutely questioning eyes; how he had succumbed
again and again, and then struggled no more,
seeing only in them the suggestion of childhood
made incarnate in the Holy Babe. And yet,
even as he thought, he drew from his gown a
little shoe, and laid it beside his breviary. It
was Francisco's baby slipper, a duplicate to
those worn by the miniature waxen figure of the
Holy Virgin herself in her niche in the transept.

Had he felt during these years any qualms of
conscience at this concealment of the child's sex?
None. For to him the babe was sexless, as most
befitted one who was to live and die at the foot
of the altar. There was no attempt to deceive
God; what mattered else? Nor was he with-
holding the child from the ministrations of the
sacred sisters; there was no convent near the
Mission, and as each year passed, the difficulty

of restoring her to the position and duties of her sex became greater and more dangerous. And then the acolyte's destiny was sealed by what again appeared to Father Pedro as a direct interposition of Providence. The child developed a voice of such exquisite sweetness and purity that an angel seemed to have strayed into the little choir, and kneeling worshipers below, transported, gazed upwards, half expectant of a heavenly light breaking through the gloom of the raftered ceiling. The fame of the little singer filled the valley of San Carmel; it was a miracle vouchsafed the Mission; Don José Peralta remembered, ah yes, to have heard in old Spain of boy choristers with such voices!

And was this sacred trust to be withdrawn from him? Was this life which he had brought out of an unknown world of sin, unstained and pure, consecrated and dedicated to God, just in the dawn of power and promise for the glory of the Mother Church, to be taken from his side? And at the word of a self-convicted man of sin —a man whose tardy repentance was not yet absolved by the Holy Church. Never! never! Father Pedro dwelt upon the stranger's rejection of the ministrations of the Church with a pitiable satisfaction; had he accepted it, he would have had a sacred claim upon Father Pedro's sympathy and confidence. Yet he rose

again, uneasily and with irregular steps returned to the corridor, passing the door of the
familiar little cell beside his own. The window,
the table, and even the scant toilette utensils
were filled with the flowers of yesterday, some
of them withered and dry; the white gown of
the little chorister was hanging emptily against
the wall. Father Pedro started and trembled;
it seemed as if the spiritual life of the child
had slipped away with its garments.

In that slight chill, which even in the hottest
days in California always invests any shadow
cast in that white sunlight, Father Pedro shivered in the corridor. Passing again into the
garden, he followed in fancy the wayfaring
figure of Francisco, saw the child arrive at the
rancho of Don Juan, and with the fateful blind-
ness of all dreamers projected a picture most
unlike the reality. He followed the pilgrims
even to San José, and saw the child deliver the
missive which gave the secret of her sex and
condition to the Father Superior. That the authority at San José might dissent with the Padre
of San Carmel, or decline to carry out his de-
signs, did not occur to the one-idea'd priest.
Like all solitary people, isolated from passing
events, he made no allowances for occurrences
outside of his routine. Yet at this moment a
sudden thought whitened his yellow cheek.

What if the Father Superior deemed it necessary to impart the secret to Francisco? Would
the child recoil at the deception, and, perhaps,
cease to love him? It was the first time, in his
supreme selfishness, he had taken the acolyte's
feelings into account. He had thought of him
only as one owing implicit obedience to him as
a temporal and spiritual guide.

"Reverend Father!"

He turned impatiently. It was his muleteer,
José. Father Pedro's sunken eye brightened.

"Ah, José! Quickly, then; hast thou found
Sanchicha?"

"Truly, your reverence! And I have brought
her with me, just as she is; though if your
reverence make more of her than to fill the six-
foot hole and say a prayer over her, I'll give
the mule that brought her here for food for the
bull's horns. She neither hears nor speaks, but
whether from weakness or sheer wantonness, I
know not."

"Peace, then! and let thy tongue take example from hers. Bring her with thee into the
sacristy and attend without. Go!"

Father Pedro watched the disappearing figure
of the muleteer and hurriedly swept his thin,
dry hand, veined and ribbed like a brown November leaf, over his stony forehead, with a
sound that seemed almost a rustle. Then he

suddenly stiffened his fingers over his breviary, dropped his arms perpendicularly before him, and with a rigid step returned to the corridor and passed into the sacristy.

For a moment in the half-darkness the room seemed to be empty. Tossed carelessly in the corner appeared some blankets topped by a few straggling black horse tails, like an unstranded *riata*. A trembling agitated the mass as Father Pedro approached. He bent over the heap and distinguished in its midst the glowing black eyes of Sanchicha, the Indian centenarian of the Mission San Carmel. Only her eyes lived. Helpless, boneless, and jelly-like, old age had overtaken her with a mild form of deliquescence.

"Listen, Sanchicha," said the father, gravely. "It is important that thou shouldst refresh thy memory for a moment. Look back fourteen years, mother; it is but yesterday to thee. Thou dost remember the baby—a little *muchacha* thou broughtest me then—fourteen years ago?"

The old woman's eyes became intelligent, and turned with a quick look towards the open door of the church, and thence towards the choir.

The Padre made a motion of irritation. "No, no! Thou dost not understand; thou dost not attend me. Knowest thou of any mark of clothing, trinket, or amulet found upon the babe?"

The light of the old woman's eyes went out.

She might have been dead. Father Pedro waited a moment, and then laid his hand impatiently on her shoulder.

"Dost thou mean there are none?"

A ray of light struggled back into her eyes.

"None."

"And thou hast kept back or put away no sign nor mark of her parentage? Tell me, on this crucifix."

The eyes caught the crucifix, and became as empty as the orbits of the carven Christ upon it.

Father Pedro waited patiently. A moment passed; only the sound of the muleteer's spurs was heard in the courtyard.

"It is well," he said at last, with a sigh of relief. "Pepita shall give thee some refreshment, and José will bring thee back again. I will summon him."

He passed out of the sacristy door, leaving it open. A ray of sunlight darted eagerly in, and fell upon the grotesque heap in the corner. Sanchicha's eyes lived again; more than that, a singular movement came over her face. The hideous caverns of her toothless mouth opened— she laughed. The step of José was heard in the corridor, and she became again inert.

The third day, which should have brought the return of Antonio, was nearly spent. Father Pedro was impatient but not alarmed. The good fathers at San José might naturally detain Antonio for the answer, which might require deliberation. If any mischance had occurred to Francisco, Antonio would have returned or sent a special messenger. At sunset he was in his accustomed seat in the orchard, his hands clasped over the breviary in his listless lap, his eyes fixed upon the mountain between him and that mysterious sea that had brought so much into his life. He was filled with a strange desire to see it, a vague curiosity hitherto unknown to his preoccupied life; he wished to gaze upon that strand, perhaps the very spot where she had been found; he doubted not his questioning eyes would discover some forgotten trace of her; under his persistent will and aided by the Holy Virgin, the sea would give up its secret. He looked at the fog creeping along the summit, and recalled the latest gossip of San Carmel; how that since the advent of the Americanos it was gradually encroaching on the Mission. The hated name vividly recalled to him the features of the stranger as he had stood before him three nights ago, in this very garden; so vividly that he sprang to his feet with an exclamation. It was no fancy, but Señor Cranch himself advancing from under the shadow of a pear tree.

"I reckoned I'd catch you here," said Mr.

Cranch, with the same dry, practical business fashion, as if he was only resuming an interrupted conversation, "and I reckon I ain't going to keep you a minit longer than I did t' other day." He mutely referred to his watch, which he already held in his hand, and then put it back in his pocket. "Well! we found her!"

"Francisco," interrupted the priest with a single stride, laying his hand upon Cranch's arm, and staring into his eyes.

Mr. Cranch quietly removed Father Pedro's hand. "I reckon that wasn't the name as *I* caught it," he returned dryly. "Hadn't you better sit down?"

"Pardon me—pardon me, Señor," said the priest, hastily sinking back upon his bench, "I was thinking of other things. You—you—came upon me suddenly. I thought it was the acolyte. Go on, Señor! I am interested."

"I thought you'd be," said Cranch, quietly. "That's why I came. And then you might be of service too."

"True, true," said the priest, with rapid accents; "and this girl, Señor, this girl is—"

"Juanita, the *mestiza,* adopted daughter of Don Juan Briones, over on the Santa Clare Valley," replied Cranch, jerking his thumb over his shoulder, and then sitting down upon the bench beside Father Pedro.

The priest turned his feverish eyes piercingly upon his companion for a few seconds, and then doggedly fixed them upon the ground. Cranch drew a plug of tobacco from his pocket, cut off a portion, placed it in his cheek, and then quietly began to strap the blade of his jack-knife upon his boot. Father Pedro saw it from under his eyelids, and even in his preoccupation despised him.

"Then you are certain she is the babe you seek?" said the father, without looking up.

"I reckon as near as you can be certain of anything. Her age tallies; she was the only foundling girl baby baptized by you, you know," —he partly turned round appealingly to the Padre,—"that year. Injin woman says she picked up a baby. Looks like a pretty clear case, don't it?"

"And the clothes, friend Cranch?" said the priest, with his eyes still on the ground, and a slight assumption of easy indifference.

"They will be forthcoming, like enough, when the time comes," said Cranch; "the main thing at first was to find the girl; that was *my* job; the lawyers, I reckon, can fit the proofs and say what's wanted, later on."

"But why lawyers," continued Padre Pedro, with a slight sneer he could not repress, "if the child is found and Señor Cranch is satisfied?"

"On account of the property. Business is business!"

"The property?"

Mr. Cranch pressed the back of his knife-blade on his boot, shut it up with a click, and putting it in his pocket said calmly,—

"Well, I reckon the million of dollars that her father left when he died, which naturally belongs to her, will require some proof that she is his daughter."

He had placed both his hands in his pockets, and turned his eyes full upon Father Pedro. The priest arose hurriedly.

"But you said nothing of this before, Señor Cranch," said he, with a gesture of indignation, turning his back quite upon Cranch, and taking a step towards the refectory.

"Why should I? I was looking after the girl, not the property," returned Cranch, following the Padre with watchful eyes, but still keeping his careless, easy attitude.

"Ah, well! Will it be said so, think you? Eh! *Bueno.* What will the world think of your sacred quest, eh?" continued the Padre Pedro, forgetting himself in his excitement, but still averting his face from his companion.

"The world will look after the proofs, and I reckon not bother if the proofs are all right," replied Cranch, carelessly; "and the girl won't

think the worse of me for helping her to a
fortune. Hallo! you've dropped something."
He leaped to his feet, picked up the breviary
which had fallen from the Padre's fingers, and
returned it to him with a slight touch of gentle-
ness that was unsuspected in the man.

The priest's dry, tremulous hand grasped the
volume without acknowledgment.

"But these proofs?" he said hastily; "these
proofs, Señor?"

"Oh, well, you'll testify to the baptism, you
know."

"But if I refuse; if I will have nothing to do
with this thing! If I will not give my word
that there is not some mistake," said the priest,
working himself into a feverish indignation.
"That there are not slips of memory, eh? Of
so many children baptized, is it possible for me
to know which, eh? And if this Juanita is not
your girl, eh?"

"Then you'll help me to find who is," said
Cranch, coolly.

Father Pedro turned furiously on his tor-
mentor. Overcome by his vigil and anxiety he
was oblivious of everything but the presence of
the man who seemed to usurp the functions of
his own conscience. "Who are you, who speak
thus?" he said hoarsely, advancing upon Cranch
with outstretched and anathematizing fingers.

"Who are you, Señor Heathen, who dare to dictate to me, a Father of Holy Church? I tell you, I will have none of this. Never! I will not. From this moment, you understand—nothing. I will never . . ."

He stopped. The first stroke of the Angelus rang from the little tower. The first stroke of that bell before whose magic exorcism all human passions fled, the peaceful bell that had for fifty years lulled the little fold of San Carmel to prayer and rest, came to his throbbing ear. His trembling hands groped for the crucifix, carried it to his left breast; his lips moved in prayer. His eyes were turned to the cold, passionless sky, where a few faint, far-spaced stars had silently stolen to their places. The Angelus still rang, his trembling ceased, he remained motionless and rigid.

The American, who had uncovered in deference to the worshiper rather than the rite, waited patiently. The eyes of Father Pedro returned to the earth, moist as if with dew caught from above. He looked half absently at Cranch.

"Forgive me, my son," he said, in a changed voice. "I am only a worn old man. I must talk with thee more of this—but not to-night—not to-night;—to-morrow—to-morrow—to-morrow."

He turned slowly and appeared to glide rather

than move under the trees, until the dark shadow of the Mission tower met and encompassed him. Cranch followed him with anxious eyes. Then he removed the quid of tobacco from his cheek.

"Just as I reckoned," remarked he, quite audibly. "He's clean gold on the bed rock after all!"

CHAPTER IV.

THAT night Father Pedro dreamed a strange dream. How much of it was reality, how long it lasted, or when he awoke from it, he could not tell. The morbid excitement of the previous day culminated in a febrile exaltation in which he lived and moved as in a separate existence.

This is what he remembered. He thought he had risen at night in a sudden horror of remorse, and making his way to the darkened church had fallen upon his knees before the high altar, when all at once the acolyte's voice broke from the choir, but in accents so dissonant and unnatural that it seemed a sacrilege, and he trembled. He thought he had confessed the secret of the child's sex to Cranch, but whether the next morning or a week later he did not know. He fancied, too, that Cranch had also confessed some trifling deception to him, but what, or why, he could not remember; so much greater seemed the enormity of his own transgression. He thought Cranch had put in his hands the letter he had written to the Father Superior, saying that his secret was still safe, and that he had been spared the avowal and the scandal that might have ensued. But through all, and above all, he was conscious of one fixed idea: to seek the seashore with Sanchicha, and upon the spot where she had found Francisco, meet the young girl who had taken his place, and so part from her forever. He had a dim recollection that this was necessary to some legal identification of her, as arranged by Cranch, but how or why he did not understand; enough that it was a part of his penance.

It was early morning when the faithful Antonio, accompanied by Sanchicha and José, rode forth with him from the Mission of San Carmel. Except on the expressionless features of the old woman, there was anxiety and gloom upon the faces of the little cavalcade. He did not know how heavily his strange abstraction and hallucinations weighed upon their honest hearts. As they wound up the ascent of the mountain he noticed that Antonio and José conversed with bated breath and many pious crossings of themselves, but with eyes always wistfully fixed upon him. He wondered if, as part of his penance, he ought not to proclaim his sin and abase himself before them; but he knew that his devoted followers would insist upon sharing his punishment; and he remembered his promise to Cranch, that for *her* sake he would say nothing. Before they reached the summit he turned once or twice to look back upon the Mission. How small it looked, lying there in the peaceful valley, contrasted with the broad sweep of the landscape beyond, stopped at the further east only by the dim, ghost-like outlines of the Sierras. But the strong breath of the sea was beginning to be felt; in a few moments more they were facing it with lowered *sombreros* and flying *serapes,* and the vast, glittering, illimitable Pacific opened out beneath them.

Dazed and blinded, as it seemed to him, by the shining, restless expanse, Father Pedro rode forward as if still in a dream. Suddenly he halted, and called Antonio to his side.

"Tell me, child, didst thou not say that this coast was wild and desolate of man, beast, and habitation?"

"Truly I did, reverend father."

"Then what is that?" pointing to the shore.

Almost at their feet nestled a cluster of houses, at the head of an *arroyo* reaching up from the beach. They looked down upon the smoke of a manufactory chimney, upon strange heaps of material and curious engines scattered along the sands, with here and there moving specks of human figures. In a little bay a schooner swung at her cables.

The *vaquero* crossed himself in stupefied alarm. "I know not, your reverence; it is only two years ago, before the *rodeo,* that I was here for strayed colts, and I swear by the blessed bones of San Antonio that it was as I said."

"Ah! it is like these Americanos," responded the muleteer. "I have it from my brother Diego that he went from San José to Pescadero two months ago, across the plains, with never a hut nor *fonda* to halt at all the way. He returned in seven days, and in the midst of the plain there were three houses and a mill, and many people. And why was it? Ah! Mother of God! one had picked up in the creek where he drank that much of gold;" and the muleteer tapped one of the silver coins that fringed his jacket sleeves in place of buttons.

"And they are washing the sands for gold there now," said Antonio, eagerly pointing to some men gathered round a machine like an enormous cradle. "Let us hasten on."

Father Pedro's momentary interest had passed. The words of his companions fell dull and meaningless upon his dreaming ears. He was conscious only that the child was more a stranger to him as an outcome of this hard, bustling life, than when he believed her borne to him over the mysterious sea. It perplexed his dazed, disturbed mind to think that if such an antagonistic element could exist within a dozen miles of the Mission, and he not know it, could not such an atmosphere have been around him, even in his monastic isolation, and he remain blind to it? Had he really lived in the world without knowing it? Had it been in his blood? Had it impelled him to— He shuddered and rode on.

They were at the last slope of the zigzag descent to the shore, when he saw the figures of a man and woman moving slowly through a field of wild oats, not far from the trail. It seemed to his distorted fancy that the man was Cranch. The woman! His heart stopped beating. Ah! could it be? He had never seen her in her proper garb: would she look like that? Would she be as tall? He thought he bade José and Antonio go on slowly before with Sanchicha, and dismounted, walking slowly between the high stalks of grain, lest he should disturb them. They evidently did not hear his approach, but were talking earnestly. It seemed to Father Pedro that they had taken each other's hands, and as he looked Cranch slipped his arm round her waist. With only a blind instinct of some dreadful sacrilege in this act, Father Pedro would have rushed forward, when the girl's voice struck his ear. He stopped, breathless. It was not Francisco, but Juanita, the little *mestiza*.

"But are you sure you are not pretending to love me now, as you pretended to think I was the *muchacha* you had run away with and lost? Are you sure it is not pity for the deceit you practiced upon me—upon Don Juan—upon poor Father Pedro?"

It seemed as if Cranch had tried to answer with a kiss, for the girl drew suddenly away from him with a coquettish fling of the black braids, and whipped her little brown hands behind her.

"Well, look here," said Cranch, with the same easy, good-natured, practical directness which the priest remembered, and which would have passed for philosophy in a more thoughtful man, "put it squarely, then. In the first place, it was Don Juan and the alcalde who first suggested you might be the child."

"But you have said you knew it was Francisco all the time," interrupted Juanita.

"I did; but when I found the priest would not assist me at first, and admit that the acolyte was a girl, I preferred to let him think I was deceived in giving a fortune to another, and leave it to his own conscience to permit it or frustrate it. I was right. I reckon it was pretty hard on the old man, at his time of life, and wrapped up as he was in the girl; but at the moment he came up to the scratch like a man."

"And to save him you have deceived me? Thank you, Señor," said the girl with a mock curtsey.

"I reckon I preferred to have you for a wife than a daughter," said Cranch, "if that's what you mean. When you know me better, Juanita," he continued, gravely, "you'll know that I would never have let you believe I sought in you the one if I had not hoped to find in you the other."

"*Bueno!* And when did you have that pretty hope?"

"When I first saw you."

"And that was—two weeks ago."

"A year ago, Juanita. When Francisco visited you at the rancho. I followed and saw you."

Juanita looked at him a moment, and then suddenly darted at him, caught him by the lapels of his coat and shook him like a terrier.

"Are you sure that you did not love that Francisco? Speak!" (She shook him again.) "Swear that you did not follow her!"

"But—I did," said Cranch, laughing and shaking between the clenching of the little hands.

"Judas Iscariot! Swear you do not love her all this while."

"But, Juanita!"

"Swear!"

Cranch swore. Then to Father Pedro's intense astonishment she drew the American's face towards her own by the ears and kissed him.

"But you might have loved her, and married a fortune," said Juanita, after a pause.

"Where would have been my reparation—my duty?" returned Cranch, with a laugh.

"Reparation enough for her to have had you," said Juanita, with that rapid disloyalty of one loving woman to another in an emergency. This provoked another kiss from Cranch, and then Juanita said demurely,—

"But we are far from the trail. Let us return, or we shall miss Father Pedro. Are you sure he will come?"

"A week ago he promised to be here to see the proofs to-day."

The voices were growing fainter and fainter; they were returning to the trail.

Father Pedro remained motionless. A week ago! Was it a week ago since—since what? And what had he been doing here? Listening! He! Father Pedro, listening like an idle *peon* to the confidences of two lovers. But they had talked of him, of his crime, and the man had

pitied him. Why did he not speak? Why
did he not call after them? He tried to
raise his voice. It sank in his throat with
a horrible choking sensation. The nearest heads
of oats began to nod to him, he felt himself swaying backwards and forwards. He fell
—heavily, down, down, down, from the summit
of the mountain to the floor of the Mission
chapel, and there he lay in the dark.

.   .   .   .

"He moves."

"Blessed Saint Anthony preserve him!"

It was Antonio's voice, it was José's arm, it
was the field of wild oats, the sky above his head,
—all unchanged.

"What has happened?" said the priest feebly.

"A giddiness seized your reverence just now,
as we were coming to seek you."

"And you met no one?"

"No one, your reverence."

Father Pedro passed his hand across his forehead.

"But who are these?" he said, pointing to
two figures who now appeared upon the trail.

Antonio turned.

"It is the Americano, Señor Cranch, and his
adopted daughter, the *mestiza* Juanita, seeking
your reverence, methinks."

"Ah!" said Father Pedro.

Cranch came forward and greeted the priest cordially. "It was kind of you, Father Pedro," he said, meaningly, with a significant glance at José and Antonio, "to come so far to bid me and my adopted daughter farewell. We depart when the tide serves, but not before you partake of our hospitality in yonder cottage."

Father Pedro gazed at Cranch and then at Juanita.

"I see," he stammered. "But she goes not alone. She will be strange at first. She takes some friend, perhaps—some companion?" he continued, tremulously.

"A very old and dear one, Father Pedro, who is waiting for us now."

He led the way to a little white cottage, so little and white and recent, that it seemed a mere fleck of sea foam cast on the sands. Disposing of José and Antonio in the neighboring workshop and outbuildings, he assisted the venerable Sanchicha to dismount, and, together with Father Pedro and Juanita, entered a white palisaded enclosure beside the cottage, and halted before what appeared to be a large, folding trap-door, covering a slight sandy mound. It was locked with a padlock; beside it stood the American alcalde and Don Juan Briones. Father Pedro looked hastily around for another figure, but it was not there.

"Gentlemen," began Cranch, in his practical business way, "I reckon you all know we've come here to identify a young lady, who"—he hesitated—"was lately under the care of Father Pedro, with a foundling picked up on this shore fifteen years ago by an Indian woman. How this foundling came here, and how I was concerned in it, you all know. I've told everybody here how I scrambled ashore, leaving that baby in the dingy, supposing it would be picked up by the boat pursuing me. I've told some of you," he looked at Father Pedro, "how I first discovered, from one of the men, three years ago, that the child was not found by its father. But I have never told any one, before now, I *knew* it was picked up here.

"I never could tell the exact locality where I came ashore, for the fog was coming on as it is now. But two years ago I came up with a party of gold hunters to work these sands. One day, digging near this creek, I struck something embedded deep below the surface. Well, gentlemen, it wasn't gold, but something worth more to me than gold or silver. Here it is."

At a sign the alcalde unlocked the doors and threw them open. They disclosed an irregular trench, in which, filled with sand, lay the half-excavated stern of a boat.

"It was the dingy of the Trinidad, gentlemen; you can still read her name. I found hidden away, tucked under the stern sheets, mouldy and water-worn, some clothes that I recognized to be the baby's. I knew then that the child had been taken away alive for some purpose, and the clothes were left so that she should carry no trace with her. I recognized the hand of an Indian. I set to work quietly. I found Sanchicha here, she confessed to finding a baby, but what she had done with it she would not at first say. But since then she has declared before the alcalde that she gave it to Father Pedro, of San Carmel, and that here it stands—Francisco that was! Francisca that it is!"

He stepped aside to make way for a tall girl, who had approached from the cottage.

Father Pedro had neither noticed the concluding words nor the movement of Cranch. His eyes were fixed upon the imbecile Sanchicha,—Sanchicha, on whom, to render his rebuke more complete, the Deity seemed to have worked a miracle, and restored intelligence to eye and lip. He passed his hand tremblingly across his forehead, and turned away, when his eye fell upon the last comer.

It was she. The moment he had longed for and dreaded had come. She stood there, animated, handsome, filled with a hurtful consciousness in her new charms, her fresh finery, and the pitiable trinkets that had supplanted her scapulary, and which played under her foolish fingers. The past had no place in her preoccupied mind; her bright eyes were full of eager anticipation of a substantial future. The incarnation of a frivolous world, even as she extended one hand to him in half-coquettish embarrassment she arranged the folds of her dress with the other. At the touch of her fingers, he felt himself growing old and cold. Even the penance of parting, which he had looked forward to, was denied him; there was no longer sympathy enough for sorrow. He thought of the empty chorister's robe in the little cell, but not now with regret. He only trembled to think of the flesh that he had once caused to inhabit it.

"That's all, gentlemen," broke in the practical voice of Cranch. "Whether there are proofs enough to make Francisca the heiress of her father's wealth, the lawyers must say. I reckon it's enough for me that they give me the chance of repairing a wrong by taking her father's place. After all, it was a mere chance."

"It was the will of God," said Father Pedro, solemnly.

They were the last words he addressed them. For when the fog had begun to creep inshore, hastening their departure, he only answered their farewells by a silent pressure of the hand, mute lips, and far-off eyes.

When the sound of their laboring oars grew fainter, he told Antonio to lead him and San-chicha again to the buried boat. There he bade her kneel beside him. "We will do penance here, thou and I, daughter," he said gravely. When the fog had drawn its curtain gently around the strange pair, and sea and shore were blotted out, he whispered, "Tell me, it was even so, was it not, daughter, on the night she came?" When the distant clatter of blocks and rattle of cordage came from the unseen vessel, now standing out to sea, he whispered again, "So, this is what thou didst hear, even then." And so during the night he marked, more or less audibly to the half-conscious woman at his side, the low whisper of the waves, the murmur of the far-off breakers, the lightening and thickening of the fog, the phantoms of moving shapes, and the slow coming of the dawn. And when the morning sun had rent the veil over land and sea, Antonio and José found him, haggard, but erect, beside the trembling old woman, with a blessing on his lips, pointing to the horizon where a single sail still glimmered:—

"Va Usted con Dios."

A BLUE GRASS PENELOPE

SHE was barely twenty-three years old. It is probable that up to that age, and the beginning of this episode, her life had been uneventful. Born to the easy mediocrity of such compensating extremes as a small farm-house and large lands, a good position and no society, in that vast grazing district of Kentucky known as the "Blue Grass" region, all the possibilities of a Western American girl's existence lay before her. A piano in the bare-walled house, the latest patented mower in the limitless meadows, and a silk dress sweeping the rough floor of the unpainted "meeting-house" were already the promise of those possibilities. Beautiful she was, but the power of that beauty was limited by being equally shared with her few neighbors. There were small, narrow, arched feet besides her own that trod the uncarpeted floors of outlying log-cabins with

equal grace and dignity; bright, clearly opened
eyes that were equally capable of looking unabashed upon princes and potentates, as a few
later did, and the heiress of the county judge
read her own beauty without envy in the frank
glances and unlowered crest of the blacksmith's
daughter. Eventually she had married the male
of her species, a young stranger, who, as schoolmaster in the nearest town, had utilized to some
local extent a scant capital of education. In
obedience to the unwritten law of the West,
after the marriage was celebrated the doors of
the ancestral home cheerfully opened, and bride
and bridegroom issued forth, without regret and
without sentiment, to seek the further possibilities of a life beyond these already too familiar
voices. With their departure for California as
Mr. and Mrs. Spencer Tucker, the parental nest
in the Blue Grass meadows knew them no more.

They submitted with equal cheerfulness to
the privations and excesses of their new conditions. Within three years the schoolmaster developed into a lawyer and capitalist, the Blue
Grass bride supplying a grace and ease to these
transitions that were all her own. She softened
the abruptness of sudden wealth, mitigated the
austerities of newly acquired power, and made
the most glaring incongruity picturesque. Only
one thing seemed to limit their progress in the

region of these possibilities. They were childless. It was as if they had exhausted the future
in their own youth, leaving little or nothing for
another generation to do.

A southwesterly storm was beating against
the dressing-room windows of their new house
in one of the hilly suburbs of San Francisco,
and threatening the unseasonable frivolity of
the stucco ornamentation of cornice and balcony. Mrs. Tucker had been called from the
contemplation of the dreary prospect without
by the arrival of a visitor. On entering the
drawing-room she found him engaged in a half-
admiring, half-resentful examination of its new
furniture and hangings. Mrs. Tucker at once
recognized Mr. Calhoun Weaver, a former Blue
Grass neighbor; with swift feminine intuition
she also felt that his slight antagonism was
likely to be transferred from her furniture to
herself. Waiving it with the lazy amiability
of Southern indifference, she welcomed him by
the familiarity of a Christian name.

"I reckoned that mebbee you opined old Blue
Grass friends wouldn't naturally hitch on to
them fancy doins," he said, glancing around
the apartment to avoid her clear eyes, as if resolutely setting himself against the old charm of
her manner as he had against the more recent

glory of her surroundings, "but I thought I'd
just drop in for the sake of old times."

"Why shouldn't you, Cal?" said Mrs. Tucker
with a frank smile.

"Especially as I'm going up to Sacramento
to-night with some influential friends," he continued, with an ostentation calculated to resist
the assumption of her charms and her furniture. "Senator Dyce of Kentucky, and his
cousin Judge Briggs; perhaps you know 'em,
or may be Spencer—I mean Mr. Tucker—
does."

"I reckon," said Mrs. Tucker smiling; "but
tell me something about the boys and girls at
Vineville, and about yourself. *You're* looking
well, and right smart too." She paused to give
due emphasis to this latter recognition of a huge
gold chain with which her visitor was somewhat ostentatiously trifling.

"I didn't know as you cared to hear anything
about Blue Grass," he returned, a little abashed.
"I've been away from there some time myself,"
he added, his uneasy vanity taking fresh alarm
at the faint suspicion of patronage on the part
of his hostess. "They're doin' well, though;
perhaps as well as some others."

"And you're not married yet," continued
Mrs. Tucker, oblivious of the innuendo. "Ah,
Cal," she added archly, "I am afraid you are

as fickle as ever. What poor girl in Vineville
have you left pining?"

The simple face of the man before her flushed
with foolish gratification at this old-fashioned,
ambiguous flattery. "Now look yer, Belle," he
said, chuckling, "if you're talking of old times
and you think I bear malice agin Spencer,
why—"

But Mrs. Tucker interrupted what might
have been an inopportune sentimental retrospect with a finger of arch but languid warning.
"That will do! I'm dying to know all about
it, and you must stay to dinner and tell me.
It's right mean you can't see Spencer too; but
he isn't back from Sacramento yet."

Grateful as a *tête-à-tête* with his old neighbor in her more prosperous surroundings would
have been, if only for the sake of later gossip-
ing about it, he felt it would be inconsistent
with his pride and his assumption of present business. More than that, he was uneasily conscious
that in Mrs. Tucker's simple and unaffected
manner there was a greater superiority than he
had ever noticed during their previous acquaintance. He would have felt kinder to her had
she shown any "airs and graces," which he
could have commented upon and forgiven. He
stammered some vague excuse of preoccupation,
yet lingered in the hope of saying something

which, if not aggressively unpleasant, might at least transfer to her indolent serenity some of his own irritation. "I reckon," he said, as he moved hesitatingly towards the door, "that Spencer has made himself easy and secure in them business risks he's taking. That 'ere Alameda ditch affair they're talking so much about is a mighty big thing, rather *too* big if it ever got to falling back on him. But I suppose he's accustomed to take risks?"

"Of course he is," said Mrs. Tucker gayly. "He married *me*."

The visitor smiled feebly, but was not equal to the opportunity offered for gallant repudiation. "But suppose *you* ain't accustomed to risks?"

"Why not? I married *him*," said Mrs. Tucker.

Mr. Calhoun Weaver was human, and succumbed to this last charming audacity. He broke into a noisy but genuine laugh, shook Mrs. Tucker's hand with effusion, said, "Now that's regular Blue Grass and no mistake!" and retreated under cover of his hilarity. In the hall he made a rallying stand to repeat confidentially to the servant who had overheard them: "Blue Grass, all over, you bet your life," and, opening the door, was apparently swallowed up in the tempest.

Mrs. Tucker's smile kept her lips until she had returned to her room, and even then languidly shone in her eyes for some minutes after, as she gazed abstractedly from her window on the storm-tossed bay in the distance. Perhaps some girlish vision of the peaceful Blue Glass plain momentarily usurped the prospect; but it is to be doubted if there was much romance in that retrospect, or that it was more interesting to her than the positive and sharply cut outlines of the practical life she now held. Howbeit she soon forgot this fancy in lazily watching a boat that, in the teeth of the gale, was beating round Alcatraz Island. Although at times a mere blank speck on the gray waste of foam, a closer scrutiny showed it to be one of those lateen-rigged Italian fishing boats that so often flecked the distant bay. Lost in the sudden darkening of rain, or reappearing beneath the lifted curtain of the squall, she watched it weather the island, and then turn its laboring but persistent course towards the open channel. A rent in the Indian-inky sky, that showed the narrowing portals of the Golden Gate beyond, revealed, as unexpectedly, the destination of the little craft, a tall ship that hitherto lay hidden in the mist of the Saucelito shore. As the distance lessened between boat and ship, they were again lost in the downward swoop of another squall. When it lifted, the ship was creeping under the headland towards the open sea, but the boat was gone. Mrs. Tucker in vain rubbed the pane with her handkerchief; it had vanished. Meanwhile the ship, as she neared the Gate, drew out from the protecting headland, stood outlined for a moment with spars and canvas hearsed in black against the lurid rent in the horizon, and then seemed to sink slowly into the heaving obscurity beyond. A sudden onset of rain against the windows obliterated the remaining prospect; the entrance of a servant completed the diversion.

"Captain Poindexter, ma'am!"

Mrs. Tucker lifted her pretty eyebrows interrogatively. Captain Poindexter was a legal friend of her husband, and had dined there frequently; nevertheless she asked: "Did you tell him Mr. Tucker was not at home?"

"Yes, 'm."

"Did he ask for *me?*"

"Yes, 'm."

"Tell him I'll be down directly."

Mrs. Tucker's quiet face did not betray the fact that this second visitor was even less interesting than the first. In her heart she did not like Captain Poindexter. With a clever woman's instinct she had early detected the fact that he had a superior, stronger nature than

her husband; as a loyal wife, she secretly resented the occasional unconscious exhibition of
this fact on the part of his intimate friend in
their familiar intercourse. Added to this slight
jealousy, there was a certain moral antagonism
between herself and the captain which none but
themselves knew. They were both philosophers,
but Mrs. Tucker's serene and languid optimism
would not tolerate the compassionate and kind-
hearted pessimisms of the lawyer. "Knowing
what Jack Poindexter does of human nature,"
her husband had once said, "it's mighty fine
in him to be so kind and forgiving. You ought
to like him better, Belle." "And qualify myself to be forgiven," said the lady pertly. "I
don't see what you're driving at, Belle; I give
it up," had responded the puzzled husband.
Mrs. Tucker kissed his high but foolish forehead tenderly, and said: "I'm glad you don't,
dear."

Meanwhile her second visitor had, like the
first, employed the interval in a critical survey
of the glories of the new furniture, but with
apparently more compassion than resentment in
his manner. Once only had his expression
changed. Over the fireplace hung a large photograph of Mr. Spencer Tucker. It was re-
touched, refined, and idealized in the highest
style of that polite and diplomatic art. As

Captain Poindexter looked upon the fringed hazel eyes, the drooping raven moustache, the clustering ringlets, and the Byronic full throat and turned-down collar of his friend, a smile of exhausted humorous tolerance and affectionate impatience curved his lips. "Well, you *are* a fool, aren't you?" he apostrophized it half-audibly.

He was standing before the picture as she entered. Even in the trying contiguity of that peerless work he would have been called a fine-looking man. As he advanced to greet her, it was evident that his military title was not one of the mere fanciful sobriquets of the locality. In his erect figure and the disciplined composure of limb and attitude there were still traces of the refined academic rigors of West Point. The pliant adaptability of Western civilization which enabled him, three years before, to leave the army and transfer his executive ability to the more profitable profession of the law, had loosed sash and shoulder-strap, but had not entirely removed the restraint of the one, or the bearing of the other.

"Spencer is in Sacramento," began Mrs. Tucker in languid explanation, after the first greetings were over.

"I knew he was not here," replied Captain Poindexter gently, as he drew the proffered

chair towards her, "but this is business that
concerns you both." He stopped and glanced
upwards at the picture. "I suppose you know
nothing of his business? Of course not," he
added reassuringly, "nothing, absolutely nothing, certainly." He said this so kindly, and
yet so positively, as if to promptly dispose of
that question before going further, that she
assented mechanically. "Well, then, he's taken
some big risks in the way of business, and—
well, things have gone bad with him, you know.
Very bad! Really, they couldn't be worse! Of
course it was dreadfully rash and all that," he
went on, as if commenting upon the amusing
waywardness of a child; "but the result is the
usual smash-up of everything, money, credit,
and all!" He laughed and added: "Yes, he's
got cut off—mules and baggage regularly routed
and dispersed! I'm in earnest." He raised his
eyebrows and frowned slightly, as if to deprecate any corresponding hilarity on the part of
Mrs. Tucker, or any attempt to make *too* light
of the subject, and then rising, placed his hands
behind his back, beamed half-humorously upon
her from beneath her husband's picture, and
repeated: "That's so."

Mrs. Tucker instinctively knew that he spoke
the truth, and that it was impossible for him
to convey it in any other than his natural man-

ner; but between the shock and the singular influence of that manner she could at first only say, "You don't mean it!" fully conscious of the utter inanity of the remark, and that it seemed scarcely less cold-blooded than his own.

Poindexter, still smiling, nodded.

She arose with an effort. She had recovered from the first shock, and pride lent her a determined calmness that more than equaled Poindexter's easy philosophy.

"Where is he?" she asked.

"At sea, and I hope by this time where he can not be found or followed."

Was her momentary glimpse of the outgoing ship a coincidence, or only a vision? She was confused and giddy, but, mastering her weakness, she managed to continue in a lower voice:

"You have no message for me from him? He told you nothing to tell me?"

"Nothing, absolutely nothing," replied Poindexter. "It was as much as he could do, I reckon, to get fairly away before the crash came."

"Then you did not see him go?"

"Well, no," said Poindexter. "I'd hardly have managed things in this way." He checked himself and added, with a forgiving smile, "But he was the best judge of what he needed, of course."

"I suppose I will hear from him," she said quietly, "as soon as he is safe. He must have had enough else to think about, poor fellow."

She said this so naturally and quietly that Poindexter was deceived. He had no idea that the collected woman before him was thinking only of solitude and darkness, of her own room, and madly longing to be there. He said, "Yes, I dare say," in quite another voice, and glanced at the picture. But as she remained standing, he continued more earnestly, "I didn't come here to tell you what you might read in the newspapers to-morrow morning, and what everybody might tell you. Before that time I want you to do something to save a fragment of your property from the ruin; do you understand? I want you to make a rally, and bring off something in good order."

"For him?" said Mrs. Tucker, with brightening eyes.

"Well, yes, of course—if you like—but as if for yourself. Do you know the Rancho de los Cuervos?"

"I do."

"It's almost the only bit of real property your husband hasn't sold, mortgaged, or pledged. Why it was exempt, or whether only forgotten, I can't say."

"I'll tell you why," said Mrs. Tucker, with a slight return of color. "It was the first land we ever bought, and Spencer always said it should be mine and he would build a new house on it."

Captain Poindexter smiled and nodded at the picture. "Oh, he did say that, did he? Well, *that's* evidence. But you see he never gave you the deed, and by sunrise to-morrow his creditors will attach it—unless—"

"Unless—" repeated Mrs. Tucker, with kindling eyes.

"Unless," continued Captain Poindexter, "they happen to find *you* in possession."

"I'll go," said Mrs. Tucker.

"Of course you will," returned Poindexter, pleasantly; "only, as it's a big contract to take, suppose we see how you can fill it. It's forty miles to Los Cuervos, and you can't trust yourself to steamboat or stage-coach. The steamboat left an hour ago."

"If I had only known this then!" ejaculated Mrs. Tucker.

"*I* knew it, but you had company then," said Poindexter, with ironical gallantry, "and I wouldn't disturb you." Without saying how he knew it, he continued, "In the stage-coach you might be recognized. You must go in a private conveyance and alone; even I can not go with you, for I must go on before and meet you there. Can you drive forty miles?"

Mrs. Tucker lifted up her abstracted pretty lids. "I once drove fifty—at home," she returned simply.

"Good! and I dare say you did it then for fun. Do it now for something real and personal, as we lawyers say. You will have relays and a plan of the road. It's rough weather for a *pasear*, but all the better for that. You'll have less company on the road."

"How soon can I go?" she asked.

"The sooner the better. I've arranged everything for you already," he continued with a laugh. "Come now, that's a compliment to you, isn't it?" He smiled a moment in her steadfast, earnest face, and then said, more gravely, "You'll do. Now listen."

He then carefully detailed his plan. There was so little of excitement or mystery in their manner that the servant, who returned to light the gas, never knew that the ruin and bankruptcy of the house was being told before her, or that its mistress was planning her secret flight.

"Good afternoon; I will see you to-morrow then," said Poindexter, raising his eyes to hers as the servant opened the door for him.

"Good afternoon," repeated Mrs. Tucker,

quietly answering his look. "You need not light the gas in my room, Mary," she continued in the same tone of voice as the door closed upon him; "I shall lie down for a few moments, and then I may run over to the Robinsons for the evening."

She regained her room composedly. The longing desire to bury her head in her pillow and "think out" her position had gone. She did not apostrophize her fate, she did not weep; few real women do in the access of calamity, or when there is anything else to be done. She felt that she knew it all; she believed she had sounded the profoundest depths of the disaster, and seemed already so old in her experience that she almost fancied she had been prepared for it. Perhaps she did not fully appreciate it; to a life like hers it was only an incident, the mere turning of a page of the illimitable book of youth; the breaking up of what she now felt had become a monotony. In fact, she was not quite sure she had ever been satisfied with their present success. Had it brought her all she expected? She wanted to say this to her husband, not only to comfort him, poor fellow, but that they might come to a better understanding of life in the future. She was not perhaps different from other loving women who, believing in this unattainable goal of mat-

rimony, have sought it in the various episodes
of fortune or reverses, in the bearing of children, or the loss of friends. In her childless
experience there was no other life that had
taken root in her circumstances and might suffer transplantation; only she and her husband
could lose or profit by the change. The "perfect" understanding would come under other
conditions than these.

She would have gone superstitiously to the
window to gaze in the direction of the vanished
ship, but another instinct restrained her. She
would put aside all yearning for him until she
had done something to help him, and earned
the confidence he seemed to have withheld. Perhaps it was pride—perhaps she never really
believed his exodus was distant or complete.

With a full knowledge that to-morrow the
various ornaments and pretty trifles around her
would be in the hands of the law, she gathered
only a few necessaries for her flight and some
familiar personal trinkets. I am constrained
to say that this self-abnegation was more fastidious than moral. She had no more idea of
the ethics of bankruptcy than any other charming woman; she simply did not like to take with
her any contagious memory of the chapter of
the life just closing. She glanced around the
home she was leaving without a lingering re-

gret; there was no sentiment of tradition or
custom that might be destroyed; her roots lay
too near the surface to suffer from dislocation;
the happiness of her childless union had de-
pended upon no domestic centre, nor was its
flame sacred to any local hearthstone. It was
without a sigh that, when night had fully fallen,
she slipped unnoticed down the staircase. At
the door of the drawing-room she paused and
then entered with the first guilty feeling of
shame she had known that evening. Looking
stealthily around she mounted a chair before
her husband's picture, kissed the irreproach-
able moustache hurriedly, said, "You foolish
darling, you!" and slipped out again. With
this touching indorsement of the views of a
rival philosopher, she closed the door softly and
left her home forever.

CHAPTER II.

THE wind and rain had cleared the unfrequented suburb of any observant lounger, and
the darkness, lit only by far-spaced, gusty
lamps, hid her hastening figure. She had barely
crossed the second street when she heard the
quick clatter of hoofs behind her; a buggy
drove up to the curbstone, and Poindexter

leaped out. She entered quickly, but for a moment he still held the reins of the impatient horse. "He's rather fresh," he said, eying her keenly; "are you sure you can manage him?"

"Give me the reins," she said simply.

He placed them in the two firm, well-shaped hands that reached from the depths of the vehicle, and was satisfied. Yet he lingered.

"It's rough work for a lone woman," he said, almost curtly. "*I* can't go with you, but, speak frankly, is there any man you know whom you can trust well enough to take? It's not too late yet; think a moment!"

He paused over the buttoning of the leather apron of the vehicle.

"No, there is none," answered the voice from the interior; "and it's better so. Is all ready?"

"One moment more." He had recovered his half-bantering manner. "You *have* a friend and countryman already with you, do you know? Your horse is Blue Grass. Good night."

With these words ringing in her ears she began her journey. The horse, as if eager to maintain the reputation which his native district had given his race, as well as the race of the pretty woman behind him, leaped impatiently forward. But pulled together by the fine and firm fingers that seemed to guide rather

than check his exuberance, he presently struck
into the long, swinging pace of his kind, and
kept it throughout without "break" or accelera-
tion.   Over the paved streets the light buggy
rattled, and the slender shafts danced around
his smooth barrel, but when they touched the
level high-road, horse and vehicle slipped forward through the night, a swift and noiseless
phantom.   Mrs. Tucker could see his graceful
back dimly rising and falling before her with
tireless rhythm, and could feel the intelligent
pressure of his mouth until it seemed the re-
sponsive grasp of a powerful but kindly hand.
The faint glow of conquest came to her cold
cheek; the slight stirrings of pride moved her
preoccupied heart.   A soft light filled her hazel
eyes.   A desolate woman, bereft of husband
and home, and flying through storm and night,
she knew not where, she still leaned forward
towards her horse.   "Was he Blue Grass, then,
dear old boy ?" she gently cooed at him in the
darkness.   He evidently *was,* and responded by
blowing her an ostentatious equine kiss.   "And
he would be good to his own forsaken Belle,"
she murmured caressingly, "and wouldn't let
any one harm her ?"   But here, overcome by
the lazy witchery of her voice, he shook his
head so violently that Mrs. Tucker, after the
fashion of her sex, had the double satisfaction

of demurely restraining the passion she had
evoked.

To avoid the more traveled thoroughfare,
while the evening was still early, it had been
arranged that she should at first take a less
direct but less frequented road. This was a
famous pleasure-drive from San Francisco, a
graveled and sanded stretch of eight miles to
the sea and an ultimate "cocktail," in a "stately
pleasure-dome decreed" among the surf and rocks
of the Pacific shore. It was deserted now, and
left to the unobstructed sweep of the wind and
rain. Mrs. Tucker would not have chosen this
road. With the instinctive jealousy of a bucolic
inland race born by great rivers, she did not
like the sea; and again the dim and dreary
waste tended to recall the vision connected with
her husband's flight, upon which she had resolutely shut her eyes. But when she had reached
it the road suddenly turned, following the trend
of the beach, and she was exposed to the full
power of its dread fascinations. The combined
roar of sea and shore was in her ears; as the
direct force of the gale had compelled her to
furl the protecting hood of the buggy to keep
the light vehicle from oversetting or drifting
to leeward, she could no longer shut out the
heaving chaos on the right from which the pallid ghosts of dead and dying breakers dimly

rose and sank as if in awful salutation. At
times through the darkness a white sheet appeared spread before the path and beneath the
wheels of the buggy, which, when withdrawn
with a reluctant hiss, seemed striving to drag
the exhausted beach seaward with it. But the
blind terror of her horse, who swerved at every
sweep of the surge, shamed her own half-super-
stitious fears, and with the effort to control his
alarm she regained her own self-possession, albeit with eyelashes wet not altogether with the
salt spray from the sea. This was followed by
a reaction, perhaps stimulated by her victory
over the beaten animal, when for a time, she
knew not how long, she felt only a mad sense
of freedom and power; oblivious of even her
sorrows, her lost home and husband, and with
intense feminine consciousness she longed to
be a man. She was scarcely aware that the
track turned again inland until the beat of the
horse's hoofs on the firm ground and an accel-
eration of speed showed her she had left the
beach and the mysterious sea behind her, and
she remembered that she was near the end of
the first stage of her journey. Half an hour
later the twinkling lights of the roadside inn
where she was to change horses rose out of the
darkness.

Happily for her, the ostler considered the

horse, who had a local reputation, of more im-
portance than the unknown muffled figure in
the shadow of the unfurled hood, and confined
his attention to the animal. After a careful
examination of his feet and a few comments
addressed solely to the superior creation,
he led him away. Mrs. Tucker would have
liked to part more affectionately from her four-
footed compatriot, and felt a sudden sense of
loneliness at the loss of her new friend, but a
recollection of certain cautions of Captain Poindexter's kept her mute. Nevertheless, the ostler's ostentatious adjuration of "Now then,
aren't you going to bring out that mustang for
the Señora?" puzzled her. It was not until
the fresh horse was put to, and she had flung
a piece of gold into the attendant's hand, that
the "*Gracias*" of his unmistakable Saxon speech
revealed to her the reason of the lawyer's caution. Poindexter had evidently represented her
to these people as a native Californian who did
not speak English. In her inconsistency her
blood took fire at this first suggestion of deceit,
and burned in her face. Why should he try to
pass her off as anybody else? Why should she
not use her own, her husband's name? She
stopped and bit her lip.

It was but the beginning of an uneasy train
of thought. She suddenly found herself think-

ing of her visitor, Calhoun Weaver, and not
pleasantly. He would hear of their ruin to-
morrow, perhaps of her own flight. He would remember his visit, and what would he think of
her deceitful frivolity? Would he believe that
she was then ignorant of the failure? It was
her first sense of any accountability to others
than herself, but even then it was rather owing
to an uneasy consciousness of what her husband
must feel if he were subjected to the criticisms
of men like Calhoun. She wondered if others
knew that he had kept her in ignorance of his
flight. Did Poindexter know it, or had he only
entrapped her into the admission? Why had
she not been clever enough to make him think
that she knew it already? For the moment she
hated Poindexter for sharing that secret. Yet
this was again followed by a new impatience
of her husband's want of insight into her ability
to help him. Of course the poor fellow could
not bear to worry her, could not bear to face
such men as Calhoun, or even Poindexter (she
added exultingly to herself), but he might have
sent her a line as he fled, only to prepare her
to meet and combat the shame alone. It did
not occur to her unsophisticated singleness of
nature that she was accepting as an error of
feeling what the world would call cowardly
selfishness.

At midnight the storm lulled and a few stars trembled through the rent clouds. Her eyes had become accustomed to the darkness, and her country instincts, a little overlaid by the urban experiences of the last few years, came again to the surface. She felt the fresh, cool radiation from outlying, upturned fields, the faint, sad odors from dim stretches of pricking grain and quickening leaf, and wondered if at Los Cuervos it might be possible to reproduce the peculiar verdure of her native district. She beguiled her fancy by an ambitious plan of retrieving their fortunes by farming; her comfortable tastes had lately rebelled against the homeless mechanical cultivation of these desolate but teeming Californian acres, and for a moment indulged in a vision of a vine-clad cottage home that in any other woman would have been sentimental. Her cramped limbs aching, she took advantage of the security of the darkness and the familiar contiguity of the fields to get down from the vehicle, gather her skirts together, and run at the head of the mustang, until her chill blood was thawed, night drawing a modest veil over this charming revelation of the nymph and woman. But the sudden shadow of a coyote checked the scouring feet of this swift Camilla, and sent her back precipitately to the buggy. Nevertheless, she was refreshed and able to pursue her journey, until the cold gray of early morning found her at the end of her second stage.

Her route was changed again from the main highway, rendered dangerous by the approach of day and the contiguity of the neighboring *rancheros*. The road was rough and hilly, her new horse and vehicle in keeping with the rudeness of the route—by far the most difficult of her whole journey. The rare wagon tracks that indicated her road were often scarcely discernible; at times they led her through openings in the half-cleared woods, skirted suspicious morasses, painfully climbed the smooth, dome-like hills, or wound along perilous slopes at a dangerous angle. Twice she had to alight and cling to the sliding wheels on one of those treacherous inclines, or drag them from impending ruts or immovable mire. In the growing light she could distinguish the distant, low-lying marshes eaten by encroaching sloughs and insidious channels, and beyond them the faint gray waste of the Lower Bay. A darker peninsula in the marsh she knew to be the extreme boundary of her future home: the Rancho de los Cuervos. In another hour she began to descend to the plain, and once more to approach the main road, which now ran nearly parallel with her track. She scanned it cautiously for any early traveler;

it stretched north and south in apparent un-
ending solitude. She struck into it boldly, and
urged her horse to the top of his speed, until
she reached the cross road that led to the rancho.
But here she paused and allowed the reins to
drop idly on the mustang's back. A singular
and unaccountable irresolution seized her. The
difficulties of her journey were over; the rancho
lay scarcely two miles away; she had achieved
the most important part of her task in the ap-
pointed time, but she hesitated. What had she
come for? She tried to recall Poindexter's
words, even her own enthusiasm, but in vain.
She was going to take possession of her husband's property, she knew, that was all. But
the means she had taken seemed now so exaggerated and mysterious for that simple end that
she began to dread an impending something, or
some vague danger she had not considered, that
she was rushing blindly to meet. Full of this
strange feeling she almost mechanically stopped
her horse as she entered the cross road.

From this momentary hesitation a singular
sound aroused her. It seemed at first like the
swift hurrying by of some viewless courier of
the air, the vague alarm of some invisible flying
herald, or like the inarticulate cry that precedes
a storm. It seemed to rise and fall around her
as if with some changing urgency of purpose.

Raising her eyes she suddenly recognized the
two far-stretching lines of telegraph wire above
her head, and knew the æolian cry of the morning wind along its vibrating chords. But it
brought another and more practical fear to her
active brain. Perhaps even now the telegraph
might be anticipating her! Had Poindexter
thought of that? She hesitated no longer, but
laying the whip on the back of her jaded mustang again hurried forward.

As the level horizon grew more distinct, her
attention was attracted by the white sail of a
small boat lazily threading the sinuous channel
of the slough. It might be Poindexter arriving
by the more direct route from the steamboat
that occasionally lay off the ancient *embarcadero* of the Los Cuervos Rancho. But even
while watching it her quick ear caught the
sound of galloping hoofs behind her. She
turned quickly and saw she was followed by a
horseman. But her momentary alarm was
succeeded by a feeling of relief as she recognized the erect figure and square shoulders of
Poindexter. Yet she could not help thinking that he looked more like a militant scout,
and less like a cautious legal adviser, than
ever.

With unaffected womanliness she rearranged
her slightly disordered hair as he drew up beside

her. "I thought you were in yonder boat," she said.

"Not I," he laughed; "I distanced you by the high road two hours, and have been reconnoitring, until I saw you hesitate at the cross roads."

"But who is in the boat?" asked Mrs. Tucker, partly to hide her embarrassment.

"Only some early Chinese market gardener, I dare say. But you are safe now. You are on your own land. You passed the boundary monument of the rancho five minutes ago. Look! All you see before you is yours from the *embarcadero* to yonder Coast Range."

The tone of half-raillery did not, however, cheer Mrs. Tucker. She shuddered slightly and cast her eyes over the monotonous sea of *tule* and meadow.

"It doesn't look pretty, perhaps," continued Poindexter, "but it's the richest land in the State, and the *embarcadero* will some day be a town. I suppose you'll call it Blue Grassville. But you seem tired!" he said, suddenly dropping his voice to a tone of half-humorous sympathy.

Mrs. Tucker managed to get rid of an impending tear under the pretense of clearing her eyes. "Are we nearly there?" she asked.

"Nearly. You know," he added with the

same half-mischievous, half-sympathizing gayety, "it's not exactly a palace you're coming to.
Hardly. It's the old *casa* that has been deserted for years, but I thought it better you
should go into possession there than take up
your abode at the shanty where your husband's
farm-hands are. No one will know when you
take possession of the *casa,* while the very hour
of your arrival at the shanty would be known;
and if they should make any trouble—"

"If they should make any trouble?" repeated
Mrs. Tucker, lifting her frank, inquiring eyes
to Poindexter.

His horse suddenly rearing from an apparently accidental prick of the spur, it was a
minute or two before he was able to explain.
"I mean if this ever comes up as a matter of
evidence, you know. But here we are!"

What had seemed to be an overgrown mound
rising like an island out of the dead level of the
grassy sea now resolved itself into a collection
of adobe walls, eaten and incrusted with shrubs
and vines, that bore some resemblance to the
usual uninhabited-looking exterior of a Spanish-
American dwelling. Apertures that might have
been lance-shaped windows or only cracks and
fissures in the walls were choked up with weeds
and grass, and gave no passing glimpse of the
interior. Entering a ruinous corral they came

to a second entrance, which proved to be the *patio* or courtyard. The deserted wooden corridor, with beams, rafters, and floors whitened by the eternal sun and wind, contained a few withered leaves, dryly rotting skins, and thongs of leather, as if undisturbed by human care. But among these scattered *débris* of former life and habitation there was no noisome or unclean suggestion of decay. A faint, spiced odor of desiccation filled the bare walls. There was no slime on stone or sun-dried brick. In place of fungus or discolored moisture the dust of efflorescence whitened in the obscured corners. The elements had picked clean the bones of the crumbling tenement ere they should finally absorb it.

A withered old *peon* woman, who in dress, complexion, and fibrous hair might have been an animated fragment of the *débris,* rustled out of a low vaulted passage and welcomed them with a feeble crepitation. Following her into the dim interior Mrs. Tucker was surprised to find some slight attempt at comfort and even adornment in the two or three habitable apartments. They were scrupulously clean and dry, two qualities which in her feminine eyes atoned for poverty of material.

"I could not send anything from San Bruno, the nearest village, without attracting atten-

tion," explained Poindexter; "but if you can
manage to picnic here for a day longer, I'll get
one of our Chinese friends here," he pointed to
the slough, "to bring over, for his return cargo
from across the bay, any necessaries you may
want.   There is no danger of his betraying
you," he added, with an ironical smile; "Chinamen and Indians are, by an ingenious provision
of the statute of California, incapable of giving
evidence against a white person.   You can trust
your handmaiden perfectly—even if she can't
trust *you*.   That is your sacred privilege under
the constitution.   And now, as I expect to catch
the up boat ten miles from hence, I must say
'good-by' until to-morrow night.   I hope to
bring you then some more definite plans for the
future.   The worst is over."   He held her hand
for a moment, and with a graver voice continued, "You have done it very well—do you
know—very well!"

In the slight embarrassment produced by his
sudden change of manner she felt that her
thanks seemed awkward and restrained.   "Don't
thank me," he laughed, with a prompt return
of his former levity, "that's my trade.   I only
advised.   You have saved yourself like a plucky
woman—shall I say like Blue Grass?   Good-
by!"   He mounted his horse, but, as if struck
by an after-thought, wheeled and drew up by

her side again. "If I were you I wouldn't see many strangers for a day or two, and listen to as little news as a woman possibly can." He laughed again, waved her a half-gallant, half-military salute, and was gone. The question she had been trying to frame, regarding the probability of communication with her husband, remained unasked. At least she had saved her pride before him.

Addressing herself to the care of her narrow household, she mechanically put away the few things she had brought with her, and began to readjust the scant furniture. She was a little discomposed at first at the absence of bolts, locks, and even window-fastenings until assured, by Concha's evident inability to comprehend her concern, that they were quite unknown at Los Cuervos. Her slight knowledge of Spanish was barely sufficient to make her wants known, so that the relief of conversation with her only companion was debarred her, and she was obliged to content herself with the sapless, crackling smiles and withered genuflexions that the old woman dropped like dead leaves in her path. It was staring noon when, the house singing like an empty shell in the monotonous wind, she felt she could stand the solitude no longer, and, crossing the glaring *patio* and whistling corridor, made her way to the open gateway.

But the view without seemed to intensify her desolation. The broad expanse of the shadowless plain reached apparently to the Coast Range, trackless and unbroken save by one or two clusters of dwarfed oaks, which at that distance were but mossy excrescences on the surface, barely raised above the dead level. On the other side the marsh took up the monotony and carried it, scarcely interrupted by undefined water-courses, to the faintly marked out horizon line of the remote bay. Scattered and apparently motionless black spots on the meadows that gave a dreary significance to the title of "the Crows" which the rancho bore, and sudden gray clouds of sand-pipers on the marshes, that rose and vanished down the wind, were the only signs of life. Even the white sail of the early morning was gone.

She stood there until the aching of her straining eyes and the stiffening of her limbs in the cold wind compelled her to seek the sheltered warmth of the courtyard. Here she endeavored to make friends with a bright-eyed lizard, who was sunning himself in the corridor; a graceful little creature in blue and gold, from whom she felt at other times she might have fled, but whose beauty and harmlessness solitude had made known to her. With misplaced kindness she tempted it with bread-crumbs, with no other

effect than to stiffen it into stony astonishment.
She wondered if she should become like the
prisoners she had read of in books, who poured
out their solitary affections on noisome creatures, and she regretted even the mustang, which
with the buggy had disappeared under the
charge of some unknown retainer on her arrival. Was she not a prisoner? The shutterless windows, yawning doors, and open gate
refuted her suggestion, but the encompassing
solitude and trackless waste still held her captive. Poindexter had told her it was four miles
to the shanty; she might walk there. Why had
she given her word that she would remain at
the rancho until he returned?

The long day crept monotonously away, and
she welcomed the night which shut out the
dreary prospect. But it brought no cessation of
the harassing wind without, nor surcease of the
nervous irritation its perpetual and even activity
wrought upon her. It haunted her pillow even
in her exhausted sleep, and seemed to impatiently beckon her to rise and follow it. It
brought her feverish dreams of her husband,
footsore and weary, staggering forward under
its pitiless lash and clamorous outcry; she would
have gone to his assistance, but when she reached
his side and held out her arms to him it hurried her past with merciless power, and, bear-

ing her away, left him hopelessly behind. It was broad day when she awoke. The usual night showers of the waning rainy season had left no trace in sky or meadow; the fervid morning sun had already dried the *patio;* only the restless, harrying wind remained.

Mrs. Tucker arose with a resolve. She had learned from Concha on the previous evening that a part of the shanty was used as a *tienda* or shop for the laborers and *rancheros.* Under the necessity of purchasing some articles, she would go there and for a moment mingle with those people, who would not recognize her. Even if they did, her instinct told her it would be less to be feared than the hopeless uncertainty of another day. As she left the house the wind seemed to seize her as in her dream, and hurry her along with it, until in a few moments the walls of the low *casa* sank into the earth again and she was alone, but for the breeze on the solitary plain. The level distance glittered in the sharp light, a few crows with slant wings dipped and ran down the wind before her, and a passing gleam on the marsh was explained by the far-off cry of a curlew.

She had walked for an hour, upheld by the stimulus of light and morning air, when the cluster of scrub oaks, which was her destination, opened enough to show two rambling sheds, before one of which was a wooden platform containing a few barrels and bones. As she approached nearer, she could see that one or two horses were tethered under the trees, that their riders were lounging by a horse-trough, and that over an open door the word *Tienda* was rudely painted on a board, and as rudely illustrated by the wares displayed at door and window. Accustomed as she was to the poverty of frontier architecture, even the crumbling walls of the old *hacienda* she had just left seemed picturesque to the rigid angles of the thin, blank, unpainted shell before her. One of the loungers, who was reading a newspaper aloud as she advanced, put it aside and stared at her; there was an evident commotion in the shop as she stepped upon the platform, and when she entered, with breathless lips and beating heart, she found herself the object of a dozen curious eyes. Her quick pride resented the scrutiny and recalled her courage, and it was with a slight coldness in her usual lazy indifference that she leaned over the counter and asked for the articles she wanted.

The request was followed by a dead silence. Mrs. Tucker repeated it with some *hauteur*.

"I reckon you don't seem to know this store is in the hands of the sheriff," said one of the loungers.

Mrs. Tucker was not aware of it.

"Well, I don't know any one who's a better right to know than Spence Tucker's wife," said another with a coarse laugh. The laugh was echoed by the others. Mrs. Tucker saw the pit into which she had deliberately walked, but did not flinch.

"Is there any one to serve here?" she asked, turning her clear eyes full upon the bystanders.

"You'd better ask the sheriff. He was the last one to *sarve* here. He sarved an attachment," replied the inevitable humorist of all Californian assemblages.

"Is he here?" asked Mrs. Tucker, disregarding the renewed laughter which followed this subtle witticism.

The loungers at the door made way for one of their party, who was half dragged, half pushed into the shop. "Here he is," said half a dozen eager voices, in the fond belief that his presence might impart additional humor to the situation. He cast a deprecating glance at Mrs. Tucker and said, "It's so, madam! This yer place *is* attached; but if there's anything you're wanting, why I reckon, boys,"—he turned half appealingly to the crowd,—"we could oblige a lady." There was a vague sound of angry opposition and remonstrance from the back door of the shop, but the majority, partly overcome by Mrs. Tucker's beauty, assented. "Only," continued the officer explanatorily, "ez these yer goods are in the hands of the creditors, they ought to be represented by an equivalent in money. If you're expecting they should be charged—"

"But I wish to *pay* for them," interrupted Mrs. Tucker, with a slight flush of indignation; "I have the money."

"Oh, I bet you have!" screamed a voice, as, overturning all opposition, the malcontent at the back door, in the shape of an infuriated woman, forced her way into the shop. "I'll bet you have the money! Look at her, boys! Look at the wife of the thief, with the stolen money in diamonds in her ears and rings on her fingers. *She's* got money if *we've* none. *She* can pay for what she fancies, if we haven't a cent to redeem the bed that's stolen from under us. Oh yes, buy it all, Mrs. Spencer Tucker! buy the whole shop, Mrs. Spencer Tucker, do you hear? And if you ain't satisfied then, buy my clothes, my wedding ring, the only things your husband hasn't stolen."

"I don't understand you," said Mrs. Tucker coldly, turning towards the door. But with a flying leap across the counter her relentless adversary stood between her and retreat.

"You don't understand! Perhaps you don't understand that your husband not only stole the hard labor of these men, but even the little money they brought here and trusted to his thieving hands. Perhaps you don't know that he stole my husband's hard earnings, mortgaged these very goods you want to buy, and that he is to-day a convicted thief, a forger, and a run-away coward. Perhaps, if you can't understand *me,* you can read the newspaper. Look!" She exultingly opened the paper the sheriff had been reading aloud, and pointed to the displayed headlines. "Look! there are the very words, 'Forgery, Swindling, Embezzlement!' Do you see? And perhaps you can't understand this. Look! 'Shameful Flight. Abandons his Wife. Runs off with a Notorious—' "

"Easy, old gal, easy now. D—n it! Will you dry up? I say. *Stop!*"

It was too late!

The sheriff had dashed the paper from the woman's hand, but not until Mrs. Tucker had read a single line, a line such as she had sometimes turned from with weary scorn in her careless perusal of the daily shameful chronicle of domestic infelicity. Then she had coldly wondered if there could be any such men and women; and now! The crowd fell back before her; even the virago was silenced as she looked at her face. The humorist's face was as white, but not as immobile, as he gasped,

"Christ! if I don't believe she knew nothin' of it!"

For a moment the full force of such a supposition, with all its poignancy, its dramatic intensity, and its pathos, possessed the crowd. In the momentary clairvoyance of enthusiasm they caught a glimpse of the truth, and by one of the strange reactions of human passion they only waited for a word of appeal or explanation from her lips to throw themselves at her feet. Had she simply told her story they would have believed her; had she cried, fainted, or gone into hysterics, they would have pitied her. She did neither. Perhaps she thought of neither, or indeed of anything that was then before her eyes. She walked erect to the door and turned upon the threshold. "I mean what I say," she said calmly. "I don't understand you. But whatever just claims you have upon my husband will be paid by me, or by his lawyer, Captain Poindexter."

She had lost the sympathy but not the respect of her hearers. They made way for her with sullen deference as she passed out on the platform. But her adversary, profiting by the last opportunity, burst into an ironical laugh.

"Captain Poindexter, is it? Well, perhaps he's safe to pay *your* bill, but as for your husband's—"

"That's another matter," interrupted a familiar voice with the greatest cheerfulness; "that's what you were going to say, wasn't it? Ha! ha! Well, Mrs. Patterson," continued Poindexter, stepping from his buggy, "you never spoke a truer word in your life. One moment, Mrs. Tucker. Let me send you back in the buggy. Don't mind *me*. I can get a fresh horse of the sheriff. I'm quite at home here. I say, Patterson, step a few paces this way, will you? A little further from your wife, please. That'll do. You've got a claim of five thousand dollars against the property, haven't you?"

"Yes."

"Well, that woman just driving away is your one solitary chance of getting a cent of it. If your wife insults her again, that chance is gone. And if *you* do——"

"Well?"

"As sure as there is a God in Israel and a Supreme Court of the State of California, I'll kill you in your tracks! . . . Stay!"

Patterson turned. The irrepressible look of humorous tolerance of all human frailty had suffused Poindexter's black eyes with mischievous moisture. "If you think it quite safe to confide to your wife this prospect of her improvement by widowhood, you may!"

CHAPTER III.

MR. PATTERSON did not inform his wife of the lawyer's personal threat to himself. But he managed, after Poindexter had left, to make her conscious that Mrs. Tucker might be a power to be placated and feared. "You've shot off your mouth at her," he said argumentatively, "and whether you've hit the mark or not you've had your say. Ef you think it's worth a possible five thousand dollars and interest to keep on, heave ahead. Ef you rather have the chance of getting the rest in cash, you'll let up on her." "You don't suppose," returned Mrs. Patterson contemptuously, "that she's got anything but what that man of hers—Poindexter—lets her have?" "The sheriff says," retorted Patterson surlily, "that she's notified him that she claims the *rancho* as a gift from her husband three years ago, and she's in *possession* now, and was so when the execution was out. It don't make no matter," he added, with gloomy philosophy, "who's got a full hand as long as *we* ain't got the cards to chip in. I wouldn't 'a' minded it," he continued meditatively, "ef Spence Tucker had dropped a hint to me afore he put out." "And I suppose," said Mrs. Patterson angrily, "you'd have put out too?" "I reckon," said Patterson simply.

Twice or thrice during the evening he referred, more or less directly, to this lack of confidence shown by his late debtor and employer, and seemed to feel it more keenly than the loss of property. He confided his sentiments quite openly to the sheriff in possession, over the whiskey and euchre with which these gentlemen avoided the difficulties of their delicate relations. He brooded over it as he handed the keys of the shop to the sheriff when they parted for the night, and was still thinking of it when the house was closed, everybody gone to bed, and he was fetching a fresh jug of water from the well. The moon was at times obscured by flying clouds, the *avant-couriers* of the regular evening shower. He was stooping over the well, when he sprang suddenly to his feet again. "Who's there?" he demanded sharply.

"Hush!" said a voice so low and faint it might have been a whisper of the wind in the palisades of the corral. But, indistinct as it was, it was the voice of the man he was thinking of as far away, and it sent a thrill of alternate awe and pleasure through his pulses.

He glanced quickly around. The moon was hidden by a passing cloud, and only the faint outlines of the house he had just quitted were

visible. "Is that you, Spence?" he said tremulously.

"Yes," replied the voice, and a figure dimly
emerged from the corner of the corral.

"Lay low, lay low, for God's sake," said Patterson, hurriedly throwing himself upon the
apparition. "The sheriff and his *posse* are in
there."

"But I must speak to you a moment," said
the figure.

"Wait," said Patterson, glancing towards the
building. Its blank, shutterless windows revealed no inner light; a profound silence encompassed it. "Come quick," he whispered.
Letting his grasp slip down to the unresisting
hand of the stranger, he half-dragged, half-led
him, brushing against the wall, into the open
door of the deserted bar-room he had just
quitted, locked the inner door, poured a glass
of whiskey from a decanter, gave it to him,
and then watched him drain it at a single
draught. The moon came out, and, falling
through the bare windows full upon the
stranger's face, revealed the artistic but slightly
disheveled curls and moustache of the fugitive,
Spencer Tucker.

Whatever may have been the real influence
of this unfortunate man upon his fellows, it
seemed to find expression in a singular una-

nimity of criticism. Patterson looked at him with a half-dismal, half-welcoming smile. "Well, you are a h——ll of a fellow, ain't you?"

Spencer Tucker passed his hand through his hair and lifted it from his forehead, with a gesture at once emotional and theatrical. "I am a man with a price on me!" he said bitterly. "Give me up to the sheriff, and you'll get five thousand dollars. Help me, and you'll get nothing. That's my d——d luck, and yours too, I suppose."

"I reckon you're right there," said Patterson gloomily. "But I thought you got clean away. Went off in a ship——"

"Went off in a boat to a ship," interrupted Tucker savagely; "went off to a ship that had all my things on board—everything. The cursed boat capsized in a squall just off the Heads. The ship, d——n her, sailed away, the men thinking I was drowned, likely, and that they'd make a good thing off my goods, I reckon."

"But the girl, Inez, who was with you, didn't she make a row?"

"*Quien sabe?*" returned Tucker, with a reckless laugh. "Well, I hung on like grim death to that boat's keel until one of those Chinese fishermen, in a 'dug-out,' hauled me in oppo-

site Saucelito. I chartered him and his dug-out
to bring me down here."

"Why here?" asked Patterson, with a certain
ostentatious caution that ill-concealed his pen-
sive satisfaction.

"You may well ask," returned Tucker, with
an equal ostentation of bitterness, as he slightly
waved his companion away. "But I reckoned
I could trust a white man that I'd been kind
to, and who wouldn't go back on me. No, no,
let me go! Hand me over to the sheriff!"

Patterson had suddenly grasped both the
hands of the picturesque scamp before him,
with an affection that for an instant almost
shamed the man who had ruined him. But
Tucker's egotism whispered that this affection
was only a recognition of his own superiority,
and felt flattered. He was beginning to believe
that he was really the injured party.

"What I *have* and what I have *had* is yours,
Spence," returned Patterson, with a sad and
simple directness that made any further discussion a gratuitous insult. "I only wanted to
know what you reckoned to do here."

"I want to get over across the Coast Range
to Monterey," said Tucker. "Once there, one
of those coasting schooners will bring me down
to Acapulco, where the ship will put in."

Patterson remained silent for a moment.

"There's a mustang in the corral you can take —leastways, I shan't know that it's gone—until to-morrow afternoon. In an hour from now," he added, looking from the window, "these clouds will settle down to business. It will rain; there will be light enough for you to find your way by the regular trail over the mountain, but not enough for any one to know you. If you can't push through to-night, you can lie over at the *posada* on the summit. Them greasers that keep it won't know you, and if they did they won't go back on you. And if they did go back on you, nobody would believe them. It's mighty curious," he added, with gloomy philosophy, "but I reckon it's the reason why Providence allows this kind of cattle to live among white men and others made in his image. Take a piece of pie, won't you?" he continued, abandoning this abstract reflection and producing half a flat pumpkin pie from the bar. Spencer Tucker grasped the pie with one hand and his friend's fingers with the other, and for a few moments was silent from the hurried deglutition of viand and sentiment. *"You're* a white man, Patterson, anyway," he resumed. "I'll take your horse, and put it down in our account, at your own figure. As soon as this cursed thing is blown over, I'll be back here and see you through, you bet. I

don't desert my friends, however rough things
go with me."

"I see you don't," returned Patterson, with
an unconscious and serious simplicity that had
the effect of the most exquisite irony. "I was
only just saying to the sheriff that if there
was anything I could have done for you, you
wouldn't have cut away without letting me
know." Tucker glanced uneasily at Patterson,
who continued, "Ye ain't wanting anything
else?" Then observing that his former friend
and patron was roughly but newly clothed, and
betrayed no trace of his last escapade, he added,
"I see you've got a fresh harness."

"That d—d Chinaman bought me these at
the landing; they're not much in style or fit,"
he continued, trying to get a moonlight view of
himself in the mirror behind the bar, "but that
don't matter here." He filled another glass
of spirits, jauntily settled himself back in his
chair, and added, "I don't suppose there are
any girls around, anyway."

"'Cept your wife; she was down here this
afternoon," said Patterson meditatively.

Mr. Tucker paused with the pie in his hand.
"Ah, yes!" He essayed a reckless laugh, but
that evident simulation failed before Patterson's melancholy. With an assumption of falling in with his friend's manner, rather than

from any personal anxiety, he continued, "Well?"

"That man Poindexter was down here with her. Put her in the *hacienda* to hold possession afore the news came out."

"Impossible!" said Tucker, rising hastily. "It don't belong—that is—" he hesitated.

"Yer thinking the creditors 'll get it, mebbe," returned Patterson, gazing at the floor. "Not as long as she's in it; no sir! Whether it's really hers, or she's only keeping house for Poindexter, she's a fixture, you bet. They're a team when they pull together, they are!"

The smile slowly faded from Tucker's face, that now looked quite rigid in the moonlight. He put down his glass and walked to the window as Patterson gloomily continued, "But that's nothing to you. You've got ahead of 'em both, and had your revenge by going off with the gal. That's what I said all along. When folks—especially women folks—wondered how you could leave a woman like your wife, and go off with a scallawag like that gal, I allers said they'd find out there was a reason. And when your wife came flaunting down here with Poindexter before she'd quite got quit of you, I reckon they began to see the whole little game. No sir! I knew it wasn't on account of the gal! Why, when you came here to-night and told me

quite nat'ral-like and easy how she went off in
the ship, and then calmly ate your pie and
drank your whiskey after it, I knew you didn't
care for her. There's my hand, Spence; you're
a trump, even if you are a little looney, eh?
Why, what's up?"

Shallow and selfish as Tucker was, Patterson's words seemed like a revelation that shocked
him as profoundly as it might have shocked a
nobler nature. The simple vanity and selfishness that made him unable to conceive any
higher reason for his wife's loyalty than his
own personal popularity and success, now that
he no longer possessed that _éclat,_ made him
equally capable of the lowest suspicions. He
was a dishonored fugitive, broken in fortune
and reputation—why should she not desert him!
He had been unfaithful to her from wildness,
from caprice, from the effect of those fascinating qualities; it seemed to him natural that
she should be disloyal from more deliberate
motives, and he hugged himself with that belief. Yet there was enough doubt, enough of
haunting suspicion that he had lost or alienated
a powerful affection, to make him thoroughly
miserable. He returned his friend's grasp convulsively and buried his face upon his shoulder.
But he was not above feeling a certain exultation in the effect of his misery upon the dog-

like, unreasoning affection of Patterson, nor could he entirely refrain from slightly posing his affliction before that sympathetic but melancholy man. Suddenly he raised his head, drew back, and thrust his hand into his bosom with a theatrical gesture.

"What's to keep me from killing Poindexter in his tracks ?" he said wildly.

"Nothin' but *his* shooting first," returned Patterson, with dismal practicality. "He's mighty quick, like all them army men. It's about even, I reckon, that he don't get *me* first," he added in an ominous voice.

"No!" returned Tucker, grasping his hand again. "This is not your affair, Patterson; leave him to me when I come back."

"If he ever gets the drop on me, I reckon he won't wait," continued Patterson lugubriously. "He seems to object to my passin' criticism on your wife, as if she was a queen or an angel."

The blood came to Spencer's cheek, and he turned uneasily to the window. "It's dark enough now for a start," he said hurriedly, "and if I could get across the mountain without lying over at the summit, it would be a day gained."

Patterson arose without a word, filled a flask of spirit, handed it to his friend, and silently led the way through the slowly falling rain and the now settled darkness. The mustang was quickly secured and saddled, a heavy *poncho* afforded Tucker a disguise as well as a protection from the rain. With a few hurried, disconnected words, and an abstracted air, he once more shook his friend's hand and issued cautiously from the corral. When out of earshot from the house he put spurs to the mustang, and dashed into a gallop.

To intersect the mountain road he was obliged to traverse part of the highway his wife had walked that afternoon, and to pass within a mile of the *casa* where she was. Long before he reached that point his eyes were straining the darkness in that direction for some indication of the house which was to him familiar. Becoming now accustomed to the even obscurity, less trying to the vision than the alternate light and shadow of cloud or the full glare of the moonlight, he fancied he could distinguish its low walls over the monotonous level. One of those impulses which had so often taken the place of resolution in his character suddenly possessed him to diverge from his course and approach the house. Why, he could not have explained. It was not from any feeling of jealous suspicion or contemplated revenge—that had passed with the presence of Patterson; it was not from any vague lingering sentiment for the

woman he had wronged—he would have shrunk
from meeting her at that moment. But it was
full of these and more possibilities by which he
might or might not be guided, and was at least
a movement towards some vague end, and a distraction from certain thoughts he dared not
entertain and could not entirely dismiss. In-
conceivable and inexplicable to human reason,
it might have been acceptable to the Divine
omniscience for its predestined result.

He left the road at a point where the marsh
encroached upon the meadow, familiar to him
already as near the spot where he had embarked from the Chinaman's boat the day before. He remembered that the walls of the
hacienda were distinctly visible from the *tules*
where he had hidden all day, and he now knew
that the figures he had observed near the building, which had deterred his first attempts at
landing, must have been his wife and his friend.
He knew that a long tongue of the slough filled
by the rising tide followed the marsh, and lay
between him and the *hacienda*. The sinking of
his horse's hoofs in the spongy soil determined
its proximity, and he made a *détour* to the right
to avoid it. In doing so, a light suddenly rose
above the distant horizon ahead of him, trembled
faintly, and then burned with a steady lustre.
It was a light at the *hacienda*. Guiding his

horse half abstractedly in this direction, his progress was presently checked by the splashing of the animal's hoofs in the water. But the turf below was firm, and a salt drop that had spattered to his lips told him that it was only the encroaching of the tide in the meadow. With his eyes on the light, he again urged his horse forward. The rain lulled, the clouds began to break, the landscape alternately lightened and grew dark; the outlines of the crumbling *hacienda* walls that enshrined the light grew more visible. A strange and dreamy resemblance to the long blue-grass plain before his wife's paternal house, as seen by him during his evening rides to courtship, pressed itself upon him. He remembered, too, that she used to put a light in the window to indicate her presence. Following this retrospect, the moon came boldly out, sparkled upon the overflow of silver at his feet, seemed to show the dark, opaque meadow beyond for a moment, and then disappeared. It was dark now, but the lesser earthly star still shone before him as a guide, and pushing towards it, he passed in the all-embracing shadow.

CHAPTER IV.

As Mrs. Tucker, erect, white, and rigid, drove away from the *tienda,* it seemed to her to sink again into the monotonous plain, with all its horrible realities. Except that there was now a new and heart-breaking significance to the solitude and loneliness of the landscape, all that had passed might have been a dream. But as the blood came back to her cheek, and little by little her tingling consciousness returned, it seemed as if her life had been the dream, and this last scene the awakening reality. With eyes smarting with the moisture of shame, the scarlet blood at times dyeing her very neck and temples, she muffled her lowered crest in her shawl and bent over the reins. Bit by bit she recalled, in Poindexter's mysterious caution and strange allusions, the corroboration of her husband's shame and her own disgrace. This was why she was brought hither—the deserted wife, and abandoned confederate! The mocking glitter of the concave vault above her, scoured by the incessant wind, the cold stare of the shining pools beyond, the hard outlines of the Coast Range, and the jarring accompaniment of her horse's hoofs and rattling buggy wheels alternately goaded and distracted her. She found herself repeating "No! no! no!" with the dogged

reiteration of fever. She scarcely knew when
or how she reached the *hacienda*. She was only
conscious that as she entered the *patio* the dusty
solitude that had before filled her with unrest
now came to her like balm. A benumbing
peace seemed to fall from the crumbling walls;
the peace of utter seclusion, isolation, oblivion,
death! Nevertheless, an hour later, when the
jingle of spurs and bridle were again heard in
the road, she started to her feet with bent brows
and a kindling eye, and confronted Captain
Poindexter in the corridor.

"I would not have intruded upon you so soon
again," he said gravely, "but I thought I might
perhaps spare you a repetition of the scene of
this morning. Hear me out, please," he added,
with a gentle, half-deprecating gesture, as she
lifted the beautiful scorn of her eyes to his.
"I have just heard that your neighbor, Don José
Santierra, of Los Gatos, is on his way to this
house. He once claimed this land, and hated
your husband, who bought of the rival claimant,
whose grant was confirmed. I tell you this," he
added, slightly flushing as Mrs. Tucker turned
impatiently away, "only to show you that
legally he has no rights, and you need not see
him unless you choose. I could not stop his
coming without perhaps doing you more harm
than good; but when he does come, my pres-

ence under this roof as your legal counsel will enable you to refer him to me." He stopped. She was pacing the corridor with short, impatient steps, her arms dropped, and her hands clasped rigidly before her. "Have I your permission to stay?"

She suddenly stopped in her walk, approached him rapidly, and fixing her eyes on his, said,—

"Do I know *all,* now—everything?"

He could only reply that she had not yet told him what she had heard.

"Well," she said scornfully, "that my husband has been cruelly imposed upon—imposed upon by some wretched woman, who has made him sacrifice his property, his friends, his honor—everything but me?"

"Everything but whom?" gasped Poindexter. "But ME!"

Poindexter gazed at the sky, the air, the deserted corridor, the stones of the *patio* itself, and then at the inexplicable woman before him. Then he said gravely, "I think you know everything."

"Then if my husband has left me all he could —this property," she went on rapidly, twisting her handkerchief between her fingers, "I can do with it what I like, can't I?"

"You certainly can."

"Then sell it," she said, with passionate vehemence. "Sell it—all! everything! And sell these." She darted into her bedroom, and returned with the diamond rings she had torn from her fingers and ears when she entered the house. "Sell them for anything they'll bring, only sell them at once."

"But for what?" asked Poindexter, with demure lips but twinkling eyes.

"To pay the debts that this—this—woman has led him into; to return the money she has stolen!" she went on rapidly, "to keep him from sharing her infamy! Can't you understand?"

"But, my dear madam," began Poindexter, "even if this could be done—"

"Don't tell me 'if it could'—it *must* be done. Do you think I could sleep under this roof, propped up by the timbers of that ruined *tienda?* Do you think I could wear those diamonds again, while that termagant shop-woman can say that her money bought them? No. If you are my husband's friend you will do this—for—for his sake." She stopped, locked and interlocked her cold fingers before her, and said, hesitating and mechanically, "You meant well, Captain Poindexter, in bringing me here, I know! You must not think that I blame you for it, or for the miserable result of it that you have just witnessed. But if I have gained anything by it, for God's sake let me reap it quickly, that I may give it to these people and go! I have a friend who can aid me to get to my husband or to my home in Kentucky, where Spencer will yet find me, I know. I want nothing more." She stopped again. With another woman the pause would have been one of tears. But she kept her head above the flood that filled her heart, and the clear eyes fixed upon Poindexter, albeit pained, were undimmed.

"But this would require time," said Poindexter, with a smile of compassionate explanation; "you could not sell now, nobody would buy. You are safe to hold this property while you are in actual possession, but you are not strong enough to guarantee it to another. There may still be litigation; your husband has other creditors than these people you have talked with. But while nobody could oust you—the wife who would have the sympathies of judge and jury—it might be a different case with any one who derived title from you. Any purchaser would know that you could not sell, or if you did, it would be at a ridiculous sacrifice."

She listened to him abstractedly, walked to the end of the corridor, returned, and without looking up, said,—

"I suppose you know her?"

"I beg your pardon?"

"This woman. You have seen her?"

"Never, to my knowledge."

"And you are his friend! That's strange." She raised her eyes to his. "Well," she continued impatiently, "who is she? and what is she? You know that surely?"

"I know no more of her than what I have said," said Poindexter. "She is a notorious woman."

The swift color came to Mrs. Tucker's face as if the epithet had been applied to herself. "I suppose," she said in a dry voice, as if she were asking a business question, but with an eye that showed her rising anger,—"I suppose there is some law by which creatures of this kind can be followed and brought to justice— some law that would keep innocent people from suffering for their crimes?"

"I am afraid," said Poindexter, "that arresting her would hardly help these people over in the *tienda*."

"I am not speaking of them," responded Mrs. Tucker, with a sudden sublime contempt for the people whose cause she had espoused: "I am talking of my husband."

Poindexter bit his lip. "You'd hardly think of bringing back the strongest witness against him," he said bluntly.

Mrs. Tucker dropped her eyes and was silent. A sudden shame suffused Poindexter's cheek; he felt as if he had struck that woman a blow. "I beg your pardon," he said hastily, "I am talking like a lawyer to a lawyer." He would have taken any other woman by the hand in the honest fullness of his apology, but something restrained him here. He only looked down gently on her lowered lashes, and repeated his question if he should remain during the coming interview with Don José. "I must beg you to determine quickly," he added, "for I already hear him entering the gate."

"Stay," said Mrs. Tucker, as the ringing of spurs and clatter of hoofs came from the corral. "One moment." She looked up suddenly, and said, "How long had he known her?" But before he could reply there was a step in the doorway, and the figure of Don José Santierra emerged from the archway.

He was a man slightly past middle age, fair and well shaven, wearing a black broadcloth *serape,* the deeply embroidered opening of which formed a collar of silver rays around his neck, while a row of silver buttons down the side seams of his riding trousers, and silver spurs, completed his singular equipment. Mrs. Tucker's swift feminine glance took in these details, as well as the deep salutation, more formal than the exuberant frontier politeness she was accustomed to, with which he greeted her. It was enough to arrest her first impulse to retreat. She hesitated and stopped as Poindexter stepped forward, partly interposing between them, acknowledging Don José's distant recognition of himself with an ironical accession of his usual humorous tolerance. The Spaniard did not seem to notice it, but remained gravely silent before Mrs. Tucker, gazing at her with an expression of intent and unconscious absorption.

"You are quite right, Don José," said Poindexter, with ironical concern, "it is Mrs. Tucker. Your eyes do *not* deceive you. She will be glad to do the honors of her house," he continued, with a simulation of appealing to her, "unless you visit her on business, when I need not say *I* shall be only too happy, to attend you, as before.

Don José, with a slight lifting of the eyebrows, allowed himself to become conscious of the lawyer's meaning. "It is not of business that I come to kiss the Señora's hand to-day," he replied, with a melancholy softness; "it is as her neighbor, to put myself at her disposition. Ah! the what have we here for a lady?" he continued, raising his eyes in deprecation of the surroundings; "a house of nothing, a place of winds and dry bones, without refreshments, or satisfaction, or delicacy. The Señora will not refuse to make us proud this day to send her of that which we have in our poor home at Los Gatos, to make her more complete. Of what shall it be? Let her make choice. Or if she would commemorate this day by accepting of our hospitality at Los Gatos, until she shall arrange herself the more to receive us here, we shall have too much honor."

"The Señora would only find it the more difficult to return to this humble roof again, after once leaving it for Don José's hospitality," said Poindexter, with a demure glance at Mrs. Tucker. But the innuendo seemed to lapse equally unheeded by his fair client and the stranger. Raising her eyes with a certain timid dignity which Don José's presence seemed to have called out, she addressed herself to him.

"You are very kind and considerate, Mister Santierra, and I thank you. I know that my husband"—she let the clear beauty of her translucent eyes rest full on both men—"would thank you too. But I shall not be here long enough to accept your kindness in this house or in your own. I have but one desire and object now. It is to dispose of this property, and indeed all I possess, to pay the debt of my husband. It is in your power, perhaps, to help me. I am told that you wish to possess Los Cuervos," she went on, equally oblivious of the consciousness that appeared in Don José's face, and a humorous perplexity on the brow of Poindexter. "If you can arrange it with Mr. Poindexter, you will find me a liberal vendor. That much you can do, and I know you will believe I shall be grateful. You can do no more, unless it be to say to your friends that Mrs. Belle Tucker remains here only for that purpose, and to carry out what she knows to be the wishes of her husband." She paused, bent her pretty crest, dropped a quaint curtsey to the superior age, the silver braid, and the gentlemanly bearing of Don José, and with the passing sunshine of a smile disappeared from the corridor.

The two men remained silent for a moment, Don José gazing abstractedly on the door through which she had vanished, until Poindexter, with a return of his tolerant smile, said, "You have heard the views of Mrs. Tucker. You know the situation as well as she does."

"Ah, yes; possibly better."

Poindexter darted a quick glance at the grave, sallow face of Don José, but detecting no unusual significance in his manner, continued, "As you see, she leaves this matter in my hands. Let us talk like business men. Have you any idea of purchasing this property?"

"Of purchasing, ah, no."

Poindexter bent his brows, but quickly relaxed them with a smile of humorous forgiveness. "If you have any other idea, Don José,
I ought to warn you, as Mrs. Tucker's lawyer,
that she is in legal possession here, and that
nothing but her own act can change that position."

"Ah, so."

Irritated at the shrug which accompanied
this, Poindexter continued haughtily, "If I am
to understand, you have nothing to say—"

"To say, ah, yes, possibly. But"—he glanced
toward the door of Mrs. Tucker's room—"not
here." He stopped, appeared to recall himself,
and with an apologetic smile and a studied but
graceful gesture of invitation, he motioned to
the gateway, and said, "Will you ride?"

"What can the fellow be up to?" muttered
Poindexter, as with an assenting nod he proceeded to remount his horse. "If he wasn't an
old *hidalgo,* I'd mistrust him. No matter! here
goes!"

The Don also remounted his half-broken mustang; they proceeded in solemn silence through
the corral, and side by side emerged on the open
plain. Poindexter glanced around; no other
being was in sight. It was not until the lonely
hacienda had also sunk behind them that Don
José broke the silence.

"You say just now we shall speak as business men. I say no, Don Marco; I will not. I shall speak, we shall speak, as gentlemen."

"Go on," said Poindexter, who was beginning to be amused.

"I say just now I will not purchase the *rancho* from the Señora. And why? Look you, Don Marco;" he reined in his horse, thrust his hand under his *serape,* and drew out a folded document: "this is why."

With a smile, Poindexter took the paper from his hand and opened it. But the smile faded from his lips as he read. With blazing eyes he spurred his horse beside the Spaniard, almost unseating him, and said sternly, "What does this mean?"

"What does it mean?" repeated Don José, with equally flashing eyes, "I'll tell you. It means that your client, this man Spencer Tucker, is a Judas, a traitor! It means that he gave Los Cuervos to his mistress a year ago, and that she sold it to me——to me, you hear!——*me,* José Santierra, the day before she left! It means that the coyote of a Spencer, the thief, who bought these lands of a thief, and gave them to a thief, has tricked you all. Look," he said, rising in his saddle, holding the paper like a *bâton,* and defining with a sweep of his arm the whole level plain, "all these lands were once

mine, they are mine again to-day. Do I want
to purchase Los Cuervos? you ask, for you will
speak of the *business*. Well, listen. I *have* purchased Los Cuervos, and here is the deed."

"But it has never been recorded," said Poindexter, with a carelessness he was far from
feeling.

"Of a verity, no. Do you wish that I should
record it?" asked Don José, with a return of
his simple gravity.

Poindexter bit his lip. "You said we were
to talk like gentlemen," he returned. "Do you
think you have come into possession of this
alleged deed like a gentleman?"

Don José shrugged his shoulders. "I found
it tossed in the lap of a harlot. I bought it for
a song. Eh, what would you?"

"Would you sell it again for a song?" asked
Poindexter.

"Ah! what is this?" said Don José, lifting
his iron-gray brows; "but a moment ago we
would sell everything, for any money. Now we
would buy. Is it so?"

"One moment, Don José," said Poindexter,
with a baleful light in his dark eyes. "Do I
understand that you are the ally of Spencer
Tucker and his mistress, that you intend to turn
this doubly betrayed wife from the only roof
she has to cover her?"

"Ah, I comprehend not. You heard her say she wished to go. Perhaps it may please *me* to distribute largess to these cattle yonder, I do not say no. More she does not ask. But *you,* Don Marco, of whom are you advocate? You abandon your client's mistress for the wife, is it so?"

"What I may do you will learn hereafter," said Poindexter, who had regained his composure, suddenly reining up his horse. "As our paths seem likely to diverge, they had better begin now. Good morning."

"Patience, my friend, patience! Ah, blessed St. Anthony, what these Americans are! Listen. For what *you* shall do, I do not inquire. The question is to me what I"—he emphasized the pronoun by tapping himself on the breast— "I, José Santierra, will do. Well, I shall tell you. To-day, nothing. To-morrow, nothing. For a week, for a month, nothing! After, we shall see."

Poindexter paused thoughtfully. "Will you give your word, Don José, that you will not press the claim for a month?"

"Truly, on one condition. Observe! I do not ask you for an equal promise, that you will not take this time to defend yourself." He shrugged his shoulders. "No! It is only this. You shall promise that during that time the

Señora Tucker shall remain ignorant of this document."

Poindexter hesitated a moment. "I promise," he said at last.

"Good. Adios, Don Marco."

"Adios, Don José."

The Spaniard put spurs to his mustang and galloped off in the direction of Los Gatos. The lawyer remained for a moment gazing on his retreating but victorious figure. For the first time the old look of humorous toleration with which Mr. Poindexter was in the habit of regarding all human infirmity gave way to something like bitterness. "I might have guessed it," he said, with a slight rise of color. "He's an old fool; and she—well, perhaps it's all the better for her!" He glanced backwards almost tenderly in the direction of Los Cuervos, and then turned his head towards the *embarcadero*.

As the afternoon wore on, a creaking, antiquated ox-cart arrived at Los Cuervos, bearing several articles of furniture, and some tasteful ornaments from Los Gatos, at the same time that a young Mexican girl mysteriously appeared in the kitchen, as a temporary assistant to the decrepit Concha. These were both clearly attributable to Don José, whose visit was not so remote but that these delicate attentions might have been already projected before Mrs. Tucker had declined them, and she could not, without marked discourtesy, return them now. She did not wish to seem discourteous; she would like to have been more civil to this old gentleman, who still retained the evidences of a picturesque and decorous past, and a repose so different from the life that was perplexing her. Reflecting that if he bought the estate these things would be ready to his hand, and with a woman's instinct recognizing their value in setting off the house to other purshasers' eyes, she took a pleasure in tastefully arranging them, and even found herself speculating how she might have enjoyed them herself had she been able to keep possession of the property. After all, it would not have been so lonely if refined and gentle neighbors, like this old man, would have sympathized with her; she had an instinctive feeling that, in their own hopeless decay and hereditary unfitness for this new civilization, they would have been more tolerant of her husband's failure than his own kind. She could not believe that Don José really hated her husband for buying of the successful claimant, as there was no other legal title. Allowing herself to become interested in the guileless gossip of the new handmaiden, proud of her broken English, she was drawn into a sympathy with the grave simplicity of Don José's character, a relic of that true nobility which placed this descendant of the Castilians and the daughter of a free people on the same level.

In this way the second day of her occupancy of Los Cuervos closed, with dumb clouds along the gray horizon, and the paroxysms of hysterical wind growing fainter and fainter outside the walls; with the moon rising after nightfall, and losing itself in silent and mysterious confidences with drifting scud. She went to bed early, but woke past midnight, hearing, as she thought, her own name called. The impression was so strong upon her that she rose, and, hastily enwrapping herself, went to the dark embrasures of the oven-shaped windows, and looked out. The dwarfed oak beside the window was still dropping from a past shower, but the level waste of marsh and meadow beyond seemed to advance and recede with the coming and going of the moon. Again she heard her name called, and this time in accents so strangely familiar that with a slight cry she ran into the corridor, crossed the *patio,* and reached the open gate. The darkness that had, even in this brief interval, again fallen upon the prospect she tried in vain to pierce with eye and voice. A blank silence followed. Then the veil was suddenly withdrawn; the vast plain, stretching from the mountain to the sea, shone as clearly

as in the light of day; the moving current of
the channel glittered like black pearls, the stagnant pools like molten lead; but not a sign of
life nor motion broke the monotony of the broad
expanse.. She must have surely dreamed it. A
chill wind drove her back to the house again;
she entered her bedroom, and in half an hour
she was in a peaceful sleep.

CHAPTER V.

THE two men kept their secret. Mr. Poindexter convinced Mrs. Tucker that the sale of
Los Cuervos could not be effected until the no-
toriety of her husband's flight had been fairly
forgotten, and she was forced to accept her fate.
The sale of her diamonds, which seemed to her
to have realized a singularly extravagant sum,
enabled her to quietly reinstate the Pattersons
in the *tienda* and to discharge in full her husband's liabilities to the *rancheros* and his hum-
bler retainers.

Meanwhile the winter rains had ceased. It
seemed to her as if the clouds had suddenly one
night struck their white tents and stolen away,
leaving the unvanquished sun to mount the vacant sky the next morning alone, and possess it
thenceforward unchallenged. One afternoon

she thought the long sad waste before her window had caught some tint of gayer color from the sunset; a week later she found it a blazing landscape of poppies, broken here and there by blue lagoons of lupine, by pools of daisies, by banks of dog-roses, by broad outlying shores of dandelions that scattered their lavish gold to the foot of the hills, where the green billows of wild oats carried it on and upwards to the darker crest of pines. For two months she was dazzled and bewildered with color. She had never before been face to face with this spendthrift Californian Flora, in her virgin wastefulness, her more than goddess-like prodigality. The teeming earth seemed to quicken and throb beneath her feet; the few circuits of a plough around the outlying corral were enough to call out a jungle growth of giant grain that almost hid the low walls of the *hacienda*. In this glorious fecundity of the earth, in this joyous renewal of life and color, in this opulent youth and freshness of soil and sky, it alone remained, the dead and sterile Past, left in the midst of buoyant rejuvenescence and resurrection, like an empty churchyard skull upturned on the springing turf. Its bronzed adobe walls mocked the green vine that embraced them, the crumbling dust of its courtyard remained ungerminating and unfruitful; to the thousand stirring voices without, its dry lips alone remained mute, unresponsive and unchanged.

During this time Don José had become a frequent visitor at Los Cuervos, bringing with him at first his niece and sister in a stately precision of politeness that was not lost on the proud Blue Grass stranger. She returned their visit at Los Gatos, and there made the formal acquaintance of Don José's grandmother, a lady who still regarded the decrepit Concha as a giddy *muchacha,* and who herself glittered as with the phosphorescence of refined decay. Through this circumstance she learned that Don José was not yet fifty, and that his gravity of manner and sedateness was more the result of fastidious isolation and temperament than years. She could not tell why the information gave her a feeling of annoyance, but it caused her to regret the absence of Poindexter, and to wonder, also somewhat nervously, why he had lately avoided her presence. The thought that he might be doing so from a recollection of the innuendoes of Mrs. Patterson caused a little tremor of indignation in her pulses. "As if—" but she did not finish the sentence even to herself, and her eyes filled with bitter tears.

Yet she had thought of the husband who had so cruelly wronged her less feverishly, less impatiently than before. For she thought she loved him now the more deeply, because, although she was not reconciled to his absence, it seemed to keep alive the memory of what he had been before his one wild act separated them. She had never seen the reflection of another woman's eyes in his; the past contained no haunting recollection of waning or alienated affection; she could meet him again, and, clasping her arms around him, awaken as if from a troubled dream without reproach or explanation. Her strong belief in this made her patient; she no longer sought to know the particulars of his flight, and never dreamed that her passive submission to his absence was partly due to a fear that something in his actual presence at that moment would have destroyed that belief forever.

For this reason the delicate reticence of the people at Los Gatos, and their seclusion from the world which knew of her husband's fault, had made her encourage the visits of Don José, until from the instinct already alluded to she one day summoned Poindexter to Los Cuervos, on the day that Don José usually called. But to her surprise the two men met more or less awkwardly and coldly, and her tact as hostess was tried to the utmost to keep their evident antagonism from being too apparent. The effort to reconcile their mutual discontent, and some other feeling she did not quite understand, produced a nervous excitement which called the blood to her cheek and gave a dangerous brilliancy to her eyes, two circumstances not unnoticed nor unappreciated by her two guests. But instead of reuniting them, the prettier Mrs. Tucker became, the more distant and reserved grew the men, until Don José rose before the usual hour, and with more than usual ceremoniousness departed.

"Then my business does not seem to be with *him?*" said Poindexter, with quiet coolness, as Mrs. Tucker turned her somewhat mystified face towards him. "Or have you anything to say to me about him in private?"

"I am sure I don't know what you both mean," she returned with a slight tremor of voice. "I had no idea you were not on good terms. I thought you were! It's very awkward." Without coquetry and unconsciously she raised her blue eyes under her lids until the clear pupils coyly and softly hid themselves in the corners of the brown lashes, and added, "You have both been so kind to me."

"Perhaps that is the reason," said Poindexter, gravely. But Mrs. Tucker refused to accept the suggestion with equal gravity, and began to laugh. The laugh, which was at first frank, spontaneous, and almost child-like, was becoming hysterical and nervous as she went on, until it was suddenly checked by Poindexter.

"I have had no difficulties with Don José Santierra," he said, somewhat coldly ignoring her hilarity, "but perhaps he is not inclined to be as polite to the friend of the husband as he is to the wife."

"Mr. Poindexter!" said Mrs. Tucker quickly, her face becoming pale again.

"I beg your pardon!" said Poindexter, flushing; "but—"

"You want to say," she interrupted coolly, "that you are not friends, I see. Is that the reason why you have avoided this house?" she continued gently.

"I thought I could be of more service to you elsewhere," he replied evasively. "I have been lately following up a certain clue rather closely. I think I am on the track of a confidante of—of—that woman."

A quick shadow passed over Mrs. Tucker's face. "Indeed!" she said coldly. "Then I am to believe that you prefer to spend your leisure moments in looking after that creature to calling here?"

Poindexter was stupefied. Was this the woman who only four months ago was almost vindictively eager to pursue her husband's paramour! There could be but one answer to it—Don José! Four months ago he would have smiled compassionately at it from his cynical preëminence. Now he managed with difficulty to stifle the bitterness of his reply.

"If you do not wish the inquiry carried on," he began, "of course—"

"I? What does it matter to me?" she said coolly. "Do as you please."

Nevertheless, half an hour later, as he was leaving, she said, with a certain hesitating timidity, "Do not leave me so much alone here, and let that woman go."

This was not the only unlooked-for sequel to her innocent desire to propitiate her best friends. Don José did not call again upon his usual day, but in his place came Doña Clara, his younger sister. When Mrs. Tucker had politely asked after the absent Don José, Doña Clara wound her swarthy arms around the fair American's waist and replied, "But why did you send for the *abogado* Poindexter when my brother called?"

"But Captain Poindexter calls as one of my friends," said the amazed Mrs. Tucker. "He is a gentleman, and has been a soldier and an officer," she added with some warmth.

"Ah, yes, a soldier of the law, what you call an *oficial de policia,* a chief of *gendarmes,* my sister, but not a gentleman—a *camarero* to protect a lady."

Mrs. Tucker would have uttered a hasty reply, but the perfect and good-natured simplicity of Doña Clara withheld her. Nevertheless, she treated Don José with a certain reserve at their next meeting, until it brought the simple-minded Castilian so dangerously near the point of demanding an explanation which implied too much that she was obliged to restore him temporarily to his old footing. Meantime she had a brilliant idea. She would write to Calhoun Weaver, whom she had avoided since that memorable day. She would say she wished to consult him. He would come to Los Cuervos; he might suggest something to lighten this weary waiting; at least she would show them all that she had still old friends. Yet she did not dream of returning to her Blue Grass home; her parents had died since she left; she shrank from the thought of dragging her ruined life before the hopeful youth of her girlhood's companions.

Mr. Calhoun Weaver arrived promptly, ostentatiously, oracularly, and cordially, but a little coarsely. He had—did she remember? —expected this from the first. Spencer had lost his head through vanity, and had attempted too much. It required foresight and firmness, as he himself—who had lately made successful "combinations" which she might perhaps have heard of—well knew. But Spencer had got the "big head." "As to that woman—a devilish handsome woman too!—well, everybody knew that Spencer always had a weakness that way, and he would say—but if she didn't care to hear any more about her—well, perhaps she was right. That was the best way to take it." Sitting before her, prosperous, weak, egotistical, incompetent, unavailable, and yet filled with a vague kindliness of intent, Mrs. Tucker loathed him. A sickening perception of her own weakness in sending for him, a new and aching sense of her utter isolation and helplessness, seemed to paralyze her.

"Nat'rally you feel bad," he continued, with the large air of a profound student of human nature. "Nat'rally, nat'rally you're kept in an uncomfortable state, not knowing jist how you stand. There ain't but one thing to do. Jist rise up, quiet like, and get a divorce agin Spencer. Hold on! There ain't a judge or jury in California that wouldn't give it to you right off the nail, without asking questions. Why, you 'ld get it by default if you wanted to; you 'ld just have to walk over the course! And then, Belle," he drew his chair still nearer her, "when you've settled down again—well!—I don't mind renewing that offer I once made ye,

before Spencer ever came round ye—I don't
mind, Belle, I swear I don't! Honest Injin!
I'm in earnest, there's my hand!"

Mrs. Tucker's reply has not been recorded.
Enough that half an hour later Mr. Weaver appeared in the courtyard with traces of tears on
his foolish face, a broken falsetto voice, and
other evidence of mental and moral disturbance.
His cordiality and oracular predisposition remained sufficiently to enable him to suggest the
magical words "Blue Grass" mysteriously to
Concha, with an indication of his hand to the
erect figure of her pale mistress in the doorway,
who waved to him a silent but half-compassion-
ate farewell.

At about this time a slight change in her
manner was noticed by the few who saw her
more frequently. Her apparently invincible
girlishness of spirit had given way to a certain
matronly seriousness. She applied herself to
her household cares and the improvement of the
hacienda with a new sense of duty and a settled earnestness, until by degrees she wrought
into it not only her instinctive delicacy and
taste, but part of her own individuality. Even
the rude *rancheros* and tradesmen who were permitted to enter the walls in the exercise of their
calling began to speak mysteriously of the
beauty of this garden of the *almarjal*. She

went out but seldom, and then accompanied by
the one or the other of her female servants, in
long drives on unfrequented roads.   On Sundays she sometimes drove to the half-ruined
mission church of Santa Inez, and hid herself,
during mass, in the dim monastic shadows of
the choir.   Gradually the poorer people whom
she met in these journeys began to show an almost devotional reverence for her, stopping in
the roads with uncovered heads for her to pass,
or making way for her in the *tienda* or *plaza*
of the wretched town with dumb courtesy. She
began to feel a strange sense of widowhood, that,
while it at times brought tears to her eyes, was
not without a certain tender solace.   In the
sympathy and simpleness of this impulse she
went as far as to revive the mourning she had
worn for her parents, but with such a fatal accenting of her beauty, and dangerous misin-
terpreting of her condition to eligible bachelors
strange to the country, that she was obliged to
put it off again.   Her reserve and dignified
manner caused others to mistake her nationality
for that of the Santierras, and in "Doña Bella"
the simple Mrs. Tucker was for a while forgotten.   At times she even forgot it herself.
Accustomed now almost entirely to the accents
of another language and the features of another
race, she would sit for hours in the corridor,

whose massive bronzed inclosure even her tasteful care could only make an embowered mausoleum of the Past, or gaze abstractedly from
the dark embrasures of her windows across the
stretching *almarjal* to the shining lagoon beyond
that terminated the estuary. She had a strange
fondness for this tranquil mirror, which under
sun or stars always retained the passive reflex
of the sky above, and seemed to rest her weary
eyes. She had objected to one of the plans
projected by Poindexter to redeem the land and
deepen the water at the *embarcadero,* as it would
have drained the lagoon, and the lawyer had
postponed the improvement to gratify her fancy.
So she kept it through the long summer unchanged save by the shadows of passing wings
or the lazy files of sleeping sea-fowl.

On one of these afternoons she noticed a
slowly moving carriage leave the high road and
cross the *almarjal* skirting the edge of the lagoon. If it contained visitors for Los Cuervos
they had evidently taken a shorter cut without
waiting to go on to the regular road which inter-
sected the highway at right angles a mile farther on. It was with some sense of annoyance
and irritation that she watched the trespass, and
finally saw the vehicle approach the house. A
few moments later the servant informed her that
Mr. Patterson would like to see her alone.

When she entered the corridor, which in the dry season served as a reception hall, she was surprised to see that Patterson was not alone. Near him stood a well-dressed handsome woman, gazing about her with good-humored admiration of Mrs. Tucker's taste and ingenuity.

"It don't look much like it did two years ago," said the stranger cheerfully. "You've improved it wonderfully."

Stiffening slightly, Mrs. Tucker turned inquiringly to Mr. Patterson. But that gentleman's usual profound melancholy appeared to be intensified by the hilarity of his companion. He only sighed deeply and rubbed his leg with the brim of his hat in gloomy abstraction.

"Well! go on, then," said the woman, laughing and nudging him. "Go on—introduce me —can't you? Don't stand there like a tombstone. You won't? Well, I'll introduce myself." She laughed again, and then, with an excellent imitation of Patterson's lugubrious accents, said, "Mr. Spencer Tucker's wife that *is,* allow me to introduce you to Mr. Spencer Tucker's sweetheart that *was!* Hold on! I said *that was.* For true as I stand here, ma'am —and I reckon I wouldn't stand here if it wasn't true—I haven't set eyes on him since the day he left you."

"It's the Gospel truth, every word," said Patterson, stirred into a sudden activity by Mrs. Tucker's white and rigid face. "It's the frozen truth, and I kin prove it. For I kin swear that when that there young woman was sailin' outer the Golden Gate, Spencer Tucker was in my bar room; I kin swear that I fed him, lickered him, give him a hoss and set him in his road to Monterey that very night."

"Then, where is he now?" said Mrs. Tucker, suddenly facing them.

They looked at each other, and then looked at Mrs. Tucker. Then both together replied slowly and in perfect unison, "That's—what—we—want—to—know." They seemed so satisfied with this effect that they as deliberately repeated, "Yes—that's—what—we—want—to—know."

Between the shock of meeting the partner of her husband's guilt and the unexpected revelation to her inexperience, that in suggestion and appearance there was nothing beyond the recollection of that guilt that was really shocking in the woman—between the extravagant extremes of hope and fear suggested by their words, there was something so grotesquely absurd in the melodramatic chorus that she with difficulty suppressed a hysterical laugh.

"That's the way to take it," said the woman, putting her own good-humored interpretation upon Mrs. Tucker's expression. "Now, look here! I'll tell you all about it." She carefully selected the most comfortable chair, and sitting down, lightly crossed her hands in her lap. "Well, I left here on the 13th of last January on the ship Argo, calculating that your husband would join the ship just inside the Heads. That was our arrangement, but if anything happened to prevent him, he was to join me in Acapulco. Well! He didn't come aboard, and we sailed without him. But it appears now he did attempt to join the ship, but his boat was capsized. There, now, don't be alarmed! he wasn't drowned, as Patterson can swear to—no, catch *him!* not a hair of him was hurt; but *I—I* was bundled off to the end of the earth in Mexico, alone, without a cent to bless me. For true as you live, that hound of a captain, when he found, as he thought, that Spencer was nabbed, he just confiscated all his trunks and valuables and left me in the lurch. If I hadn't met a man down there that offered to marry me and brought me here, I might have died there, I reckon. But I did, and here I am. I went down there as your husband's sweetheart, I've come back as the wife of an honest man, and I reckon it's about square!"

There was something so startlingly frank, so hopelessly self-satisfied, so contagiously good-

humored in the woman's perfect moral uncon-
sciousness, that even if Mrs. Tucker had been
less preoccupied her resentment would have
abated. But her eyes were fixed on the gloomy
face of Patterson, who was beginning to unlock
the sepulchres of his memory and disinter his
deeply buried thoughts.

"You kin bet your whole pile on what this
Mrs. Capting Baxter—ez used to be French Inez
of New Orleans—hez told ye. Ye kin take
everything she's unloaded. And it's only doin'
the square thing to her to say, she hain't done
it out o' no cussedness, but just to satisfy herself, now she's a married woman and past such
foolishness. But that ain't neither here nor
there. The gist of the whole matter is that
Spencer Tucker was at the *tienda* the day after
she sailed and after his boat capsized." He
then gave a detailed account of the interview, with the unnecessary but truthful
minutiæ of his class, adding to the particulars already known that the following
week he visited the Summit House and was
surprised to find that Spencer had never
been there, nor had he ever sailed from
Monterey.

"But why was this not told to me before?"
said Mrs. Tucker, suddenly. "Why not at the
time? Why," she demanded almost fiercely,

turning from the one to the other, "has this been
kept from me?"

"I'll tell ye why," said Patterson, sinking
with crushed submission into a chair. "When
I found he wasn't where he ought to be, I got
to lookin' elsewhere. I knew the track of the
hoss I lent him by a loose shoe. I examined,
and found he had turned off the high road somewhere beyond the lagoon, jist as if he was makin'
a bee line here."

"Well," said Mrs. Tucker, breathlessly.

"Well," said Patterson, with the resigned
tone of an accustomed martyr, "mebbe I'm a
God-forsaken idiot, but I reckon he *did* come
yer. And mebbe I'm that much of a habitooal
lunatic, but thinking so, I calkilated you'ld
know it without tellin'."

With their eyes fixed upon her, Mrs. Tucker
felt the quick blood rush to her cheeks, although
she knew not why. But they were apparently
satisfied with her ignorance, for Patterson resumed, yet more gloomily:—

"Then if he wasn't hidin' here beknownst to
you, he must have changed his mind agin and
got away by the *embarcadero*. The only thing
wantin' to prove that idea is to know how he
got a boat, and what he did with the hoss. And
thar's one more idea, and ez that can't be
proved," continued Patterson, sinking his voice

still lower, "mebbe it's accordin' to God's laws."

Unsympathetic to her as the speaker had always been and still was, Mrs. Tucker felt a vague chill creep over her that seemed to be the result of his manner more than his words. "And that idea is . . . ?" she suggested with pale lips.

"It's this! Fust, I don't say it means much to anybody but me. I've heard of these warnings afore now, ez comin' only to folks ez hear them for themselves alone, and I reckon I kin stand it, if it's the will o' God. The idea is then—that—Spencer Tucker—*was drownded* in that boat; the idea is"—his voice was almost lost in a hoarse whisper—"that it was no living man that kem to me that night, but a spirit that kem out of the darkness and went back into it! No eye saw him but mine—no ears heard him but mine. I reckon it weren't intended it should." He paused, and passed the flap of his hat across his eyes. "The pie, you'll say, is agin it," he continued in the same tone of voice,—"the whiskey is agin it—a few cuss words that dropped from him, accidental like, may have been agin it. All the same they mout have been only the little signs and tokens that it was him."

But Mrs. Baxter's ready laugh somewhat

rudely dispelled the infection of Patterson's
gloom. "I reckon the only spirit was that
which you and Spencer consumed," she said,
cheerfully. "I don't wonder you're a little
mixed. Like as not you've misunderstood his
plans." Patterson shook his head. "He'll turn
up yet, alive and kicking! Like as not, then,
Poindexter knows where he is all the time."

"Impossible! He would have told me," said
Mrs. Tucker, quickly.

Mrs. Baxter looked at Patterson without
speaking. Patterson replied by a long lugubrious whistle.

"I don't understand you," said Mrs. Tucker,
drawing back with cold dignity.

"You don't?" returned Mrs. Baxter. "Bless
your innocent heart! Why was he so keen to
hunt me up at first, shadowing my friends and
all that, and why has he dropped it now he
knows I'm here, if he didn't know where Spencer was?"

"I can explain that," interrupted Mrs.
Tucker, hastily, with a blush of confusion.
"That is—I—"

"Then mebbe you kin explain too," broke in
Patterson with gloomy significance, "why he
has bought up most of Spencer's debts himself,
and perhaps you're satisfied it *isn't* to hold the
whip hand of him and keep him from coming

back openly. Pr'aps you know why he's movin' heaven and earth to make Don José Santierra sell the ranch, and why the Don don't see it all."

"Don José sell Los Cuervos! Buy it, you mean?" said Mrs. Tucker. "*I* offered to sell it to him."

Patterson arose from the chair, looked despairingly around him, passed his hand sadly across his forehead, and said: "It's come! I knew it would. It's the warning! It's suthing betwixt jim-jams and doddering idjiocy. Here I'd hev been willin' to swear that Mrs. Baxter here told me *she* had sold this yer ranch nearly two years ago to Don José, and now you—"

"Stop!" said Mrs. Tucker, in a voice that chilled them.

She was standing upright and rigid, as if stricken to stone. "I command you to tell me what this means!" she said, turning only her blazing eyes upon the woman.

Even the ready smile faded from Mrs. Baxter's lips as she replied hesitatingly and submissively: "I thought you knew already that Spencer had given this ranch to me. I sold it to Don José to get the money for us to go away with. It was Spencer's idea—"

"You lie!" said Mrs. Tucker.

There was a dead silence. The wrathful

blood that had quickly mounted to Mrs. Baxter's cheek, to Patterson's additional bewilderment, faded as quickly. She did not lift her eyes again to Mrs. Tucker's, but, slowly raising herself from her seat, said, "I wish to God I did lie; but it's true. And it's true that I never touched a cent of the money, but gave it all to him!" She laid her hand on Patterson's arm, and said, "Come! let us go," and led him a few steps towards the gateway. But here Patterson paused, and again passed his hand over his melancholy brow. The necessity of coherently and logically closing the conversation impressed itself upon his darkening mind. "Then you don't happen to have heard anything of Spencer?" he said sadly, and vanished with Mrs. Baxter through the gate.

Left alone to herself, Mrs. Tucker raised her hands above her head with a little cry, interlocked her rigid fingers, and slowly brought her palms down upon her upturned face and eyes, pressing hard as if to crush out all light and sense of life before her. She stood thus for a moment motionless and silent, with the rising wind whispering without and flecking her white morning dress with gusty shadows from the arbor. Then, with closed eyes, dropping her hands to her breast, still pressing hard, she slowly passed them down the shapely contours

of her figure to the waist, and with another cry
cast them off as if she were stripping herself
of some loathsome garment. Then she walked
quickly to the gateway, looked out, returned to
the corridor, unloosening and taking off her
wedding-ring from her finger as she walked.
Here she paused, then slowly and deliberately
rearranged the chairs and adjusted the gay-
colored rugs that draped them, and quietly re-
entered her chamber.

Two days afterwards the sweating steed of
Captain Poindexter was turned loose in the
corral, and a moment later the captain entered
the corridor. Handing a letter to the decrepit
Concha, who seemed to be utterly disorganized
by its contents, and the few curt words with
which it was delivered, he gazed silently upon
the vacant bower, still fresh and redolent
with the delicacy and perfume of its graceful
occupant, until his dark eyes filled with un-
accustomed moisture. But his reverie was interrupted by the sound of jingling spurs without,
and the old humor struggled back in his eyes
as Don José impetuously entered. The Spaniard started back, but instantly recovered himself.

"So I find you here. Ah! it is well!" he said
passionately, producing a letter from his bosom.

"Look! Do you call this honor? Look how you keep your compact!"

Poindexter coolly took the letter. It contained a few words of gentle dignity from Mrs. Tucker, informing Don José that she had only that instant learned of his just claims upon Los Cuervos, tendering him her gratitude for his delicate intentions, but pointing out with respectful firmness that he must know that a moment's further acceptance of his courtesy was impossible.

"She has gained this knowledge from no word of mine," said Poindexter, calmly. "Right or wrong, I have kept my promise to you. I have as much reason to accuse you of betraying my secret in this," he added coldly, as he took another letter from his pocket and handed it to Don José.

It seemed briefer and colder, but was neither. It reminded Poindexter that as he had again deceived her she must take the government of her affairs in her own hands henceforth. She abandoned all the furniture and improvements she had put in Los Cuervos to him, to whom she now knew she was indebted for them. She could not thank him for what his habitual generosity impelled him to do for any woman, but she could forgive him for misunderstanding her like any other woman, perhaps she should say, like a child. When he received this she would be already on her way to her old home in Kentucky, where she still hoped to be able by her own efforts to amass enough to discharge her obligations to him.

"She does not speak of her husband, this woman," said Don José, scanning Poindexter's face. "It is possible she rejoins him, eh?"

"Perhaps in one way she has never left him, Don José," said Poindexter, with grave significance.

Don José's face flushed, but he returned carelessly, "And the *rancho,* naturally you will not buy it now?"

"On the contrary, I shall abide by my offer," said Poindexter, quietly.

Don José eyed him narrowly, and then said, "Ah, we shall consider of it."

He did consider it, and accepted the offer. With the full control of the land, Captain Poindexter's improvements, so indefinitely postponed, were actively pushed forward. The thick walls of the *hacienda* were the first to melt away before them; the low lines of corral were effaced, and the early breath of the summer trade winds swept uninterruptedly across the now leveled plain to the *embarcadero,* where a newer structure arose. A more vivid green alone marked the spot where the crumbling

adobe walls of the *casa* had returned to the
parent soil that gave it. The channel was deepened, the lagoon was drained, until one evening
the magic mirror that had so long reflected the
weary waiting of the Blue Grass Penelope lay
dull, dead, lustreless, an opaque quagmire of
noisome corruption and decay to be put away
from the sight of man forever. On this spot the
crows, the titular tenants of Los Cuervos, assembled in tumultuous congress, coming and
going in mysterious clouds, or laboring in thick
and writhing masses, as if they were continuing
the work of improvement begun by human
agency. So well had they done the work that
by the end of a week only a few scattered white
objects remained glittering on the surface of
the quickly drying soil. But they were the
bones of the missing outcast, Spencer Tucker!

.   .   .   .

The same spring a breath of war swept over
a foul, decaying quagmire of the whole land,
before which such passing deeds as these were
blown as vapor. It called men of all rank and
condition to battle for a nation's life, and among
the first to respond were those into whose boyish
hands had been placed the nation's honor. It
returned the epaulets to Poindexter's shoulder
with the addition of a double star, carried him
triumphantly to the front, and left him, at the

end of a summer's day and a hard-won fight, sorely wounded, at the door of a Blue Grass farmhouse. And the woman who sought him out and ministered to his wants said timidly, as she left her hand in his, "I told you I should live to repay you."

LEFT OUT ON LONE STAR MOUNTAIN.

CHAPTER I.

THERE was little doubt that the Lone Star claim was "played out." Not dug out, worked out, washed out, but *played* out. For two years its five sanguine proprietors had gone through the various stages of mining enthusiasm; had prospected and planned, dug and doubted. They had borrowed money with hearty but unredeeming frankness, established a credit with unselfish abnegation of all responsibility, and had borne the disappointment of their creditors with a cheerful resignation which only the consciousness of some deep Compensating Future could give. Giving little else, however, a singular dissatisfaction obtained with the traders, and, being accompanied with a reluctance to make further advances, at last touched the gentle stoicism of the proprietors themselves. The youthful enthusiasm which

449

had at first lifted the most ineffectual trial, the most useless essay, to the plane of actual achievement, died out, leaving them only the dull, prosaic record of half-finished ditches, purposeless shafts, untenable pits, abandoned engines, and meaningless disruptions of the soil upon the Lone Star claim, and empty flour sacks and pork barrels in the Lone Star cabin.

They had borne their poverty, if that term could be applied to a light renunciation of all superfluities in food, dress, or ornament, ameliorated by the gentle depredations already alluded to, with unassuming levity. More than that: having segregated themselves from their fellow-miners of Red Gulch, and entered upon the possession of the little manzanita-thicketed valley five miles away, the failure of their enterprise had assumed in their eyes only the vague significance of the decline and fall of a general community, and to that extent relieved them of individual responsibility. It was easier for them to admit that the Lone Star claim was "played out" than confess to a personal bankruptcy. Moreover, they still retained the sacred right of criticism of government, and rose superior in their private opinions to their own collective wisdom. Each one experienced a grateful sense of the entire responsibility of the other four in the fate of their enterprise.

On December 24, 1863, a gentle rain was still falling over the length and breadth of the Lone Star claim. It had been falling for several days, had already called a faint spring color to the wan landscape, repairing with tender touches the ravages wrought by the proprietors, or charitably covering their faults. The ragged seams in gulch and cañon lost their harsh outlines, a thin green mantle faintly clothed the torn and abraded hillside. A few weeks more, and a veil of forgetfulness would be drawn over the feeble failures of the Lone Star claim. The charming derelicts themselves, listening to the raindrops on the roof of their little cabin, gazed philosophically from the open door, and accepted the prospect as a moral discharge from their obligations. Four of the five partners were present. The Right and Left Bowers, Union Mills, and the Judge.

It is scarcely necessary to say that not one of these titles was the genuine name of its possessor. The Right and Left Bowers were two brothers; their sobriquets, a cheerful adaptation from the favorite game of euchre, expressing their relative value in the camp. The mere fact that Union Mills had at one time patched his trousers with an old flour sack legibly bearing that brand of its fabrication, was a tempting baptismal suggestion that the other partners could not forego. The Judge, a singularly inequitable Missourian, with no knowledge whatever of the law, was an inspiration of gratuitous irony.

Union Mills, who had been for some time sitting placidly on the threshold with one leg exposed to the rain, from a sheer indolent inability to change his position, finally withdrew that weather-beaten member, and stood up. The movement more or less deranged the attitudes of the other partners, and was received with cynical disfavor. It was somewhat remarkable that, although generally giving the appearance of healthy youth and perfect physical condition, they one and all simulated the decrepitude of age and invalidism, and after limping about for a few moments, settled back again upon their bunks and stools in their former positions. The Left Bower lazily replaced a bandage that he had worn around his ankle for weeks without any apparent necessity, and the Judge scrutinized with tender solicitude the faded cicatrix of a scratch upon his arm. A passive hypochondria, born of their isolation, was the last ludicrously pathetic touch to their situation.

The immediate cause of this commotion felt the necessity of an explanation.

"It would have been just as easy for you to have stayed outside with your business leg, in-

stead of dragging it into private life in that
obtrusive way," retorted the Right Bower; "but
that exhaustive effort isn't going to fill the pork
barrel. The grocery man at Dalton says—
what's that he said?" he appealed lazily to the
Judge.

"Said he reckoned the Lone Star was about
played out, and he didn't want any more in his
—thank you!" repeated the Judge with a mechanical effort of memory utterly devoid of personal or present interest.

"I always suspected that man, after Grim-
shaw begun to deal with him," said the Left
Bower. "They're just mean enough to join
hands against us." It was a fixed belief of the
Lone Star partners that they were pursued by
personal enmities.

"More than likely those new strangers over
in the Fork have been paying cash and filled
him up with conceit," said Union Mills, trying
to dry his leg by alternately beating it or rubbing
it against the cabin wall. "Once begin wrong
with that kind of snipe and you drag everybody
down with you."

This vague conclusion was received with dead
silence. Everybody had become interested in
the speaker's peculiar method of drying his leg,
to the exclusion of the previous topic. A few
offered criticism, no one assistance.

"Who did the grocery man say that to?" asked the Right Bower, finally returning to the question.

"The Old Man," answered the Judge.

"Of course," ejaculated the Right Bower sarcastically.

"Of course," echoed the other partners together. "That's like him. The Old Man all over!"

It did not appear exactly what was like the Old Man, or why it was like him, but generally that he alone was responsible for the grocery man's defection. It was put more concisely by Union Mills.

"That comes of letting him go there! It's just a fair provocation to any man to have the Old Man sent to him. They can't, sorter, restrain themselves at him. He's enough to spoil the credit of the Rothschilds."

"That's so," chimed in the Judge. "And look at his prospecting. Why, he was out two nights last week, all night, prospecting in the moonlight for blind leads, just out of sheer foolishness."

"It was quite enough for me," broke in the Left Bower, "when the other day, you remember when, he proposed to us white men to settle down to plain ground sluicing, making 'grub' wages just like any Chinaman.

It just showed his idea of the Lone Star claim."

"Well, I never said it afore," added Union Mills, "but when that one of the Mattison boys came over here to examine the claim with an eye to purchasin', it was the Old Man that took the conceit out of him. He just as good as admitted that a lot of work had got to be done afore any pay ore could be realized. Never even asked him over to the shanty here to jine us in a friendly game; just kept him, so to speak, to himself. And naturally the Mattisons didn't see it."

A silence followed, broken only by the rain monotonously falling on the roof, and occasionally through the broad adobe chimney, where it provoked a retaliating hiss and splutter from the dying embers of the hearth. The Right Bower, with a sudden access of energy, drew the empty barrel before him, and taking a pack of well-worn cards from his pocket, began to make a "solitaire" upon the lid. The others gazed at him with languid interest.

"Makin' it for anythin'?" asked Mills.

The Right Bower nodded.

The Judge and Left Bower, who were partly lying in their respective bunks, sat up to get a better view of the game. Union Mills slowly disengaged himself from the wall and leaned

over the "solitaire" player. The Right Bower
turned the last card in a pause of almost thrilling suspense, and clapped it down on the lid
with fateful emphasis.

"It went!" said the Judge in a voice of
hushed respect. "What did you make it for?"
he almost whispered.

"To know if we'd make the break we talked
about and vamose the ranch. It's the *fifth* time
today," continued the Right Bower in a voice of
gloomy significance. "And it went agin bad
cards too."

"I ain't superstitious," said the Judge, with
awe and fatuity beaming from every line of his
credulous face, "but it's flyin' in the face of
Providence to go agin such signs as that."

"Make it again, to see if the Old Man must
go," suggested the Left Bower.

The suggestion was received with favor, the
three men gathering breathlessly around the
player. Again the fateful cards were shuffled
deliberately, placed in their mysterious combination, with the same ominous result. Yet
everybody seemed to breathe more freely, as if
relieved from some responsibility, the Judge
accepting this manifest expression of Providence
with resigned self-righteousness.

"Yes, gentlemen," resumed the Left Bower,
serenely, as if a calm legal decision had just

been recorded, "we must not let any foolishness or sentiment get mixed up with this thing, but look at it like business men. The only sensible move is to get up and get out of the camp."

"And the Old Man?" queried the Judge.

"The Old Man—hush! he's coming."

The doorway was darkened by a slight lissome shadow. It was the absent partner, otherwise known as "the Old Man." Need it be added that he was a *boy* of nineteen, with a slight down just clothing his upper lip!

"The creek is up over the ford, and I had to 'shin' up a willow on the bank and swing myself across," he said, with a quick, frank laugh; "but all the same, boys, it's going to clear up in about an hour, you bet. It's breaking away over Bald Mountain, and there's a sun flash on a bit of snow on Lone Peak. Look! you can see it from here. It's for all the world like Noah's dove just landed on Mount Ararat. It's a good omen."

From sheer force of habit the men had momentarily brightened up at the Old Man's entrance. But the unblushing exhibition of degrading superstition shown in the last sentence recalled their just severity. They exchanged meaning glances. Union Mills uttered hopelessly to himself: "Hell's full of such omens."

Too occupied with his subject to notice this

ominous reception, the Old Man continued: "I reckon I struck a fresh lead in the new grocery man at the Crossing. He says he'll let the Judge have a pair of boots on credit, but he can't send them over here; and considering that the Judge has got to try them anyway, it don't seem to be asking too much for the Judge to go over there. He says he'll give us a barrel of pork and a bag of flour if we'll give him the right of using our tail-race and clean out the lower end of it."

"It's the work of a Chinaman, and a four days' job," broke in the Left Bower.

"It took one white man only two hours to clean out a third of it," retorted the Old Man triumphantly, "for *I* pitched in at once with a pick he let me have on credit, and did that amount of work this morning, and told him the rest of you boys would finish it this afternoon."

A slight gesture from the Right Bower checked an angry exclamation from the Left. The Old Man did not notice either, but, knitting his smooth young brow in a paternally reflective fashion, went on: "You'll have to get a new pair of trousers, Mills, but as he doesn't keep clothing, we'll have to get some canvas and cut you out a pair. I traded off the beans he let me have for some tobacco for the Right Bower at the other shop, and got them to throw in a new pack of cards. These are about played out. We'll be wanting some brushwood for the fire; there's a heap in the hollow. Who's going to bring it in? It's the Judge's turn, isn't it? Why, what's the matter with you all?"

The restraint and evident uneasiness of his companions had at last touched him. He turned his frank young eyes upon them; they glanced helplessly at each other. Yet his first concern was for them, his first instinct paternal and protecting. He ran his eyes quickly over them; they were all there and apparently in their usual condition. "Anything wrong with the claim?" he suggested.

Without looking at him the Right Bower rose, leaned against the open door with his hands behind him and his face towards the landscape, and said, apparently to the distant prospect: "The claim's played out, the partnership's played out, and the sooner we skedaddle out of this the better. If," he added, turning to the Old Man, "if *you* want to stay, if you want to do Chinaman's work at Chinaman's wages, if you want to hang on to the charity of the traders at the Crossing, you can do it, and enjoy the prospects and the Noah's doves alone. But we're calculatin' to step out of it."

"But I haven't said I wanted to do it *alone*,"

protested the Old Man with a gesture of bewilderment.

"If these are your general ideas of the partnership," continued the Right Bower, clinging to the established hypothesis of the other partners for support, "it ain't ours, and the only way we can prove it is to stop the foolishness right here. We calculated to dissolve the partnership and strike out for ourselves elsewhere. You're no longer responsible for us, nor we for you. And we reckon it's the square thing to leave you the claim and the cabin, and all it contains. To prevent any trouble with the traders, we've drawn up a paper here—"

"With a bonus of fifty thousand dollars each down, and the rest to be settled on my children," interrupted the Old Man, with a half-uneasy laugh. "Of course. But—" he stopped suddenly, the blood dropped from his fresh cheek, and he again glanced quickly round the group. "I don't think—I—I quite *sabe*, boys," he added, with a slight tremor of voice and lip. "If it's a conundrum, ask me an easier one."

Any lingering doubt he might have had of their meaning was dispelled by the Judge. "It's about the softest thing you kin drop into, Old Man," he said confidentially; "if *I* hadn't promised the other boys to go with them, and if I didn't need the best medical advice in Sacra-

mento for my lungs, I'd just enjoy staying
with you."

"It gives a sorter freedom to a young fellow
like you, Old Man, like goin' into the world on
your own capital, that every Californian boy
hasn't got," said Union Mills, patronizingly.

"Of course it's rather hard papers on us, you
know, givin' up everything, so to speak; but it's
for your good, and we ain't goin' back on you,"
said the Left Bower, "are we, boys?"

The color had returned to the Old Man's
face a little more quickly and freely than usual.
He picked up the hat he had cast down, put it
on carefully over his brown curls, drew the flap
down on the side towards his companions, and
put his hands in his pockets. "All right," he
said, in a slightly altered voice. "When do you
go?"

"To-day," answered the Left Bower. "We
calculate to take a moonlight *pasear* over to the
Cross Roads and meet the down stage at about
twelve to-night. There's plenty of time yet,"
he added, with a slight laugh; "it's only three
o'clock now."

There was a dead silence. Even the rain
withheld its continuous patter, a dumb, gray
film covered the ashes of the hushed hearth.
For the first time the Right Bower exhibited
some slight embarrassment.

"I reckon it's held up for a spell," he said, ostentatiously examining the weather, "and we might as well take a run round the claim to see if we've forgotten nothing. Of course, we'll be back again," he added hastily, without looking at the Old Man, "before we go, you know."

The others began to look for their hats, but so awkwardly and with such evident preoccupation of mind that it was not at first discovered that the Judge had his already on. This raised a laugh, as did also a clumsy stumble of Union Mills against the pork barrel, although that gentleman took refuge from his confusion and secured a decent retreat by a gross exaggeration of his lameness, as he limped after the Right Bower. The Judge whistled feebly. The Left Bower, in a more ambitious effort to impart a certain gayety to his exit, stopped on the threshold and said, as if in arch confidence to his companions, "Darned if the Old Man don't look two inches higher since he became a proprietor," laughed patronizingly, and vanished.

If the newly-made proprietor had increased in stature, he had not otherwise changed his demeanor. He remained in the same attitude until the last figure disappeared behind the fringe of buckeye that hid the distant highway. Then he walked slowly to the fire-place, and, leaning against the chimney, kicked the dying embers together with his foot. Something dropped and spattered in the film of hot ashes. Surely the rain had not yet ceased!

His high color had already fled except for a spot on either cheek-bone that lent a brightness to his eyes. He glanced around the cabin. It looked familiar and yet strange. Rather, it looked strange *because* still familiar, and therefore incongruous with the new atmosphere that surrounded it—discordant with the echo of their last meeting, and painfully accenting the change. There were the four "bunks," or sleeping berths, of his companions, each still bearing some traces of the individuality of its late occupant with a dumb loyalty that seemed to make their light-hearted defection monstrous. In the dead ashes of the Judge's pipe, scattered on his shelf, still lived his old fire; in the whittled and carved edges of the Left Bower's bunk still were the memories of bygone days of delicious indolence; in the bullet-holes clustered round a knot of one of the beams there was still the record of the Right Bower's old-time skill and practice; in the few engravings of female loveliness stuck upon each headboard there were the proofs of their old extravagant devotion—all a mute protest to the change.

He remembered how, a fatherless, truant schoolboy, he had drifted into their adventurous, nomadic life, itself a life of grown-up truancy like his own, and became one of that gypsy family. How they had taken the place of relations and household in his boyish fancy, filling it with the unsubstantial pageantry of a child's play at grown-up existence, he knew only too well. But how, from being a pet and *protégé,* he had gradually and unconsciously asserted his own individuality and taken upon his younger shoulders not only a poet's keen appreciation of that life, but its actual responsibilities and half-childish burdens, he never suspected. He had fondly believed that he was a neophyte in their ways, a novice in their charming faith and indolent creed, and they had encouraged it; now their renunciation of that faith could only be an excuse for a renunciation of *him.* The poetry that had for two years invested the material and sometimes even mean details of their existence was too much a part of himself to be lightly dispelled. The lesson of those ingenuous moralists failed, as such lessons are apt to fail; their discipline provoked but did not subdue; a rising indignation, stirred by a sense of injury, mounted to his cheek and eyes. It was slow to come, but was none the less violent that it had been preceded by the benumbing shock of shame and pride.

I hope I shall not prejudice the reader's

sympathies if my duty as a simple chronicler
compels me to state, therefore, that the sober
second thought of this gentle poet was to burn
down the cabin on the spot with all its contents.
This yielded to a milder counsel—waiting for
the return of the party, challenging the Right
Bower, a duel to the death, perhaps himself
the victim, with a crushing explanation *in
extremis*, "It seems we are *one* too many. No
matter; it is settled now. Farewell!" Dimly
remembering, however, that there was something of this in the last well-worn novel they
had read together, and that his antagonist might
recognize it, or even worse, anticipate it himself, the idea was quickly rejected. Besides,
the opportunity for an apotheosis of self-sacri-
fice was past. Nothing remained now but to
refuse the proffered bribe of claim and cabin
by letter, for he must not wait their return. He
tore a leaf from a blotted diary, begun and
abandoned long since, and essayed to write.
Scrawl after scrawl was torn up, until his fury
had cooled down to a frigid third personality.
"Mr. John Ford regrets to inform his late partners that their tender of house, of furniture,"
however, seemed too inconsistent with the pork-
barrel table he was writing on; a more eloquent
renunciation of their offer became frivolous and
idiotic from a caricature of Union Mills, label

and all, that appeared suddenly on the other side of the leaf; and when he at last indited a satisfactory and impassioned exposition of his feelings, the legible *addendum* of "Oh, ain't you glad you're out of the wilderness!"—the forgotten first line of a popular song, which no scratching would erase—seemed too like an ironical postscript to be thought of for a moment. He threw aside his pen and cast the discordant record of past foolish pastime into the dead ashes of the hearth.

How quiet it was. With the cessation of the rain the wind too had gone down, and scarcely a breath of air came through the open door. He walked to the threshold and gazed on the hushed prospect. In this listless attitude he was faintly conscious of a distant reverberation, a mere phantom of sound—perhaps the explosion of a distant blast in the hills—that left the silence more marked and oppressive. As he turned again into the cabin a change seemed to have come over it. It already looked old and decayed. The loneliness of years of desertion seemed to have taken possession of it; the atmosphere of dry rot was in the beams and rafters. To his excited fancy the few disordered blankets and articles of clothing seemed dropping to pieces; in one of the bunks there was a hideous resemblance in the longitudinal heap of clothing to a withered and mummied corpse. So it might look in after years when some passing stranger—but he stopped. A dread of the place was beginning to creep over him; a dread of the days to come, when the monotonous sunshine should lay bare the loneliness of these walls; the long, long days of endless blue and cloudless, overhanging solitude; summer days when the wearying, incessant trade winds should sing around that empty shell and voice its desolation. He gathered together hastily a few articles that were especially his own—rather that the free communion of the camp, from indifference or accident, had left wholly to him. He hesitated for a moment over his rifle, but, scrupulous in his wounded pride, turned away and left the familiar weapon that in the dark days had so often provided the dinner or breakfast of the little household. Candor compels me to state that his equipment was not large nor eminently practical. His scant pack was a light weight for even his young shoulders, but I fear he thought more of getting away from the Past than providing for the Future.

With this vague but sole purpose he left the cabin, and almost mechanically turned his steps towards the creek he had crossed that morning. He knew that by this route he would avoid meeting his companions; its difficulties and circuitousness would exercise his feverish limbs and give him time for reflection. He had determined to leave the claim, but whence he had not yet considered. He reached the bank of the creek where he had stood two hours before; it seemed to him two years. He looked curiously at his reflection in one of the broad pools of overflow, and fancied he looked older. He watched the rush and outset of the turbid current hurrying to meet the South Fork, and to eventually lose itself in the yellow Sacramento. Even in his preoccupation he was impressed with a likeness to himself and his companions in this flood that had burst its peaceful boundaries. In the drifting fragments of one of their forgotten flumes washed from the bank, he fancied he saw an omen of the disintegration and decay of the Lone Star claim.

The strange hush in the air that he had noticed before—a calm so inconsistent with that hour and the season as to seem portentous— became more marked in contrast to the feverish rush of the turbulent water-course. A few clouds lazily huddled in the west apparently had gone to rest with the sun on beds of somnolent poppies. There was a gleam as of golden water everywhere along the horizon, washing out the cold snowpeaks, and drowning even the rising moon. The creek caught it here

and there, until, in grim irony, it seemed to
bear their broken sluice-boxes and useless engines on the very Pactolian stream they had
been hopefully created to direct and carry. But
by some peculiar trick of the atmosphere, the
perfect plenitude of that golden sunset glory
was lavished on the rugged sides and tangled
crest of the Lone Star mountain. That isolated
peak, the landmark of their claim, the gaunt
monument of their folly, transfigured in the
evening splendor, kept its radiance unquenched
long after the glow had fallen from the encompassing skies, and when at last the rising moon,
step by step, put out the fires along the winding
valley and plains, and crept up the bosky sides
of the cañon, the vanishing sunset was lost only
to reappear as a golden crown.

The eyes of the young man were fixed upon
it with more than a momentary picturesque
interest. It had been the favorite ground of his
prospecting exploits, its lowest flank had been
scarred in the old enthusiastic days with hydraulic engines, or pierced with shafts, but its
central position in the claim and its superior
height had always given it a commanding view
of the extent of their valley and its approaches,
and it was this practical preëminence that alone
attracted him at that moment. He knew that
from its crest he would be able to distinguish

the figures of his companions, as they crossed the valley near the cabin, in the growing moonlight. Thus he could avoid encountering them on his way to the high road, and yet see them, perhaps, for the last time. Even in his sense of injury there was a strange satisfaction in the thought.

The ascent was toilsome, but familiar. All along the dim trail he was accompanied by gentler memories of the past, that seemed, like the faint odor of spiced leaves and fragrant grasses wet with the rain and crushed beneath his ascending tread, to exhale the sweeter perfume in his effort to subdue or rise above them. There was the thicket of manzanita, where they had broken noonday bread together; here was the rock beside their maiden shaft, where they had poured a wild libation in boyish enthusiasm of success; and here the ledge where their first flag, a red shirt heroically sacrificed, was displayed from a long-handled shovel to the gaze of admirers below. When he at last reached the summit, the mysterious hush was still in the air, as if in breathless sympathy with his expedition. In the west, the plain was faintly illuminated, but disclosed no moving figures. He turned towards the rising moon, and moved slowly to the eastern edge. Suddenly he stopped. Another step would have been his last! He stood upon the crumbling edge of a precipice. A landslip had taken place on the eastern flank, leaving the gaunt ribs and fleshless bones of Lone Star mountain bare in the moonlight. He understood now the strange rumble and reverberation he had heard; he understood now the strange hush of bird and beast in brake and thicket!

Although a single rapid glance convinced him that the slide had taken place in an unfrequented part of the mountain, above an inaccessible cañon, and reflection assured him his companions could not have reached that distance when it took place, a feverish impulse led him to descend a few rods in the track of the avalanche. The frequent recurrence of outcrop and angle made this comparatively easy. Here he called aloud; the feeble echo of his own voice seemed only a dull impertinence to the significant silence. He turned to reascend; the furrowed flank of the mountain before him lay full in the moonlight. To his excited fancy, a dozen luminous star-like points in the rocky crevices started into life as he faced them. Throwing his arm over the ledge above him, he supported himself for a moment by what appeared to be a projection of the solid rock. It trembled slightly. As he raised himself to its level, his heart stopped beating. It was simply a fragment detached from the outcrop, lying loosely on the ledge but upholding him by *its own weight only*. He examined it with trembling fingers; the encumbering soil fell from its sides and left its smoothed and worn protuberances glistening in the moonlight. It was virgin gold!

Looking back upon that moment afterwards, he remembered that he was not dazed, dazzled, or startled. It did not come to him as a discovery or an accident, a stroke of chance or a caprice of fortune. He saw it all in that supreme moment; Nature had worked out their poor deduction. What their feeble engines had essayed spasmodically and helplessly against the curtain of soil that hid the treasure, the elements had achieved with mightier but more patient forces. The slow sapping of the winter rains had loosened the soil from the auriferous rock, even while the swollen stream was carrying their impotent and shattered engines to the sea.

What mattered that his single arm could not lift the treasure he had found! What mattered that to unfix those glittering stars would still tax both skill and patience! The work was done, the goal was reached! even his boyish impatience was content with that. He rose slowly to his feet, unstrapped his long-handled shovel from his back, secured it in the crevice, and quietly regained the summit.

It was all his own! His own by right of discovery under the law of the land, and without accepting a favor from *them*. He recalled even the fact that it was *his* prospecting on the mountain that first suggested the existence of gold in the outcrop and the use of the hydraulic. *He* had never abandoned that belief, whatever the others had done. He dwelt somewhat indignantly to himself on this circumstance, and half unconsciously faced defiantly towards the plain below. But it was sleeping peacefully in the full sight of the moon, without life or motion. He looked at the stars; it was still far from midnight. His companions had no doubt long since returned to the cabin to prepare for their midnight journey. They were discussing him, perhaps laughing at him, or worse, pitying him and his bargain. Yet here was his bargain! A slight laugh he gave vent to here startled him a little, it sounded so hard and so unmirthful, and so unlike, as he oddly fancied, what he really *thought*. But *what* did he think?

Nothing mean or revengeful; no, they never would say *that*. When he had taken out all the surface gold and put the mine in working order, he would send them each a draft for a thousand dollars. Of course, if they were ever ill or poor

he would do more. One of the first, the very
first things he should do would be to send them
each a handsome gun and tell them that he only
asked in return the old-fashioned rifle that once
was his. Looking back at the moment in after
years, he wondered that, with this exception, he
made no plans for his own future, or the way
he should dispose of his newly acquired wealth.
This was the more singular as it had been the
custom of the five partners to lie awake at night,
audibly comparing with each other what they
would do in case they made a strike. He remembered how, Alnaschar-like, they nearly
separated once over a difference in the disposal
of a hundred thousand dollars that they never
had, nor expected to have. He remembered how
Union Mills always began his career as a mil-
lionnaire by a "square meal" at Delmonico's;
how the Right Bower's initial step was always
a trip home "to see his mother"; how the Left
Bower would immediately placate the parents of
his beloved with priceless gifts (it may be par-
enthetically remarked that the parents and the
beloved one were as hypothetical as the fortune); and how the Judge would make his
first start as a capitalist by breaking a certain
faro bank in Sacramento. He himself had
been equally eloquent in extravagant fancy in
those penniless days, he who now was quite

cold and impassive beside the more extravagant reality.

How different it might have been! If they had only waited a day longer! if they had only broken their resolves to him kindly and parted in good will! How he would long ere this have rushed to greet them with the joyful news! How they would have danced around it, sung themselves hoarse, laughed down their enemies, and run up the flag triumphantly on the summit of the Lone Star Mountain! How they would have crowned him "the Old Man," "the hero of the camp!" How he would have told them the whole story; how some strange instinct had impelled him to ascend the summit, and how another step on that summit would have precipitated him into the cañon! And how—but what if somebody else, Union Mills or the Judge, had been the first discoverer? Might they not have meanly kept the secret from him; have selfishly helped themselves and done—

"What *you* are doing now."

The hot blood rushed to his cheek, as if a strange voice were at his ear. For a moment he could not believe that it came from his own pale lips until he found himself speaking. He rose to his feet, tingling with shame, and began hurriedly to descend the mountain.

He would go to them, tell them of his discovery, let them give him his share, and leave them forever. It was the only thing to be done, strange that he had not thought of it at once. Yet it was hard, very hard and cruel to be forced to meet them again. What had he done to suffer this mortification? For a moment he actually hated this vulgar treasure that had forever buried under its gross ponderability the light and careless past, and utterly crushed out the poetry of their old, indolent, happy existence.

He was sure to find them waiting at the Cross Roads where the coach came past. It was three miles away, yet he could get there in time if he hastened. It was a wise and practical conclusion of his evening's work, a lame and impotent conclusion to his evening's indignation. No matter. They would perhaps at first think he had come to weakly follow them, perhaps they would at first doubt his story. No matter. He bit his lips to keep down the foolish rising tears, but still went blindly forward.

He saw not the beautiful night, cradled in the dark hills, swathed in luminous mists, and hushed in the awe of its own loveliness! Here and there the moon had laid her calm face on lake and overflow, and gone to sleep embracing them, until the whole plain seemed to be lifted into infinite quiet. Walking on as in a dream, the black, impenetrable barriers of skirting thickets opened and gave way to vague distances that it appeared impossible to reach, dim vistas that seemed unapproachable. Gradually he seemed himself to become a part of the mysterious night. He was becoming as pulseless, as calm, as passionless.

What was that? A shot in the direction of the cabin! yet so faint, so echoless, so ineffective in the vast silence, that he would have thought it his fancy but for the strange instinctive jar upon his sensitive nerves. Was it an accident, or was it an intentional signal to him? He stopped; it was not repeated, the silence reasserted itself, but this time with an ominous death-like suggestion. A sudden and terrible thought crossed his mind. He cast aside his pack and all encumbering weight, took a deep breath, lowered his head and darted like a deer in the direction of the challenge.

CHAPTER II.

THE exodus of the seceding partners of the Lone Star claim had been scarcely an imposing one. For the first five minutes after quitting the cabin, the procession was straggling and vagabond. Unwonted exertion had exaggerated the lameness of some, and feebleness of moral purpose had predisposed the others to obtrusive musical exhibition. Union Mills limped and whistled with affected abstraction; the Judge whistled and limped with affected earnestness. The Right Bower led the way with some show of definite design; the Left Bower followed with his hands in his pockets. The two feebler natures, drawn together in unconscious sympathy, looked vaguely at each other for support.

"You see,'" said the Judge, suddenly, as if triumphantly concluding an argument, "there ain't anything better for a young fellow than independence. Nature, so to speak, points the way. Look at the animals."

"There's a skunk hereabouts," said Union Mills, who was supposed to be gifted with aristocratically sensitive nostrils, "within ten miles of this place; like as not crossing the Ridge. It's always my luck to happen out just at such times. I don't see the necessity anyhow of trapesing round the claim now, if we calculate to leave it to-night."

Both men waited to observe if the suggestion was taken up by the Right and Left Bower moodily plodding ahead. No response following, the Judge shamelessly abandoned his companion.

"You wouldn't stand snoopin' round instead

of lettin' the Old Man get used to the idea
alone? No; I could see all along that he was
takin' it in, takin' it in, kindly but slowly, and
I reckoned the best thing for us to do was to
git up and git until he'd got round it." The
Judge's voice was slightly raised for the benefit
of the two before him.

"Didn't he say," remarked the Right Bower,
stopping suddenly and facing the others, "didn't
he say that that new trader was goin' to let him
have some provisions anyway?"

Union Mills turned appealingly to the Judge;
that gentleman was forced to reply, "Yes; I remember distinctly he said it. It was one of
the things I was particular about on his account," responded the Judge, with the air of
having arranged it all himself with the new
trader. "I remember I was easier in my mind
about it."

"But didn't he say," queried the Left Bower,
also stopping short, "suthin' about it's being
contingent on our doing some work on the
race?"

The Judge turned for support to Union Mills,
who, however, under the hollow pretense of pre-
paring for a long conference, had luxuriously
seated himself on a stump. The Judge sat down
also, and replied, hesitatingly, "Well, yes! Us
or him."

"Us or him," repeated the Right Bower, with gloomy irony. "And you ain't quite clear in your mind, are you, if *you* haven't done the work already? You're just killing yourself with this spontaneous, promiscuous, and premature overwork; that's what's the matter with you."

"I reckon I heard somebody say suthin' about it's being a Chinaman's three-day job," interpolated the Left Bower, with equal irony, "but I ain't quite clear in my mind about that."

"It'll be a sorter distraction for the Old Man," said Union Mills, feebly—"kinder take his mind off his loneliness."

Nobody taking the least notice of the remark, Union Mills stretched out his legs more comfortably and took out his pipe. He had scarcely done so when the Right Bower, wheeling suddenly, set off in the direction of the creek. The Left Bower, after a slight pause, followed without a word. The Judge, wisely conceiving it better to join the stronger party, ran feebly after him, and left Union Mills to bring up a weak and vacillating rear.

Their course, diverging from Lone Star Mountain, led them now directly to the bend of the creek, the base of their old ineffectual operations. Here was the beginning of the famous tail-race that skirted the new trader's claim, and then lost its way in a swampy hollow. It was choked with débris; a thin, yellow stream that once ran through it seemed to have stopped work when they did, and gone into greenish liquidation.

They had scarcely spoken during this brief journey, and had received no other explanation from the Right Bower, who led them, than that afforded by his mute example when he reached the race. Leaping into it without a word, he at once began to clear away the broken timbers and drift-wood. Fired by the spectacle of what appeared to be a new and utterly frivolous game, the men gayly leaped after him, and were soon engaged in a fascinating struggle with the impeded race. The Judge forgot his lameness in springing over a broken sluice-box; Union Mills forgot his whistle in a happy imitation of a Chinese coolie's song. Nevertheless, after ten minutes of this mild dissipation, the pastime flagged; Union Mills was beginning to rub his leg when a distant rumble shook the earth. The men looked at each other; the diversion was complete; a languid discussion of the probabilities of its being an earthquake or a blast followed, in the midst of which the Right Bower, who was working a little in advance of the others, uttered a warning cry and leaped from the race. His companions had barely time to follow before a sudden and inexplicable rise in the waters of the creek sent a swift irruption of the flood through the race. In an instant its choked and impeded channel was cleared, the race was free, and the scattered débris of logs and timber floated upon its easy current. Quick to take advantage of this labor-saving phenomenon, the Lone Star partners sprang into the water, and by disentangling and directing the eddying fragments completed their work.

"The Old Man oughter been here to see this," said the Left Bower; "it's just one o' them climaxes of poetic justice he's always huntin' up. It's easy to see what's happened. One o' them high-toned shrimps over in the Excelsior claim has put a blast in too near the creek. He's tumbled the bank into the creek and sent the back water down here just to wash out our race. That's what I call poetical retribution."

"And who was it advised us to dam the creek below the race and make it do the thing?" asked the Right Bower, moodily.

"That was one of the Old Man's ideas, I reckon," said the Left Bower, dubiously.

"And you remember," broke in the Judge with animation, "I allus said, 'Go slow, go slow. You just hold on and suthin' will happen.' And," he added, triumphantly, "you see suthin' has happened. I don't want to take credit to myself, but I reckoned on them Excelsior boys bein' fools, and took the chances."

"And what if I happen to know that the Excelsior boys ain't blastin' to-day?" said the Right Bower, sarcastically.

As the Judge had evidently based his hypothesis on the alleged fact of a blast, he deftly evaded the point. "I ain't saying the Old Man's head ain't level on some things; he wants a little more *sabe* of the world. He's improved a good deal in euchre lately, and in poker—well! he's got that sorter dreamy, listenin'-to-the-angels kind o' way that you can't exactly tell whether he's bluffin' or has got a full hand. Hasn't he?" he asked, appealing to Union Mills.

But that gentleman, who had been watching the dark face of the Right Bower, preferred to take what he believed to be his cue from him. "That ain't the question," he said virtuously; "we ain't takin' this step to make a card sharp out of him. We're not doin' Chinamen's work in this race to-day for that. No, sir! We're teachin' him to paddle his own canoe." Not finding the sympathetic response he looked for in the Right Bower's face, he turned to the Left.

"I reckon we were teachin' him our canoe was too full," was the Left Bower's unexpected reply. "That's about the size of it."

The Right Bower shot a rapid glance under his brows at his brother. The latter, with his hands in his pockets, stared unconsciously at the rushing waters, and then quietly turned away. The Right Bower followed him. "Are you goin' back on us?" he asked.

"Are you?" responded the other.

"No!"

"*No*, then it is," returned the Left Bower quietly. The elder brother hesitated in half-angry embarrassment.

"Then what did you mean by saying we reckoned our canoe was too full?"

"Wasn't that our idea?" returned the Left Bower, indifferently. Confounded by this practical expression of his own unformulated good intentions, the Right Bower was staggered.

"Speakin' of the Old Man," broke in the Judge, with characteristic infelicity, "I reckon he'll sort o' miss us, times like these. We were allers runnin' him and bedevilin' him, after work, just to get him excited and amusin', and he'll kinder miss that sort o' stimulatin'. I reckon we'll miss it too, somewhat. Don't you remember, boys, the night we put up that little sell on him and made him believe we'd struck it rich in the bank of the creek, and got him so conceited, he wanted to go off and settle all our debts at once?"

"And how I came bustin' into the cabin with a pan full of iron pyrites and black sand," chuckled Union Mills, continuing the reminiscences, "and how them big gray eyes of his nearly bulged out of his head. Well, it's some satisfaction to know we did our duty by the young fellow even in those little things." He turned for confirmation of their general disinterestedness to the Right Bower, but he was already striding away, uneasily conscious of the lazy following of the Left Bower, like a laggard conscience at his back. This movement again threw Union Mills and the Judge into feeble complicity in the rear, as the procession slowly straggled homeward from the creek.

Night had fallen. Their way lay through the shadow of Lone Star Mountain, deepened here and there by the slight, bosky ridges that, starting from its base, crept across the plain like vast roots of its swelling trunk. The shadows were growing blacker as the moon began to assert itself over the rest of the valley, when the Right Bower halted suddenly on one of these ridges. The Left Bower lounged up to him, and stopped also, while the two others came up and completed the group.

"There's no light in the shanty," said the Right Bower in a low voice, half to himself and half in answer to their inquiring attitude. The men followed the direction of his finger. In the distance the black outline of the Lone Star cabin stood out distinctly in the illumined space. There was the blank, sightless, external glitter of moonlight on its two windows that seemed to reflect its dim vacancy, empty alike of light, and warmth, and motion.

"That's sing'lar," said the Judge in an awed whisper.

The Left Bower, by simply altering the position of his hands in his trousers' pockets, managed to suggest that he knew perfectly the meaning of it, had always known it; but that being now, so to speak, in the hands of Fate, he was callous to it. This much, at least, the elder brother read in his attitude. But anxiety at that moment was the controlling impulse of the Right Bower, as a certain superstitious remorse was the instinct of the two others, and without heeding the cynic, the three started at a rapid pace for the cabin.

They reached it silently, as the moon, now riding high in the heavens, seemed to touch it with the tender grace and hushed repose of a tomb. It was with something of this feeling that the Right Bower softly pushed open the door; it was with something of this dread that the two others lingered on the threshold, until the Right Bower, after vainly trying to stir the

dead embers on the hearth into life with his
foot, struck a match and lit their solitary candle.
Its flickering light revealed the familiar interior
unchanged in aught but one thing. The bunk
that the Old Man had occupied was stripped of
its blankets; the few cheap ornaments and photo-
graphs were gone; the rude poverty of the bare
boards and scant pallet looked up at them un-
relieved by the bright face and gracious youth
that had once made them tolerable. In the grim
irony of that exposure, their own penury was
doubly conscious. The little knapsack, the tea-
cup and coffee-pot that had hung near his bed,
were gone also. The most indignant protest,
the most pathetic of the letters he had composed
and rejected, whose torn fragments still littered
the floor, could never have spoken with the eloquence of this empty space! The men exchanged no words: the solitude of the cabin,
instead of drawing them together, seemed to iso-
late each one in selfish distrust of the others.
Even the unthinking garrulity of Union Mills
and the Judge was checked. A moment later,
when the Left Bower entered the cabin, his
presence was scarcely noticed.

The silence was broken by a joyous exclamation from the Judge. He had discovered the
Old Man's rifle in the corner, where it had been
at first overlooked. "He ain't gone yet, gentle-

men—for yer's his rifle," he broke in, with a feverish return of volubility, and a high excited falsetto. "He wouldn't have left this behind. No! I knowed it from the first. He's just outside a bit, foraging for wood and water. No, sir! Coming along here I said to Union Mills —didn't I?—'Bet your life the Old Man's not far off, even if he ain't in the cabin.' Why, the moment I stepped foot—"

"And I said coming along," interrupted Union Mills, with equally reviving mendacity, "Like as not he's hangin' round yer and lyin' low just to give us a surprise.' He! ho!"

"He's gone for good, and he left that rifle here on purpose," said the Left Bower in a low voice, taking the weapon almost tenderly in his hands.

"Drop it, then!" said the Right Bower. The voice was that of his brother, but suddenly changed with passion. The two other partners instinctively drew back in alarm.

"I'll not leave it here for the first comer," said the Left Bower, calmly, "because we've been fools and he too. It's too good a weapon for that."

"Drop it, I say!" said the Right Bower, with a savage stride towards him.

The younger brother brought the rifle to a half charge with a white face but a steady eye.

"Stop where you are!" he said collectedly. "Don't row with *me*, because you haven't either the grit to stick to your ideas or the heart to confess them wrong. We've followed your lead, and—here we are! The camp's broken up— the Old Man's gone—and we're going. And as for the d—d rifle—"

"Drop it, do you hear!" shouted the Right Bower, clinging to that one idea with the blind pertinacity of rage and a losing cause. "Drop it!"

The Left Bower drew back, but his brother had seized the barrel with both hands. There was a momentary struggle, a flash through the half-lighted cabin, and a shattering report. The two men fell back from each other; the rifle dropped on the floor between them.

The whole thing was over so quickly that the other two partners had not had time to obey their common impulse to separate them, and consequently even now could scarcely understand what had passed. It was over so quickly that the two actors themselves walked back to their places, scarcely realizing their own act.

A dead silence followed. The Judge and Union Mills looked at each other in dazed astonishment, and then nervously set about their former habits, apparently in that fatuous belief common to such natures, that they were ignoring a painful situation. The Judge drew the barrel towards him, picked up the cards, and began mechanically to "make a patience," on which Union Mills gazed with ostentatious interest, but with eyes furtively conscious of the rigid figure of the Right Bower by the chimney and the abstracted face of the Left Bower at the door. Ten minutes had passed in this occupation, the Judge and Union Mills conversing in the furtive whispers of children unavoidably but fascinatedly present at a family quarrel, when a light step was heard upon the crackling brushwood outside, and the bright panting face of the Old Man appeared upon the threshold. There was a shout of joy; in another moment he was half-buried in the bosom of the Right Bower's shirt, half-dragged into the lap of the Judge, upsetting the barrel, and completely encompassed by the Left Bower and Union Mills. With the enthusiastic utterance of his name the spell was broken.

Happily unconscious of the previous excitement that had provoked this spontaneous unanimity of greeting, the Old Man, equally relieved, at once broke into a feverish announcement of his discovery. He painted the details, with, I fear, a slight exaggeration of coloring, due partly to his own excitement, and partly to justify their own. But he was strangely conscious that these bankrupt men appeared less elated with their personal interest in their stroke of fortune than with his own success. "I told you he'd do it," said the Judge, with a reckless unscrupulousness of statement that carried everybody with it; "look at him! the game little pup." "Oh no! he ain't the right breed, is he?" echoed Union Mills with arch irony, while the Right and Left Bower, grasping either hand, pressed a proud but silent greeting that was half new to him, but wholly delicious. It was not without difficulty that he could at last prevail upon them to return with him to the scene of his discovery, or even then restrain them from attempting to carry him thither on their shoulders on the plea of his previous prolonged exertions. Once only there was a momentary embarrassment. "Then you fired that shot to bring me back?" said the Old Man, gratefully. In the awkward silence that followed, the hands of the two brothers sought and grasped each other, penitently. "Yes," interposed the Judge, with delicate tact, "ye see the Right and Left Bower almost quarreled to see which should be the first to fire for ye. I disremember which did"—"I never touched the trigger," said the Left Bower, hastily. With a hurried backward kick, the Judge resumed, "It went off sorter spontaneous."

The difference in the sentiment of the procession that once more issued from the Lone Star cabin did not fail to show itself in each individual partner according to his temperament. The subtle tact of Union Mills, however, in expressing an awakened respect for their fortunate partner by addressing him, as if unconsciously, as "Mr. Ford" was at first discomposing, but even this was forgotten in their breathless excitement as they neared the base of the mountain. When they had crossed the creek the Right Bower stopped reflectively.

"You say you heard the slide come down before you left the cabin?" he said, turning to the Old Man.

"Yes; but I did not know then what it was. It was about an hour and a half after you left," was the reply.

"Then look here, boys," continued the Right Bower with superstitious exultation; "it was the *slide* that tumbled into the creek, overflowed it, and helped *us* clear out the race!"

It seemed so clear that Providence had taken the partners of the Lone Star directly in hand that they faced the toilsome ascent of the mountain with the assurance of conquerors. They paused only on the summit to allow the Old Man to lead the way to the slope that held their treasure. He advanced cautiously to the edge

of the crumbling cliff, stopped, looked bewildered, advanced again, and then remained
white and immovable. In an instant the Right
Bower was at his side.

"Is anything the matter? Don't—don't look
so, Old Man, for God's sake!"

The Old Man pointed to the dull, smooth,
black side of the mountain, without a crag,
break, or protuberance, and said with ashen
lips:—

"It's gone!"

And it was gone! A *second* slide had taken
place, stripping the flank of the mountain, and
burying the treasure and the weak implement
that had marked its side deep under a chaos
of rock and *débris* at its base.

"Thank God!" The blank faces of his companions turned quickly to the Right Bower.
"Thank God!" he repeated, with his arm
round the neck of the Old Man. "Had he
stayed behind he would have been buried too."
He paused, and, pointing solemnly to the depths
below, said, "And thank God for showing us
where we may yet labor for it in hope and
patience like honest men."

The men silently bowed their heads and
slowly descended the mountain. But when they
had reached the plain one of them called out to

the others to watch a star that seemed to be rising and moving towards them over the hushed and sleeping valley.

"It's only the stage coach, boys," said the Left Bower, smiling; "the coach that was to take us away."

In the security of their new-found fraternity they resolved to wait and see it pass. As it swept by with flash of light, beat of hoofs, and jingle of harness, the only real presence in the dreamy landscape, the driver shouted a hoarse greeting to the phantom partners, audible only to the Judge, who was nearest the vehicle.

"Did you hear—*did* you hear what he said, boys?" he gasped, turning to his companions. "No! Shake hands all round, boys! God bless you all, boys! To think we didn't know it all this while!"

"Know what?"

"Merry Christmas!"